THE HATESICK DIARIES

ST. MARY'S REBELS
BOOK 5

SAFFRON A. KENT

COPYRIGHT

This is a work of fiction. Names, characters, places, and incidents are either the product of the author's imagination or are used fictitiously, and any resemblance to actual persons living or dead, business establishments, events, or locales, is entirely coincidental.

The Hatesick Diaries © 2023 by Saffron A. Kent
All rights reserved. No part of this book may be used or reproduced in any manner whatsoever without written permission of the author except in the case of brief quotations embodied in critical articles or reviews.

Cover Art by Najla Qamber Designs
Editing by Olivia Kalb & Leanne Rabesa
Proofreading by Virginia Tesi Carey

Jan 2023 Edition

Published in the United States of America

DEDICATION

For every good girl who's dreamed of her happily ever after with a bad boy. And written about it in her diary.

For my husband, now and always. The only guy I've ever written about in my diary.

Lovesick (n.):

In love with someone. Or loving someone to the point of obsession. To the point of sickness.

Hatesick (n.):

In hate with someone. And as a result, being obsessed and possessed; being sick and consumed by them. Much like its antonym, lovesick.

CHAPTER ONE

Six years ago. Bardstown

He's a criminal.

He has to be.

First, he's wearing all black: black jeans and a black hoodie with the hood up. In summer, no less.

And second, he's very carefully and cautiously laying out a string on the ground.

It's a very long string too.

It at least circles around the thick bushes that border this massive back yard, and goes well into the woods *behind* that back yard. Where I'm currently standing behind the thick trunk of a tree and watching him secretly.

Or more like watching his back, because he's facing away from me, walking backward.

When he's come far enough I guess, he stops and kneels on the ground, completely blocking my view.

I can't see what he's doing.

Why he's bent over that string.

Whatever it is though, it can't be good.

It might even be dangerous.

The prudent thing to do — prudent means practical; also known as feasible, realistic, sensible, matter of fact — is to turn around and run. To get away from him. Especially when no one knows that I'm here, wandering around the woods in the middle of the night, and not up in my bedroom, sleeping like I should be.

In my defense, tonight is special.

Plus I couldn't sleep in my new bed, in the new house, in a new place.

We — my parents and I — only arrived here last week, see.

Both of them got a new job and so we packed up and left our old apartment in Brooklyn and came to Bardstown to start a new life. As opposed to Brooklyn, everything is super open here: our big two-story house; these woods that I'm taking an impromptu walk in; the back yard beyond it, the giant manor beyond the back yard.

But I'm not going to lie, I miss Brooklyn. I miss my friends, my old school, even our old rundown apartment that had more leaks and squeaky floorboards than not. But it's okay. My mom always says that you make sacrifices for people you love. That this is what love is.

To compromise. To make adjustments and to be good to the people you love.

So I'm happy as long as my parents are happy.

Except for *this*.

I'm not happy about this, whatever it is that this boy is doing.

I mean, if he's really doing something bad then shouldn't I confront him? Shouldn't I stop him? I'm new here, yes, but these are my woods now. This is my house, my property and estate.

Well, not technically.

We only live here, but...

"I know you're there."

My thoughts come to a screeching halt at those words.

His words.

He said them, right?

Yes, he did.

Even though he hasn't turned around or stopped doing whatever it is that he's doing.

What is he *doing* though?

"I can hear you fucking thinking from over there."

This time, I have no confusion as to who spoke because his shoulders tense up and his arms jerk, as if his entire body is speaking along with his lips.

Or more like snapping at me.

Which gets my back up and I dig my fingers into the trunk. "I'm not *fucking* thinking."

At this, he finally stops and straightens up, cocking his head to the side slightly as if paying attention to me. The only thing he doesn't do is turn around as he says, "What?"

I know he can't see me but still I lift my chin as I reply, "I'm just thinking. *Period*. No fucking."

Okay, that sounded so much better and *smarter* in my head, I swear.

Also, not funny.

But apparently it is because it makes him chuckle in response, his shoulders moving again.

And this time I notice that they're broad.

Probably because he's straightened up now and isn't hunched over that string of his. In fact, his shoulders are broader than any guy's shoulders in my class, either at my old school or the new.

"No fucking, huh," he drawls. "Well, there's a lot to unpack there, in that statement. But I don't think you wanna go there." I frown as to what he means but he keeps going. "So instead, why don't you tell me what you're *just thinking* about?"

His tone makes me narrow my eyes.

Actually *everything* about him is making me narrow my eyes.

The fact that he sounds so amused, his voice thick and raspy — something else that I've come across for the first time ever; no boys at my old school or new sound like him — and that he still hasn't turned around to face me while speaking, like he doesn't think I'm worthy of being looked in the eye while talking.

The sheer arrogance.

The sheer conceit, haughtiness, hubris.

The *egotism*!

It makes me come out of hiding — it wasn't a very good hiding spot anyway, since he'd already spotted me — and put my hands on my hips as I say, "I'm *just thinking* how rude it is that you're talking to me and yet you haven't turned around and shown me your face."

This time I don't think I've said anything remotely funny, but he still chuckles.

It's almost a laugh, actually, and I breathe out sharply, ready to say something else, something even more stern, but he springs up to his feet so quickly and so suddenly turning around that I snap my mouth closed.

And simply stare.

And gaze, gape, goggle and gawp at his face for the first time.

A face that looks like... summer.

That's my first and very nonsensical thought. How can *anyone* look like a *season*?

He does though.

Despite his all-black clothing, he looks like my favorite season.

Probably because his skin is so tanned.

It's so beachy and bronzed. Like he's been out in the sun for a long time. And that he could potentially stay out there for even longer and never ever get burned. Plus all that hair.

That I can see now that his hood has fallen off.

And even though his hair's dark, as dark as his clothing, I still think that it's a surfer's look.

Probably because it's on the long side, falling over his brows and the side of his face, skimming the neck of his hoodie, all loose, slightly wavy and messy.

So yeah, summer.

Despite being all dark and... dangerous.

"You done staring, Bubblegum?"

Startled, my eyes snap up to his.

They're dark too.

Probably black or a very dark shade of brown; I can't tell right now.

All I can tell is that they have a glint in them.

"I wasn't..." I say, my hands coming off my hips and simply falling limp at my sides now. "Staring."

Liar.

You're a liar, Echo.

He knows that too, and so again he finds my words amusing.

But this time, he doesn't chuckle.

He simply lets his mouth quirk up in a lopsided smile. And I think it's worse because his smile isn't just a smile. It's a smirk, and it makes him look even more arrogant.

"Good," he says. "Because then I'd have to tell you what I was *just thinking*."

"What were you thinking?" I ask before I can stop myself.

His eyes glint some more. "About how rude it is that you're staring at me and yet you haven't told me your name."

Your name...

His words, again all arrogant sounding, catch me up to the fact that he called me something just now, didn't he?

Bubblegum.

He called me Bubblegum.

Just the thought of it makes things zoom and whoosh around in my belly.

Ignoring it, I ask, "What did you just call me?"

His lips stay quirked up as he shrugs. "I had two choices: bubblegum or strawberry." Then, "I don't like strawberries, so I picked bubblegum."

Why would he call me that? What does that...

You know what, I don't care.

Folding my arms across my chest, I fire back, "Well, I don't like bubblegum."

"Then you should tell me your name."

"I'm never telling you my name."

"Never is a long time, Bubblegum."

"Stop calling me that."

"Can't." He shakes his head slowly. "You're a little too pink."

"What?"

"Pink..." he repeats before trailing off and moving his eyes away from my face, letting them go down my body.

My belly whooshes again as I follow his gaze, looking down at myself.

Which is when I finally figure it out.

What he's saying and why he called me Bubblegum in the first place.

"You," he finishes his statement and my eyes spring back to his.

It's glowing even more, his gaze.

And it makes my belly whoosh harder. Which is not helped by the fact that he's correct.

As in, I *am* pink.

Or rather, my dress is.

My brand new dress with a lace overlay — the first thing my parents bought for me in celebration of their new jobs and tonight's special occasion — that I absolutely adore.

"I'm not pink," I tell him. "My dress is pink."

Keeping his eyes on me, he adds, "And your toes. Your sandals." He jerks his chin up. "Plus that ribbon in your hair. All pink. Like bubblegum."

Okay, it's official now.

I don't think I like him very much.

Whoever he is.

"So I'm wearing all pink. So what? It's not like I wear it every day. It's a special occasion today, okay?"

"Yeah, what's the special occasion?"

I purse my lips. "I'm not going to tell you."

His eyes flash as he drawls, "You're starting to break my heart a little bit, Bubblegum."

At his low words, all the air gets sucked out of my lungs.

Not to mention, at his actions too.

At the fact that he puts a hand on his chest and rubs the spot just above his heart, like I'm really breaking it.

God, who is this guy?

I've never ever met anyone like him before.

I didn't even know guys like him *existed*.

I force myself to breathe though and ask, "What are you doing out here, in the woods?"

My question doesn't faze him in the least. In fact, he's all ready with an answer. "Getting interrogated by some bubblegum."

My nostrils flare and his lips twitch at my displeasure.

"Why do you have that string?" I look at it, lying on the ground just by his side. "What are you going to do with it?"

"Magic."

"Is it something bad?"

"Define bad."

"It is, isn't it?"

"Are you afraid?"

"No."

I don't sound very convincing, even to myself. And he smiles. As if he likes it. As if the prospect of scaring me sounds fun to him. Then, "Because if you were, I'd tell you then you've got nothing to worry about."

"But someone else... does?"

"Not you." He shakes his head slowly. "That's all you need to know."

"I don't think —"

"Besides, it's none of your business," he cuts me off, raising an arrogant eyebrow. "Is it?"

"Actually it *is* my business."

"And how is that?"

"Because these are my woods."

"Your woods."

"Yes, I live here."

Finally, *freaking finally*, all amusement and arrogance get wiped off his face.

I'm so happy that it's a struggle to not smile and maintain my own arrogant expression but I do it.

Anything to turn the tables on him.

Anything.

"You live here."

I nod. "Yup."

"*Here*," he goes, his eyes going up and down my body again. "At the manor?"

My heart jerks in my chest.

For a variety of reasons.

First, this is a very specific question. And the answer to it is no.

I do not live at the manor.

I live in the carriage house, right *across* from the manor, also known as the servant's quarters. Truth be told, I haven't even been inside the manor yet.

And second, because I've decided to lie and tell him yes anyway.

I do realize that lying is bad.

My parents are going to be very unhappy about it, if they ever find out.

But I have thought about it and lying is the only logical next step.

If I tell him that this is my house and my property, he's going to be intimidated. He's going to be afraid of me and that should take care of his stupid smug expression. Plus it might also stop him from carrying out his nefarious — also known as wicked, sinful, appalling, odious and so on — intentions.

So it's a win-win really.

It's lying for a good cause.

Breathing a lungful of air, I reply, "Yes."

His eyes narrow as he studies me for a second or two. It's okay. It's understandable.

He's likely stunned by my revelation.

And the fact that he's messing with the wrong girl.

A powerful girl.

"So you're one of the Davidsons then," he says.

"I am."

I am not.

I'm one of the Adlers — Echo Adler — who work for the Davidsons. My mom's one of the new cooks and my dad is the new head groundskeeper. But he's not going to know that. He's...

Wait a second.

What if he does know?

I mean, he's here, isn't he? On the Davidsons' estate, and what if he knows all the Davidsons? What if he's friends with them, with one of their sons? I hear they have two, both older than me and both living out of town, one in college and the other in a boarding school.

Oh my God.

Oh my *God*.

"Have you... do you know th-them?" I ask, or more like squeak really.

He's silent for a second or two and I think I see a smile, or rather a smirk, forming on his mouth but it vanishes so quickly that I definitely think I imagined it.

Shrugging, he says, "Heard of them." Then with his eyes sweeping across my face, "Didn't know they had a cute little Bubblegum living among them though."

Okay, thank God.

Thank. God.

I'm so relieved that I'm not even going to take offense at him calling me by that ridiculous — belly-whooshing — name. But...

Did he just say 'cute little Bubblegum?'

He called me... cute.

"Now you know. So..." I clear my throat, ignoring everything once again. "Whatever it is that you're trying to do, don't."

"Yeah?"

"Yes."

His eyes flick back and forth between mine. "Or what?"

I frown. "Or I..."

"You," he prods.

I breathe out sharply. "Or I call security on you."

Strangely, my threat makes his mouth stretch up into a smile.

And yet again, air gets knocked out of my lungs for a second or two. Because *this* smile of his is really just a smile — small, lopsided and... fond even — and not a smirk.

"Because you're one of the Davidsons and this is your manor," he murmurs.

"Yes."

Humming, he jerks his chin at me. "So what's this party for?"

Right.

There's a party.

It's happening in the backyard right now, just beyond the woods.

I can hear the laughter, the talking, the music wafting through the trees. Another one of the reasons why I couldn't sleep tonight and decided to take a walk. Because of the noise and because my parents are both working and so sneaking out was easy. Not that I'm the sneaking out type but still.

The party is in honor of the Davidsons' oldest son, Homer Davidson. I think he just graduated from business school and is now set to travel abroad in order to handle Davidson Hotel's European division.

"Why?" I ask suspiciously.

"The same occasion you mentioned before, I assume."

"I..."

"Wait, *special* occasion. That requires you to be so," he looks me up and down again, "pink."

"I'm not..." I shake my head. "It's none of your business, what occasion it is. All you need to know is that you can't ruin it."

"How about you tell me what the special occasion is and I promise not to ruin it for you."

"How about you promise not to ruin it and I won't call security on you."

Again my threat has a minimal effect on him. "Well then, I'm afraid we can't come to an agreement."

With that, he reaches his arm back to his pocket, quite possibly fishing for something, and I blurt out, "It's my birthday."

He pauses, his focus completely on me.

Damn it.

I can't believe I gave in. I can't believe I *told* him.

The first true thing in all of this.

It *is* my birthday.

That's the occasion.

That's why when I couldn't sleep, I decided to put on my birthday dress and take a midnight stroll.

"Your birthday."

Sighing, I continue, "Yes." My eyes go to his arm that's still in its position, at his back, quite possibly in his pocket. "And you can't do whatever it is you were going to."

"How old are you today?"

I draw back. "I'm not telling you that."

"Fifteen?"

"That wasn't part of the deal."

"Nah," he muses, his eyes searching my face, "fourteen, yeah?"

"I told you what you wanted to know. Now can you bring your arm up front please?"

"Jesus Christ, don't tell me you're thirteen," he keeps guessing, emphasizing 'thirteen.'

"What, why?"

"Because that would make you too young."

"For what?" I'm so confused right now but I don't care about that. I only care about his hand at his back. "Listen, you promised, okay? You promised that you wouldn't ruin the party if I told you what you wanted to know and I did. And a promise is a promise. A promise is an oath. It's a pledge; it's a word of honor. It's a covenant, commitment, contract and a vow. It's a *freaking bond*."

I do realize that I could probably not have gone this crazy with rattling off all the synonyms.

But then I'm stressed out. He's stressing me out. And when I'm stressed out, I find solace — also known as comfort, consolation and relief — in language and words.

"I didn't know that a promise could be so many things," he says, quietly for some reason, his eyes becoming serious.

"It could be because…" I take a moment to catch my breath. "Synonyms."

"Synonyms."

"Yes."

"What about them?"

Another moment to breathe. "I like them. I like synonyms. And, uh, words. I'm a logophile."

"What's a logophile?"

"It's what you call someone when they love words in general."

He keeps staring at me and staring at me and I open my mouth to tell him to stop when he speaks. "Tell me you're not thirteen."

His voice has gone lower. Deeper.

And my heart is beating even louder now because of it. "I'm not."

"So fourteen then."

"First *you* tell *me* that you'll keep your promise and won't ruin my birthday party."

He stares at me a beat. "I won't."

I breathe in a sigh of relief, or I would have if he hadn't done what he does in the next moment.

He brings his arm forward, but not because he has abandoned his plan. But because he has in his grip what he wanted out of his pocket, a black rectangular thing that he turns on with a flick of his thumb.

An orange flame bursts to life, making his summer skin glow for a second or two before he turns around and drops to the ground. In a flash, he sets the string on fire.

I watch it all with a thundering heart, as if in slow motion.

That lone spark of fire racing along the string. Just as it disappears around the corner, I come out of my shock and dash over to where he's standing, facing away from me.

"What did you..." I breathe out, my chest heaving. "You promised. You *promised* that you wouldn't ruin my party. You —"

It happens then.

This huge explosion. This boom that destroys all my words.

And it keeps happening.

The blasts keep coming until they're are a continuous, nonstop cacophony of sounds. Mixed in with shocked gasps and screams from people. I'm about to scream too when something lights up.

Up in the sky.

Red and green sparkles.

Hundreds and hundreds of tiny twinkling sparks showering down from the sky.

Like the rain.

So thick and bright that night turns into day.

Fireworks.

He lit up fireworks.

It's so unexpected after what I'd been just thinking, this magnificent display of light and sound, that I do something unexpected as well.

I let out a lone but loud laugh.

"This is..." I whisper over the crackling sounds of fireworks, and shocked gasps and screams of people. "This is beautiful."

"Yeah."

His softly spoken word makes me look at him.

Only to find that he's already watching me, shadows dancing on his face, his eyes sparkling even more. And I realize two things at once.

First, that he isn't talking about the fireworks. His quiet 'yeah' was meant for something else.

Some*one* else. Someone like me.

And as shocking as this revelation is — kinda like when he called me cute — the second realization is much more shocking to me.

The fact that those dancing shadows make him look... beautiful.

And sexy.

God, he's sexy.

I've never thought that about a guy before. Sure, I've seen a lot of cute guys, handsome guys. But I don't think I've ever seen a guy who's equal parts beautiful and sexy.

This is crazy.

Isn't it?

But wait, there's more. There's a third realization.

That his eyes are dark, yes — chocolate brown to be specific — but that's not all. There are hues of red in them too. That I only notice now because I'm so close to him and the night sky seems to be on fire.

"And I didn't," he says, watching me.

"You didn't what?"

"Ruin your party."

"You —"

"Because this isn't your party, is it?"

My eyes go wide. As does *his* smile.

But before either of us can say anything, a strange voice distracts us both.

"Found him." Some static comes on before that voice continues, "Yeah, bringing him in now."

His words sound ominous, and when he comes into view, with his walkie talkie and all, I don't like the look of him either. He's big and broad and from the looks of it, a security guard.

He comes to a stop a few feet away from us and addresses the guy who just set the sky on fire. "Having fun?"

At the guard's irritated question, he turns toward him and shrugs. "You could say that."

"You scared a lot of people, kid."

"I heard, yeah."

The man shakes his head. "Your father wants to see you."

"Thought he might."

"You going to come easily?"

"I could," he muses, "but since I do like to have fun, I'm gonna say no."

The man sighs. "I'm not running after you, kid. They don't pay me enough for that shit, all right?"

"Yeah, my father is a penny-pinching asshole. Despite the popular belief." Cocking his head to the side, he continues, "Fortunately for you though, I don't take after the old man. How about you let me go and I'll pay you double whatever it is they pay you for a month."

The man stares at him for a few seconds before stepping forward. "Come on, Reign. Let's go."

"Reign..."

That was me.

I said that.

His name is Reign.

I know that name. I know who Reign is.

I *know*.

I snap my eyes up to him and again, I find him already staring at me. He completes his name for me. "Davidson. That's me. Probably not for long though. Since my dad wants to see me."

"This is..."

Again, he finishes the sentence for me. "My party, yeah. Well, my brother's."

I swallow, horrified, blushing. "I... I didn't..."

His eyes, so unique and interesting and still on fire, roam over my features. "Yeah, not helping, Bubblegum."

"W-what?"

"If you don't want me to call you Bubblegum, then you should stop being so pink."

Before I can say something else, the guard speaks. "Let's go, kid. I don't have all day."

The guy — *Reign* — doesn't move though.

He keeps staring at me. "Tell me your name."

"Echo."

Something moves over his features then.

Something like... relief mixed in with a mysterious emotion.

Whatever it is, it makes my breaths choppy. It makes me feel relief too.

That I said it. I told him.

Which is weird because I didn't want to.

"Echo."

I nod and now that I've told him my name, the rest of my story comes out. "Adler. Echo Adler. I... My parents work for your parents. They just started. M-my mom's on the cooking staff and my dad's the groundskeeper. I live —"

My words come to a jerking halt when the man steps forward and in a shocking display of aggression, grabs hold of Reign's arm.

"Hey, what the hell?" I go, all loudly and angrily. "Let him go."

The guard throws me a dismissive look before he jerks on Reign's arms and begins to drag him away.

I open my mouth to protest again but Reign doesn't let me. "Where do you live?"

Swallowing, I answer, "In the carriage house. Right across from... your mansion. Are you..."

"Am I what?"

I watch him move further and further away, his arm still in the grip of the man. And it's a strong grip too. It must be hurting him. It has to be.

"Going to be okay?" I ask, worried.

A lopsided smile stretches his lips. Then, ignoring my question, he asks one of his own. "How old are you?"

"T-twelve."

I don't get to see what passes over his features at my reply though. Because he's almost at the end, the corner of the woods and the backyard, too far away for me to see anything, but I do think that I hear a muttered curse.

Then, "Well, happy birthday, Echo."

Those are his last words before he disappears.

And I stand here, staring at the spot where he was only a second ago.

Hearing my name echo — like its namesake — in his voice, through the woods.

And in my heart.

CHAPTER TWO

Five years ago. Bardstown

Sometimes I still hear it.

My name in his voice, echoing around the woods.

I know it's crazy and I know it's been a year since that night but still.

It's even crazier when you think about the fact that he doesn't even live here, at the manor, in Bardstown. He lives in Connecticut, at a posh boarding school.

Rumor has it that it was a way for his parents to wash their hands of him.

Rumor also has it that there are a million rumors about him.

About the second son of the Davidsons.

The bad son, the rebel son.

The son who has brought them nothing but trouble for as long as anyone on the Davidson staff can remember. And they remember a lot.

Like the time when he was arrested at the age of twelve for vandalizing his school, which is when they sent him off to that boarding school. He was then suspended from said boarding school for getting caught selling the final exam *before* finals; they had to make a large donation to the school to keep his place.

Then there was a time, even before this, when he stole his dad's new car — he was eleven, they say — and took it on a joyride around town. Until the cops caught up to him, somewhere out in the neighboring town of Wuthering

Garden, parked in a grocery store parking lot, where he'd paid someone to buy him beer.

And this is just scratching the surface.

There isn't a rule he's not broken or crime/misdemeanor he hasn't committed.

You name it and he's done it.

Meanwhile, the Davidsons' older son, Homer Davidson, is the epitome of good behavior. He's an obedient son and a brilliant young businessman, every inch the heir of the Davidson dynasty.

It was easy to find it all out, all the rumors, the stories, the anecdotes.

People talk about him a lot around here, the cooking staff, the cleaning staff, the chauffeurs, the groundkeepers, the guards and so on. They talk about how unfortunate it is that the Davidsons have a son that's always hell bent on bringing shame to their name, how unfair it is for the Davidsons because they've done nothing to deserve it.

Howard Davidson is a good employer. A respected citizen and businessman, generous and kind. And I guess I can attest to that firsthand; Mr. Davidson gave my parents jobs when they most needed them. Gave us a place to stay, helped us move and so on.

But that's not the point.

The point is that I too have a story about him.

An anecdote.

About how I met him on the night of my twelfth birthday and he set the sky on fire. How he turned night into day.

But I haven't told anyone about it.

Because I don't indulge in gossip or judgement. But mostly because he hasn't told anyone about it either.

About how I lied to him.

How I spun stories the night we met.

I've wondered about that, actually.

Once the shock of the night wore off, the enormity of what I had done set in. The wickedness, the awfulness, the horror and depravity of my lie had started to sink in.

And I got so worried.

I kept waiting and waiting for my parents to call me downstairs from my room and ask me about the bad thing that I'd done. About sneaking out and wandering in the woods at midnight. About the lie that I'd told and how that lie had gotten them fired.

I essentially pretended to be the daughter of the king when in reality, I'm the daughter of the king's groundskeeper and the cook, didn't I? Of course they would've gotten fired for it.

And oh my God, that would've been such a disaster.

Especially given my dad's condition. He used to work construction back in Brooklyn, but an accident made it so that he can't work long hours anymore. Meaning he not only got fired – on a mere technicality to justify it – but also couldn't find a job for the longest time. So my mom had to work two different jobs to pick up the slack.

Their jobs at the Davidson manor came as a blessing.

My reckless lie could've ruined all that.

But nothing happened.

No one found out about what I did, and I knew it was because of him.

Because he never told on me.

He kept my secret, didn't he?

He didn't have to but he did.

And I'm not going to repay that by gossiping about him.

So whenever they talk and speculate, all I do is be quiet and simply listen. And well, listen carefully.

Which is how I know that he's back.

After a whole entire year, he's back from Connecticut for a few days. And that's why I'm here.

Wandering in the same woods.

Coincidentally, also on the same day as last year, while another party goes on in the back yard.

Again, this one's in honor of Homer Davidson; his parents throw a lot of parties for him. His parents throw a lot of parties in general but again, that's not the point.

The point is that I know this is crazy. What I'm doing doesn't make sense.

There's no logic to it.

There's no guarantee that I'm going to run into him again.

But I...

I had to do something; he's here.

I mean, I have to see him.

I just have to.

"Looking for me?"

At the voice coming from behind me, my heart jumps in my chest.

And I spin around.

And I... God, he's bigger.

Than he was the last time I saw him.

He's taller. Broader. And he was already plenty tall and broad from what I remember.

Those shoulders of his — the ones that were already bigger than the shoulders of any other guy I know — now look like they can span the door of my bedroom. His chest looks like it can block off the view of the woods and the manor from my window.

Not to mention, it looks like he can so easily tower over the canopy bed that I sleep in.

He can so easily tower over me.

Plus he still looks like my favorite season.

Despite the fact that he still has dark clothes on.

He still looks like the end of June with his bronzed skin and that long dark surfer's hair.

"You done staring, Bubblegum?"

My eyes shoot up to his and since his words are a repetition of what he said to me a year ago, my words are too. "I wasn't... staring."

His lips — which I now notice look fuller than last year too — stretch up into a smirk. His typical arrogant smirk that makes my already racing heart race more.

"Good," he drawls. "Because if you were, then I'd have to tell you what I was just thinking."

"What were you thinking?"

His eyes that I know have red hues in them stare at me something fierce before he says, "About how I wasn't wrong and that I didn't dream it up."

"Dream what up?"

"You." Then, "Or how pink you are."

Breathless, I fist my dress. Which is pink. Again.

"It's, uh, a special occasion," I tell him.

"I know."

Okay, I have a confession to make.

When my mom asked me what I wanted for my birthday this year and I told her a pink dress, I wasn't ready to admit it. When I put it on tonight before I came out for my midnight stroll, I wasn't ready to admit it then either.

But I have to now, I think.

That I did it all for him.

I wanted him to notice it, in case I ran into him again.

And now that he has, I don't know what to do.

I don't know what to say except, "And don't call me that."

"It's either Strawberries or Bubblegum." His eyes gleam and he slowly shakes his head. "Don't like strawberries."

"How about just using my name?"

The one that I've been hearing in his voice for the past year.

Not that I'm going to tell him that.

Because as I said, this is crazy.

All of this is crazy.

The fact that I'm here, wearing pink, and he's here, calling me Bubblegum *because* I'm wearing pink, and we're seeing each other after exactly a year.

But something occurs to me.

"You do know... As in, you do *remember* what my name is, don't you?"

Because what if he doesn't?

There's a possibility of that, right?

Just because I'm crazy doesn't mean he is too. And yes, from the looks of it he does seem to remember a lot of things from that night, but maybe he... forgot?

This one little thing.

My question turns his smirk into a smile. A very tiny one.

Actually it's not even a smile per se. It's more like a twitching of his lips.

"Yeah," he replies, still studying me intensely.

Feeling a blush come onto my cheeks, I tuck a wayward strand back and push, "Well, what is it?"

At this, his smile widens.

As if I said something amusing.

As if me asking him whether or not he remembers my name is such a funny thing.

And you know what, despite constantly thinking about that night all year long, I'd forgotten one little thing too. I'd *forgotten* how angry he made me last time.

How arrogant he was and how easily he ruffled my feathers.

"Your name, huh? Well, let's see…" He squints his eyes as if thinking and gosh, I'm this close to strangling him. "From what I *remember*, your name is also known as reverberation, reflection and resounding. Isn't it," he pauses before adding, "Echo?"

Oh.

Okay.

I mean…

So he does remember.

Not only that, he also remembers my love for words. And gosh, my heart is pounding. My veins are buzzing and there's a fluttering in my tummy.

"You're a jerk," I say, for making me think that he didn't remember it.

His smile widens as he says, "Your turn."

"At what?"

"Say my name."

The crazy pounding of my heart gets crazier as I reply, "Reign." His eyes turn even more glow-y and I swallow before continuing, "Also known as to rule and govern. Or be in power or dominate."

"Dominate."

"Yes."

"I do like the sound of that," he says, still watching me with the same intensity.

"You're back," I say then.

"What?"

"From Connecticut," I continue. "Your school."

He chooses to remain silent at this.

Self-conscious, I shift on my feet. "Are you, uh, back for your brother's party?"

"No."

"Oh." Then, "Well, it's just that you don't come home very often and..."

"And what?"

"I was just wondering why that is and just... Yeah."

"I think you know, don't you?"

"I know what?"

"Why I don't come back," he narrows his eyes as if gauging me, "often."

I do.

I do know that.

It's because of his behavior. Rumors have it that his parents don't want him here. They love him but he's a handful, and so it's best for everyone involved if he stays away. So it's very rare for him to visit his home, and despite all the rumors and despite not knowing him all that well, my heart clenches for him. And I can't help but say, "You should."

"What?"

"This is your home." I swallow. "You should come back and visit. Often."

Again he maintains his silence, staring at me. And I hate that I brought this up.

All I wanted to do was talk to him, but I've unintentionally broached a topic that obviously is a sore spot for him.

I open my mouth to say something, anything, but he says, "So what else do you know?"

"What?"

"You know what school I go to," he continues, widening his stance. "You know why I don't come back here. I'm guessing you know a lot more."

"It doesn't matter what I know. It's not important."

"It's kinda important."

"Can't we just forget about it?"

"No."

"We should talk about something else."

"Let's talk about this."

"Look," I say, feeling like an idiot for ruining everything so quickly. "I don't think you're going to like it very much. What I know and what they say."

"I think I can handle it."

"I don't agree with them."

"You probably should."

That actually doesn't sit well with me. That he said that.

Not to mention that somehow we got here.

To this ugly, touchy topic.

"You want to know what I know, what they say about you? Fine, I'll tell you. They say that you're a rebel. That you're a rule-breaker. A lawbreaker, a delinquent, an offender, a villain, a criminal. A bandit. They say that you're dangerous and you're always making trouble. It's a good thing that you don't come back because when you do, you always make things difficult. You always make it hard for everyone to deal with you, especially your parents who love you and just want what's best for you. And that if I do see you when you're back, I should run the other way. That I shouldn't talk to you."

Or at least that's what they've told my mom over the last year.

I have to admit that I lied to her, or rather, never told her that I did talk to him that one time. And I know that I'm not going to tell her that I met him tonight either.

I'm not a liar, I swear.

I'm a good girl, a rule-follower.

But for some reason, in this scenario, I don't want to follow the rules.

"But I want you to know something. I don't put much stock in what I hear. I never judge a person based on rumors. Especially when you're not here to defend yourself or tell your side of the story. The only thing that I believe in is that you helped me. Last time." I swallow, my chest heaving with my rapid breaths. "I-I lied to you. I made up stories and... I shouldn't have done that. I usually don't lie. I'm not... I'm not a liar, but I did lie that night and you had every right to go to your parents about me, tell on me. But you didn't. And I... I'm thankful. So that's what I believe in. What you did, not what I hear."

By the time I finish I realize that he's much closer to me now than he was when I first started talking.

Only he hasn't moved. I don't think.

I think it's me. *I* moved.

I'm not at the spot where I was standing before. I'm right in front of him.

Somewhere during my speech, my legs moved, as if coming alive on their own, and they brought me here.

Where he is.

Where I can see, can confirm, that whatever I thought he could do with his body — tower and block and span — he really can. He's doing it right now in fact.

He's towering over me and blocking the woods and spanning my entire world with his broad shoulders and muscular chest.

Plus his eyes.

The red in them is glowing.

"You're kind of drama, aren't you?" he murmurs, looking down at me.

"What?"

"That was a very good speech."

"I –"

"And a bandit," he says, ignoring me, his lips twitching. "That's new."

"That's mine."

"Yours."

"I call you that." Then, "You gave me a name so I gave you one too."

Something flashes through his expression, probably pleasure I think. "The Bandit and the Bubblegum."

I watch him, mesmerized and also marveling.

If his jaw was this square last time I saw him or if, along with his body growing up, his jaw got broader as well. More square, more mature and masculine.

Still sexy though.

Still beautiful.

And *still* the only guy I've thought this about.

"It was in this book that I was reading," I tell him. "A bandit."

"Yeah?"

"Yes. He always wore black and he always came out in the middle of the night but..."

"But what?"

"But he still had this, uh, tanned, summer skin."

"Summer skin."

"Like yours," I explain. "You know, like when it's the end of June and you're out in the sun for a long time. Because it's so warm and bright and you don't want to go home yet. And you spend your days eating watermelon and drinking lemonade and lying on the beach. Summer."

"What else?"

This time when I move, I'm aware of it.

I'm aware of me taking a step toward him, the leaves crunching beneath my pink sandals, my pink-nailed toes curling when I take in the long, delicious strands of his hair. "He also had thick dark hair. All wavy and messy. It fell on his forehead all the time, kinda like yours. And he wore a bandana to push it back."

"Don't think I've got a bandana."

I look back into his eyes, which are somehow even more fiery now. "He also rode a horse and carried a gun at his hip. And he'd ride along the highway, kidnapping girls from the side of the road."

"Don't think I've kidnapped a girl either." Then, after a pause, "Not yet."

A rush, both hot and cold, washes over my skin. "He was a real scourge of society. Everybody was afraid of him."

"Now *that*," he says, his voice low, "sounds like me."

"I liked him though," I quickly point out, swallowing.

"You did."

"Yes. He lets the last girl he kidnaps go. He even saves her, from a bad home life. It's a very good comment on," I clear my throat, blushing, "how bad guys can be good guys. And how people aren't all bad or all good. We all have sides."

He sweeps his gaze over my features once before saying, "Is that why you're standing so close to me? The Bandit. Because you think I've got a good side. Despite what they say about me."

"Yes."

"What about you?"

"What about me?"

"You're a good girl, aren't you?"

"Yes."

"Do you have a bad side?"

"Not really. Except that I lied to you. But mostly I try to be good. I try to follow all the rules and be good for my parents."

"So what are you doing, reading books about criminals and bandits," he asks then, "and walking around these woods at midnight?"

I came here to see you.

I don't say that.

Because crazy, remember?

Instead I reply, "These woods are perfectly safe."

"Not with a bandit in them, no."

"And I love books."

"Apart from the color pink and words you mean."

"Do you like words?"

"No more than the next person."

"What's your favorite color?"

He takes my face in at that, my birthday dress, my sandals and my toes. The pink ribbon in my hair. "Don't have one."

"Do you like books then?"

"Fuck no."

I bite my lip. "Well, one day I'm going to write my own book."

I am.

That's my plan. My dream.

To be a writer.

To write stories, big and short. To create something. To build a castle of words.

"You are, huh?"

"Yes." I sigh. "But for now, I write in my journal."

That throws him off a little bit; I can tell.

There's a light frown between his brows and his eyes turn even more penetrating as he says, "A journal."

"I have a diary. I write in it every night."

That light frown of his is still in place and it stays there while he studies me in a strange way. Like he's seeing me for the first time, or maybe in a new light. Or maybe it's all in my head because as soon as I blink that mysterious look from his eyes is gone and he's back to being his irreverent self.

"Dear Diary, huh."

"More like Dear Holly." Then, "I sort of name my diaries, depending on how they feel. This one feels like a Holly, all cute and pink."

"Maybe you should call it Bubblegum then."

"Don't —"

"Because it sounds like you. And I'll remember that for next time."

"What?"

"That you like diaries."

"I don't underst..."

My words trail off when he steps back and does the most astonishing thing. The most bizarre — outlandish and strange and surreal — thing.

He goes down on his knees.

Or rather one knee.

And I'm...

I'm so shocked that all I can do is sputter. "What's... What are you..."

"Giving you your gift," he replies, apparently understanding my half-baked sentences.

"What?"

Like last year, he reaches back into his pocket and fishes something out. For a second or so, I think it's a lighter and my belly whooshes. Not in fear but excitement.

In anticipation that he might set fire to the sky again.

For my birthday.

But it's not a lighter.

It's something else. Something shiny.

Something *chiming*.

And then he's touching me.

He's *touching* me.

My ankle.

He's touching, *gripping* my ankle.

And before I can process that, he lifts my foot and places it on his thigh. My arms shoot up and fly, landing on his shoulders. All of this happens so fast, like in a second or two, that it feels like magic.

Or maybe it's him.

He feels like magic.

The heat of his fingers around my ankle and the roughness of his summer skin feel like magic. Or the fact that everything about him is so hard and muscular, the slant of his shoulders, the bulge in his thigh.

He is all… boy.

Hard and heated and muscled. Masculine.

He's the first guy I've touched like this. Or who's touched *me* like this.

"What are you doing?"

I know I won't get an answer though.

Because he's busy elsewhere.

His entire focus is on my foot.

So I focus on it as well and what I see makes me fist his t-shirt — gosh it's so soft — all tight and hard. He's wrapping something around my ankle, that shiny thing that he'd gotten out of his pocket. Which makes me realize what it is.

"An anklet," I whisper.

I watch in fascination as he — his big and strong fingers — deftly closes a very delicate and fragile-looking clasp as he puts his gift on me. When he's done and I feel it rustling against my skin, my toes curl again. "You're giving me an anklet."

Finally he looks up. "So you can't sneak up on me again."

I swallow, my curled toes flexing. "I didn't though. You caught me last time."

His reddish-brown eyes flash with the memory. "I did, yeah."

My fingers in his t-shirt tighten even more. "It's beautiful."

Just like the fireworks last year.

Just like his eyes, his face, *him*.

"Yeah," he whispers back and I know, I *know* for a fact, that he isn't talking about the anklet.

He's talking about me.

Me.

Exactly like last time.

"Is that why," I swallow, "you came here tonight? To give me a birthday gift."

He did, didn't he?

Running into him wasn't a coincidence.

He was looking for me like I was looking for him.

"Thirteen, yeah?" he rasps.

My heart skips a beat and I nod. "Yes."

And he's sixteen.

He's a sophomore and I'm not even in high school yet.

Maybe that's why he thought that I was too young for him, and I bet he still thinks that.

I don't like it though.

I do not like it one bit.

Tightening my fist in his shirt and digging my heel in his thigh, I say, "I... It's not that young. I-I mean I'm not, I've never been, very young. It's all the books I read. I've always been super worldly and mature because of it. And like, my teachers and all, they've always called me precocious and smart. I mean," I blush, "I think we... I *don't* think that there's any reason why we can't be friends. We —"

"There's a reason."

"What?"

I'm not sure what he meant just then. And unfortunately, I don't get an explanation from him because we get interrupted again.

Just like last year.

By another voice.

"Jesus, there you are."

My eyes swivel in the direction the voice had come from, thinking that this cannot be happening again. Another guard *cannot* be coming to take him away.

But it's not a guard.

It's a boy.

More importantly, it's a boy Reign's age, I think.

He stands at a distance from us and his gaze — puzzled and confused — is pinned on me. Before he shifts his focus to Reign and then lower.

To my foot.

Which I realize is still on Reign's thigh.

Blushing furiously, I take it off and jump apart from him.

"Did I interrupt something?" the guy asks.

"No," I quickly reply even though the question was for Reign.

I'm not sure why I'm so flustered but I am. Maybe because he *is* interrupting something and the urge to tell him off for that is so strong that I had to say no.

At my answer, the guy's eyes come back to me and he tilts his head to the side slightly. As if trying to figure out what's going on.

It makes me self-conscious enough that I tuck my hair behind my ear.

Noticing my action, the guy says, "Hey."

"Hi," I say politely.

Again, he looks at Reign — who's come up to his feet now — as if expecting something from him, but Reign is weirdly silent and I think broody. I wonder if it's because he's thinking what I'm thinking, that this new guy did interrupt us.

Then the guy looks back at me and jerks his chin. "I'm Lucas."

"Oh, um, I'm Echo," I say automatically because it's only polite.

But then I freeze because I hear an honest to God growl.

A *growl*.

And I swear it's coming from Reign.

But before I can confirm it, the new guy — Lucas — says, "Echo." Then, smiling, "Pretty name."

Okay, this time I'm sure there's a growl. But I'm too polite to switch my focus back to Reign and ignore Lucas's compliment. "Thank you."

Still I glance over at Reign from the corner of my eye and notice that his fists are clenched.

"You have to forgive him," Lucas says, shrugging, stealing my focus again. "Reign and good manners don't mix well. I'm used to it by now though. I'm this asshole's best friend."

"Best friend?"

"Yeah. I know it's hard to believe." Lucas chuckles. "Seeing how charming I am."

Well, he is charming, I guess.

Also easy-going and friendly.

But my mind is too much on Reign to really appreciate that.

My silence doesn't deter Lucas though. "So I've never seen you around before this. Who are —"

"Let's go."

Those are the first words Reign has spoken since Lucas got here. And even though they're curt, I can't help but breathe in a sigh of relief.

That he spoke. Maybe now I can figure out what's wrong.

Why is Reign glaring at his own best friend?

"But I'm having a conversation here," Lucas protests good-naturedly, smiling.

Not that it affects Reign in the slightest. His mysterious bad mood doesn't thaw at all. In fact, it becomes worse and he growls, "Yeah? I don't fucking care. Come on."

With that, he moves.

He starts to walk away and I'm not going to lie, every step that he takes away from me, my chest grows tighter, my breaths faster.

Where is he going? We haven't finished our talk yet and we were in the middle of the most important part. Shouldn't we finish that?

Also, when am I going to see him again?

I *am* going to see him again, right?

I'm not even sure how long he's staying here for and...

I'm about to call out to him but Lucas gets there first. "Jesus, what's your problem? I —"

Reign comes to a halt then, his shoulders tight and his back moving on a wave of a breath. Turning around to face Lucas, he goes, "She's no one."

"What?"

He raises his eyebrows. "You wanted to know who she is, yeah? She's no one. At least, not someone who matters."

"What the fuck does that mean?"

"It means," he grits out, "that she's the staff. Or at least her mother is. And her father." When Lucas keeps frowning, Reign continues, "You see the food they're all stuffing their faces with? I hear that her mother's quite the chef. And her father's very handy with the lawnmower."

Lucas stares at him before coming back to me for a second. "O-kay. I —"

"So you understand what I'm saying to you?" He gestures with his chin. "She's a little servant girl. You're mixing with the wrong crowd. The right crowd is over there. Come on."

For a few seconds after that, there's silence.

No one says anything, not Reign, not Lucas and definitely not me.

I couldn't. Even if I wanted to.

Because enough's already been said, I guess. By Reign.

Who I very weirdly notice stands in such a way that we make a triangle, him and me and Lucas. I'm not sure why I'm noticing that. What a strange thing to notice in a moment like this, but nevertheless I do.

I notice.

The distance. The shape.

The fact that he still won't look at me.

But Lucas does. I feel the moment his eyes swivel over and land on me. My cheeks burn when I notice the pity in them. "I'm... Fuck, I'm so sorry. I —"

His words get interrupted again when Reign turns back and begins walking away.

Widening the distance. Ruining the triangle.

And all I can do is stand here and watch him leave.

Unable to process what just happened.

CHAPTER THREE

Who: The Bubblegum
Where: The second-floor bedroom in the carriage house on the Davidson estate
When: 1:15AM; five years ago, one day after Echo's thirteenth birthday

Dear Holly,
He lives here now.
Or rather, he's going to live here now.
At the manor.
Not only that, he's also going to go to my school as well, Bardstown High West.
I don't know what's more shocking, him coming back to live in Bardstown from Connecticut or that he's going to go to a public school like mine rather than a posh private school like most of the rich kids go to.
But apparently, from what I hear, this is a punishment for him.
For being expelled from that boarding school.
The whole manor is abuzz with the news that the second son of the Davidsons finally got expelled for having drugs in

his dorm room. Marijuana. Since this was his like, tenth offense or whatever, no amount of donation or Davidson influence could save him. And his dad is furious. So sending him to Bardstown High West is his way of teaching him a lesson. Sort of like going from riches to rags for not appreciating the riches.

So he isn't here for only a couple of days or the weekend, he's home forever.

And I'm going to see him, not only on the estate, but also around campus. Because we share one with the high school.

I'm also going to see his best friend, Lucas.

Because he's back too.

Lucas Wayne.

Actually, he's more than his best friend.

Lucas is Reign's brother, or rather the brother he never had, even though he does have a brother, Homer. But not only is Homer eight years older than Reign, he's never home and so Homer and Reign have never been close. In fact, Homer finds his younger brother as disappointing as the rest of their family.

Anyway, Lucas and Reign are inseparable and have been since the age of eight.

Where one goes the other follows.

What one does, the other does as well.

Which means that if Reign was caught with drugs, Lucas was caught too and so he was expelled as well. And since Lucas's dad — his mom died when he was little, according to the manor gossip — is great friends with Reign's dad, they decided to send their son to the same poor public school for punishment.

So yeah.

That's what happened to me today.

The guy who I haven't been able to stop thinking about for a year is back. And he's back for good. And I'd be super happy about the news. I'd be overjoyed, ecstatic, thrilled and positively giddy about the news if he hadn't done what he had done.

If he hadn't said what he'd said.
Servant girl.
He thinks I'm a servant girl.
He thinks that I'm the wrong crowd.
And it would've been okay. It would've been totally fine, if he'd only said that. But then he had to go and insult my mom and dad, with his stupid chef and lawnmower comment.
I mean, what does that mean?
Why did he do that?
And if that's what he thinks about me, then why give me that gift?
Why give me the stupid anklet?
You know what, I'm going to give it back. I'm going to just... throw it at his arrogant, smug face and then demand an explanation.
Demand to know what his problem is.
That stupid, idiot jerk.
That Bandit.
~Echo

Who: The Bandit
Where: The second-floor bedroom in the manor on the Davidson estate
When: 1:15AM; five years ago, one day after Echo's thirteenth birthday

He wants her.
He fucking wants her.
And he wants her a lot.
He wants her so much that he couldn't stop talking about her last night. He couldn't stop asking me questions. How I knew her; what I was doing there with her; why was her foot on my thigh; was she hurt; should we go back and look.

He wants her like a lovesick puppy.

Like she's the most beautiful girl he's ever seen. Like her quirks, her love of pink, her synonyms, her honey-blonde hair, the fact that she has a diary makes something move in his chest. Because he keeps a diary too.

But he doesn't, does he?

Because I do.

I keep a diary. And when I found out that she does too, things moved in my fucking chest. For the first time, those things weren't laced in embarrassment, in shame that I keep a journal like a fucking pussy. A stupid fucking habit formed at a therapist's office that has proven hard to break.

Not only that, I want her so much that the first thing I did when I came back to this hellhole town, to this nightmarish manor, was to go look for her, in the same woods, at the same time that I'd met her a year ago.

With a piece of jewelry in my back pocket.

That I actually bought with my own money. Well, from selling pot, but still.

And it makes me angry.

For so many, many reasons.

Firstly, because I want her in the first place. Enough to do the things that I just mentioned.

And it doesn't make sense that I do.

She's fucking thirteen. She's a baby and I hardly know her.

And secondly, I'm angry because of how angry it makes me that my best friend wants her too.

So angry that I want to fucking punch his face.

I wanted to fucking punch his face last night to make him stop talking. I wanted to fucking stab his eyes for looking at her.

And since I couldn't do any of those things, I warned him off her. I told him who she was and how she wasn't the girl for him because she's the staff, or the daughter of the staff anyway. Something me and him have been warned time and again to stay away from, by both our fathers. Apparently, you can't consort with the staff.

Whatever.

That's not important.

Important thing is that I warned him.

And not because of some stupid made-up rule but because I fucking hated how he was looking at her.

So yeah, I'm angry.

I'm so fucking angry that I can't stop looking at my window every five seconds. Because the first thing that I see when I look out of it, is the carriage house.

I wonder if the window that I see when I do look out belongs to her.

I wonder what she must be doing right now. I wonder if she's writing in her diary.

I wonder what is it about her.

She's just a girl, Jesus. There are a million girls out there. A million.

Which means girls are expendable. They're inconsequential. They don't matter.

And they especially don't matter when your best friend wants them too.

So here's what I'm gonna do next: nothing.

Absolutely fucking nothing.

I'm not letting a girl ruin our friendship.

It doesn't matter how pure and pink and goddamn sweet she appears to be. It doesn't matter how weirdly fascinated I am with her; my fascination will wear off.

She's not worth it.

She's not fucking worth my friendship with my best friend.

CHAPTER FOUR

Who: The Bubblegum
Where: The second-floor bedroom in the carriage house on the Davidson estate
When: 11:04 PM; four years ago, a week after Echo's fourteenth birthday

Dear Holly,
He asked me out.
Today. At school.
He came up to me in the library for our regular tutoring session and just came out with it.
I'm going to be honest, I did have a feeling that he's wanted to do this for some time now. Quite possibly ever since he asked me to tutor him to help him with his grades. The whole fact that he came to the library on our side of the school and asked me to tutor him even though I'm still in the eighth grade tipped me off a little bit.
But I was still shocked.
It's not as if he has any shortage of interested girls at school. Being a soccer superstar and the team captain comes with many advantages, especially in Bardstown, the so-called soccer nation.
But ever since I started to tutor him, he always invites me to

his games. And if I do end up going, he makes sure to look at me whenever he scores a goal.

So yeah, I knew.

But as I said, I'm shocked.

Or more like, I don't know what to do.

Well, there are reasons to say no.

First and foremost, I'm only fourteen. I'm not even allowed to date yet. Second, even if my parents lift that restriction, they're going to totally freak out when they find out who they're lifting the restriction for.

We're not really allowed to consort with our employers.

And even though the Waynes are not our employers, they're still our employers' friends.

They're our employers' best friends, aren't they?

Which brings me to the most important reason to say no to Lucas: him.

The guy who hates me.

And there's no doubt now that he hates me, right?

Not after a year.

Not after a year of him looking at me like I'm the lowest of low.

A bug beneath his black boots. That he wants to crush and wreck and ruin and destroy.

His servant girl.

All because my parents work for his parents.

Because I'm poor and he's rich.

Because I'm the wrong crowd.

I still remember what he said about me that night, on my thirteenth birthday. I still remember how he looked at me, or rather how he didn't look at me, because he didn't think I was even worthy of that little courtesy.

Oh, and let's not forget how in the beginning I gave him the benefit of the doubt and tried to actually be nice to him, tried to befriend him, and how he rejected — no, crushed — all my attempts, making me feel like an idiot for even entertaining the thought that a rich boy like him would ever consort with a servant girl like me. I thought he deserved my kindness because rumors can be false and exaggerated but he proved me wrong. He taught me that every rumor about him is true.

And ever since I started tutoring his best friend, his hatred for me has only grown.

Now, I can feel his eyes on me. His reddish-brown eyes boring into me, making my skin prickle every time we pass each other by in the school hallways. Or every time I go to the soccer games. Because like Lucas, he's a soccer player too.

A rockstar soccer player.

Who, like Lucas, doesn't have any shortage of interested girls either.

In fact, I saw them ogling him this afternoon. While he was running laps around the soccer field.

Shirtless.

Please, what a show-off.

And he is a show-off.

While Lucas is more level-headed and methodical — hence the captain, I suppose — he's more reckless. He's more spontaneous. He likes to play around on the field, do backflips or jumps and cartwheels during the game, just so girls will scream his name.

Freaking jerk.

Freaking Bandit.

And the Daredevil. That's what they call him, his soccer nickname.

Which is appropriate.

Because he is the devil.

So I don't even want to think about how he'd react, what he'd do, if he found out that Lucas has asked me out. That I'd be going out on a date with his best friend.

But wait a second.

What am I thinking?

What the hell am I thinking?

Who is he to stop me from dating his best friend? Who is he to have any effect on my decisions whatsoever?

I mean, I like Lucas, right?

He's friendly. He's easygoing. He's always been nice to me, which is why I agreed to tutor him in the first place. Best of all, he doesn't look at me like I'm nothing. Like I don't belong in his social circle.

He looks at me like he likes me, like he thinks I'm beautiful.

So why can't I go out with him if I want to?

And you know what, I will.

I will go out with him and if Reign Davidson doesn't like it, he can go fuck himself.

~Echo

Who: The Bandit
Where: The second-floor bedroom in the manor on the Davidson estate
When: 11:04 PM; four years ago, a week after Echo's fourteenth birthday.

He asked her out. He fucking asked her out.
He fucking. Asked. Her. Out.

Who: The Bandit
Where: The second-floor bedroom in the manor on the Davidson estate
When: 1:27 AM; four years ago, the day Echo says yes to Lucas.

Fuck.
Fuck. Fuck. Fuck.
Fucking fuck.

Who: The Bandit
Where: The second-floor bedroom in the manor on the Davidson estate
When: 3:11 AM; four years ago, the day Echo says yes to Lucas

He's my best friend.
He's like my brother.
Don't kill him. Do not fucking kill him.
Do not punch him.
Do not break his nose.
Do. Not.

Who: The Bandit
Where: The second-floor bedroom in the manor on the Davidson estate
When: 3:19 AM; four years ago, the day Echo says yes to Lucas

FUCK.

CHAPTER FIVE

Who: The Bubblegum
Where: The second-floor bedroom in the carriage house on the Davidson estate
When: 10:13 PM; three years ago, on Echo's fifteenth birthday

Dear Holly,

He loves me.

He told me that today. He took me to this fancy restaurant for my birthday dinner and he told me that he loved me.

Again, like the first time he asked me out, I had a feeling that he was going to say that.

He'd been dropping enough hints about forever and future and what will happen when he goes off to college next year on his soccer scholarship and I'm still in school.

It was still shocking though, I'm not going to lie.

But what was more shocking was that I told him that I loved him too.

I didn't know that I was going to say that until the words came out of my mouth and he looked so... happy. He looked so thrilled and relieved and just glad.

So I didn't know how to take it back, and now I'm glad I didn't.

Because if you really think about it, I do love him.

I do.

I mean, let's talk about how amazing he is.

He's the most amazing boyfriend ever.

The most amazing.

He's attentive, affectionate, caring.

He's loyal. He doesn't even look at other girls and there are still plenty of girls who'd love to be looked at by him, given his rockstar soccer player status.

Oh, and my parents like him too.

Something that I was worried about because of our different social status. But he won them over and now he's like a part of our little family.

So yay!

Not to mention...

Okay, this might sound really petty but I'm just going to say it because this is my diary, and these are my secrets. But just imagine — imagine — how he'd react to this. How he'd take this news.

He's going to lose his shit, isn't he?

He so is.

My boyfriend's best friend. The Bandit.

I shouldn't grin or dance around in my bed gleefully as I write this because it's the least important thing right now. But oh my God, he's really going to lose his freaking shit when he finds out that Lucas and I love each other. That his best friend has fallen for the Servant Girl, someone so beneath him.

Especially when he's spent the entire last year either wishing or trying to break us up.

I still haven't forgotten the Halloween incident last year, by the way. When he got Lucas drunk at this soccer party and set a pregnant nun and a Catwoman on him so they could seduce him.

That freaking asshole.

It's a good thing that my boyfriend is loyal and came back the next day to tell me all about it. Because who knows what would've happened.

Well, I mean something did happen though.

I kissed him.

Yup, after he finished telling me the sorry tale and promised to give Reign a piece of his mind, I kissed Lucas. Not only to show my appreciation but also because he could go tell his best friend to suck it. He could tell his best friend that he didn't need to be seduced by other girls because his girlfriend was enough.

The fact that that was our very first kiss and that I partially — okay, seventy percent — did it to prove a point to his best friend is not something that I care to think about a lot.

I look at it this way: we had to kiss sometime, right? So we did. Plus I'd been holding out for weeks.

Which is another point in Lucas's favor. That he'd waited for me.

He's still waiting for me.

Because even though we kiss and make out regularly, we haven't taken it to the next level. We haven't done it yet. Mostly because, again, I'm the hold-up.

Maybe I'm terrified of the pain that comes with losing your virginity, and trust me, I'm plenty scared of that. Maybe it's my age; I'm only fifteen. There's no need to rush. Or maybe it's something else, but I'm not there yet.

And Lucas doesn't pressure me.

So yeah, there's no reason to not love him and so I do.

And if that pisses my boyfriend's best friend off then that's just a bonus.

Because as much as he hates me, I hate him more. I hate him with every fiber of my being. I hate my boyfriend's best friend so much that it makes me sick.

Hatesick.

~Echo

Who: The Bandit
Where: The second-floor bedroom in the manor on the Davidson estate
When: 12:37 AM; three years ago, on Echo's fifteenth birthday

She loves him.
She's in love with him. And he's in love with her.
What the fuck is love?
What does it mean, to be in love?
Does it mean that she's it for him? That he'll stay with her for the rest of his fucking life? And that he'll die for her, kill for her? Does it mean that he'll do anything to see her smile at him or have her light brown eyes light up when she looks at him?
What the fuck does it mean?
I wanted to ask him that when he told me the joyous news. I also wanted to do a million other things that I've been increasingly thinking about ever since he started going out with her.
The usual, you know.
Punch him in the face. Break a few ribs. Put him in the hospital.
Kill him.
But I didn't.
Even when he told me to behave.
To fucking rein myself in when she's around because as it turns out, she's going to be around for a long, long time. He wants me to be his best friend and support him, and make it less obvious that I hate her.
Hate.
Now that I know something about.
I know what it feels like to hate. To loathe, to detest, abhor, abominate and fucking despise.
It's like you're burning up.
It's like you're being slashed open, constantly bleeding.

Every second of every hour. Of every day.

And since you're in constant agony, you want others to be in agony too.

You want others to suffer as well.

You want her to suffer.

Because she's the one, isn't she?

She's the one who has managed to ruin the one good thing in my life. She's the one who makes me want to kill my best friend every time she smiles at him, every time she gets close to him, laughs with him, talks to him, touches him.

It's because of her that I can't stand my best friend's happiness. I can't stand to be around him.

I can't stand to be his friend anymore.

So yeah, I know about hate. I know how sick it makes me.

How sick she makes me.

Fucking hatesick.

CHAPTER SIX

Two years ago. Bardstown

At first I ignore it.

The *tap tap tap* echoing around my room.

It must be the tree just outside my window. The branches have a habit of knocking on the glass when the weather turns windy. My friends, when they come over, have a tendency of getting scared, but when you practically live in the middle of the woods, you become used to it.

But then the *tap tap tap* almost becomes a *boom boom boom*, and I jump out of my bed, my heart in my throat.

This does not sound like a tree at all.

This sounds like…

Like someone is knocking at my window.

Like someone is rapping their knuckles on the glass.

And I realize that I can see them.

Whoever they are.

The drapes are closed and I'm used to seeing the blurry silhouette of the branches swaying gently. However, tonight I can see the silhouette of someone else as well.

The head, the shoulders.

The freaking arm that reaches out and bangs at the window once more, this time louder and more insistent. Like they're getting impatient at the delay.

Oh Jesus *Christ.*

What do I do, what do I do, what do I fucking *do*?

The knock comes again and instead of running toward my door and dashing out of my room, I dash toward the window. Before I even realize it, I'm tearing the drapes open and then I'm... numb.

I'm dazed. I'm dreaming.

I am, aren't I?

This has to be a dream.

No, a nightmare.

If I'm seeing what I'm seeing then it's definitely a nightmare.

Because what I'm seeing, or rather *who* I'm seeing, lives there.

His eyes live there.

Reddish brown and so unique with crazy thick eyelashes.

That jaw, square and sculpted and stubbled.

Perpetually tight and clenched. *Offended.*

Like I make his life difficult simply by existing.

So yeah, a nightmare.

Only I don't remember falling asleep and I don't think he ever talks in my nightmares. He's too busy shooting me condescending and hateful glares.

But he's talking now.

His lips are moving and oh my God, this is not a nightmare at all. This is worse. This is reality.

He is here.

Here.

Outside of my bedroom window.

"Open the window."

I shudder at his words. At his gravelly and deep voice, now that I can hear it.

Squinting at his crouched form, I try to speak. "What the..."

"Open the window."

"What?"

Finally he seems to be getting to the end of his patience with me and that stubbled jaw of his clenches. "Open the fucking window."

"How did you..." I shake my head. "What are you doing out there?"

"Trying to get you to open this fucking window."

"Why... I don't..." I shake my head again and breathe deep. "Why didn't you use the front door?"

I don't think that's the right question, given how absurd and bizarre this is.

Him, outside my window. Him, *on a branch of that tree* outside my window.

"How did you even get up there?" I ask then, without giving him the chance to answer.

He shoots me a look. "How do you think? I climbed."

"You *climbed*?"

His jaw clenches again. And that's the extent of his response.

"But it's a tree," I add.

"Hence the *climbing*." Then, "Unless you think I've got magical powers and I can fly, that's pretty much what you do with a fucking tree. You *climb* it."

Okay, not two minutes, *not two freaking minutes*, into this conversation and I want to strangle him.

"You're such a —"

"And you really think your parents would've let me in? If I had knocked at your front door."

No, not at all.

I don't think my parents would've let him in.

They're both downstairs right now, watching TV, winding down for the night after a long day of work in his family's employ. If their boss's second son had showed up at the door, they would've freaked out and slammed it in his face. Because my parents are the best and they know everything, all the rumors about him and about how he's treated me all these years. Which means they would've sent him away and given him a piece of their minds.

Even at the risk of losing their jobs.

I sigh and he takes that as my agreement to the point he made.

Then, in a softer and somehow also rougher voice, "Open the window, Bubblegum."

And the breath that escapes me then is all shivery and trembling.

Bubblegum.

His name for me.

It's been exactly three years since he called me that.

The last time was the night of my thirteenth birthday. And today, I turn sixteen and I…

I hated that name.

I *did*.

And I hate that he's calling me by it. Probably to throw me off or something. So I get my trembles under control and, reaching forward, I open the window and immediately step back as he enters my bedroom.

This is so absurd, isn't it?

I haven't seen him in a year, not since he went away to college last year. Since then he hasn't been back, not even for the holidays. Which is not really out of the norm and now he's standing in my bedroom.

What is he doing here?

"Is this the first time you've been back? Since you went away to college," I ask, watching him rake his fingers through his hair, which I realize has grown out even more.

His surfer's hair, only dark.

"Why," he asks, his reddish-brown eyes flashing, "did you miss me?"

"Yes," I tell him, taking in his sharply honed, slightly more mature features. "I missed you like I miss getting stabbed in the eye."

He rakes his eyes over my features. "Very wild for someone very…"

"Very what?"

"Pink." Then, "And girly. And good."

"Well, I'm a girl and I'm good, so," I say in a prickly tone. "And from what I remember I told you not to call me that."

At my words, his lips tilt up slightly. "If you remember that then you probably also remember that I never really cared about what you told me."

"That's because you're selfish, arrogant and despicable."

"More synonyms to describe me," he murmurs. "Nice to see that I still take up way too much room in your pretty little head."

"You do not —"

"Besides," he continues over me, "still can't blame me for calling you that, can you?"

"What?"

Instead of answering me, he looks down. At my dress.

And before I can stop myself, I blush.

Because of course, my dress is pink.

And I hate that he can so easily make me do that. He can so easily make me blush and leave me breathless.

"You," he says in a raspy tone when he's done looking me over. "Bubblegum pink."

"I'm..."

I forget what I was going to say because after he's done with his once-over of me, he moves on to my room. And I realize that this is the first time he's staring at it, my personal sanctuary, my personal things.

My bedroom walls, the rugs on the floor, the desk by the window he climbed into.

All of which are soft and pastel shades of pink.

But it's nothing compared to how hard he stares when his gaze finally reaches my bed.

At my rumpled sheets and my strewn-about pillows.

My diary.

He stares at it the hardest.

"You still call it Holly?" he asks when his eyes — super intense all of a sudden — come back to me.

My heart slams in my chest. "No."

"Because it's not pink."

I swallow. "No, it's not."

"It's the only thing in your room that's not pink."

"Yes."

Yup, the only thing.

The most precious thing in the world to me is not pink. I know it doesn't fit. It doesn't make sense, but one day I got this urge to pack up my pink diaries and get a new one that's brown leather.

Dark brown leather.

"So what is it called then?"

My heart beats so forcefully then that I feel like my chest is turning black and blue.

My *whole body* is turning black and blue.

"That's…" I clear my throat. "None of your business."

It isn't.

Nothing about me or what I do is any of his business.

So I'm not sure why I feel a pinch in my chest when his expression shutters and a cool mask takes its place. "You're right. Not my business at all." He sweeps his eyes over my room once again before coming back to me. "But good to see that not everything in your room is covered in unicorn vomit."

I purse my lips. "Now that you've insulted me to your heart's content, do you mind telling me what you're doing here."

"Saying hey."

"What?"

"We've got things to talk about."

"What things?"

I'm confused.

Very, very confused.

I'm also distracted.

By his biceps.

Because they're flexed right now. Taut and bulging.

And that's because his arms are folded across his chest as he casually stands by my window, his hip propped against it, his ankles crossed.

As if we're having a normal conversation.

As if this is a regular occurrence.

What *in the fuck* is going on?

"For starters," he rumbles, unfolding his arms and pushing off the window, "let's talk about how we have so much in common."

"What?"

He takes a step toward me. "How you live in my house."

I glance down at his boots before looking up and taking a step back. "This isn't your house. This is your family's house."

Another step forward. "How you work for my family."

I take another step back. "My parents work for your family."

"How that dress you're wearing right now," he motions with a jerk of his chin, "was bought with my money."

"It's your parents' money that *my* parents have earned. Through hard work. Which you probably don't understand the meaning of."

My dig doesn't faze him, however.

His expression is unmoved as he takes yet another step toward me. "How the cake that you had last night was bought from my money too."

I'm forced to take another step back. "What? That's... How did you..."

I did have a cake last night.

And well, since my mom was super busy with her job, she didn't have time to bake so she bought me one from the bakery, promising that she'd bake for me next weekend. But how did he know that? How...

"And the little party you're planning to have tomorrow," he goes on, "with your little school friends, my money's gonna pay for that too."

Oh God.

How does he... *know*?

"How do you know all that? How —"

"But most importantly," he takes that last step, his eyes swirling with something, "how you're dating my best friend."

My spine hits the bedpost then, my body coming to a jarring halt.

But his words hit me harder.

They hit me right in the center of my chest and I know.

I finally know why he's here.

I can see it in his eyes, how heated they are, how harsh.

How his jaw is pulsing, how tense his large frame is.

"I —"

"How he came all the way from New York to see you tonight. For your fucking birthday."

"Reign, I —"

He puts his arm up, gripping the bedpost that I'm glued to, up above my head. "And *how,*" his grip on the post tightens, those distracting biceps of his bulging, threatening to rip his dark t-shirt, "you broke his heart in return."

I'm threatening to rip mine as well, my dress, at this.

With how tight I'm clutching it.

"I... I'm..."

"You did," he growls, "didn't you?"

I swallow thickly, looking up at his angry face, my heart twisting and clenching in my chest.

And I can't help but ask, "Did he... Did he call you?"

"What *the fuck* do you think?"

"I-I didn't mean to... I didn't..."

"Well, that's great then, isn't it? That you didn't mean to."

"I'm so sorry. I'm —"

"Do it."

"What?"

He clenches his jaw for a second before growling, "Say yes."

"W-what?" I repeat, my eyes wide and my breaths all fearful.

But apparently, it's not enough for him.

He wants me even more afraid, even more shivery and shaky because he leans down, his eyes burning so bright that I feel harsh sun staring down at me. "Pick up your phone right the fuck now and tell him."

"Tell him what?"

His nostrils flare as he grinds his teeth.

As he pushes himself to say the next words like he can't bear to say them but he has to.

He needs to.

Because that's why he came here.

"Tell him," he says slowly, "that you'll marry him."

"No," I blurt out.

And hate myself for it.

Even more than I did before he arrived here so abruptly and I was on the bed, pouring all my angst into my diary. I hate myself even more for saying no now, than I did when I'd said it to my boyfriend.

Who did come here to surprise me on my birthday.

He wasn't supposed to be here, let alone take me out for a birthday dinner. He was supposed to be back in New York like he's been for the past year, for college, practicing for an upcoming soccer game. But he left all that to come to me. He said that he didn't want me to be alone, not today, not for my birthday.

And I was so happy to see him too.

But then I went and ruined everything.

I hurt him.

All because at the end of our meal, he asked me a question and produced a ring.

He said that even though we're young, it feels right. It feels like forever. And this ring, even though it's an engagement ring, doesn't mean that we have to marry as soon as I turn eighteen. I could treat it as a promise ring and we could wait until I finished college, if I wanted to. But he couldn't not give me a ring and propose because he could see our future so clearly.

Him being a pro-soccer player and me being his wife.

Unlike all the other times before — when he'd asked me out for the first time or told me that he loved me — I couldn't see this coming. And to say that I freaked out is an understatement.

I freaked the fuck out.

I felt trapped. Suffocated.

I felt like someone was standing on my chest, not letting me breathe.

And so I ran.

I told him that I wanted to go back home. That I couldn't be here. I couldn't do this. And like the best boyfriend in the whole wide world, he did what I asked him to. He drove me back home and I've been shut up in my room ever since.

"No," he repeats, softly.

"I-I can't."

"And why not?"

"I just..."

"You just what?"

"I-I can't. I..."

"You *what*?"

"Because it's too soon," I blurt out the first thing that comes into my head.

Even though as soon as I say it, I know it's a lie.

It's not too soon.

It's not why I said no. I said no because I was feeling trapped and I have a feeling I'd feel trapped even if he asked me this question years down the lane.

And oh my God, the hate that I feel for myself keeps growing.

Because why do I feel this way? Why do I feel trapped when I love Lucas so much?

"You've been dating him for two years," his best friend snaps, his chest undulating on a sharp breath.

"I'm —"

"Two years that have felt like two fucking centuries."

"What?"

"So which part of that is too *goddamn fucking soon*?"

"I don't know, okay? *I don't know*."

All I know is that I can't do it.

I can't marry the boy I love for some reason. I can't say yes to him and I don't know what's wrong with me. I don't understand how I could've done something like this to him.

How I could've hurt Lucas like this.

"Maybe I can enlighten you then," he says, breaking into my confused thoughts.

He inches even closer, his body bending forward.

His broad shoulders dipping, his sculpted face looming over me as he rasps, "It's hard, isn't it?"

"What's hard?"

"This whole long-distance shit," he goes on, his eyes flicking over my face. "It's hard for him. I can tell. The fact that he doesn't get to see you as much, or as often as he'd like. He doesn't get to see your pretty dresses, all nice and tight up top but fluttering and flying around your creamy thighs. Doesn't get to see your thick long honey-colored braids, always bound with a ribbon, sometimes a hairclip with butterflies. Or the way you tilt your face up whenever there's sun out, like you want to absorb every inch of the sunshine, and you do, don't you? Because your fucking skin glows, somehow both pale and golden at the same time. Or that you always have a tiny smile whenever you open a book. Doesn't matter which book, your mouth always tips up. And that you never fucking watch where you're going and so he has to put his hand on you, grip your elbow or your tiny waist, your delicate shoulders, so he can steer you away from trouble. He can protect you because you don't have the common fucking sense to do it yourself. He doesn't get to do all that now and he hates it. He fucking hates that you're not close. Where he can get to you whenever he wants, touch you, smell you," he breathes in deep then as if smelling me, as if *he's* the one who misses my scent, "or hear your voice. Your laugh."

Somewhere along the way, while he was talking, rasping, my belly has bottomed out. It's fallen through my body and it's like I'm in the air.

I'm flying.

There's wind beneath my feet and I don't think I'm coming down any time soon.

Not with the way he's watching my lips.

My mouth.

As if *he's* the one who misses my laughter and not Lucas.

"Reign," I whisper.

His eyes snap up and as soon as they look into mine, his jaw clenches. "It's hard for him. So I bet it's hard for you too." Then, after a pause, "Is it?"

"Yes," I somehow manage to say even though I'm still reeling and breathless.

Another clench. "You miss him, huh."

"A lot."

"A lot."

I nod.

"So maybe you found a way to make it easy."

"What?"

"Maybe," he drawls, "you found *someone* to make it easy."

"S-someone?"

This time, the pulse on his jaw lingers longer, turning all his features harsh, his eyes all violent. "Who is he?"

"Who's who?"

"The asshole who keeps sniffing around you."

"What asshole? What are you talking about?"

"At the school library."

"At the school..." Then, "Are you... Are you talking about Evan?"

"Is that what his name is? Fucking Evan."

"How do you... How do you know about Evan?" I ask, studying his face in return. When his nostrils flare and a muscle jumps on his cheek at 'Evan,' I continue, "Are you... Are you like, *spying* on me? Is that how you know about my birthday cake and the party and... and Evan."

Oh my God, I'm...

He's...

He's a freaking stalker. He's a freaking criminal.

Bandit.

"Relax," he drawls, probably reading how horrified I am on my face. "Your boyfriend has a big mouth when it comes to you and your mundane fucking life. And as for spying on you, I make sure to keep tabs on things that matter. And you do. To my best friend. Unfortunately. And it's a good thing too, isn't it? Because now I know."

"You know what?" I snap.

"Why it's too fucking soon."

"And why is it too fucking soon, Reign?"

"It's too fucking soon, *Echo*, because you're stepping out on my best friend, aren't you?"

Maybe if he'd said it in a different way, in a way not so hostile or in a way that doesn't make it seem like he's talking about himself. Like I'm stepping out on *him* and not on his best friend, and that's why he's so freaking angry.

Then I probably wouldn't have done what I did.

I probably wouldn't have raised my arm, my palms wide open, so I could smack his face.

But I did and no, I don't manage to.

Slap him I mean.

Because he stops me mid-strike.

My wrist being caught in a tight grip.

His grip.

"How dare you?" My chest is heaving. "How fucking *dare* you? You're an asshole."

"And you still haven't answered my question."

"Because it's a bullshit question." Before he can say anything else, I get up in his face and continue, "And where do you get off asking me questions? When you're the one who's always tried your best to take him away from me. Weren't you the one who got him drunk at the Halloween party that one time? You were the one who set girls on him so he'd step out on *me*."

He makes a face like he doesn't know what I'm talking about. "What?"

"Don't lie to me. I know what you did."

He stares at me a beat, still looking clueless but then speaks. "I have no idea what the fuck you're talking about and I've got no interest in finding out. Because we have more important matters to discuss, don't you think? Now answer the fucking question."

"No." I clench my teeth. "Because as I said, it's a bullshit question. Especially coming from you. *Especially* when I'd never, not ever, do anything to hurt Lucas."

As soon as I say it, I realize that I shouldn't have.

I shouldn't have said that last part because it's not true, is it?

I did do something to hurt him.

I refused to give him what he asked for.

I ran away.

"But then you did, didn't you?" he says, digging his fingers into my wrist.

His words make my eyes sting. "Evan is a guy I tutor. Like I did with Lucas. I meet up with him at the library three times a week so we can go over his assignments and class work. There's nothing..."

I shake my head, breathing in deeply. "I wouldn't do that. To Lucas. I love him. I love him more than I could ever imagine loving someone. And yes, this last year has been hard. I miss him so much it hurts. It makes me ache. But not once, not for a single moment, did I think about going behind his back. I-I could never... I'm not like that. But apparently, I am because... Because look what I did. Tonight. Instead of appreciating that he left everything and drove down just to surprise me, I broke his heart.

And I don't even know how to make it right because I... I felt so suffocated."

"What?"

A tear drops down my cheeks and his frown is so big and thick that I could settle my thumb in that groove. "You've always hated me, since the beginning. Because of who I am, who my parents are, how I don't fit into your sparkly and lavish lifestyle. How Lucas could do so much better than me, a servant girl. And you know what, you're right. You're absolutely right. Because when he asked me to make a commitment to him, I felt suffocated."

There. It's out there.

I told him.

My secret.

And what an odd choice for a confidant.

The guy who's always hated me.

But now that I have said it out loud, I can't stop. "I felt trapped. I felt like someone was sitting on my chest. Like I couldn't breathe, and how stupid is that, right? How crazy and insane to feel that way. When I love him so much. When he's the most amazing guy I've ever met. So loyal and loving and God, I know how lucky I am. I know that. All my girlfriends at school tell me. They tell me that Lucas is the best because their boyfriends are all so selfish and inconsiderate and disloyal and..."

"And what?" he prods lowly, roughly.

I blink a couple of times to clear my vision, dislodging a thick drop of tear. "Like you."

He watches it drip down.

Making its way past my flushed cheeks, the side of my parted mouth, clinging to my jaw for half a second. Before it plops.

Down on his thumb.

I flinch when that happens.

When he catches my tear with the pad of his thick digit.

And I realize that he's let my wrist go and not only does he catch my tear with the same hand that he was using to grip mine, he's also wiping the wetness off my cheek with those same fingers.

"Like me," he rasps.

My heart is beating, drumming, flapping its wings inside my chest as if it were a bird.

And standing still is such a struggle that before I can think about it, my newly-freed hand finds his t-shirt and grips it tightly.

"Yes," I whisper, my cheek tingling where he's touching me. "They're all jerks like you are."

"Like I am."

"Like you, they can't be trusted."

"No."

"They're all assholes."

"They are."

"And dangerous."

His eyes appear liquid then. "Like a bandit."

My winged heart skips a beat and I can't help but whisper, "That's what I call it."

"Call what?"

"My diary."

"What?"

Twisting his t-shirt, I reply, "I call it Bandit now."

His lips part and a long breath escapes, misty and warm. "Why?"

"Because I was trying to turn something bad in my life into something good," I tell him, my neck craned up, my eyes flicking over his downturned face. "Reform it, if you will. Because every time I thought about you, I got so angry. I got so furious and enraged. And it was so exhausting. I didn't want to feel that anymore. I didn't want to be sick with hate. So I named the most precious thing in the world to me after you."

"You did."

"Yes. Turning something bad into something good. I read that in a book."

And as soon as I did, it reminded me of him. So I got myself a new diary. The one whose color matched the color of his eyes. Dark brown with red hues.

The only non-pink thing in my room.

"Did it help?" he asks, his thumb on my jaw now, only millimeters away from my lips.

"Not yet."

"It's not going to."

"It might. I haven't lost hope."

"You should."

I don't know what's happening.

But everything feels so... lazy and heavy and lethargic and hot.

His breaths. My breaths.

His eyes. My skin.

His thumb on my cheek, so close to my parted mouth now.

My knuckles almost caressing his hard, ridged abdomen.

"Sixteen, huh," he whispers.

"Yes."

He runs his gaze all over my face, which I know must be all flushed. "You still too mature for your age?"

My breath hitches.

And I want to hide my face now.

I want to clench my eyes shut and burrow my nose in his massive chest.

Because he's bringing up that long ago conversation.

The *embarrassing* and one-sided conversation I had with him back when I was naive and stupid and thought that I wanted to be his friend. Before he taught me that all rumors about him are true and that I should believe them and not what my heart was telling me.

"Yes," I reply.

His thumb inches closer to my mouth. "But you can see why we can't be friends now though, can't you?"

"Because we make each other hatesick."

"Yeah."

"Why did you," I ask, my lips trembling, "give me that anklet?"

My question makes him frown. "What?"

Swallowing, I bring my other hand forward, the one that was up until now gripping the bedpost behind me, and clutch his t-shirt. Because I need something sturdier.

To hold on to.

Something more grounding and solid.

Something like him in this moment.

Because he's the only one who seems stable when everything else is shifting and sliding around me.

"Why did you bring me that gift?" I explain. "If you hated me so much, why did you give it to me?"

Was it his way of mocking me somehow, hurting me? Making me feel important so it's more fun when he snatches the rug from under me?

It still sits in my nightstand drawer, his gift.

Shoved to the back but still there.

So many times I thought about giving it back to him. Just leaving it where he'd find it later so I didn't have to do it face to face. But I couldn't do it for some reason.

I couldn't let it go.

Pressing his thumb down on my lip, tugging at it, he whispers, "Happy birthday, Echo."

I know I should say something right now.

Something like, *thank you and please can you move away from me? Can you please stop looking at me like that?*

But I can't say a single thing.

I can't make a sound.

All I can do is look up at him. And *think.*

What I thought so long ago.

That he's sexy and beautiful.

Symmetrical.

One sharp feature giving way to another. Proud cheekbones hollowing out and slanting down to a stubbled jaw. Smooth forehead and arrogant brows sculpted down to thickly lashed eyes. His straight nose off setting his wide mouth.

His mouth.

Smooth and curved and gosh, looking like the softest pillow.

And I don't know how it happens. I don't know who makes the first move but I'm pressing against that plush pillow.

My mouth is pressing against his mouth.

And I'm…

I'm devouring them, his lips. I'm swallowing them.

Or maybe it's him who's doing that. He's devouring me, my lips, swallowing them with his own.

No, wait.

I think it's both of us.

We're both doing the devouring and swallowing.

And holy God, I don't understand how that happened. I don't understand how we came to this.

To me pressed up against the bedpost and him pressed up against me.

As we kiss each other.

As he kisses me and I kiss him back.

And not just with our mouths either. We're kissing each other with our whole bodies.

We're tangled up in each other.

Somehow his hands are in my hair, fisting it, pulling at it, messing up my braid. Like this is the very first thing that he wanted to do as soon as he got his hands on me. And my own fingers are on his shoulders, his biceps, scratching his skin, pulling at his t-shirt. Like that is what *I* wanted to do.

Feel the thickness of those arms and rake my nails on his skin because he makes me so mad.

And apparently, I also wanted to suck on his tongue.

Because I had a feeling that it was going to be tasty.

His tongue was going to be sweet and delicious and so heated.

And gosh, it is.

It's like sucking on summer.

It's like sucking on sunshine and watermelon and lemonade.

All the things that I love.

All the things that I crave all year round.

I have a feeling that I taste like all the things he craves too. Because he's sucking on my tongue as well. In fact, he's going harder at it, at me, at my mouth. Thrusting his tongue inside, going deep, reaching the back of my mouth.

And when I moan because I don't think anyone has ever been so deep inside of me, it drives him wild.

It makes him groan and growl and I think that I have never heard a sound like that before.

Such a needy sound.

I want more of that. I want to hear that sound forever.

But a second later, it gets drowned out by another sound.

A big one.

A bang. Loud enough to break us apart. To have reality zap in.

And the moment we break apart, I feel such a chill, such a cold stark fear that I shake with it.

But that's nothing compared to how much I tremble and shake when I swing my eyes to the left and find the source of that loud noise. It was the door to my bedroom opening, crashing against the wall. And it was him who did it. Who opened the door.

My boyfriend.

Who at this very second stands on the threshold, watching me.

In his best friend's arms.

CHAPTER SEVEN

Present. St. Mary's School for Troubled Teenagers

I'm a criminal.

A troublemaker. A delinquent, a lawbreaker, a culprit, an offender.

Or at least people think I am.

I don't blame them.

I mean, I do wear a mustard-colored skirt, white knee-high socks and black Mary Janes: the uniform of St. Mary's School for Troubled Teenagers. An all-girls reform school located in the middle of the woods in the town of St. Mary's.

And as the name suggests, only criminals go there.

Criminals who have done bad things. Who have broken laws, caused mayhem, wreaked havoc.

Criminals like me.

So this should be easy for me. What I'm doing tonight.

This being stalking.

Well technically, it's not stalking.

It's not like I'm going to hide in the bushes and crouch under the window while I spy using my binoculars. I don't even have binoculars. And there's no crouching and spying involved. There *may* be some hiding involved though, I can't be sure.

"Echo?"

My frantic thoughts break when I hear my name.

For a second, I can't quite figure out where the voice is coming from.

Because there's no one here.

I'm alone. And I'm sitting. On something.

Blinking, I look around, trying to gauge where exactly I am; how did I get here and all that.

"Echo," the voice says again, this time accompanied by a couple of loud, banging sounds. "Open the door."

The door.

Right.

The voice is coming through the door.

Of the bathroom where I'm currently sitting on a closed toilet seat, my hands fisted in my lap and my eyes pinned to the tiled floor. And that voice belongs to my friend, Jupiter.

Straightening up, I take a deep breath and reply, "I'm busy."

"No, you aren't."

"What?"

"Fine. Busy with what exactly?"

Honestly, I should've known.

It's Jupiter.

She's feisty and fiery and a little too nosy.

All qualities I usually appreciate.

Because if it wasn't for her, we never would've been friends in the first place. We never would've gotten to know each other and discover that we're not just friends but the best of friends.

Not because I have bad social skills. I actually have very good social skills and I have always been able to make friends easily. But as it turns out, St. Mary's School for Troubled Teenagers has a way of squelching the best in you. My friend on the other side of the door though, was granted this one good quality. The ability to break down barriers.

And so here we are.

Best of friends ever since we both arrived at St. Mary's two years ago.

"It's a bathroom, Jupiter," I tell her, eyeing the white door. "What do you think people are busy with? In a bathroom."

I can see Jupiter roll her eyes at my reply. "As if you're using the bathroom for any of its intended purposes."

I draw back and repeat, "What?"

"I can always tell when the bathroom is not being used for its intended purposes."

"That's..." I shake my head. "The most ridiculous thing I've ever heard."

"*Or*," she goes, "is it the most awesome thing you've ever heard? That I'm so in tune with human emotion that I can sense someone's distress from a mile away."

"No," I say, decidedly. "It's definitely the most ridiculous thing. And I'm not in distress. All I need is a little privacy, thank you."

"Right," she scoffs, "to do what, overthink?"

"I'm —"

"Because I know that's exactly what you're doing in there. And I have two very good reasons to believe that." Then, "No, wait. Three. *Three* very good reasons to believe that." Before I can say anything, she begins listing them, "A: You've been in there for like, thirty minutes even though you know that we need to get going soon and you hate being late to anything because you're such a good girl. *Annoyingly* good. B: You left in the middle of a conversation when we both know that you're too polite to ever do that. Like, you'd stand there with your ears bleeding if you had to but you won't leave. Again because you're so annoyingly good. And the third reason why I think you're overthinking is because that's exactly what you've been doing for the past two weeks. Ever since you came up with the plan."

I have to admit — as much as it pains me — that she's right. On all three points.

I hate being late to places, and from the looks of it we're going to be at least fifteen minutes late to our destination. I hate interrupting someone or cutting someone short when they're talking. And that's exactly what I did before I fled to the bathroom.

To be alone. To, yes, overthink.

Because of the plan.

The stupid stupid plan.

That *I* came up with, by the way.

All alone. Single-handedly.

"It's wrong," I say after several seconds of silence. "What I'm about to do."

"No, it's not."

"It's stalking, Jupiter."

"It's almost stalking."

I narrow my eyes at the door. "I don't think that that's going to matter. That it's almost stalking."

"To whom exactly?"

"To the cops, for one."

I hear a long sigh. "No one's going to call the cops on you."

"Oh, they're not?"

"Well," she admits. "Not again."

Yeah, not again.

Because they have before, haven't they?

Yes, I'm one of the many, many unlucky people who have had the misfortune of cops being called on them. In fact that's the very reason I'm at a reform school.

Because two years ago, I did something stupid *and* illegal.

Which means cops had to get involved.

Look, I'm not saying that I didn't deserve it.

I absolutely deserved it.

I absolutely deserved being arrested and interrogated. In fact, I think I got off easy. I could've spent months in a juvenile detention center for the horrible thing that I did. Instead, I was let out free. On the condition that I attend a reform school.

But that's not the point.

The point is that I shouldn't do this.

I should never have come up with this plan.

"I'm just," I take a deep but shaky breath, "very afraid."

I hear her sigh as well. But I can sense that it's in solidarity rather than in exasperation. "I know. And it's not crazy to feel that way after everything that you've been through. So if you want to back out, we totally can. It's up to you. Whatever you decide, we'll stand behind it."

"We absolutely will."

This is a second voice.

And it belongs to my second best friend, Poe.

It's slightly crazy that I'm calling her my best friend when we've only just met. I mean, we go to the same school and have had all the same classes for the past two years. But it's only recently that we started interacting more and realized that we totally missed out on being friends before.

In fact, it's her bathroom that I've shut myself in.

It's her house.

Ever since I decided to do this, Jupiter and Poe both have stood behind me and supported me wholeheartedly. The fact that we're here, at Poe's house, when we aren't allowed to go anywhere off campus is testament to that support.

It sounds archaic, doesn't it?

That we aren't *allowed* to go anywhere off campus.

But it's our reality, given our school.

Since it's a reform school and the girls who go there are all troublemakers, the main goal of St. Mary's is restoration. So we can rejoin society as responsible citizens, and in order to accomplish that, they have ironclad and rigid rules.

Ranging from the obvious ones such as showing up to classes on time, never missing a homework deadline, and getting good grades, to less apparent ones like you can only watch TV for a certain amount of time in a day; or that every night they switch off the lights at 9:30; or you can only go off campus if you have a signed permission slip, and so on.

Oh, and if you misbehave or if your grades fall below the set minimum, you get punished.

By losing privileges.

TV privileges, going out privileges, telephone privileges.

Alternatively, if you do well in classes and follow all the rules, your privileges are increased.

All of this, however, only applies during regular school months.

During summer school, the rules are even stricter.

Because having to go to summer school — when you're supposed to be off enjoying summer vacation — in itself is a major red flag. It means you probably didn't follow enough rules and/or get good enough grades during the regular school months.

It's summer now.

Meaning we're in summer school.

What's even worse is that we're all seniors.

Or rather *still* seniors.

We were supposed to graduate last month but... didn't.

Couldn't.

Lack of grades, lack of good behavior. Lack of common sense.

Which means I shouldn't be here, in Poe's bathroom, at Poe's big mansion-like house. None of us should be. But Poe has connections and she used them to get us out of St. Mary's for the weekend.

Because she's awesome that way, she got Jupiter out too.

And they're both being awesome right now as well.

Being so supportive and understanding after everything that they've already done for me. And I'm aware that I can't let them do this, not anymore.

There's a *reason* why I came up with this plan. A reason why I'm doing this. And yes, doing this might be stupid and reckless, maybe even dangerous for me, but I have to.

So as much as I'd like to stay in here, hidden away like a coward, I can't.

Taking a deep breath, I come up to my feet and walk over to the door. I open it to reveal my two best friends peering at me with concerned gazes. To put them at ease, I smile and hope that it's not as shaky as I feel it is.

"It's okay," I say. "I'm just being silly. I can do this."

"Are you sure?" Jupiter asks, her emerald eyes clouded with worry.

"Yeah."

"Like, absolutely?" Poe asks gently. "Again, you don't have to do this if you don't want to."

"I know." I smile again but this one's calmer; how can it not be when my friends are so amazing? "But I think it's going to be fine."

Maybe if I say it enough times, it's going to be.

They both stare at me for a beat or two before Jupiter nods. "Okay. Let's do this."

Poe nods as well. "So remember, we're going to be there the whole time."

"Right," I say with determination.

"Which means all of us will have your back."

All of us, yeah.

Have I mentioned how awesome Poe is?

If I have, then it bears repeating.

Because not only has she supported me herself, she's recruited other people to support me too: her own friends. Who have all adopted me and Jupiter into their fold like we've been friends forever.

Again, they all went to St. Mary's — they just graduated on time — and we all had the same classes over the years, so I've known them from afar. But it's only recently, ever since summer school started and Poe became my and Jupiter's friend, that we started to get closer. And when I told Poe of my plan, she gathered everyone to lend me all the support that I could want.

"Yes," I say.

"And we can leave any time you want us to," Jupiter chimes in.

"Got it."

"So there's nothing to worry about," Poe concludes. "If he says something or, you know, does something, we'll be there for you."

I want to respond to Poe but I find that I can't.

Not because I'm suddenly afraid again — I mean, the nerves are still there but I've mostly got a handle on it — but because I feel a tremble go through my body.

I feel my belly clench and my toes curl.

If he says something...

I wonder what he will say. When he sees me for the first time in two years.

I wonder what he'll sound like.

Will he be angry? Enraged that I'm here when he specifically told me to stay away from him.

Or will he be too shocked, too stunned to say anything at all?

Or maybe he'll see me after such a long time and for a few seconds, he'll forget.

What I did to him.

How I hurt him.

I don't know.

All I know is that whatever he'll say, however he'll sound, I can't wait for it.

I can't *wait* to hear his voice after two long years.

"I know," I finally gather my voice to reply to Poe. "But it's okay. It's going to be fine. Besides, as you guys already told me, no guy in his right mind would be able to say anything upsetting, when he takes a look at this."

I wave my hand up and down my body to tell them what I mean. And as expected, their grins come out and I'm relieved; I don't want them to worry about me anymore.

Plus it's the truth anyway. The dress that I have on is the most beautiful thing I've ever seen.

All thanks to Poe.

Along with being an awesome friend, Poe is a fashionista. Her eye for design and colors and fabric is second to none, and the corset-style dress that she's chosen for me makes me look prettier than I am. It clings to my body in all the right places, accentuating my tiny waist and my C-cup boobs. Not to mention, my pale skin and my dirty blonde hair shine against the backdrop of the suede fabric.

Plus it's blue.

His favorite color.

Now that my temporary freak-out is over, we all finish up getting dressed and head to our destination: a bar called The Horny Bard.

Despite what the name suggests — probably a strip club or something similar — The Horny Bard is a sports bar in Bardstown. It's a very popular hangout for all the soccer players, and given that I've been living in Bardstown since I was twelve, I've heard of it. But this is the first time I'm going to set foot in it.

And I have to say that it's the loudest place I've ever been in.

It's not just the music either.

Which is extremely loud and heavily bass-centric; so much so that I swear the liquor bottles at the bar and the glasses on the table are freaking vibrating. It's also the big TV screens up on the dark walls and the people who are shouting and cheering and swearing at them.

Plus it has to be the most dungeon-y place that I've ever been in.

Everything is not only dark but bathed in a reddish glow. From the crazy mob to the shiny liquor bottles, the brick walls, the pool tables in the back, the furniture.

I don't see how this place can be remotely popular, but it is and it's okay.

I'm keeping my mind on important things.

Like how if the information that I have is correct, he's going to be here tonight.

And it should be.

I mean, the Bardstown High West chat group — comprised of girls from my old school —wouldn't spread false information about this at least. Especially when he's coming back to town after two whole years and is apparently... *single*.

So I forge ahead, ignoring the loud music, scary swearing and even the fact that I step into something super sticky and have to almost rip my heel off the floor in order to keep going.

I will let nothing, least of all the tackiness of the bar, stand in my way tonight.

But then a few moments later, I see something that makes me think — jarringly and abruptly — that I spoke too quickly.

Because I think I *would* let something stand in my way.

Or someone.

The only one.

With skin like my favorite season and eyes like dark melted chocolate. Only they're not all melted chocolate. There are tones of rich red wine. Which you only see when you're close to him.

Super close.

So close that you know that his skin doesn't just look like summer, it *feels* like summer too. It feels hot and smooth and like basking in the sunshine.

So close that you know he's also hard and strong all over. He feels like a mountain made of packed muscles and dense bones, and you feel all fragile and delicate when he wraps his arms around you.

And when he...

When he puts his mouth on you, the mouth that he's putting on the rim of that beer bottle he's drinking from, you become cursed.

You make mistakes. You do stupid things.

And then you pay for them.

I know all that.

I know it all first-hand.

Because I've been that close to him. I have felt all those things.

His heat. His strength.

And his curse.

Because two years ago, on the night of my sixteenth birthday, I was foolish enough to kiss him.

My boyfriend's best friend.

And I'm still paying for it.

CHAPTER EIGHT

I'm a slut.

That's explanation number one.

Of why I kissed my boyfriend's best friend when I was sixteen.

Why I kissed one boy when I was in love with another.

Explanation number two is that I'm stupid.

I'm a stupid slut.

For ruining the best thing that ever happened to me.

For hurting the guy I love.

Both things, I never thought I was or ever would be. Both things, I sometimes wonder why I was in the first place.

When I was dating Lucas, I never looked at another guy. He was it for me. He was the one. So I don't know why I would do what I did.

I have no explanation for my stupid and slutty behavior.

Just like I have no explanation — *still* — for what I'd done *before* I turned into the slut of Bardstown.

Freaking out and running away.

I did that, didn't I?

When Lucas had asked me to marry him.

I still don't know why I felt the way I did.

Trapped and suffocated and strangled.

All I know is that I did and I wish I hadn't.

I wish I could turn back time and undo all the damage. I wish I could go back and *hear* that knock on my bedroom door. The knock by my boyfriend who'd come back to talk about what had happened at the restaurant but instead found me cheating on him.

I can't change any of that though.

All I can do is try to make *some* amends.

Something that I've wanted to do for two years now and haven't been able to. Because Lucas wouldn't let me; he's cut off all contact with me. So a couple of weeks ago when I read in that chat group that he was coming back to town, I thought this was my chance.

They had his whole itinerary posted, all the parties he was going to go to, all the get-togethers that were being thrown in his honor. While I did pay attention to the itinerary — I'm here, aren't I? — I was more concerned about his reason for coming back: his father is ill and they say that he might be dying.

His father is not a good person. That's the very first thing.

He used to abuse Lucas when he was growing up, and I know that Lucas hates his dad. But I also know that despite everything, he's a good son. Which means even though he's had a difficult relationship with his father, this must be tough for him, his imminent passing.

Only that stupid freaking chat never mentioned anything about *him*.

Or maybe they did but beyond Lucas I didn't pay attention to anything else.

To the one thing — the one person — who could potentially stop me.

My biggest mistake, all six feet and three inches of him.

My boyfriend's — *ex*-boyfriend's — best friend.

And get this: instead of standing at the far end of this very tacky bar, he's right here.

He's sitting in front of me.

Sitting.

It's surreal, isn't it?

How is this even *happening*?

Okay, you know what, let me just do the run-down of everything that has happened ever since I arrived here, that led to this very dream-like moment.

So first, I came with all my friends. *And* their boyfriends.

Actually, there are boyfriends and also brothers.

One of the girls, Calliope Thorne, has like four big brothers.

Yup, *four*. Of which three are here.

When Poe gathered all her friends to accompany me to The Horny Bard, Callie was the one who pointed out that we were going to need help getting inside a bar since we were all underage. So it might be a good idea to involve her brothers plus her boyfriend — oh wait, husband; she's married to this gorgeous-looking guy who somehow always manages to stay within her touching distance — who are all over twenty-one.

It was a difficult road, from what Poe tells me, to get them to agree, but they did. And I'm so thankful for it. That so many people came out to support me.

But anyway, I came to the bar and then I saw.

Him I mean, standing with a group of *his* friends.

And then I froze.

For a moment or two.

And *then* I dove for the nearest brick pillar and hid.

Because what the fuck was I thinking? Why *wasn't* I thinking actually?

Of course he'd be here.

He's my boyfriend's — *ex*-boyfriend's — best friend.

He goes where Lucas goes. And vice-versa.

And if I had even a little bit of common sense, I would've paid attention to this fact and prepared myself. And then I wouldn't have taken cover like a coward behind a pillar. Thank God my friends were there to build me back up and get me out of there. So I could face the situation head-on. Only I never could've imagined, not in a million years, that the situation would become this.

So the boyfriends and the brothers? Turns out, they know *him*.

Yeah.

Apparently, they're all soccer buddies from high school. They used to play each other, one of Callie's brothers — Ledger I think his name is — her husband and *him*. Bardstown East and Bardstown West. So they know each other.

Again, if I'd paid even a little bit of attention to soccer back when I went to all those games, I probably would've known this little tidbit of information. But I didn't and from the looks of it, they don't just know each other, they're all really good friends.

And they're just so happy to see each other.

So happy to be catching up and mingling and talking like the long-lost friends that they are.

Laughing even.

Him, laughing right in front of me when I'm going to *fucking pieces* right now.

I can't compute that.

I can't compute any of this, any of what's happening. And I need to because time's running out. I need to get my head on straight so I can do what I came here to do.

Talk to the boy I love.

Whose heart I broke, not once but twice, in one night.

He's here too, sitting ten feet away from me and…

"He's looking at you."

The voice whispering in my ear sort of wakes me up and helps me focus.

Sitting on the couch, surrounded by my friends, I've been keeping my eyes glued to the glass of orange juice in my lap. Trying to look all cool and unaffected. Not like the desperate quivering mess of an ex-girlfriend that I am.

"What?" I whisper back.

"He," Jupiter repeats slowly, her green eyes sparkling, "is *looking*. At you."

My heart thuds in my chest. "W-who?"

She rolls her eyes at me. "Who do you think?"

"Him?"

"Um, yes."

My heart thuds again and then starts to beat really rapidly and loudly and chaotically.

Because it's been two years. Two whole years and so I'd forgotten.

I'd forgotten that this is what he does.

He stares.

He watches.

He keeps his reddish-brown eyes pinned on me whenever we're in the same room, the same space.

And every time he did that, I'd sweat. I'd shiver.

From the heat in them.

From the *hate* in them.

But then why would he need to stare at me now? I'm not his best friend's girlfriend anymore, am I?

Shouldn't he be happy now?

Shouldn't his hate, if not gone completely, have lessened?

He got what he wanted.

He won.

I fist my fingers around the tumbler of orange juice. "I can't believe he's doing that. I can't *believe* he's looking at me in front of his best friend. After what…"

I trail off because Jupiter is giving me weird looks. Ones that suggest that she's confused at my reaction, that she doesn't know what I'm talking about.

And then I realize that she probably doesn't.

Because she isn't talking about what I think she's talking about — or whom.

"You…" I clear my throat, squirming in my seat. "You mean him, don't you? You mean, *Lucas* is looking at me."

She studies me for a second or two. "Who else did you think I was talking about?"

"No one."

She narrows her eyes suspiciously. "No one."

"Yes." I clear my throat again. "I-I mean, I knew you were talking about Lucas." Before she can say anything else, I add, "I'm just really stressed."

Not a lie.

I am. And probably that's why while she was referring to my ex-boyfriend, I thought she was talking about his best friend.

"I know," she says, sighing. "I'm sorry. I wish we could do something. I wish I could go over there and punch that son of a bitch in his goddamn gorgeous face."

This time, I know that she's talking about *him* for sure.

Needless to say, Jupiter knows who he is and my entire history with him.

Although I will say that I've left a few details out.

As in, what *exactly* happened on the night of the breakup.

I never told her how I was partially responsible for it too. I never told her about the kiss.

Not deliberately though.

I didn't set out to lie or omit things.

Two years ago, when I shared this story with her, everything was so fresh and I was so ashamed at what I'd done. So I glossed over it. And given my history with him, she simply assumed that he might have been responsible for the breakup and I didn't correct her.

"No, it's fine," I tell Jupiter, feeling guilty for hiding things from her. "I'm just —"

"Are we talking about the gorgeous villain who's so disgustingly gorgeous that all I want to do is look at him and not look at him at the same time?"

That's Callie.

She's sitting to my right, followed by Bronwyn Littleton or simply Wyn, Poe's other friend. Then comes Poe herself and Tempest.

Who says, "Don't let my brother hear you say that. He's going to blow his lid."

Tempest doesn't go to St. Mary's but she's good friends with Callie — has been for years — and now her sister-in-law. Because she's Reed's, Callie's husband, little sister.

Callie glances at Reed, who somehow senses that she's looking at him and meets her gaze with his own. And God, his eyes are all heated and intense. And I have to turn away because I don't want to intrude in their private moment.

Callie bites her lip at the way Reed's staring at her before turning back to us. "Okay, sorry. You guys are right. That name belongs to him." She sighs happily. "And only him."

"Which means we need a new name," says Wyn.

Poe turns to her. "How about Thorn? Because you know, he's a thorn in her side and all that."

Wyn bumps her with her shoulder. "Shut up. There can only be one Thorn and you know it."

"Well technically, there are five Thornes," Callie teases. "Including me and my four older brothers."

Wyn shoots her a flat look. "There may be five *Thornes* but still there's only one original thorn. My Thorn. And no one else can use that name."

"Ooh," Poe goes, grinning. "Possessive."

Wyn narrows her eyes at Poe. "Yes, I am."

And why wouldn't she be?

When we're talking about Conrad Thorne, the love of her life.

In my experience, Wyn is pretty chill and easy-going. But when it comes to Conrad, Callie's oldest brother and her boyfriend, she can be pretty intense.

Which I totally understand and love.

Poe sticks her tongue out at Wyn. Then, "But we do need to call him something."

"Yup, so we can bitch about him right in front of him," Jupiter adds.

"Bandit," I blurt out.

And feel my heart slam against my ribs.

Slam and batter and bruise.

I feel my mouth tingling, my cheeks heating up.

Probably because it's been two years since I said that name out loud.

Two years since I wrote it as well.

After that night, I knew nothing I did would ever turn the one bad thing in my life into anything remotely good. So I switched back to calling my diary Holly.

I promised myself that I would never ever say that name out loud.

Saying it now feels like a bad omen.

"Bandit," Jupiter repeats.

"That's actually a good one," Callie says.

"Very artistic," Wyn, who's an artist herself, adds.

"Yup," Tempest agrees as well. "I would've thought criminal or something. But Bandit is much better."

Poe smiles. "Totally goes with his dark and mysterious persona. Plus how he's robbing us and Echo here of a very important fact."

"What's that?" I frown.

"That your ex is staring at you. Which was how we got started in the first place."

Holy shit.

Holy *fucking* shit.

Yes.

Poe is right.

That's exactly how we got here. Jupiter had pointed out that Lucas was staring at me. Which I misunderstood, but it's sinking in.

This fact.

That Lucas, my ex-boyfriend, the boy I lost because of my mistakes, the boy I still love, is staring at me.

Oh God.

Oh God, oh God, *oh God*.

What does that mean?

Clutching my glass of orange juice even tighter, I ask in a halting voice, "Is that... Is that like a good staring or you know, bad staring?"

"Good," Jupiter answers. "Definitely good."

"Kind of like he can't take his eyes off you staring," Callie informs me with a smile.

"Told ya." Poe grins.

Before giving me advice.

They all give me advice actually. On what to do next.

How to play it cool and how to show him that he doesn't affect me. That I'm not still pining over him.

Which is all great.

And I do listen to them.

Not because I want to show him how okay I am after the breakup — I'm not and it's fine if he sees that — but because I don't want to freak him out. I don't want him to think that I came here for him or that I'm stalking him.

I want this to look natural and non-threatening.

Me running into him here to talk. To apologize and to start building bridges.

So the fact that he's looking at me in a good way helps my confidence a bit.

I try to peek at him through my eyelashes or the corner of my eyes, trying to catch his eyes, make some contact. It takes a while but during one of these surveys, my eyes clash with his.

And my heart soars in my chest.

With happiness. With glee.

Because in his gaze, I find the old Lucas. The one who looked at me with adoration and love.

With warmth.

The last time I looked into his eyes, they appeared hurt. Angry and betrayed.

So I excuse myself to go to the bathroom then, hoping that he'll get the signal. That he'll follow me.

God, please let him follow me.

In the restroom, which is thankfully and surprisingly empty, I look myself in the mirror. I pat my hair. I wash my hands.

"He's looking at you," I tell myself. "Maybe he misses you. Maybe he missed you like you've missed him and maybe…"

No, I'm not going there. I'm not thinking about getting back together with him.

Not right now.

Not ever even.

This isn't about that.

I'm just happy that I may have a chance to apologize to him. I can't possibly hope for anything else, anything more. Not after what I did.

I smile at myself in the mirror.

Then with another deep breath, I turn around and walk out, hoping to find him standing outside.

But instead, I find someone else.

Someone who makes me come to a screeching, jarring halt. As if I've run into a wall.

An obstacle, a hurdle.

A problem.

And I have, haven't I?

Because who I find outside the restroom is the very last person I'd hoped to find.

In fact, I wish that I'd never run into him.

I wish that I'd never set my eyes on him in the first place.

On Reign Davidson.

My ex-boyfriend's best friend.

CHAPTER NINE

You're a slut.

That's what he said to me. The very last time we talked.

His exact words were: "*Maybe it's a good thing you said no to him. Because I think he's better off without you after all. He's better off without the hungry fucking slut who pounced on the guy she claims to hate. Stay the fuck away from him. And me.*"

I went to him, see. For help.

After everything happened, Lucas wouldn't pick up my calls so like an idiot, I called *him* up as my last resort. I wanted us to go together to Lucas so we could explain that it meant nothing, that our *stupid kiss* meant nothing. It was a mistake — a horrible, horrendous, grave, awful mistake — and that I'd do anything to make up for it.

But he rejected the idea. He refused to help me.

He refused to lift *even a finger* to help me.

And why would he? He never wanted us to get together in the first place. In fact, I bet he must've used this opportunity to put even a greater wedge between me and Lucas.

So yeah, I called him to ask for help and he kicked me when I was already so down.

And here he is again.

Looking at me. *Staring* at me.

And my heart is beating right now like it used to beat back then. My body is shaking the way it used to back then as well. My skin is trembling.

"Nice dress," he drawls, his eyes going up and down my body.

And I have to press my back up against the wall.

Not only at his voice — that two years later sounds so much deeper and rougher, more sanded down, as if he barely uses it — but also because of what he just said.

What he always says. What he always *notices*.

When he sees me.

My dress.

It feels like no time has passed at all. It feels like I saw him only yesterday. That only yesterday, I turned sixteen and he climbed through my window. Only yesterday, he had me trapped between my bedpost and himself.

And I made the biggest mistake of my life and I lost everything.

No.

No, no, no.

I don't want to think about that. I don't want to think about that night or anything else that came before.

So I shut those thoughts down and thank God that I'm not wearing pink.

With my heart a pulpy mess in my chest, I ask, "What do you want?"

Leaning against the opposite wall, he stands all casually, his hands in his pockets, taking stock of me. At my question, his eyes come back to my face. "It's pretty."

Of course he completely ignores my question.

Because when has he ever cared about what I want?

"Why are you here?" I try again.

"Blue suits you," he murmurs, determined to not answer me.

As opposed to what, pink?

I almost say it.

Almost.

But thankfully, I pull myself back from it. I don't want to engage him. I don't want to go down memory lane with him. As if we're old friends, sharing some kind of an inside joke.

We're not friends.

We never were and we never will be.

Not to mention, I don't have *time* to do this with him.

I need to get back to the people who actually are my friends. His friends too by the way.

His best friend.

I need to get back to his best friend and do what I came here to do.

"What do you *want*?" I ask again, this time with a more severe voice.

Hoping that it might get through to him.

But of course not.

Cocking his head to the side, he replies, kinda amused, kinda not, "I want you to say thank you."

"What?"

"It was a compliment."

"Yeah, right," I scoff, unable to help myself.

He frowns slightly. "What, you don't think so?"

Don't say it.

Just give him what he wants. Say thank you so you can get back.

"No."

Damn it, Echo.

"And why's that?"

"Because it's you."

"And?"

"And you never give anyone compliments."

His lips twitch as if on the verge of a smile. Which I already know can't be the case.

Not with him.

If anything, his lips are going to be on the verge of a smirk.

Arrogant, condescending, I'm-too-cool-for-this-world smirk.

"I'm pretty sure I do."

"Well okay, so let me rephrase," I say. "You never give compliments to me."

And there it is: his smirk.

All dark and in its glory.

"Ah," he drawls again, nodding as if reaching a conclusion of some sort. "I hear hurt feelings."

"There are no —"

"Well, allow me to rectify that."

"You don't —"

"You look pretty in blue," a pause, "Echo."

Happy birthday, Echo.

Echo...

He said that. That night, I mean.

In fact, he said it *right before.*

The thing that ruined my life. The kiss.

I realize that except for my name, his words just now are completely different from before.

But somehow it doesn't matter.

It doesn't *fucking matter.*

Because the things that happen inside of me, the tidal wave of feelings that emerge, are exactly the same.

I combust. I go up in flames. I die.

I fly.

Like I did that night.

And this is not good. This is very, very bad.

I want this déjà vu feeling to go away. I want *him* to go away.

Why won't he just go away?

"What do you want, Reign? Why are you here?"

Now it's his turn to clench his teeth, his jaw. Narrow his eyes slightly.

As if me calling his name affects him the same way, as if it makes him sick as well.

If it does, then I'm glad.

I hope he's sick to his stomach like I am right now.

To my dismay though, he recovers quickly and his features go all relaxed and nonchalant as he says, "To say hi. I mean, how long has it been, huh? Since we saw each other."

"Two years." Then, I add, "Not long enough though."

He chuckles. "And you were sitting out there, surrounded by all your friends. We didn't get a chance to talk, let alone catch up."

"If I wanted to talk to you, I would have."

"Now that wasn't very nice, was it?" he says, shaking his head slightly. "I give you a compliment and you break my heart."

"You don't have a heart."

"Yeah?"

"Yes. You're heartless."

At my words, he takes one hand out of his pocket and puts it on his chest. On the left side of it.

He splays his fingers wide and with sparkling eyes, he says, "Well, whatever it is, it's racing right now."

I swallow at his gesture.

Because yet another memory from a night long ago, longer than two years, teases my mind. When he did something exactly like this, clutching the left side of his chest. But I'm happy to report that I shut it down before I drown in it.

Instead I distract myself with his large, dusky hand on his sculpted chest.

The chest that looks even broader and thicker than before. And his tanned fingers that look even more summery. Probably from all the soccer playing. Running around the field, kicking the ball, under the sun.

I haven't heard much about his career or even Lucas's career for that matter, because I don't live at the manor anymore. So I'm cut off from all the gossip and rumors. But I'm sure they're both doing great. I'm sure they're both killing it over there with their skills and talent.

"I hope it's racing fast enough for a heart attack," I retort.

He chuckles again. "I wouldn't rule it out, no. Especially since I'm seeing you after so long."

"Are you —"

"Because I wasn't lying, Echo. You are pretty." Then in a grave voice, "You're fucking breathtaking."

My heart practically punches my chest then.

It practically digs a hole through my bones, trying to burst out of my body.

Knowing him, that would be his goal. Snatching my heart right out of my chest and leaving me here to die.

And I'm proven right — God, so so right — when in a flash, he appears in front of me. One second, he was leaning against the opposite wall and the next, he's standing right in front of me with hardly any gap between our bodies.

"Get away from me," I somehow manage to say.

It's difficult though. So very difficult.

Not only because my déjà vu isn't going anywhere but also because the very thing that I was hoping to avoid is right in front of me now.

Him.

His face. His body.

And how it's all changed.

How there are subtle and not-so-subtle differences.

How there are a couple of lines around his eyes that weren't there before. A tiny mark slashing through his right eyebrow that makes me think that it's a result of an injury, something he got in the last two years because that mark wasn't there when I knew him.

A bump on his nose. No, wait, two bumps.

Maybe he broke it a couple of times.

Plus his cheekbones are even more pronounced now. They always made hollows slanting down to his scruffy jaw but now they're deeper, his jaw is even more square. Like time has chiseled away at his features, his body, making everything even sleeker and sharper.

The biggest change, however, is in his hair.

Something that's been really hard for me not to look at and ponder over.

Before, his hair used to be long and messy, falling over his forehead in disarray. A surfer's hair, only dark. But now it's short. Much shorter, cut so close to the scalp on the sides and thick and spiky up top.

It makes me realize how naive I was, how innocent to think that he looked like a criminal before.

He didn't.

He looks like it now.

He looks dangerous now with his hair buzzed short, with his slightly crooked nose and hollow cheekbones. All hardened and rough.

Dipping his scruffy jaw, he rasps, "But I hope it was a gift."

"What?"

"A little too," he searches for a word, "classy and expensive for a servant girl such as yourself to afford."

My heart clenches in pain.

It always comes down to this, doesn't it?

That I have no money. That I'm poor. My family is poor.

I'm beneath him.

I'm beneath Lucas. I'm practically beneath everyone.

"I'm not your servant girl."

"You wore it for him," he says, ignoring me, "didn't you?"

"Don't talk about him," I warn.

His eyes swipe across my features. "Because you came here for him."

My heart skips a beat at his right conclusion. "I came here with my friends, okay?"

"I'd believe you, you know." He dips down even further as his mouth pulls up on the side in his signature smirk. "If you didn't reek of a little thing called desperation."

I flinch. "Get away from me right now."

"All dressed up and pretty," he rasps, ignoring my command. "But as I said, I hope it was a gift. Because I'd hate to see you waste money that you don't have. For something you'll never get."

"And what is that?"

"Him."

It shouldn't have stung the way it does. I knew what he was going to say.

But hearing it and *expecting* to hear it are two different things.

And even though he got my intentions for tonight wrong — I'm not here to get him back — he knew where to hit me to exact maximum pain for me and pleasure for himself.

"And you'd make sure of that this time, wouldn't you?" I say bitterly.

"Make sure of what?"

"That I *don't* get him. Because you never liked me with him anyway."

"No, I didn't."

Pain stabs my chest. "So what, do you pop champagne every night now? In celebration."

"And snort a couple of lines of cocaine on Sunday, just for good measure."

"That I've disappeared from your best friend's life."

I expect him to answer. To make a quip. Rub it in my face, make it hurt more. But he goes silent for a few seconds, his reddish brown and glinting-a-second-ago eyes shut down. Then, murmuring, "Best friend."

"Yes."

One more sweep of his gaze over my face before he goes back to being his usual arrogant self. And I'm left wondering what that was.

That momentary flicker on his features.

But as always, he makes me realize that I have other things to worry about when he says, "Sure, yeah. Life's pretty fun."

"I —"

"Although," he continues over me, "not as much fun as it was watching you out there. Pretending to be all aloof and unaffected, pretending that you don't care, that you don't notice. When we both know that you do. You did."

"I know about his dad," I blurt out.

"What?"

"I know he's dying, okay?"

His face screws up in disgust. "His dad's a fucking piece of shit."

Well, yeah. I can't argue with him there.

But that doesn't mean it doesn't hurt Lucas.

"Even so. Lucas must be having a tough time of it. He always cared about his dad." And then, because I can't resist, I add, "Not that you're capable of understanding that."

Because he's a shitty son, isn't he?

While Lucas has an excuse to be a shitty son — but he isn't — Reign actually is. And he doesn't even have an excuse. His parents have always been good to him. They've always tried to help him, reach out to him so he could reform his ways. But he's always been a disappointment to them.

He's always been a rebel and a troublemaker.

Freaking Bandit.

But if my dig made a dent on his cockiness, I can't see it.

Because he's as casual as ever. "Your point being?"

"My point being that maybe you should stop thinking about how much you hate me for once and start thinking about Lucas. Because maybe I'm here tonight to be there for him. As friends. He's going to need all the support that he can get and I'm here to give it to him."

"Yeah, no. He doesn't need anything from you."

God, I hate him.

I hate him so so much.

"He was noticing me too, you know," I say then, unable to stop myself.

Probably not the wisest thing to say to him.

But I'm getting a little tired of his taunts.

And his fucking gatekeeping.

"Well," he says, tilting his head to the side, "you can't blame him, can you? You look pretty as fuck."

"You know what, I —"

"But I don't think he's going for desperation these days." I flinch again and he goes on, "So really, I'm saving you all the trouble here." He dips his chin. "You're welcome."

I would've laughed.

If I wasn't so furious.

Because the idea of him saving me from anything is ludicrous.

It's ridiculous, farcical, absurd. Preposterous.

"I didn't say thank you."

"I didn't mind."

"And I can save myself. I don't need your help."

"I seem to recall differently though."

I stiffen. "Don't go there."

"Yeah, why?" He looks me up and down. "You threatening my armoire again?"

He did not just say that.

He did not just *mock* my actions from two years ago.

The ones that I regret down to my bones.

Down to my very soul.

The stupid, reckless actions that destroyed my life. That changed the course of it by sending me to a reform school.

So when he refused to help me and called me names, I got angry. I got crazy angry. So much so that I snuck into his bedroom and destroyed it like he destroyed my heart.

But that's not the worst part.

The worst part is that he's right. I *am* threatening his armoire again; apparently it was from Italy, something that his grandmother had given him and his brother a few years back. I didn't know that when I broke it though; they told me later, at the police station.

I am also threatening his nightstand, his desk, his fucking computer, his bed, the mirror in his bathroom, his stupid windows, the lamps and everything else that I broke that night.

Sometimes I still can't believe that I did all that. That I was angry enough, heartbroken enough, *crazy* enough to actually commit a crime.

And that's the scary part, isn't it?

That he can make me do that. That this guy can make me hate him so much that I destroyed my life for him.

I ruined it. I wrecked it.

My life. My parents' life.

I vandalized their employer's son's room. It's a miracle that they didn't get fired. A miracle that they still get to work there.

And that's exactly why I can't be in his presence.

Reign Davidson is my kryptonite.

He's my catnip.

My personal poison. My insanity drug.

He's my anti-soulmate who makes me sick with hate.

"I want *you*," I repeat on a low voice, "to get away from me or I'm going to end you."

Amused, he drawls, "You've always been a little too drama, haven't you?"

I clench my teeth at his reminder. "I swear to fucking God, I'll do it. I swear it. I promise it."

"And a promise is a fucking oath, isn't it?"

If I could cover my ears, I would do it.

If I could reach into my brain and take out the piece of it that has Reign Davidson written all over it, I'd do that.

As it is, I don't think it's going to help, covering my ears. And I don't have a fucking knife to stab myself with and perform a lobotomy.

So I can't stop the memories flashing through my mind. The memories of when I said the same thing to him, the very first night we'd met.

I do it though.

I somehow shut it down and growl, "You're dead. I —"

"Take my advice," he speaks over me, all amusement vanished, "return the dress and forget about him."

And then he steps back.

Shoving his hands down into his pockets again, he says, "It was nice seeing you, Echo. I hope we don't have to do it again." Then, "And it's been two years, two months and twelve days."

With that, he leaves.

And I realize that things have changed. That we still hate each other but now he has the upper hand. He has Lucas and I don't. And he'll do everything in his power to keep us away from each other.

He'll do everything in his power to keep me from getting to my ex-boyfriend.

CHAPTER TEN

Who: The Bubblegum
Where: Jupiter's bedroom in Bardstown, where Echo's staying for the
    weekend
When: 3:10 AM; the night of The Horny Bard

Dear Holly,
I saw him tonight.
For the first time in two years. Very first time since that night. And I don't think I handled it very well.
It didn't go anything like I'd imagined and you already know how much and how many times I've imagined it. Imagined seeing the guy I kissed on the night of my sixteenth birthday.
The guy I hate. The wrong guy.
The guy who called me a slut for kissing him.
And I wish, I freaking wish, that that was all.
That me running into him was the only bad thing that happened tonight.
But no, something else happened too.
I realized that I still remember it.
His taste.

And when he cornered me in that hallway and pounced on me like the predator he is, that was all I could think about.

That I know his taste.

I know what my ex-boyfriend's best friend tastes like.

His cruel and mean and smirking lips taste like summer.

Watermelon and lemonade.

God, what's wrong with me, Holly? How could I still be thinking about it?

When will I stop thinking about it?

When will I stop letting him get to me?

Not only that, I let him ruin my plans for the night.

After our stupid encounter, I had to take a few minutes to gather myself, and so by the time I got back, Lucas was gone.

My friends didn't have to tell me why; I already knew who was behind it.

Now that he's back, I know that this won't be the last time. He'll try to ruin all my plans. He'll try to sabotage me at every step. He won't let me get what I want that easily.

Which means I can't let him.

He's taken a lot from me over the years. He's robbed me of my control, my emotions, my happiness. My common sense even, and as a result, I've lost everything important to me.

But not this.

He won't take this from me.

I'm going to find a way to get to Lucas.

And I'm also going to find a way to forget it.

Forget what he tastes like.

My ex-boyfriend's best friend.

~Echo

CHAPTER ELEVEN

The Bandit

I'm the second son.

The son born after the first. Obviously.

And as a second son, I only have one job: to be like the first.

To do as the first son does.

To talk like him. To walk like him. To like the things that he likes.

Basically, I'm supposed to follow his lead and be a second version of him.

My older brother.

Who's good and responsible. Straitlaced and a star in all things he does.

Or at least that's what I've been told all my life.

One thing about me: I don't like being told what to do. Not sure where that comes from but it's my major personality trait. I tend to get pissed off when people try to order me around and so I do the exact opposite.

Which means that all my life I've taken a job of my own: to do everything that I can to screw up the first job I was given, and emerge as my own person.

Bad and irresponsible.

A rebel and a disappointment.

It's pretty fun actually, to be all those things. Quite easy too.

You get to do whatever the fuck you want. You get to screw people over, go against expectations. You get to be selfish, reckless, careless. You're not bound by the mundane laws and rules like other people are. Not to mention, you get to party a lot, drink and smoke and fuck as much as you want.

Without actually giving a fuck.

And I don't.

I never have.

Giving a fuck is not something that I do. It's not my MO.

Or it wasn't until two years ago.

Two years, two months and twelve days.

And I have to say that I don't see the appeal. I don't see why people make such a big deal about giving a fuck. It's very annoying and inconvenient and I'd rather go back to my old ways.

But I can't.

At least not tonight.

When my best friend — the only friend that I've ever had — is hell bent on ruining his life by either getting alcohol poisoning or an STD, or both.

In the last minute or so, since I found him lurking around the makeshift bar at this very boring party thrown by one of our soccer buddies from school, he's thrown back two shots. That's a shot every minute, which puts him at at least five or six, since I started looking for him in the first place.

He told me he was going to find a restroom as soon as we arrived. Either he got waylaid by those two blondes who are hanging on his arms right now or he lied.

Stupid fucker.

Exhaling an angry breath, I push my way through people who are all trying to either thump me on the back or talk to me as I pass them by. What about my pissed off expression says, 'come talk to me, I'm a friendly guy' is beyond me right now.

Actually, what about my past behavior in high school says that they can approach me at all, I don't know. I've always tried to be as unapproachable as possible.

Thankfully though, halfway through my very irritating journey to get to my best friend, he starts making his own stumbling way to me, those two chicks in tow, and so we meet somewhere in the middle. But before I deal with Lucas, I need to deal with the girls he brought along for the ride.

I step into their paths, stopping them while Lucas carries on, probably too drunk to notice that his blonde companions have been intercepted.

Stupid *fucking* fucker.

When I see him settling himself against the pool table — the spot we'd agreed to park ourselves for the party before his whole restroom lie — and I'm satisfied that he's not going to fall on his ass and break his dumb neck, I turn to the girls.

Who are both looking at me with pretty smiles.

I should know who they are. They both look familiar and given that they're here at this party, there's a very good chance that they both went to the same school as Lucas and me. But for the life of me I can't place them.

"Hey, Reign," one of the girls says.

I'm going to call her girl number one.

"Having fun?" the second girl, let's call her girl number two, asks.

Fuck no.

I'm not having fun.

Watching your best friend practically kill himself is not fun.

Watching him do it over and over for the past two years is not fun either.

It's all pretty un-fun actually.

Nonetheless, I reply, "Sure." So I can get to the main part. "I think he's had enough."

"What?" girl number one says, confused.

"It's time for you to take off."

Girl number two is confused as well. "Take off?"

I don't see how any of what I said could possibly be confusing but still, I try to explain. "You both should leave."

"Leave?" girl number two asks again. "What do you mean?"

"We just got here," girl number one states the obvious.

"And we've been really looking forward to this party," girl number two goes.

"Yeah." Girl number one bounces, grinning. "Ever since we heard that you guys were coming back."

Then girl number two steps forward, touching me on the arm. "I know it's been a while but..." She flutters her long, curled eyelashes. "We were hoping to drive out to the woods and have some fun. Like we did last time."

Girl number one adds, "And this time we could bring Lucas too."

"Since he missed out on all the fun the last time around," girl number two chirps.

"I'm so glad he's single now," girl number one keeps going.

"Although I don't think I ever really understood why him being in a relationship stopped him from going with us in the first place. But it's okay. We can make up for that this time," girl number two finishes, still fluttering her eyelashes up at me.

Two things: It not only looks like they're both from the same school as me and Lucas, but also that I may have fucked them. Quite possibly both at the same time and out in the woods. Which means we must've done it in the car. And since I've done it a lot in the woods and in my car, I still don't seem to remember who they are.

And second, I really wanna ask her this. "That work on me last time?"

"What?"

"That." I tip my chin up to point to her eyes. "Where it looks like your eye is having a seizure."

She draws back and repeats, "What?"

"It couldn't have," I muse. "I'm not that shallow, am I?"

"Excuse me?"

"Well." I shrug then. "I kinda am. Gimme a fantastic pair of tits in a tight dress and I don't usually discriminate." She takes it as a compliment — given that her peeved expression wears off and she's smiling — and goes to say something but I don't let her. "But as tight as your dress is tonight, it's time for you to leave."

Girl number one goes, "But we —"

"If you don't want it to get hurled on."

"What?" girl number two squeaks.

I point a thumb over my shoulder. "Which he's clearly heading toward. My friend, back there, does not have more than one liver and one pair of kidneys, despite what he seems to think. So I repeat: leave."

They both frown up at me, still not budging, and I sigh.

"Look," I begin, pinning them both with my meanest, cruelest look, "it's not gonna happen. You want a dick to jump up and down on, it's not gonna be mine. Or his. I don't even think he's capable of getting it up at this point and mine doesn't get up for girls I've already fucked once before. So turn around and go back to the party so you can look for another target, okay? Night's still young and I'm sure someone will fall for your eye-seizure routine."

The last thing I see before I turn around is their open mouths.

Mission accomplished.

Now onto the next task: my best friend with a death wish.

Completely oblivious to the fact that I just sent his little friends away, he's throwing darts at the board as he takes long pulls of his beer. Something that I hadn't noticed he'd brought back with him.

My bad.

It stops now though.

I charge over to him. "It's time to leave."

He doesn't stop throwing — and missing — as he says, "So leave."

"You're going with me."

"No."

"Yeah, you are."

"Nope."

"You really want me to drag you out of here like a five-year-old, don't you?"

His mouth quirks up in a humorless smile. "One, you aren't capable of dragging me out of anywhere. And two," another pull of beer, "it depends."

"On fucking what?"

He glances at me for a second before throwing another dart. "On whether or not you've decided to play my babysitter for the night."

"I prefer bodyguard, but it's your call," I shoot back. "You're the kid here who doesn't know when to stop."

He chuckles. "Well, I learned from the best, didn't I?"

He did though.

I taught him all this, partying, drinking, smoking.

Being the stubborn shithead he's being.

I'm regretting that though.

"Listen —"

"And now you won't get to play with the chick I brought you. They're both mine."

"They're both gone."

That gives him a pause. "What?"

"I sent them away."

He looks around to confirm and when he does, he comes back to me. "Fuck you, man. I was gonna let you have the blonde one."

"They were both blondes."

That gives him pause also. As if he didn't know that himself.

He probably didn't.

Given how fucked up he is right now.

Then, shrugging, "Whatever. They talked too much anyway. Not in the mood to go through the motions and have a conversation before getting my dick sucked."

"Charming."

"Yeah, kinda like you when you open your mouth."

Right.

I'm the asshole between the two of us. Understood.

"Now that we've established that we're both charming," I try again, "I think it's time —"

"How about we play for it?"

"What?"

He tilts his head to the side, gesturing to the board. "How about if you win, we go? If I win, we stay."

I take in his face.

His eyes mostly.

They look all drunk and drugged up. Fuck knows what else he did — besides getting shitfaced drunk — while he was hunting for that restroom. Knowing him, he probably would've popped a pill or two.

Usually, I don't mind.

I'm very pro-recreational drugs. Fuck, I was a small-time drug dealer back in school, prescription drugs and pot mostly, but yeah. I'm very pro-anything that gets you as fucked up as you wanna be so you don't have to think about stuff too much.

In fact, I'd kill for a joint right now.

But ever since I became the babysitter, as Lucas calls it — two years, two months and twelve days ago — I've given all that up. I don't get to forget about stuff. I don't deserve to.

And maybe I deserve this too.

Jumping through all the fucking hoops and playing his games.

Because it's not his fault that he's this way.

It's *mine*.

"You sure you wanna make that bet?" I jerk a chin up at him. "Given that you're probably seeing double right now and that's not really the condition you wanna be in when you're trying to make a shot."

It makes him chuckle again.

And then without answering me, he turns to the board and sends the dart flying.

Which tears through the air and hits the bullseye a second later.

Then, "Again, I learned from the best."

That's true also.

I taught him how to shoot.

Way back when we'd just become friends and he'd come over to my house to hang out.

For a second, I see us. Like we used to be. Back when we were kids, both eight years old, both second sons and hence all fucked up already. But most importantly, both never had a friend before each other.

We both were rejects so we made our own club. We made our own rules. We made our own family.

Brothers.

We were that.

At least until I ruined everything and he started hating me.

Fuck.

Fuck.

Taking a deep breath, I state, "I'm not playing you."

Admiring his handiwork for a second, he turns back to me, a challenge apparent in his gaze, "Why, you scared you can't win?"

"Look, I don't wanna win, all right? Let's just go back before you start throwing up your organs."

"No, I don't think I will."

Fucking Christ.

He's really not giving me any choice, is he?

I don't want to do it.

I don't *fucking* want to do it.

But I will.

"So what, you're gonna stay here and drink yourself to oblivion," I say in a flat voice.

He doesn't pay any attention to me as he replies, "That's the plan."

"And you don't think you're being kinda obvious right now. Kinda cliché."

Fuck.

Fuck, fuck, fuck.

Don't let me do this, Lucas. Don't fucking let me do this.

But he does.

"You see her after two years and the first thing you do is get shitfaced and pick up two chicks, both *blondes*, so you can get your dick sucked." I watch his body grow tight in front of my eyes and I feel something black and sharp lodge beneath my rib cage. "And you do it so you can prove to yourself how okay you are with all this. How you saw your ex-girlfriend after a long time and didn't feel a thing."

His frame gets even tighter and that dark thing in my chest twists.

"Hate to break it to you though," I continue, despite not wanting to, "that wasn't even the right shade of blonde. And this is the exact opposite of what someone might do after seeing their ex-girlfriend that they're still hung up on."

There.

Now it's only going to be a matter of seconds before it happens.

One. Two. Three. Fo —

His fist hits my jaw and my head snaps to the side.

The sting is sharp, throbbing.

So fucking unbearable that I have a strong urge to rub it away. But that's how you know that you shouldn't. You should let it hurt because you deserve it.

I'm hoping for another punch to rack my entire frame again — maybe it'll be harder, sharper, stingier, with throbs like little earthquakes — but it doesn't come and I look at my best friend.

My brother.

The guy I've betrayed.

He's breathing hard. Any signs of his drunkenness are gone, leaving his eyes alert and full of anger. Full of hatred and disgust and yeah, disappointment.

I've been looked at that way all my life.

My father, my mother, my brother. Everyone I know and who knows me, has looked at me like this at one time or another. And I've always been okay with it. I've survived, reveled even, in being the bad guy, the train wreck.

But this cuts.

This fucking stings more than his punch.

"Stay the fuck away from me."

With those heated words, he spins around and leaves, heading for the back yard.

If he thinks I'm going to do as he says, then he hasn't been paying attention to the last two years, two months and twelve days.

I'm not going anywhere.

In fact, he's the reason I'm back in this shithole town.

Because I knew coming back to Bardstown would be hard for him.

His father is dying.

While there's no love lost between them — his father is a fucking abusive monster — it still sucks. That the man who raised you, whose approval you've always craved but never gotten, is going to be dead soon. I went through that myself a couple of years ago when my monster father died, so I know.

Plus he hasn't been back since that night.

The night I ruined everything.

So yes, coming back here I knew he'd be bombarded by memories. I knew he was going to be even more reckless, more of a loose cannon than he's become in recent years. Which means there was no way I was going to leave him alone at a time like this. Even though I knew he wouldn't like it.

He hasn't liked me hanging around him these past couple of years.

But I don't care.

If he insists on trying to wreck his life every chance he gets, I will insist on playing the babysitter and looking out for him.

Even now, I follow him out to the back yard and find him standing in a dimly lit corner, staring off into the distance. At least he's not drinking any more. And maybe after taking some of his anger out on me, he'll be a little more receptive to the idea of leaving. Which is all I wanted to begin with.

He speaks as soon as I reach him. "You remember the first time we met?"

"What?"

He's staring at the dark and expansive ground in front of us so I can't get an exact read on him. But he looks as if he's in a trance. "You saved me from those bullies. On the playground. You beat the shit out of them."

I did.

Beat the shit out of them and yes, I do remember.

I was eight and even at that age, I was a little shit.

Causing trouble, raising hell, breaking all the rules set forth by my dad or any form of authority. All because my big brother was the epitome of good behavior; the gold standard against which everyone else, especially me — the second son — was measured.

And of course, failed.

So I broke rules. I broke things. I picked fights. I beat up other kids at school.

Just for the record, I never picked on smaller kids. That was against *my own* rules. I usually went for the bigger ones, the ones who would use their size to terrorize other kids at school. It was fun to put them in their place.

Which is why I saved Lucas.

He was the new kid, a small kid, and a group of guys were messing with him.

"I remember," I tell him, swallowing thickly.

"You taught me how to fight," he murmurs.

I did that too, yes.

When I found out that he was not only being picked on at school but also at his own home, by his own father, I taught him a few moves.

"And you taught me how to play soccer," I reply.

His mouth splits into a tiny smile. "Because you fucking sucked at it."

"Only because it's a sucky game."

I don't like soccer.

I never did.

In fact I hate the sport because I was forced into it. It's something all Davidsons are into. Needless to say, my brother was a star.

A natural, according to my dad.

And I was a natural fucking disaster.

Lucas fixed that however.

In exchange for saving his ass, he promised to teach me soccer — something he played to escape his home life. And over time, I got good at it. I got fucking excellent at it. So much so that I won a soccer scholarship to go to college.

Lucas also fixed my pissed-off attitude, or rather compensated for it with his own charming one. And in turn, I fixed his problem of always getting friend-zoned by the girls.

Long story short, we've been inseparable since we were eight years old.

Well, until now.

"I'd never had a friend before you. You were my first friend. My only friend." Then, finally turning to look at me, "My brother."

It's getting harder and harder to breathe now. To stand and not go to my knees, fall under the pressure in my chest, the burden on my shoulders.

But he deserves it.

He deserves me standing here, giving him the courtesy to look him in the eyes like a man.

"You were my motherfucking *brother*, Reign," he growls, taking a step toward me. "Until you ruined it. Until you fucking destroyed everything. Every fucking thing that I cared about."

I stay silent.

Because he's right.

I did destroy everything that he cared about. His happiness. His dreams. His love. His fucking life. And if I don't find some way to stop what he's been doing, he might even lose his life-long goal of becoming a pro soccer player. It's testament to how good of a soccer player he is that even though he drinks himself half to death every night, he still shows up for practice and manages to kick ass. Or rather, it's a testament of how much he hates me that he shows up to practice to kick *my* ass specifically. And I let him because yes, he deserves all the chances to annihilate me.

So there's nothing for me to say or do except take it.

Take whatever he wants to dish out.

"You know what I saw when I looked at her tonight?" he asks, taking another step toward me. "I saw *you*. I saw your hands on her. Your fucking mouth on her. Like it was, that night. Every time I think about her, I think about you. About your betrayal. About the fact that the person I trusted the most in this world screwed me over. You fucking screwed me over, Reign. And apparently, you've been doing it for years." He clenches his jaw. "That's what you told me, didn't you? When I asked you why. When I fucking asked why the fuck would you kiss my girl, you told me that you'd wanted to kiss her for a long time. That you'd wanted *her* all the while she was mine."

I did.

I did tell him that when he asked me.

I could've lied.

I could've said that it was temporary insanity, that I'd forgotten myself there for a moment. And while all of that was true — I *did* forget myself for a moment — it wasn't the whole truth.

The whole truth was much uglier. Much more of a betrayal than a mere two-minute kiss. And he needed to know that. He fucking deserved to know who I was.

What I was.

A snake. A betrayer.

A fucking piece of shit who broke the very first rule of friendship: coveting my best friend's girl.

"So it should be obvious, isn't it?" he continues, his eyes narrowed and dripping venom. "Why I'm drinking myself into oblivion and wanting to get my dick sucked by a blonde. You did this to me. You *reduced* me to this. So you can take your babysitter routine and fuck off."

It's my turn to step forward then.

My turn to grit my teeth and narrow my eyes.

"Yeah," I growl, low. "It was me. And don't you dare forget that."

"What?"

"I'm the one to blame. *Me.*" I thump a hand on my chest. "Which means you need to stop drinking yourself to death. You need to stop ruining your life, because I've already ruined it enough for you. Do you understand? You want me gone, I'll be gone. You won't see me again. But you need to stop punishing yourself for the things that I did. Before it's too late. Before you lose everything that you've worked for. Before you do something that you might regret later."

"Yeah? And what's that?"

"You want to punish her too," I say then.

He drags in a sharp breath, his eyes becoming slits, but I don't let it deter me.

"At least, that's what you wanted to do, back there. At the bar tonight. Punish her for what happened. I saw you. I fucking saw you eyeing *her* and then that chick on the dance floor."

I drag a heavy breath of my own as I remember it.

I've known the guy almost all his life; I can read him like a book. And back there, he was gearing up to punish her too. And it was going to involve this random girl who hadn't stopped staring at him ever since we'd arrived.

Very middle school-ish but effective.

If you want to hurt the girl who's hurt you.

"Is that why you dragged me out of there?" he asks. "Because I was going to *punish* her."

"I dragged you out of there because you're not yourself," I reply, "not anymore."

"A little too worried about her," he sneers, "aren't you?"

I clench my teeth harder at his words, almost giving in and looking away from him.

But somehow I find enough strength to hold on.

To not rob him of this chance to take a stab at me.

"It's okay, she's a big girl. She could've handled it. And if not, I'm sure you would've been there. To lick her wounds and make it all better for her. She likes that, by the way. *Licking.* Not that I have to tell you, but still." Then, scoffing, "Although it's been two years now so fuck knows what else she likes."

Rage, red hot and flaming, flows through my veins.

I'm used to it. I'm used to feeling angry and hateful and bitter but for the first time in the last two years, this rage is directed toward my best friend.

"You really need to stop," I growl again, my words sounding low and rough.

"What, you don't think she's picked up new tricks along the way?"

My fists are so tight that my knuckles have their own heartbeat.

"Just a word of advice, *brother*" — he says brother like it's a dirty word — "if she can do it to me, the guy she claimed to fucking love, she could do it to you too. So I wouldn't waste my breath on her."

"Stop. *Talking*."

I barely recognize my own voice now, my words slurring together. But he has no trouble understanding me.

"Or what?"

Or I'll punch you in the face.

I'll break your nose.

Knock all your teeth out.

Rip your tongue out and shred it.

Rip your fucking lungs out of your throat so you never, not ever, say one thing against her.

I don't say it though.

I don't do anything either.

I simply stand there, vibrating with rage. With violence.

A long sigh escapes Lucas and he steps back. "Go home. What I do with my life, who I punish, is none of your goddamn business, all right? Just leave."

He turns around and starts to walk away.

"It was a kiss," I find myself saying to his back.

He pauses and twists back to look at me.

"That *I* started," I continue, even though he already knows; I told him two years ago, knowing that I wouldn't be able to save our friendship but hoping that I could at least save him and her. "I went for it first. And yes, I wanted to kiss her for a long time. That's on me. But a kiss doesn't erase years of loyalty. *Her* loyalty. To you. It doesn't erase or change how she felt about you. How much she loved you. So you wanna be angry at me for the rest of your life, it's your call. But it's time you forgave her."

And until he does, I'm not letting her get anywhere near him. I'm going to be the fucking gatekeeper if I have to be but I'm not letting my best friend hurt her with what he's become.

CHAPTER TWELVE

The Bandit

I see him as soon as I pull in to the gym parking lot.

The lighting is fucked up but there's no mistaking him. He sticks out like a fucking weirdo in his three-piece suit, his tie that still doesn't look loosened at two o'clock in the morning, and his hair that's so fucking polished that it looks wet. Not to mention his Bentley among the junkyard of rusted trucks and secondhand cars, which he's leaning against.

He might as well be wearing a sign that says, 'Hey, I'm loaded. Muggers welcome.'

What the fuck is he thinking?

This isn't the part of Bardstown that he usually frequents. I didn't even think he knew about this place.

Yo Mama's So Fit — that's actually the name of the gym — isn't exactly a high-end establishment. It's mostly frequented by people with rage issues, who need a place to smash things and not get constantly arrested for it.

But apparently he did know, and now I have to have the confrontation that I've been avoiding ever since I came back.

Fuck.

His eyes land on me as soon as I get off my bike, a Harley Davidson that I saved my fucking ass off for. He straightens up when I start walking toward him.

My big fucking brother.

"What happened to your face?" he asks as soon as I stop, eyeing my jaw where Lucas took a shot at me only an hour ago.

"That's very rude. I was born this way."

"Did you get in a fight?"

"If you have a problem with it though, you should take it up with Mom."

He stares at me for a few seconds before he deadpans, "She's in Italy for the summer."

"Ah, well it shall remain a mystery then."

His lips twitch for a second or two or at least, it looks like it. But it can't be true; my brother has zero sense of humor.

"Where's your helmet?" he asks next.

"Back in New York."

Disapproval lines his features like I knew it would.

That's why I lied.

It's back in my room, *somewhere*. I'm reckless but I'm not so reckless that I'd forget my helmet in a different city.

"Not exactly a smart choice," he says then, "when you're riding that death machine."

"It's also the machine that might help remove that stick up your ass. So maybe you should try it sometime."

He glances at my bike before saying, "No, thank you."

I shrug. "Fine. Be that way."

He stares at me for a few moments. Then, "You're staying at a motel."

"Should probably ask you how you know that. Or how you knew that I was going to be here, at the gym, and that it's fucking creepy that my own brother is stalking me, but I guess why bother, yeah? It's not as if you're gonna stop."

"I won't, no. But it's not me personally who's stalking you," he says. "I have a guy. And from what he told me, these are the only two places you've been frequenting since you came back."

I have.

Actually, these are the only two places I go to *whenever* I come back. Because this isn't the first time I've been back. Not that I've told anyone as to why I come back — it's not anyone's business — and I only come back during summer for a few weeks.

So far my brother has never cared, but apparently something's changed this summer.

"So when you didn't show up at the motel, I came here," he finishes. Then, he reaches into his suit's breast pocket and fishes out a very pristine looking handkerchief. "Although I can't say that I've enjoyed being here."

First: I can't believe I'm even saying the word, handkerchief.

Second: my brother always carries one.

With his initials embroidered on them in black: HAD.

Homer Alexander Davidson.

And third: with a flourish, he opens that piece of cloth and wipes his fingers.

"What the fuck are you doing?" I can't help but ask.

"Wiping my fingers."

"Why?"

"Because I touched the doorknob when I went into the gym to ask about you."

"How tragic."

"Indeed." He nods. "My car sanitizer is out. So I'm stuck wiping my hand every five seconds. Not that I think it's going to help, you understand."

"Of course not."

"But hope springs eternal."

My big brother, ladies and gentlemen.

Stuck-up fucking ass.

"Thrilled to see how you haven't changed," I say. "Do you mind telling me why you're here and why the fuck you've been blowing up my phone these past couple of weeks?"

He puts back his handkerchief, all neatly folded, and thrusts his hands down into his pockets, watching me silently again. "How are you?"

What the fuck?

Are we exchanging pleasantries now?

We haven't seen each other in two fucking years, haven't *talked to each other* even in two fucking years, and this is what he says to me.

I go to say something derogatory but then I take a moment.

And in that moment, I study him and as I said, he hasn't changed much.

He looks every inch like our father.

Same face — sharp and stern, devoid of any emotion — same dressing sense, same mannerisms. It's like our dad is still alive and I bet he is.

Through his first-born son.

"I'm fantastic, thank you. But forgive me if I don't care enough to ask how you are."

His eyes — exactly like dad's but a lighter shade than mine — sweep over my features, my body. "You've lost weight."

"And you've got a gut now." I pat my own. "You sure this is the look you wanna go for? No girl's ever gonna kiss you."

I'm lying, of course.

Like so many other things in his life, my big brother excels in fitness as well.

In addition to playing soccer in high school and college and now recreationally, he's a black belt in karate and does jujitsu for fun. If anything, his muscles look even more honed and stronger under that suit.

And I do know of a girl who'd die to kiss him.

Lucky fucker.

"If you'd picked up any of my calls or bothered to call me yourself, I would've…"

"You would've what?" I prod when he trails off.

And then I see something on my brother's face that for a second makes me think that it's a trick of the light.

But as I said, the lighting in this parking lot is shit, which means that the discomfort that I'm seeing on my brother's face is real. He actually fidgets before taking in a sharp breath. "I would've made arrangements for you at the hotel."

"At the hotel."

His nod is tight. "Yes."

Again, I have to take a few moments then.

To study him. To study this new expression on his face.

"You sure you're allowed to do that?" I ask finally.

His discomfort vanishing now, he clenches his jaw in irritation. "Yes, I'm allowed to do whatever I want."

"I don't think so. Because I'm pretty sure that you're still dad's little bitch."

And Dad would never have wanted me anywhere near his precious hotel. Or the manor that I grew up in. *Or* any of the Davidsons' properties, for that matter.

Something he *legally* saw to before he died.

"Look, the reason I've been calling you is," my brother says with a long sigh, not choosing to rise to the bait like he usually does, "I'd like to invite you to dinner."

"What?"

"How's next Saturday? Seven o'clock."

Next Saturday, I'm busy so I can't make it.

But more importantly, *what the fuck*?

This is even more bizarre than us exchanging pleasantries. Since when do my brother and I have dinner together?

I narrow my eyes at him. "Are you drunk right now?"

Displeasure coats his features. "No."

"High," I ask next, studying his features for the signs that he might be stoned. "Are you high? You smoke a little pot, big brother, huh? Is that why you're talking crazy?"

He doesn't dignify that with an answer.

"Because it's okay if you have. You can tell me. Not gonna judge you. It's not even real drugs, man."

"I would," he says, all serious, "smoke pot. Or do drugs or get drunk. Unfortunately, you either drank all the liquor or smoked all the pot that there was in Bardstown."

I let out a surprised chuckle. "Guilty. I can hook you up though. Just say the word. I've still got my old contacts." Then, because I can't help myself, "Maybe it'll loosen you up enough to do the deed."

He stiffens at that.

And I love it.

Jesus, how could I have forgotten?

That my brother is a fucking prude and I've always enjoyed provoking him this way.

He shifts on his feet again, this time a different kind of discomfort flashing through his features. "You know what, I think we should talk some other time. You're clearly not —"

I shake my head slowly, a smirk blooming on my lips. "No, let's talk now. So? You kiss her yet?"

His jaw clenches.

Fucking epic.

"She won't tell me," I goad. "And I've asked. Like a fucking teenage girl with a hard-on for gossip."

Another clench, then, "Do you mean to be so crass or does it come naturally?"

I spread my arms wide. "It's all natural, big brother. And I can teach you. Give you a few pointers." Then, winking suggestively, "About how to pour maple syrup all over your pancakes. Or wait, is it her pancakes and *your* maple syrup?"

Steam is coming out of his ears.

Or it would be. If we were in some cartoon.

And I wanna laugh my ass off.

God, I missed this.

The only thing I miss about my big brother: poking fun at him about his fiancée, Maple Mayflower.

Or rather, my brother's *arranged* fiancée.

So one day, our father — God fuck his soul — and her father got together and decided that their kids would marry each other when the time comes. Of course my brother agreed because when has he ever said no to Dad? She agreed too because I guess she has the same affliction as my brother, of always agreeing to whatever her father says.

Which means they've been engaged all their lives. Probably ever since my brother was a freshman and she was in like second grade or whatever. Extremely gross and archaic but what do I know.

Not that they've ever acted like a regular couple though.

Despite it being understood that they'd marry each other someday, there's no contact between the two. They don't go out on dates. They don't talk to each other or even look at each other.

Well, at least my brother doesn't.

He's always been too busy with his studies, sports, the business, to give little Maple — or pancakes as I call her, to annoy him — his time and attention. And despite my brother's callousness, she's pretty obsessed with him, has been all her life. I don't see why, honestly. She could do a lot better than a guy with the emotional range of cardboard — not that I'm any better but still — and who gets offended at the slightest mention of something intimate between a man and a woman.

Sometimes I wonder if my thirty-year-old brother is a fucking virgin.

I mean, that can't be true, right?

He must've done the deed; if not with Maple then with someone else.

Because if not, then I feel sorry for Pancakes.

Apart from Lucas, I guess you could call her my friend. Sure, it started out as a way to annoy my big brother. But then I guess she grew on me and became the little sister I never had.

"So easy," I murmur, shaking my head. "Anyway, I don't think I can make it on Saturday. Or *ever*. Have an awesome fucking night, big brother."

I'm about to step to the side but he speaks. "I know."

It sounds low and guttural, his voice.

As if the words are ripped out of his chest and I instantly go alert. "What?"

"I found something."

"You found what?"

"Dad's journal."

O-kay…

So?

Our dad had a journal; I knew that.

But only by accident.

I stumbled upon it a long time ago while I was trying to find something in his study that I could break. He was forcing me to go to the therapist's office and I hated it there. Back then he had a theory that my lack of grades and concentration was the result of an illness, like ADHD or something, because it had been very hard for him to accept that his second son wasn't like the first. That he was a rebel and not a boring puddle of mud to be molded into a shiny vase.

I was too little at the time to read the contents of the diary when I found it. But before I could even make an attempt at it, I was caught. Results were not pleasant, let's just leave it at that. And while I still snuck into his study after that incident and stole things and broke them, I never went for his journal. I did start to keep my own though. When I was old enough and when one of my therapists wanted me to keep track of my angry thoughts.

I've had enough therapy to know that it was my unconscious effort of seeking Dad's approval.

What a fucking stupid thing to do.

It doesn't matter though.

Because I don't keep a diary. Not anymore.

Not for two years, two months and twelve days.

From the looks of it though, my brother didn't know about our dad's journals. Which is surprising because I thought my dad and Homer were all buddy buddy and knew each other's secrets.

Well, not all secrets but still most of them.

He takes in another sharp breath, his chest expanding as he repeats, "So I know."

"You know what?"

"What he did to you."

I stop breathing then.

I stop thinking. I freeze.

While his chest expands on a sharp, agonized breath.

But it's not enough to calm him down. It's not enough to settle him or settle that pained expression on his face. So he shifts on his feet a few more times, runs a hand through his hair, messing up those strands — something that I'm seeing for the first time, his hair messed up — to say what he wants to next.

"He had..." He swallows. "He had it written down. What he did to... to punish you. The beatings. The starving. How he locked you up in your room, in the basement or in your closet. To teach you... To teach you a lesson. Medicating you. I knew he was taking you to doctors but I..."

Didn't know.

No, he didn't.

No one did.

Because it was a secret; my dad's long and well-kept secret.

So the first thing that comes to mind right now is how fucking stupid.

How fucking *reckless* of him.

To write down his own crimes.

Something that he went to such great lengths to hide. Something that he never ever wanted anyone to find out. Something that he told me people wouldn't believe even if I told them.

Because of his image.

Because of how generous and kind he was.

In the eyes of others, he meant.

My brother runs his fingers through his hair again, as he goes on, "I didn't know the rest of it. I didn't know how bad it was. I never... I never knew. I never saw any of what he... He wasn't..."

Like that with me.

Again, he doesn't say it because he doesn't have to.

It's implied that even though we shared a father, we really didn't.

Like the rest of the world, my brother knew a different father than I did. He got a dad who was strict but encouraging and proud and *fucking* loving instead of the one who was perpetually angry. Perpetually disappointed. Who perpetually tried to mold me into something that he wanted and when I refused, he'd become a bully.

Shouting, screaming, punching and yes, locking up and starving, medicating, whatever struck his fancy, whatever he was in the mood for that day, he'd do.

And of course in secret.

In private.

So no one would see his real face.

No one would know that the generous, upstanding Howard Davidson was a fucking monster who beat his own son.

But the stubborn motherfucker that I was, I took it all.

I didn't fucking break. I didn't fucking obey.

And that would just piss him off even more.

So again, what a stupid fucking idea to write it all down where someone could read it.

Great, Dad. Just fucking great. You're a moron, aren't you?

"Why didn't you..." he asks, his features still writhing in agony. "Why didn't you say something?"

Anger washes over me then.

Great, big wave of anger.

"To *you*, you mean," I sneer.

" I —"

"I didn't tell you anything, big brother," I growl, my voice low and vibrating, "because I didn't think you'd care. I didn't think you'd give a fuck if your wonderful father was beating on your piece of shit brother. That's what you thought about me, didn't you?"

He has enough courtesy to look ashamed. "I…"

"Because you're like everyone else." I shrug then. "Not that I blame you or anyone else. I've earned every inch of my reputation and I'm very fucking proud of it. But don't you stand there and interrogate me about what I did or didn't do."

When I actually did it.

Told someone.

Our mom.

A couple of times even, back when I was little and stupid enough to think that it would help.

Spoiler alert: it didn't.

She told me to behave and be good like Homer and it would stop. And then she went on to ignore it and keep my dad's secret like his good little accomplice.

So yeah, I didn't think my brother would care.

He's eight years older than me. By the time I was in kindergarten, he was already in boarding school, being the star student and athlete, living his life away from the house, away from me, only coming home a couple of times a year.

He had no place for me in his life.

He never did.

He was — is — my father's son and yeah, I admit to entertaining the fantasy that my big brother would come save me from our monster father when I was little, but then I grew up. I realized that no one was coming to save me, certainly not my own family when they were the ones I'd needed saving from.

So I never told anyone.

Not even Lucas.

Maybe I should have — because he was going through the same things — but I could never bring myself to after my encounters with Mom. So all Lucas knew was what everyone knew: that I was a spoiled troublemaker that my parents were very unlucky to have. Despite that, he was still my friend.

"I..." my brother begins. "I'm... I don't know what to say except that I'm sorry. I'm so fucking sorry, Reign. I wish I... I let you down. I wish I'd treated you differently. I wish I'd known. I wish I'd —"

"It doesn't matter."

Because it doesn't.

It doesn't change anything.

It doesn't change the past, the fact that he didn't know and that he knows now. And from the looks of it, is regretful. The reason I don't doubt that is because he just threw the F word at me. Homer is too polite to do that so yeah, I guess his remorse is genuine.

But as I said, it doesn't matter.

We are who we are.

He's the favored son and I'm the fuck-up.

We have different lives, different paths and nothing will ever change that.

"I'd like to," he says, his eyes staring hard at me, "make it right somehow."

"Make it right how?"

"I'd like you to come work with me."

"What?"

"At the company."

At this, I once again find myself stopping. Freezing.

Unable to say a single word.

"I know he wrote you out of the will and seized your trust fund. But I've been talking to our lawyers. There's a way that I could give it all back to you, all the money, now that I own the majority of the shares. And I want to. It belongs to you, Reign. Half of this company's yours. But I..." His chest expands. "I want you to come work with me."

"To make it happen, you mean."

His expression is cool but I see how firmly his jaw is set. "Yes."

"Even though you just said that that money belongs to me."

He lets a few seconds go by in silence. Then, "It'll be full-time for the summer. And then when your classes start, you could do part time. I understand you have soccer and other obligations. Work with me until you graduate and it's all yours."

Right.

All mine.

Fucking asshole.

"You're just like him, aren't you? Do this and I'll give you that. Get an A and I won't lock you up in your room anymore. Behave and you won't get punched in your ribs. Fall in line and I'll take you to the doctor for that broken arm I gave you."

I watch my brother flinch. "Look, you need this. You need the money, don't you? You must. I'm not sure how you've been managing but you need the money."

I have to laugh at this.

A loud, angry laugh.

"Dad cut me off two years ago, big brother. Nice of you to think of me now."

When I said our father took legal measures to keep me away from the manor, this is what I meant. He kicked me out of his will and specifically had a clause that said I could never set foot on any of his properties. And while this is a secret to most people, he had to seek help from his lawyers, some top company officials and my brother.

"Reign —"

"But I already have a job."

"What job?"

"None of your fucking business."

If my brother thought that I've been starving all this time without our father's money, then he really doesn't know shit about me.

I'm nothing but resourceful.

My college tuition is already covered by my scholarship. I always knew my dad would never pay for my education, and that he'd find a way to look like a martyr by blaming me for it. Which would've been fine; I really don't care.

Not for college or soccer.

I'm not like Lucas. I'm not interested in making a career out of soccer. The only reason I went was because he was going there. And I accidentally got a scholarship too, to the same college. So I thought why the fuck not. If it got me out of this hellhole town, which was the only thing that I've ever cared about, then I was all for it.

As for the rest of my shit, I do have a job.

I fight.

For money.

The gym that I was about to go into, before being waylaid by my brother, isn't only a boxing gym; they also organize amateur fights. Mostly, they are legal and all the fighters are paid well. Some fights, however, are not and the fighters are paid obscenely well for those.

So well that I only have to work over the summer and I'm set for the rest of the year.

Basically, this is like my summer job, has been for the last two years.

"I know I haven't been there for you," my brother begins because he doesn't know when to quit. "I've *never* been there for you. In fact, I was happy. I admit that. When Dad cut you off, I thought you deserved it. After all the years of crap you put us through, your partying, your drinking, your drugs. All the times you'd get arrested or expelled or all the times people would simply quit on you. And then, when everything happened with that girl, the Adlers... Instead of blaming her, I blamed you. I thought that it must've been you. Because it's always you, isn't it? You're the problem. You do things. You wreck things. You ruin them. And so I thought you must've done something to her; you must've pushed her into doing what she did. I thought after all that cutting you off, disowning you was the least Dad could've done and..." He shakes his head, grimacing. "I failed you. I fucking failed you, Reign. I wasn't a good big brother. I wasn't... But I —"

"No."

"But —"

"You were right."

He frowns. "About what?"

"To think that," I tell him, my hands fisted at my sides. "To think that it was me."

Because it was.

I was responsible for it. For pushing her into doing what she did.

While I make no apologies for all the other shit I've pulled in my life, I do take responsibility for this. For making her do what she did, and consequently ruining her life.

If I hadn't been so angry at myself for what I'd done, so much so that I took it out on her, she wouldn't have done what she did. If I hadn't said all those cruel things to her, she wouldn't have committed a fucking felony.

When I found out that she had though, and that she'd been arrested for it, I went to my dad. To confess. To tell him that it was me who'd provoked her and that he should let her go and punish me instead, which he did by disowning me.

Something he probably would've done one day anyway, but I guess he had the opportunity then and he took it. But while I thought that would satisfy him and save her, it didn't. He still sent her to that reform school.

So yeah, it was me.

I was the problem, not her.

The only good thing is that she's out of that place. She must've graduated by now. She must be back where she always belonged, with her parents, at the manor.

Before I fucked it all up for her.

So protecting her from the new Lucas is the least I could do.

Exhaling an angry breath, I focus on my brother. "I don't want your fucking money, all right? Don't come back here anymore."

CHAPTER THIRTEEN

Tonight, I'm a criminal.

And it's not only because I go to St. Mary's School for Troubled Teenagers but also because I'm stalking.

For real.

There's no two ways about it. No gray area.

And yes, there's tons of hiding and crouching and sneaking around involved.

First, to get out of St. Mary's.

It's the middle of the night and way past the 9:30 curfew. Which means I should be in bed, fast asleep, but I'm tiptoeing down the concrete hallway of my dorm so I can sneak out of the building and go off campus: to a house in Bardstown.

Where a party is being thrown in my ex-boyfriend's honor. And while I'm against all forms of stalking and still afraid of any dire consequences for me, I'm going there for a second chance to do what I couldn't two days ago.

This time though, I don't have my friends with me.

I didn't want to involve them and potentially get them in trouble when I knew I was going to be breaking curfew. Plus they still don't know the whole story. And until I come clean to them, I can't in good conscience keep accepting their help and support.

So I'm on my own and about an hour later, I reach my destination.

Even if I didn't know that this is where the party is happening, I'd still figure it out. It's the only house on this quiet street that's making that much noise, and taking a deep breath, I head inside.

My plan is to find Lucas and not let anything — anything *at all* — deter me.

I search for him in the crowded foyer, in the living room, dining room and all the other rooms that I can find among the throngs and throngs of bodies. When I can't find him though, I head to the back yard and oh my God, there he is.

And for a second or two, I simply stand in my spot and stare at him.

At my boyfriend — *ex*-boyfriend.

He stands in a group, holding a red cup in his hand, smiling at something someone is saying, and he looks so handsome. So familiar.

His blond hair and blue eyes.

God, I miss him.

I miss him so so much.

I don't know how I spent the last two years without him. Without seeing him, talking to him, laughing with him. And the fact that I may get to talk to him tonight is leaving me all breathless and excited.

Also terrified.

You can do this, Echo.

Yes, I can.

Another deep breath later, I start toward him. But then I come to a halt again because one second Lucas was laughing at something and the next, he's... busy doing something else.

Something like kissing.

This girl who came out of nowhere.

I mean, what the...

I was so busy staring at my ex-boyfriend that I never noticed her sidling up to him. I never noticed her trying to steal his attention until he turned away from the conversation and gave it to her. And then before I could even blink, he was bent over, claiming her mouth.

And holy fuck, before I can even blink, there's another girl in the mix.

Again, who knows where she came from but she's here now and Lucas is making out with her while the first one watches. And the group that he was standing in seems to be very happy about it. They're laughing and clapping and cheering him on, egging him on to do more, like this is some kind of a show.

And he's loving it.

He's giving them what they want.

Switching between girls. Kissing them both at once.

Pumping his fist in the air.

Obnoxious.

That's fucking obnoxious.

Distasteful, offensive, objectionable, and it reminds me of *him*.

It reminds me of something that *he'd* do, my ex-boyfriend's best friend, and I'm going to throw up.

I am going to seriously vomit right now. I'm going to…

I squeak when suddenly, I feel someone grabbing my arm and pulling me back, *dragging* me back actually, hauling me away somewhere. The only reason I let them is because my relief is so big.

At being forcefully taken away from that horrific scene.

From Lucas kissing not one but two girls.

Who were they?

Was one of them his…

Before I can finish my thought, I'm being pulled into a room.

An unknown room that at first is dark but then floods with bright, almost neon, harsh light before I hear a door snapping shut.

Making me realize that I have bigger problems right now.

Potentially *dangerous* problems.

I whirl around, ready to scream murder, but my gaze locks with a pair of familiar eyes.

Reddish brown and glowing.

And so pretty that all my screams die down.

Which I think shouldn't have happened. I should still scream. I should still call for help.

Just because I know him, the stranger I'm locked in a bathroom with — this is a bathroom; I can notice that much even though I haven't been able to look away from him — doesn't mean he's not dangerous.

He's a bandit.

Of course he's dangerous.

So I gather my wits about me, ready to scream when he growls, his features set in displeasure, "The fuck are you doing here?"

Scream, Echo.

But all I do is blink, my mouth parted. Then, "What... What happened here?"

I point at his jaw.

Apart from his brightly glowing eyes, that's the most conspicuous spot on his face. This blooming red and purple bruise on the left of his very scruffy and very sharp jaw.

Which clenches at my question.

"How'd you know he was going to be here?"

His growl is even thicker than before and I realize that his questions are probably more sensible and important than mine. More urgent and relevant to the situation at hand.

Still I can't seem to let his bruise go.

It looks vicious. Angry.

Painful.

"Were you," I swallow, eyeing it carefully, "like, in a fight or something?"

He could've been.

He's not exactly the most level-headed guy I've ever met.

Back in school, I'd see him with random bruises here and there. I'd even witness how he got some of them. By getting into fights with people all around campus, which was always followed by Lucas pulling him away and then accompanying him to the principal's office. They'd either suspend him for the day or take away his soccer privileges.

He always got them back though; he was one of the best players, and apparently it didn't matter that he was also a loose cannon as long as he could kick a ball into the net with expertise.

"Yeah, getting real tired of people asking this question," he replies with a frown.

"Why, who else asked this question?"

His jaw tenses even more. "You stalking him now?"

Stalking.

Yeah, I am.

But I'm not ready to answer him yet.

"Well, it's a normal conclusion to draw. You're always getting into fights," I say.

"What is this?" He tips that bruised jaw at me. "Your stalker goth-reject costume?"

"Hey!" I draw back, the hood that was covering my dirty blonde hair falling off, making my hair spill all over my shoulders. "There is nothing wrong with my costume. It's not even a costume. It's a pair of jeans and a hoodie."

"Since when do you wear jeans?"

"I wear jeans all the time."

"No, you don't."

"I..." I purse my lips. "Why are you always so concerned about what I'm wearing? I'm wearing what I'm wearing. It's none of your business what I'm wearing."

I hate that he knows me so well.

I'm not a jeans kind of girl. I like dresses and skirts and summery things.

But what I hate the most is the fact that he so easily figured it out, that these are my stalker clothes. Dark and designed to conceal me. Not only so I could get away undetected from St. Mary's but also because this is a party where people know me. And if people know me, then they also know what I did.

Two years ago.

And I'm not in the mood to be harassed about it, or made fun of or be laughed at or jeered at. Which is what they did back then. After everything happened, going to school was a nightmare and I have no inclination to repeat that experience tonight.

Hence my stalker, goth-reject costume.

"Now tell me about your bruise," I order.

He doesn't.

Because he's... watching.

My strewn-about hair, specifically.

And he's watching it in a way that makes me feel all exposed and self-conscious.

With his eyes all intense and heavy.

Almost in a daze.

I clear my throat then, unable to bear it, and he snaps his eyes away and brings them to my face. Then, "A bruise is a bruise. It's none of your business how I got my bruise."

Touché.

I lift my chin. "Well, I hope it hurts."

"It does."

"Good."

"You need to —"

"Is that..." I fist my hands. "Is she... one of the girls his girlfriend?"

Oh God, please no.

Please don't say yes.

I know I have no right to ask that. I have no right to feel this hurt in my chest. Especially when I did the same thing to him.

But God, it hurts.

It hurts so, so much.

His jaw tics and I can't help but hone in on that bruise again, feeling my own heart pulsing and ticking, before he replies, "No."

At this answer, a relieved breath escapes me. "So then who were they?"

He holds his silence for a few seconds. "Just some girls."

"So he doesn't know them? But how's that —"

Another sharp breath from him before he states, "I'm taking you home."

"What?"

"Come on. Let's go."

"What, no. I'm not going anywhere with you."

"Told you to stay away from him, didn't I?"

"Unfortunately for you, you don't get to tell me what to do."

"Let's," he says slowly, taking a step forward, "*go.*"

I take a step back. "No."

"Echo," he warns.

My feet tremble on my next step back but I do it. "You're taking this best friend crap a little too far, all right?"

"I'm not going to repeat myself."

"I get that you're his best buddy and you're like brothers and whatever. But you don't get to decide who speaks with him. You're not his gatekeeper or… I don't know, babysitter or —"

He takes another step forward. "Unfortunately for you, I am. So come on."

Glaring, I move back. "Maybe he wants to talk to me too."

"Very fucking unlikely."

I ignore the pain in my chest. Because there is a chance that he might be right.

I don't want him to remind me though.

"I told you he was looking at me, remember? At the bar," I goad him, despite all better judgement.

"And I told *you* that you can't blame him."

"I'm not —"

"Or any guy for that matter," he goes on. "If you keep flinging your tits under their nose."

I gasp.

I have to because he accompanies his words with a look.

A very long and lingering look at my… tits.

That are well covered by the hoodie tonight but the way he stares at them makes me feel exposed again. The way he then goes on to stare at the rest of my body, stopping in places like my jean-covered thighs and calves, makes me think that he's imagining me in a dress right now.

He's imagining me in… nothing.

And I have this great urge to cover myself from him.

From his intense, pretty, *obscene* eyes.

"You're so…" I take a deep breath. "You did not just say that. You did not just talk about my…"

My outrage makes him smirk.

And the hateful and the most obnoxious guy that he is, he deliberately stares down at my chest for a second or two before shrugging. "Well what can I say, you've got nice tits."

"Stop," I command, my chest heaving, my tits feeling all heavy and strange from his lingering glances. "Don't say that word."

His smirk turns into a low chuckle.

And I don't know how it's possible but it's even worse than his shameless stare.

Because his chuckle is downright dirty.

"I thought you liked words," he drawls.

"I'm —"

"Or maybe you're looking for another synonym here?"

"I'm not —"

"How about knockers? Jugs, fun bags, hooters. Headlights."

"Oh my *God*."

"Oh my *Reign* is the phrase you're looking for, I think."

I thought I was afraid of going to jail but I don't think I am.

I think it's going to be totally worth it if I get to kill him first.

"I'm your best friend's girlfriend, you..." God, I can't find words. "*Vulgar psycho*. So you need to stop, okay? Just stop."

"Ex though, yeah?"

"Just stop," I whisper.

Finally, it looks like I've made some progress.

Because his amusement vanishes and he says, "Then don't piss me off and do what I tell you to do."

And then I just explode.

I explode at him for being so arrogant and domineering.

So hateful that it makes me sick.

"First," I begin, my hands fisting, "no matter how much you'd like to believe it, I'm not your servant girl. Never was and never will be. I don't take orders from you. You don't tell me what to do. Second, don't come near me. Stop advancing on me like a freaking predator or something. Third, I'm here to talk to Lucas and I'm not leaving until I do so." Then, "Oh, and even when I *do* leave, I'm not leaving with you. So back off."

Good.

That was good.

I'm very proud of myself.

Or I would be. If he'd listened to anything that I just said and obeyed.

As it is, he doesn't.

He still advances on me.

In fact, he takes a very long and lunging step — at least, it looks like that to me — toward me, making me flinch. Especially when the blunt toes of his boots knock against my sneakers.

Then, dipping down, pinning his red-flecked gaze on me, he says, "First, with me is the only way you'll leave. And you *will* leave, I'll make sure of that. Second, you're not talking to Lucas when he's like this, drunk and stoned out of his mind. When he doesn't know up from down. Third, the way I see it, you've always been my servant girl and the sooner you accept that fact, the better, because then we won't have to go through this whole thing where you pretend to have all the power and I have to remind you that you have less than none. And lastly, isn't predator a synonym for criminal?"

My heart skips a beat then.

Followed by several other beats as he continues, "Not exactly but kinda though, yeah? It fits. Right there with a lawbreaker, a delinquent and a felon." Then, dipping his chin further and lowering his voice even more, "A bandit who rides a horse and kidnaps girls in the middle of the night. Although I have to say that I like my girls bold. I like 'em feisty and wild. Girls who don't run away from danger but toward it. So you with your bubblegum pink and good girl routine have got nothing to worry about. You bore me more than the books that you like to read and you're stronger than the sleeping pills that I have to take to put myself to sleep these days. Chasing after you, let alone kidnapping you, is the last thing on my agenda tonight."

I want to cover my ears again.

Reach into my brain and take out that piece containing all the memories.

Of him.

My ex-boyfriend's asshole best friend.

But I can't.

All I can do is stand here and look up into his eyes.

His flashing and glowing eyes.

Surrounded by the thickest eyelashes I've ever seen.

All I can do is breathe lungfuls of his scent, summery and sunshiny. Exactly like I remember.

And that's the thing, isn't it?

I don't want to remember. I don't want to remember anything from the past.

All I want to do is move on, move forward.

So I focus on that.

On Lucas.

"*Why*," I breathe deep and close my eyes for a second, "is Lucas drunk and stoned out of his mind?"

His best friend's answer is silence.

And a belligerent stare.

But I refuse to back down. "Why doesn't he know up from down? What does that mean?" Again he gives me nothing, and despite my better judgement, I stretch my neck, my body even further and get up in his face. "Is that why he was kissing those girls and putting on that disgusting show? Tell me. Tell me what you meant. Why's Lucas like that? What's going on? What —"

"What's going on," he speaks in a biting tone, "is that that's what Lucas does now."

"What?"

"He drinks. He smokes. He pops pills and he fucks." A pulse has started up on his cheek now. "Whoever he wants. Wherever he wants."

"But that's... That's not how he is. That's..."

"As I said, that's how he is now. Self-destructive. He parties all night and doesn't care about much else."

"He cares about soccer," I blurt out.

He does.

He's always cared about it.

About getting picked in the drafts, going pro.

About me following him wherever he goes to play.

It would actually make me feel slightly uncomfortable talking about it. Because I always wanted to end up at NYU and study creative writing, and Lucas knew that. But he'd always tell me that that you could study creative writing anywhere and us staying together was more important. And since it wasn't something super urgent, I'd simply choose not to argue.

That's not the point though.

The point is that Lucas has soccer and he loves it. And he won't do anything to risk his chances of getting picked this coming January and going pro.

"Well, if he keeps on this path, there's not going to be much left to care about."

"But that's... He wouldn't..." I have to pause, will my heart to stop beating so loudly so I can at least hear my own words. "Why? I don't... I'm..."

"Why do you think?" he tells me, his eyes intense and penetrating.

For a few seconds, I refuse to believe it.

I refuse to hear what he's telling me. I tell myself that he's lying.

That this isn't true.

It can't be.

Soccer is Lucas's life. Soccer is everything to him.

But then I was too, wasn't I?

He'd tell me that. He'd *show* me that.

He showed it to me on that night too. On my sixteenth birthday.

When I broke his heart.

I betrayed his trust. I hurt him in the worst way possible.

With his best friend.

His *best. Friend.*

With heaving breaths, I look at him. I look at his arched cheekbones, his arrogant brows. His heated eyes, his plush mouth.

That bruise on his jaw.

And I want to...

I want to bite it. I want to scratch it, scratch his ever beautiful and ever sexy face.

I want to pull at his dark, spiky hair. Punch his wildly breathing chest.

"Why aren't you doing something then?" I voice my question but I don't give him a chance to answer. "Why aren't you stopping him? Why *didn't* you stop him before he got drunk and stoned out of his mind? What are you doing here with me? Why aren't you out there, looking out for him?"

"I'm —"

"You're supposed to be his best friend," I almost scream, going up on my tiptoes. "You're supposed to look out for him. You're supposed to make sure that he's okay. You're supposed to —"

Suddenly, all my words die.

They dissolve in my throat. They turn to ash.

As I feel a searing rush of heat flowing through my veins.

And I realize it's because he's touching me.

Gripping me.

My wrist.

His long, dusky fingers are wrapped around my pale skin and as jarring as the contrast is, as jarring as the burn of his skin on my skin is, it's even breathtaking that I'm touching him too.

That I was the one who started it.

By putting my hands on his wide chest.

I don't know when I did that.

I don't know when my hands shot up and went to him and when my fingers fisted his t-shirt. And in a tight grip too because my knuckles are white and my nails are digging into my palms.

"I'm not," he rumbles.

And it's so low and thick that his chest vibrates.

Even the ground shakes beneath my feet, or at least it feels like it.

"What?" I whisper.

His fingers tighten around my wrist. "His best friend."

I suck in a breath.

"I'm not even his friend."

"I-I don't understand."

Those burning eyes of his narrow and his grip goes from tight to almost painful. "You didn't think that you were the only one, did you?"

"Y-you..."

"That you were the only fucking one who made the biggest mistake of their life that night. You didn't *think*," he growls, "that you're the only one fucking *paying* for it."

But I...

That's what I thought, yeah.

That is *exactly* what I thought.

That I'm the only one.

That I was the one banished from Lucas's life while he got to stay.

While Lucas cut me off, I thought Reign got the chance to make up for his mistake. They go to the same college. They play on the same team. Of course, Reign must've used it to his advantage and fixed his friendship with Lucas.

Not to mention, their years long history would have played a role in their reconciliation.

My grip on his t-shirt tightens too, my eyes narrowing, stinging. "B-but... You're both... You've been... You've been friends since y-you were kids and..."

"And what?" he bites out.

"I-I didn't think anything could come between you two."

"Something can."

My heart drops a beat. "Me."

"You."

I can't...

I can't comprehend this. I can't grasp the concept that they're not friends anymore.

"Turns out I'm a shitty friend," he says, something flickering in his eyes that I can't name, or maybe I'm too numb right now to name it. "Turns out I'm the kind of friend you wouldn't wish upon your worst enemy. So it's not really that much of a surprise that he's spiraling out of control. That he's fucking losing it, and the fact that I'm there for him, that I *insist* on being there for him, for every one of his fuck-ups, seems to just make everything worse. I do that though, don't I? I ruin things. I wreck them. I fucking destroy everything I touch." Another flex of his jaw. "Didn't think I'd ruin this too though. Didn't think I had it in me. To destroy the one and the only good thing in my godforsaken life."

Only when he finishes do I realize what was flickering in his eyes.

What's still flickering.

Remorse.

Regret. Contrition. Guilt.

I'm surprised that it took me so long to recognize it. When I see it every day.

In the mirror.

In my own eyes.

For hurting the most important person in my life.

He did it too, didn't he, though?

He hurt the most important person in his life as well. Only I thought he got a chance to fix it. Plus, in my very angry and low moments, I've assumed the worst.

That maybe he put the blame on me. Maybe he *told* Lucas on me.

That I was the one, *the slut*, who came on to him. That's what he said on the phone, didn't he? So then why wouldn't he say that to Lucas as well? To not only save their friendship — which I didn't think was in jeopardy to begin with — but also to keep us apart. Something that he always wanted to do.

"You didn't..." I whisper, my grip on his t-shirt still as tight and painful.

"I didn't what?"

I lick my lips. "Put the blame on me."

He glances down at my mouth for a second. "Wasn't yours."

"But I was the one who —"

His fingers flex, cutting me off. "It doesn't matter."

"But —"

He bends down then, making me press my fists on his shuddering chest even more. "Doesn't. *Fucking* matter."

"I'm sorry," I blurt out.

He flinches slightly. "What?"

God, what am I saying?

Even though he didn't take the opportunity that deep down I thought he would have, to keep me away from Lucas, doesn't mean that he isn't culpable.

He's absolutely culpable.

For a million things that came before. For years' worth of things.

But in this moment, when remorse is so thick in his gaze and I'm still reeling from his revelation — God, *how* is it even possible that they're not friends anymore? How's the world still going on — I can't help but say it.

I can't help but confess. "I-I've been jealous of you."

"Jealous."

I swallow and nod. "Because I thought... I thought you got a chance to fix it all. I thought you weren't punished. I thought you came out unscathed. After what happened. I thought that you still got to be his best friend and... and I'm the crazy ex-girlfriend who was blocked from everywhere. He wouldn't even give me a chance to apologize. That entire night, I kept calling and calling and texting and he didn't respond. And then he did, the next morning and I was..."

"Happy," he finishes for me.

"Yeah," I whisper, swallowing again. "Only he picked up to tell me to never ever call him again. That we were done and I got that, you know. I understood why after... everything. But he wouldn't let me talk. He wouldn't let me explain and I..."

And so I called him, Lucas's best friend.

To ask for help.

But we both know how that turned out.

With his room vandalized and me in a reform school.

I shake my head, "So yeah, I've been jealous. Of you. Of your friendship. Of the fact that I was the only one who lost everything."

But it feels so petty now that I say it out loud.

So vengeful.

Yes, there's no love lost between him and me.

But for some reason, I don't feel good.

I don't feel vindicated.

At the fact that I got my wish. He's suffering and guilty and miserable like me. That for the first time in my life, I see his eyes, his sharp beautiful features swimming in guilt.

All I feel is... sad. Or rather even more sad.

That so many things were destroyed that night.

Trust. Loyalty. Love. Friendship.

All lost because of one kiss.

One kiss was all it took.

To launch a war. To break hearts. To shift the ground beneath us.

"Well, I hope you like the taste of champagne," he says, breaking into my thoughts. "Because it looks like you're the one who'll be celebrating tonight."

I flinch as he throws my own words back at me, from The Horny Bard.

"I'm not —"

"But before that," his chest moves on a sigh, "you need to get out of here."

"I —"

"He isn't in any shape to listen to you. And you don't wanna listen to whatever he might have to say when he's like this." He glances down at my fists in his t-shirt. "Might break your pink little heart."

"Yeah, like you care," I scoff more from habit than anything else.

But then I pause.

Because he pauses too.

He was in the process of removing my hands from his body but at my words, he freezes for a second and I'm left... silent and thinking.

And what I'm thinking is...

It's frankly ridiculous.

It's hilarious actually.

I don't even know why the thought occurred to me. Why would it flash through my mind even for a microsecond? That he's somehow trying to... protect me.

Protect. *Me.*

I mean, it's the most nonsensical thing I've ever thought in my life.

But before I can stop myself, I ask, tightening my grip on his t-shirt, "Is that why you told me to stay away from him? Back at The Horny Bard. Because he's changed and he might break my heart."

He shoots his eyes up, again trying to dislodge my hands. "Your pink little heart, but yes."

Oh my God.

Oh my freaking God.

He *is*.

He *is* trying to protect me.

He is...

What a fucking asshole.

What a fucking jerk.

After *years* of tormenting me, putting me down, making me feel less than, *now* he swoops in to protect me. I mean, where does he get off?

For several seconds, I can't say anything.

I'm speechless. I'm fucking...

But I need to say something. I need to approach this. Whatever this is.

Whatever *ridiculous* joke this is.

"Okay, let's talk about this," I begin, looking him in the eyes, letting go of his t-shirt. "Because I feel like we need to talk about this. And it's the craziest thing that I've ever said but here goes." I take a deep breath. "You don't need to protect me."

I expect him to say something at this.

Or at least show some sort of reaction.

Shock maybe. Or amusement that I'd even say something like this.

But he doesn't.

So I keep going. "Because that's what you're doing, aren't you? You're protecting me."

Again, I give him a chance to laugh at me.

Any second now he's going to smirk and say something mean. He's going to say that I've lost my mind and that I should stop embarrassing myself.

But once again, he doesn't.

All he does is work his jaw back and forth, a pulse beating on his cheek, as he stares and stares at me. And I...

I feel angry. Again.

But now that I have *some* confirmation about my suspicions, I also feel... breathless.

My heart's racing like a crazy bird and I swallow thickly.

"You realize," I begin slowly, my chest heaving, "that this is crazy, right? You realize that the idea of *you*, Reign Marcus Davidson, protecting me, Echo Ann Adler, is fucking insane. It's beyond fucking insane. It's unreal. It's unnatural. It's fucking science fiction."

Okay, I should calm down.

Or I'll punch him in the face. *And* pass out with how fast my heart's beating.

"I don't need you to protect me," I continue in a calmer voice. "I don't even know why you'd want to. It's me and it's you. We hate each other. We make each other sick. If anything, I need protection from you. Not from my ex-boyfriend. I can handle my ex-boyfriend, okay? So I don't need your protection. What I need is..."

"The only thing you *need* to do is stay the fuck away from him," he says when I trail off, my mind churning.

"But you just said that he is spiraling."

"Yeah and I can handle him."

"You can't."

"I —"

"You're not his friend anymore."

His nostrils flare at the reminder. "And you're not his fucking girlfriend."

I take in my own deep, painful breath at that. "You had two years. *Two* years, Reign, and you haven't been able to." It looks like he's going to say something but I don't let him. "And it's not your fault. I'm sorry that I suggested that. I really am. I know you're a good friend. I mean, I'd know, right? I've seen you two together. I've put up with your hate for years because you always thought I was beneath him. So please believe me when I tell you you're a good friend. But maybe we need to try something different. Which is why I shouldn't stay away from him. Which is why *I* have to do something. I have to step in and save Lucas."

"Save Lucas."

"Yes." I nod with determination. "I think I have to fix what I broke."

Exactly.

Lucas is in pain, isn't he?

Like me, Lucas is still dealing with what happened two years ago.

Hell, like his own best friend. Well, ex-best friend now.

God, what a mess.

Anyway, *that's* why Lucas is lashing out.

That's why he's doing what he's doing.

So I need to clean it up, this mess. I need to fix everything.

"No."

"What?" I frown up at him. "What do you mean, no? What —"

"It means you're not doing anything."

"I don't —"

"You saw what happened, didn't you?" he cuts me off, almost growling, staring down at me with so much anger that I should feel scared. "You saw what he did. So you're not going to do anything. What you're going to do, is stay the fuck away from him. So I'm taking you home and you're coming with me without running your chirpy mouth a mile per second and giving me the biggest headache in the history of mankind. Do you understand? You. Me. The manor. *Right the fuck now.*"

By the time he finishes, his voice is pure growl.

And I'm so dazed by it that I don't even know what I'm saying. But I do make words. "I don't live at the manor."

He frowns. "What?"

"What?"

Which makes his frown thicker. He stares at me silently for a couple of seconds and when I don't say anything — I don't even know what he wants me to say right now — impatience flickers on his features and he bites out, "*What do you mean you don't live at the manor?*"

"It means I don't live at the manor." When his impatience increases and an actual growl comes out of his chest, I explain, my own impatience rearing its head now. "Remember how I broke your armoire two years ago? Plus a bunch of other things."

His eyes narrow, telling me that he doesn't appreciate my sarcasm.

"And remember how I got arrested for it and then got sent to a reform school?"

His eyes narrow further.

"I live there now. At St. Mary's School for Troubled Teenagers. Ergo, I do not live at the manor."

"Yes, you do."

"What?"

"Because you fucking graduated."

Oh. Okay.

Right.

He doesn't know. That I didn't.

Why would he, he doesn't live at the manor anymore. There's no way for him to find out.

And honestly, if I was more in control of my faculties, I probably would never have let it slip in front of him. I don't want him knowing that I'm still there. That I'm still in high school, a *reform high school,* while the rest of the world has moved on to bigger and better things.

But now that I've almost spilled the beans, I may as well go all the way.

Blushing, I shrug. "I didn't."

I know that he understands what I'm saying.

It's the way his body has tensed, the muscles on his chest twitching. Then, as if to confirm and really make sure that I'm saying what I'm saying, he asks, "You didn't what?"

I sigh, hating that I have to spell it out for him, hating that I have to tell him period. "I didn't graduate."

He lets another beat pass.

But *then*, he loses it.

He actually loses it and thunders, "What the fuck do you mean you didn't graduate?"

It's so unexpected that I flinch.

I don't understand his reaction.

Nevertheless, I explain, "It means I didn't graduate. I didn't have *enough credits* to graduate so I go to —"

"Bullshit."

"What?"

"Bull-fucking-shit," he snaps, his eyes so narrowed that they've become slits, his nostrils flaring like he's some kind of an enraged animal. "You're fucking smart. You're one of the smartest people I know. You're always at the top of your class. You fucking tutor people. How the fuck did you not have enough credits to graduate?"

I'm even more confused now. Than I was before, I mean.

His outburst has completely thrown me.

The fact that it looks like he... *cares*.

As unexpected as that is, it's even more unexpected that I feel a warmth blooming in my chest.

I feel a flush of pleasure.

And I can't even help it.

I can't stop it.

The racing of my heart. The hitching of my breaths.

I knew that *he* knew, about my grades and tutoring; I tutored his best friend. Plus I was his best friend's girlfriend and there were so many occasions when Lucas would announce to the world — usually in a loud voice at the cafeteria or in the courtyard — that his girl got another A, or that his girl won the debate competition.

And since Reign was always around, he'd get to listen to Lucas singing my praises.

It used to be so embarrassing and endearing as well.

So of course, Reign knows my academic record.

But I didn't know that this is what he thought of me.

That this is what he *thinks* of me.

Tucking my hair behind my ear, I say, "Well, that was... before. Before everything. I haven't been the top of my class, the top of anything really, in two years." I duck my eyes too, unable to hold his intense gaze. "Turns out, being heartbroken while you're trapped in a cage isn't very conducive to studying." I clear my throat. "Anyway, I go to summer school now and I should be able to graduate in a few weeks. And that's when I get to move back to the manor. Finally."

I'm staring down at my sneakers.

At his shoes.

At the floor.

Anywhere but up at him.

God, I'm so embarrassed.

Even more embarrassed than when I had to tell my parents that I wasn't going to be graduating after all. They've had two years of getting used to my low grades. While they were super surprised when I got arrested, this time around they almost expected it to happen.

They expected me to screw up.

He, on the other hand, still somehow thinks that I'm the same girl that I was before my sixteenth birthday.

Smart and intelligent and level-headed.

I'm not.

I'm stupid and heartbroken and desperate enough to climb over brick walls to stalk my ex-boyfriend.

"And NYU," he murmurs.

I look up. "What about it?"

His features are blank but his body is still tense. "You still going to it?"

Again, I know he knew that. Lucas talked about it often. Mostly to discourage me.

But I didn't know that he'd filed that information away to bring it up now.

I shake my head, my cheeks still burning with embarrassment. "They don't accept people who don't graduate on time." Then I can't help but add, "And even if they did, they sure as hell don't give out scholarships to them. Which is the only way I could go. Maybe next year though, I don't know. Once I have enough credits to transfer or something."

Before everything happened, my path was forged.

Or at least, it was in my mind.

I knew I'd be able to get a scholarship. My grades were excellent. My extra-curriculars were excellent too. All my teachers loved me. They knew I was going places. The only problem was Lucas's reluctance and expectation that I'd follow him wherever he went.

I thought when the time came, I'd deal with it.

But it never came.

And now here we are.

Shut up in this bathroom, while a party rages on beyond the door. And my ex-boyfriend is probably still making out with those two girls.

Which reminds me that this isn't important, this conversation.

How did we even get here?

We have more important things to worry about.

I have more important things to worry about.

"None of this is important, okay?" I tell Reign, who's staring at me like he'll never stop, mysterious emotions flickering in his eyes, all tense and brittle. "It's not important that I'm still at St. Mary's and I'm not going to NYU anymore. What's important is Lucas is spiraling. He can't go on like this. He can't keep doing what he's doing. Not to mention, your friendship. It's all broken now. Don't you want your best friend back? Maybe I can help and —"

"You still love him?"

His words are murmured but they're enough to put a stop to my own.

And I whisper, "Yes. I never stopped."

"Even after what you saw," he goes on.

"He..." I fist my hands, my heart racing painfully in my chest. "He saw me too."

With you.

This time, when his jaw tics, the bruise on the side of his mouth pulses as well.

And despite knowing better — so, *so* much better — my eyes fall to his lips and a breath escapes me.

A heated breath.

A breath that somehow smells like watermelons and lemonade.

In fact the very air smells of watermelons and lemonade. My tongue comes alive with the taste of them.

The taste of his kiss...

God, please. Not now.

Not when he's right here.

When Lucas is here too, only a short distance away.

I look away from his mouth then, shuddering.

I notice him shuddering too, his chest moving on a wave.

And I think I catch the tail end of his gaze moving away from my mouth as well. But I may be imagining things because his features are still tight and blank and I continue, "Lucas is the love of my life. Nothing will change that. Not the fact that I made a mistake, *two* very big mistakes, that night. Or that he's lashing out because of them. I will always love him."

"Always, huh," he murmurs.

I nod. "It's like you and me."

"What's like you and me?"

"This. My love for Lucas." I take in a deep breath. "I will always love him like I will always hate you."

Always. Always. *Always.*

I let that word chant in my head as I stare up at him.

Into his reddish-brown eyes. His now spiky hair. That bruised jaw.

And he stares down at me, at my flushed cheeks and my spilled hair. As if absorbing what I just said. My words. My hatred for him.

Then, stepping back from me, he goes, "Tomorrow."

"What?"

"You wanna talk to him. I'll make sure you get to."

"Y-you will?"

"I'll make sure that he's in a position to listen to you."

"I... You... How? I don't —"

"And then we fix it."

"We?"

"You and I."

"Y-you and I?"

He throws out a short nod, something flashing through his features. A thoughtful look but also something else. "We need to put you back where you belong."

"I'm sorry?"

"With him."

I blink up at him.

His eyes flick back and forth between mine. "We need to get you back together with him. That's the only way he'll stop spiraling. That's the only way we fix him. By fixing your relationship." While I'm reeling from that, he adds, "But that's it. That's all you need to worry about, you and him. Not our friendship. Not whatever the fuck comes to your mind. Just you. And him."

CHAPTER FOURTEEN

Who: The Bubblegum
Where: Dorm room at St. Mary's School for Troubled Teenagers
When: 2:30 AM; right after Reign drops Echo off at campus

Dear Holly,
I belong with him.
With Lucas.
It's not a novel idea. It's not an idea that I've never had, getting back together with him. Especially in those early days when everything had happened. But then time passed on, without any contact from him, and I lost hope.
It's back now though.
It's back and I'm afraid.
I shouldn't hope. I shouldn't dream.
I shouldn't even think about it.
But I am and it's all because of... him.
The guy who never wanted us to be together in the first place.
The guy who's always made it clear how much he hated me for his best friend, who I'd assumed would've done all that he could to keep Lucas and me apart over the years, is the one who came up with this idea.

He's the one who's going to help me get Lucas back.

Again, I should be afraid but I'm not.

I'm so very strangely not afraid at all.

Because of what I saw tonight.

In his reddish-brown eyes.

That guilt. That regret. That pain that I feel for Lucas.

And so despite years of hatred and friction between us, I'm doing this.

I'm taking his help.

I'm getting my ex-boyfriend back and I'm fixing everything.

Including my very bad habit of thinking about it. Whenever he's near.

The kiss.

That watermelon-y, lemonade-y and summery kiss.

~Echo

CHAPTER FIFTEEN

The Bandit

I'd heard stories about it.

About St. Mary's School for Troubled Teenagers, an all-girls reform school.

And I admit that like a piece of shit, I'd always assumed things about it. About the girls who go there. How wild they must be. How crazy and insane, down for whatever the fuck. I mean, you gotta be, right? For you to end up there?

I'm a pig, what can I say.

And asshole pigs like me don't think about anything deep, anything that really matters.

Things like it's a *reform* school.

Quote unquote a prison.

With brick walls and concrete buildings and fucking bars on the windows.

Things designed to trap. To suffocate.

To cage.

I realized all that later, much later. Too late actually.

After my father had sealed her fate.

And since I was responsible for that, for her life being turned upside down and shattered, I thought the least I could do was leave her alone. The least I could do was stop keeping tabs on her. Like I used to, back when she still lived at the manor and Lucas and I were in New York.

I'd tell myself that it was for Lucas.

To make sure that Lucas's girl was okay.

And it was.

Well, probably eighty percent of it.

Okay, fine. Sixty-five.

Fuck, okay.

Twenty. Twenty percent.

The rest was all me. Me being my usual piece of shit, snake best friend.

Anyway, when she was sent to St. Mary's though, I backed off. I left her alone.

And that's why I didn't know.

I had no *idea* that she was still trapped in that place. Where I had to drop her off tonight, and then *watch* her as she struggled to climb over that wall.

I say watch because she wouldn't let me help her.

She was very clear about that after she fucking freaked out and *screamed* when I put my hands on her. So like a motherfucker I had to back off.

I wanted to punch something. Wanted to break something with my rage.

"Jesus, fuck. Go down already."

I blink at the voice.

And come out of my furious thoughts, realizing where I am.

The harsh overhead lights. The smell of sweat and blood. The thuds of boots on concrete. The groans, the grunts, the sound of flesh hitting flesh.

The burning sting and the painful throb of the punch.

That Ledger, one of my good friends, just laid on me.

Among many other punches and jabs, since we're in the ring at the Yo Mama's.

Panting, I focus on him. "Then stop hitting me like a fucking girl and make it happen."

He's panting too, sweat running down his face and body in rivulets. Putting his hands on his hips, he stares at me. "You're in rare form tonight."

I am.

Mostly because I've been itching to get into the ring for a couple of days now. Especially after what my brother had sprung on me the other night.

And what I found out tonight about her.

Meaning, I need to get fucked up.

And I need him to get his act together and do it for me.

I wipe the blood off my split lip. "Yeah, you too. Except you suck."

He hums, studying me. "I think I know why."

"Why you suck? Yeah, if you do, please fucking enlighten me."

His ugly mug lights up with a slow smile. "It's her, isn't it?"

I stiffen, my eyes narrowed, my jaw clenched.

But he doesn't get the message that he needs to shut up now.

"What happened?"

I growl, my hands fisted.

He smirks. "She reject you again?"

"Stop fucking talking."

His smirk morphs into a chuckle. "Yeah, she did, didn't she? Now, if you'd listened to me and taken my advice on chicks, then none of this would be happening."

I'm gonna hit him now.

And I'm gonna keep hitting him until he's laid flat on the ground.

Which would be a fucking tragedy, because that's not why I called him. That's not why I usually call him.

I call him when I wanna get fucked up.

When I wanna get beaten within an inch of my life and be punished for all my sins. Something that I can't really do when school's on — can't go to soccer practice looking like roadkill — so summers are my only respite.

So I really need him to shut the fuck up and make me pay.

"Yeah," I goad. "Because pretending to hate a chick because she's the little sister of your high school rival — *high school*, man; it was ages ago — while secretly pining over her for three years is such a smooth move. When's the wedding again?"

That should do it.

That should make him regret telling me. Like I'm regretting telling him.

No, actually I'm regretting our whole friendship right now.

Ledger and I, we've known each other since high school. We both played soccer for our schools and frequently played each other. But while we were merely passing acquaintances while we lived in Bardstown, now we're friends since we both live in New York and run into each other a lot.

In fact, he was the one to tell me about Yo Mama.

It's run by one of his brothers' friends, Ark Reinhardt, and Ledger's been going here for years now. The guy has anger management issues. Probably from his childhood: a deadbeat father and a sick mother. And when he found out about *my* issues — how I broke everything two years, two months and fourteen days ago — he told me where to go to deal with them.

But while I took a job here as well, he hasn't.

He already has a great job, being a pro-soccer player for New York City FC. Although, the guy's been suspended for a few games. For beating up one of his teammates on the field.

Stupid hothead fucker.

At my jab, he says, "Same day as yours, motherfucker."

I puff out a breath. "Just hit me, okay? Just fucking... do it."

Finally, it gets through to him that I need it.

That I really fucking need it tonight.

And he opens and closes his fist. "Fine. But just so you know, if you don't deal with your fucking issues, you're gonna get yourself killed and end up six feet under one day."

I roll my shoulders, bracing myself. "Noted. And just so you know, if you don't deal with your issues, you're gonna kill someone and end up behind bars one day."

He spits at my feet, wipes his mouth. "Let's see who gets there first."

And with that, he throws the next punch and then the next and the next, taking out his aggression on me as if he's chasing a demon. And I accept it all as if I'm chased by one.

I'm not sure how long we go on for but finally, he does manage to put me down. I hit the ground with a massive thud and a painful but relieved breath escapes me as every part of my body throbs and pulses with its own heartbeat.

Ledger helps me up and to the locker room, where I clean up my cuts. When you've played soccer all your life, you learn how to take care of a few scrapes and bruises. Although from the looks of it, I might also have to bandage my ribs and stitch up some of the cuts along with cleaning them; Ledger did his job well.

Since this is a gym where fuckheads like us go who either love to give pain or be on the receiving end of it, it comes equipped with bunkbeds where you can spend the night if you're too fucked up to go anywhere else.

I have done that before, but I think tonight I can manage to go back to my motel. Limping, I make my way outside and find my bike in the parking lot. I climb on it but instead of starting it and driving away, I fish out my phone from my back pocket and dial the number.

I wanted to wait until the morning, but fuck it.

I don't care if it's three o'clock in the morning and he must be sleeping. I need to do it tonight and I'll keep calling until he picks up.

Which thankfully he does after only a few rings.

"Reign? Are you all right?" my brother asks in a groggy voice

"Yeah." I clear my throat. "Yes, everything's fine."

"It's three o'clock in the morning," he says as I hear the rustling of sheets in the background. "What's —"

"I'll do it."

Silence.

Complete and utter.

Which means he understood what I meant.

He understood that I'll work for him in exchange for getting my money.

"You'll do it," he says in a quiet voice.

"Yes."

"Until your graduation next year."

I work my jaw back and forth, *hating* that it's come to this.

Hating that I'm letting my brother win.

But it's fine.

It's nothing compared to what I deserve.

"Yes." Then, the main reason for why I'm calling. "But I want you to do something for me first."

Another few seconds of silence before he says, "What?"

"If I come work for you, I want you to give it to the Adlers. My money."

This time, the silence is even longer.

And I know his wheels must be turning at my request. Not that I care.

As long as he keeps his promise, I don't care what he thinks.

"The Adlers."

"Yeah." I swallow thickly. "Dress it up however you like. Tell 'em you're doing it to make up for what happened. What our old man did to them. How he..." *Sent her away, had her locked up to pursue his twisted revenge on me.* "And then I want you to make some phone calls."

"What phone calls?"

"To NYU."

"NYU," he murmurs, thoughtfully.

"I want you to get her in," I say, knowing and hating that he already knows.

Who *her* is.

"How am I supposed to get her in?"

"I don't fucking care. Find a way. You're full of fucking connections, aren't you? Find one at NYU and make it happen."

I hear a sigh before he asks, "Is this important to you?"

I clutch the phone tightly. "Do you think I'd be calling you if it wasn't?"

"I suppose not."

"You're going to do this or what?"

"If I do, then what's the guarantee that you'll still stay? Until next year."

"There isn't. But that's what it's gonna take for me to come work for you."

I expected another thoughtful silence but he's prompt in coming back with, "Fine. I'll do it." I'm releasing a breath of relief when he continues, "But not with your trust fund."

"What?"

"That money is yours. I can —"

"No," I growl. "It has to be my trust fund. It has to be *my* money. The money that belongs to *me*. You're gonna give them that money. You're gonna tell them that you're feeling generous and that they should use this money for NYU. That they should use it for... her. *My* money."

It has to be mine.

I don't know why this is so important to me.

Why I want her future to be paved by something that comes from me, but it is.

I will pay for her education, her dreams, and no one else.

Me.

"Okay," my brother says, after a few seconds. "Your money."

"Good."

"And I'll make some phone calls in the morning. See what I can do to get her in."

For the first time tonight, I feel like I'm able to breathe then.

No, it doesn't change the past and what I did.

But maybe this might fix a few broken things.

This might bring her some... happiness. Ease her heartbreak a little.

"So Monday then?" my brother asks when I stay silent.

I sigh. "Yes."

"Nine o'clock. Sharp."

If he thinks that just because he's doing me a favor, I'll become his bitch, then he has another think coming.

"Nine-thirty," I counter.

"Nine-fifteen."

"Fine."

"Wear a suit," he tells me then.

"Over your dead body." Then, "Actually, that's not a bad idea. I'll wear a suit at your funeral."

He ignores me. "A shirt then. *Not* a t-shirt."

"Don't try to change me, big brother."

"And dress shoes."

"Many have tried and failed."

He keeps ignoring me. "With socks."

"Jesus." I frown. "What kind of people you hanging with that don't wear socks with shoes?"

"People with smelly feet apparently."

My lips twitch. "Fine. I'll wear socks and a shirt. No dress pants though. My boys need room to breathe."

"Well if mine can, you can rest assured that yours can too. But you can keep your jeans if you like," a pause, then, "*little* brother."

A surprise laugh bursts out of me. "Did you just crack a joke? A *dirty* joke?"

I swear I can feel his amusement, his small smile even, through the phone. Then, "I'll see you Monday. And Reign," he sighs before adding, "you won't regret this."

And then, he's gone.

Good thing too because I came this close.

To tell him that *he* will.

He will regret this.

Because he was right. There's no guarantee that if he does all these things for me, I'll stay until next year. And I won't. I have no intention of staying.

I have every intention of going back on my word.

Because I'm going to leave.

After I've fixed things.

After I've brought Lucas back from the edge of destruction and after I've put her where she belongs — with him — I'm going to take off.

I'm going to leave this town, college, fucking soccer, everything behind.

Because I'm a bandit, aren't I?

A bandit who steals things.

Who stole their love once.

So it's best if I leave and go so far away that I won't do it again.

Steal *her* from him.

My best friend's ex-girlfriend.

CHAPTER SIXTEEN

This is hard.

I knew it would be but I didn't know how much.

This is even harder than telling Jupiter about the breakup.

As in how it happened and what I did.

I finally came clean to her at the library this afternoon. I would've come clean to Poe as well but she was at detention with the principal. But anyway, I told her what I did and then I told her what I'm going to do now. As in, my whole plan of getting my ex-boyfriend back.

She kinda wasn't happy about it.

Especially when I told her what he did, back at the party. The kiss in the backyard. But the thing is that she doesn't understand.

She doesn't get how this is my responsibility.

How I need to fix Lucas because I was the one to break him.

Which means it doesn't matter how hard this thing that I'm doing right this moment is, I have to suck it up and do it: Climbing over the fence in my dress and heeled sandals.

Well, low-heeled but heeled nonetheless.

Last night, this was much easier — even though I think I slipped a couple of times — but then I had a pair of jeans and sneakers on. As it is, I think I'm going to fall.

I am.

I have to face facts now. My heel's stuck in the gap between the bricks. My hem's stuck also. In or on something, and my grip on the wall is all slippery and sweaty. And even though it's probably been only ten to twenty seconds since I've found myself in this position, I don't think I can hold on much longer.

It's okay though.

It's fine.

It's only a few feet above the ground so it's not as if I'm going to die or get horribly injured. I should let the wall go now.

Oh God.

I'm scared. I'm fucking terrified.

Do it, Echo. Just do it.

You can't hang here for the rest of the night.

Think about Lucas.

Okay. *Okay.*

For Lucas.

I drag in a shaky breath and let go.

And fall.

Or at least start to.

My heart starts to plunge and go on a deep dive inside my body when I come to a jerking stop.

Because there's a grip.

A strong and a firm and a tight grip.

On my waist.

It's almost too tight actually. To the point of pain.

But I don't care.

I also don't care who it belongs to. Or that I could recognize it, the roughness of it, the heat, without anyone having to tell me. Well, given the fact that we were going to meet here, it's only logical who it would be, but still.

It's *him*.

It's his hands.

And for once, I'm so thankful for them.

For once, I'm so thankful that he's touching me. He's got me.

He's got me...

Just as the thought floats through my head, I'm being put on the ground and spun around. And I'm so dizzy from my near fall and his fast movements that I grip him back.

I clutch onto his biceps, my fingers digging into his hard muscles. "I didn't... I didn't need you to do that. I didn't —"

"Yeah, you did."

His whole body vibrates with the growl.

And I flinch.

He's right. I did.

But that doesn't mean it's easy for me to accept that. That I need help from him.

Especially after how he rejected me two years ago.

Especially when despite that I'm still taking his help with getting Lucas back.

"I-I was fine," I insist stupidly. "It was just my heel. It —"

"Fuck your heel."

I flinch again.

At the venom in his voice. At the violence in his fingers that are flexing and gripping my waist.

I bet his face looks violent as well.

But since the night is dark and the trees around us cover the moon in the sky, I can't really see, and thank God for that.

Swallowing jerkily, I dig my nails into his smooth skin. "A-and my dress. It —"

He digs his fingers into my waist. "Well, fuck your dress too."

I suck in my belly at this. "It was only like a six-foot drop. You don't have to growl at me like a bear."

His nostrils flare I think as he bites out, "It's *plenty* to break your reckless little dress-wearing ass. When you don't know shit about climbing over things."

I can't help but scratch him at this as my voice drips with sarcasm, "Oh, I'm sorry that I'm not an expert at climbing over things. Like you are. I've only recently started doing this, you see. Ever since I got sent to this reform school.

But if you teach classes or something, I'd be happy to take one. So you don't yell in my face the next time." Then, "And just for the record, we're working together now. Colleagues, if you will. It would be really nice if you didn't make me want to kill you every two minutes."

His jaw moves.

This, I notice clearly.

And then I notice something else.

That I'm standing on my own now. That I don't need him to support me anymore.

Which means I should move back and take my hands off his biceps. Which also means that he should move back and take his hands off me as well.

Not to mention, I should stop trying to study his face.

The nuances of it all because they're hidden by the shadows. All because I have this strong urge to study the curvature of his cheekbones and the count the number of his eyelashes.

Oh, and his mouth.

His plush, pillow-y, watermelon-y mouth.

Just as the thought flashes through my head, he moves.

As if he knew.

He knew what I was thinking about, and, embarrassed, I follow his lead.

Once we have moved away from each other, he exhales a sharp breath. "Let's go. We don't have a lot of time."

And just like that, he turns around and starts walking toward the highway. When we clear the woods, my eyes go wide.

Because there it is.

His bike.

It's real. I didn't dream that he has a bike now.

I didn't dream that I rode on it last night when he wouldn't stop insisting on bringing me back to campus, nope. While last night other things took precedence in my brain, tonight I'm super duper intrigued by his bike.

An honest to God motorcycle.

"What happened to your car?" I ask while he's busy being bent down and fiddling with something that I can't see. "Or rather cars*sss*."

Because he had a lot of them.

I guess when you're born rich, you can change cars like you change clothes. And he did. Change them a lot I mean. From cherry red to gunmetal gray, he had cars in all colors and makes and models.

So this is kind of a surprise.

This sleek bike with high handles and tires that look massive, which I now realize, I've seen on TV.

"Hey, it's a Harley Davidson," I say, noticing the logo on the front. "Reign Davidson rides a Harley Davidson." I chuckle. "Aww. Made for each other. Is that why you got it?" I join my hands in enthusiasm. "Are you going to marry your bike one day, Reign? It could be an epic love story. I mean, if you knew what love was, but maybe Harley can teach you and —"

I choke on my words when he turns around.

And I see him.

Now that we aren't under the thick canopy of trees, I see his face.

And holy God, it's... carnage.

His face is ravaged.

His lower lip is split and swollen. There's a cut on the side of his forehead, one on his right eyebrow. One of his eyes is on the verge of being swollen shut. The bridge of his nose is all dark and discolored. Not to mention, all these mini but vicious looking wounds all over his jaw and his cheeks.

"What the..." I breathe out, my gaze barely able to take and register all of the mayhem. "What happened to you?"

He doesn't answer of course.

I don't even think he can, because just look at him.

Look at his jaw. It's tightly clenched.

So tightly that I can see the muscle on his battered cheek standing taut.

Vibrating too, as if he's gritting his teeth.

It's because of the pain, isn't it?

He's in pain.

He's in *so much pain*.

How the hell did he manage to catch me back there? How the hell did he ride his bike here?

No, actually how the hell is he even standing up?

"You... I don't... What... *happened*?"

He offers me something. "Wear this."

It's the helmet.

But I ignore it.

Because now that I know he looks like that, his voice sounds pained as well, and I keep pushing. "What happened to you? I-I mean, you were fine when I last saw you. You only had that one bruise and —"

I stop talking when he steps up to me and puts the helmet on my head himself. But before he can begin to buckle the strap, I grab his wrists.

"Tell me what happened. Who did this to you?"

He grits his teeth again. "Why?"

"*Because*," I flex my fingers, noticing a gash-like wound on his cheek that's now stitched up, but still. "You look like... You look like death. You look like you're in pain."

"And?"

"And this is much worse than the bruise on your jaw the other night. This is... How could this have happened? What... What did you *do*?"

Jesus.

He got in a fight, didn't he?

Although in all the years that I've seen him get into fights, he's never looked like this. He's never looked so ravaged. I can't even imagine what he must've done for someone to beat him up like this.

I can't...

And God, I'm so... mad.

I'm so freaking *mad* at this unknown person. I'm so angry and...

"You worried about me?" he asks, his voice pure gravel right now.

Breaking into my, yes, *worried* thoughts.

And the fact that he can read me so easily makes me say, "What, no."

His gaze roves over my upturned face and I try to school my features.

I try to appear calm.

Not only because I don't want him to know that he got me but also because why would I be worried in the first place? Why do I care if he's in pain or if he looks run over by a truck?

"Because it looks like you are," he rasps.

And I let go of his wrists then. "I'm not."

I also try to move back but I can't.

Because of his stupid helmet and his fingers still clutching onto the straps.

His mouth, split and swollen as it is, stretches up in a small smirk. "Because if you were, I'd let you do it."

"Let me do what?"

"Clean up my wounds."

My breath escapes in a mad rush. "I have no interest in cleaning up your stupid wounds."

He licks his split lips. "I'll even let you bandage me up."

I throw him a mock smile. "Yes, because that's what I aspire to be. Being your nursemaid along with being your servant girl."

He chuckles. "Nursemaid, yeah. I could use a good little nursemaid like you."

I fist my hands at my sides. "Totally. Let me just knee you in your special place first and I'll get right on that."

But if I thought my sarcastic comments would bother him, then I was wrong.

Apparently nothing bothers him or stops him from scanning my face.

And the one thing he always notices about me: my dress.

This one had him cursing only moments ago but now he's watching it as if for the first time. And I guess it *is* for the first time, because just like his beaten-up face, my dress was hidden by the darkness as well.

So now he takes it in, from the spaghetti straps and the square neckline to the ruffled hem that stops an inch above my knees.

When he's done checking out my dress and making me feel all kinds of breathless, he goes, "A pretty little nursemaid *not* dressed in pink."

It's not as if what he said was wrong or untrue.

I am *not* dressed in pink.

But it still makes me squirm a little. His observation. For some reason.

But I lift my chin and say, "Yes, because blue is his favorite color."

Which is why I wore blue at The Horny Bard too. And yes, wearing a dress when I'm going to a party where people might recognize me is dangerous, but I need to look my best tonight.

I need to impress my ex-boyfriend.

Hence my choice of dress, ribbon and even my sandals.

I'm head to toe, all blue.

Although, his best friend — *ex*-best friend — tells me, "Well then I hate to say it, but you missed a spot."

I would've asked what he means by that but I don't have to.

I get it.

When those flashing reddish-brown eyes of his settle on my mouth.

Which is pink.

Painted pink I mean, with lipstick.

I was never a fan of lipstick or any sort of makeup, but Poe has made me a convert. And I needed all the confidence tonight.

"It's called lipstick, you asshole," I tell him when he won't stop staring at my lips, making them tingle, and he snaps his eyes up. "I'm trying to look my best, okay? Given the mission for tonight."

With his eyes that have become all glow-y and intense staring into mine, he rumbles, "Given the mission for tonight, why don't you worry more about your ex-boyfriend and less about what happened to my face? We're working together now, not braiding each other's hair or swapping period stories. Or whatever it is you like to do with your friends."

"I —"

"And if you think about going all drama queen on my special place, make sure you're not wearing your boyfriend's favorite color. I don't think he'd be very happy to see it ruined and *dripping* when I decide to teach you what happens to good little servant girls turned nursemaids when they don't treat my God-given gift of junk with respect." Then, "*Ex*-boyfriend."

With that he buckles the strap and steps back, ready to take off into the night.

And I'm left thinking that *this* is hard.

Working together without wanting to kill him.

"He's alone," I say to the guy who brought me to the party.

"Yeah."

"And he doesn't look drunk." I squint my eyes, trying to make him out. "I don't think, at least."

"He isn't." Then, "Yet."

"How'd you manage that?"

"Paid someone to keep an eye on him."

At this, I look away from my target, my ex-boyfriend, and look at him, his ex-best friend. "Really?"

His eyes are glued to Lucas and his bruised jaw is clamped shut.

Which he then unhinges to rasp, "Had to."

Because these days, Lucas can't stay away from liquor and self-destruction.

Right.

That's why I'm here.

Taking a deep breath, I murmur, "I guess that's my cue then."

At my words, he nods tightly and steps back.

As if putting himself in the background and letting Lucas be my entire focus.

Which is as it should be.

And so I begin walking toward the only thing that should matter to me, not Reign's bruises that I'm still thinking about even though he told me not to, or how much I hate him. Or that he actually *paid* someone to keep an eye on Lucas so I could get to talk to him.

Like he'd promised me the other night.

Until I came here and saw it, I didn't believe him.

I never thought he'd be able to pull it off, but he did.

In fact if you think about it, I never would've been able to talk to Lucas, if not for *him*. If not for his intervening and setting the whole thing up.

And despite our very recent tiff, I'm thankful.

This party, even though out in the open, still seems as crowded as the one last night, but I find him easily.

Like the other night, Lucas is standing in a group chatting, minus the red cup. He senses me as soon as I move into his periphery.

A jolt goes through my system when his eyes flare in recognition.

I'm not going to lie, what happened the other night makes me want to turn back. It makes me want to abandon this plan and ask Reign to take me back to St. Mary's. Because even though I'd said — all bravely and confidently — that I can handle myself, I have a very bad feeling that I might not be able to.

But.

It's Lucas. It's the love of my life.

I have to do this.

So I keep marching on.

Lucas watches my approach with an expression I can't read. And without taking his eyes off me, he leans toward one of the guys, probably to excuse himself, and begins walking toward me as well.

"Hi," I whisper when we reach each other.

He doesn't respond to my greeting. Simply stares at me with impassive eyes.

I swallow and fist my dress. "I... Uh, how are you?"

I want to grimace.

What a lame opener.

Lame. Lame. *Lame.*

We're talking after two years and this is what I come up with.

Although if he thinks it's weird or lame, I don't know. I can't tell because he's as blank as ever as he replies, "Okay."

"Are you," I clear my throat, feeling all kinds of awkward, "enjoying the party?"

That gets me a reaction, or a hint of it. When his lips curl into a small smile that doesn't look anything like his old warm and loving ones. And I realize why when he murmurs, "Not as much as the one last night."

Right.

Because of that threesome kissing that I'd found him in.

My heart cracks right down the middle then even though I tell myself, my heart, to not. I tell myself that I don't have the right to get sad or jealous about it.

And neither do I have the right or the luxury to turn back.

Which is what I want to do. Again.

Only the urge is much stronger now.

I fist my hands harder and try to come up with some words, any acceptable words would do right now, but he speaks first. "What are you doing here, Echo?"

"I came to see you," I blurt out, unable to come up with anything else but the truth.

His face doesn't betray any emotion as he murmurs, "What about The Horny Bard?"

My cheeks are burning. "That too."

It's okay though.

It's okay if he knows the level of my desperation. If he knows that I've been stalking him.

Wanting to see him, talk to him.

Let him see my love for him.

If it fixes things, then I don't want my dignity.

He stares at me for a few beats. Then, "What do you want?"

You.

I want you.

It's very hard not to say that.

Very hard not to spill my guts and tell him all about my intentions.

But even though I'm okay with him knowing that I'm his stalker, I also can't start declaring my undying love for him after two long years.

So I go with something neutral but important. "I heard about your dad. I'm sorry. I don't... I can't imagine what you must be feeling right now."

He stiffens for a moment or two.

But then recovers and shrugs. "It is what it is."

"I know your dad..." I shake my head, frowning. "He wasn't... good. To you. And I know this must be difficult for you to process and I wish... I... I'm just so sorry, Lucas. I'm —"

"Is that all?"

His dismissive tone throws me.

For a second or two, I can't come up with anything else to say.

But then I take a deep breath and forge ahead. "I... I wanted to apologize."

He stiffens again.

Way more than he did when I'd mentioned his father.

But then whose fault is that?

So for the umpteenth time tonight, I stand my ground and begin, "I know it sounds... It sounds ridiculous. So insufficient and small, me apologizing for something so big but... I'm such a lover of words, you know that, right? I'm such a big logophile. I'm always rattling off synonyms and jotting down new words in my diary, but I don't have any other word right now except sorry. For everything that I did. You were the last person I ever wanted to hurt, and I know people say this a lot and I can't believe I'm one of those people now but it's the truth.

"You were everything to me, Lucas, and I loved you. And I never thought, never even *dreamed*, that I could ever hurt you. But I did and for that, I will never be able to forgive myself. And you don't have to either. I'm not saying sorry for that. I'm saying sorry because you deserve that. From me. You deserve a lot of things from me and an apology is the least of it. You deserve to know that I regret it. I regret everything I did that night. Every single thing. And I live with it every day. I live with my regret. And I wish it could change things but it doesn't. And maybe my regret is meaningless to you but I... I couldn't go on without you knowing. Without taking a shot that maybe it *does* make things a little better for you. God, I hope it does. So I'm sorry, Lucas. For everything."

I wish I had more words.

Or at least better words than the ones I gave him.

But I don't and it makes me so mad at myself.

It makes me feel so inadequate and small.

More so when he says, as expressionless as ever, "Okay."

"I —"

Whatever I was going to say gets interrupted by someone calling his name. Some girl who comes rushing in, all dark hair and wide smiles, throwing her arms around him. And she's so full of energy and enthusiasm that I have to step back to give her space.

She breaks the hug, completely ignoring me, and beams at Lucas. "I've been looking all over for you." She tugs on Lucas's arm. "Come on. I have to show you something."

The way she says 'something' makes me think that it's something in the vein of what happened yesterday in that back yard.

Lucas thinks so too.

Because he glances over at me, his lips pulling into a smirk, while the girl still bounces on her feet, completely ignoring me.

Stepping back, Lucas says, "Have fun tonight, Echo."

Just like that, he turns around and walks away, wrapping his arms around the girl's shoulders. And all I can do is watch him leave as I stupidly wonder if she was a different one from the girls last night. I was more occupied with what they were doing that I never took the time to memorize their faces.

But I guess it doesn't matter.

If she's different or the same.

I'm pretty sure they're going to do the same thing that he did yesterday.

Distraught and sad and brokenhearted, I take a step back, my vision blurry with tears.

And stumble.

Really hard.

So hard that I think I'm about to fall, but for the second time tonight, someone catches me.

And it's him, isn't it?

He caught me like he did before at the wall.

This time, I'm going to thank him properly. I'm going to be nice. I'm not going to argue. I'm not going to fight. And once I've thanked him, I'll ask him to take me back. I'll ask him to take me away from this place.

"Hey, you okay?"

I freeze.

It's not his voice.

It's not his touch.

I've been so distraught that I didn't notice before. But now I blink my eyes to clear them so I can see who it is. And I go even more rigid when I finally discover the identity of the person who saved me.

Brad Cavanaugh.

Shit.

Shit, shit, *shit*.

He went to my school and he used to be on the soccer team. He wasn't very close with Lucas but they knew each other, and by association, he knew me as well. I can't say that I ever liked him very much though. He always gave me the creeps.

And turns out that there was a reason for it.

After Lucas and I broke up, Brad was the first of many guys to proposition me. He was the first person to tell me that he wanted me to be his girlfriend. When I refused, he became the first person to leave nasty notes in my locker, calling me names and generally harassing me for rejecting him.

And for being a slut and kissing my boyfriend's best friend.

I wasn't exaggerating when I said those last few weeks at my old school had been hell. And I definitely wasn't exaggerating when I wore that hoodie last night.

God, of all the people to recognize me, it *had* to be Brad.

"Yes, I'm fine. Thank you," I say, trying to step back.

He doesn't let me though, keeping his hold intact. "Echo Adler. Long time, no see." Smiling, he looks me up and down. "How the heck are you?"

His smile is slimy and creepy and all the things that make me want to run away.

And again, I try to escape but he doesn't let me go. "I'm fine, as I said. May I just have my arm back, please?"

"Still very polite. I like it."

"I'm —"

"Although, you don't have to be." He drops his voice lower. "We all know you aren't the good girl you make yourself out to be."

I flinch at his taunt.

It's not the first of its kind I've gotten.

But it still stings, and fisting my fingers, I lean back. "Look, I was just leaving, okay? Can I just have my arm back so I can do that?"

He chuckles, his eyes amused but the bad kind, the mean kind. "But you just got here."

"I'm —"

Cocking his head to the side, he cuts me off. "You're a little butt-hurt. I understand that. I saw what happened. How your boy left you high and dry just now. But listen," he twists my arm slightly, asserting his dominance as he leans in even more, "it doesn't have to be this way. How about I make you feel better, huh? You and me."

"I don't want to feel better. All I want is for you to let me go."

"Come on," he cajoles. "You know I've always liked you. I bared my heart to you back then but you shot me down. I can overlook that though. Maybe you were still heartbroken about the whole thing. But it's been two years now. This could be our chance. This could be —"

"No," I say, glaring at him. "We will never have a chance. I don't want a chance with you, with someone who has *propositioned* me. So I want you to —"

Let me go.

That's what I was going to say and maybe push him away too, if that time he hadn't listened to me.

As it is, I don't think I need to.

Because Brad has already let me go, *before* I could even finish my sentence, and is now in the process of being pushed back. Or rather *pulled* back by the neck of his t-shirt, his eyes wide and shocked.

As much as mine.

And it doesn't stop, this pulling.

Until Brad is well and truly away from me, and shoved back into a tree off to the side.

Really hard.

It's all accomplished within a few seconds: Brad letting me go and being shoved and restrained to an almost secluded corner.

And it's all accomplished by him.

This time, I'm sure it's him.

I can see the wide expanse of his back, his muscles all standing taut and twitching under his t-shirt. I can even see the elbow of his lifted arm with which he's pinning Brad to the tree.

And choking him.

My ex-boyfriend's ex-best friend.

CHAPTER SEVENTEEN

Brad is going to die.

He's so totally going to die because Reign is killing him.

Reign is fucking killing him.

Holy shit.

"What the fuck do you think you were doing?" he growls in Brad's face. "Why *the fuck* were your hands on her?"

"Reign!" I cry out, breaking into motion and running toward them. "Let him go."

It only makes him tighten his hold on Brad, who's flailing. "You know you're gonna die now, don't you? You know I'm gonna kill you. For touching her. For fucking *touching* what's mi —"

"Reign, no." I grab his t-shirt, trying to pull him away. "Let him go."

He thumps Brad's head on the tree, making him whimper and moan. "You got any last words, motherfucker? Something to say before I make you choke on your own fucking tongue."

Brad struggles harder at this, his eyes bugging out of his skull, his mouth making choking noises.

So I increase my efforts.

I pull and tug on Reign's t-shirt, his arm, as I plead, "Please, Reign. Let him go. You're killing him."

Not the right thing to say because that only amps up Reign's strength and he growls in Brad's face, baring his teeth, as if asserting his own dominance over Brad.

"Reign, just take me home, okay?" I try, still trying to snap him out of this rage. "Just please take me home. I don't like this. I don't want to be here. Please."

And finally, this works.

He loosens his hold on Brad and turns to look at me.

And I notice that his eyes are bloodshot.

His eyes are violent and stormy.

I have a feeling this is what a predator looks like, a lion or a wolf, a panther, before it rips apart its prey. But instead of moving away from him and his dangerous aura, I inch closer. I lick my dried-out lips and whisper, "Just let him go."

Those bloody eyes of his dip to my mouth for a second.

Before he clenches his bruised jaw and lets Brad go.

While Brad is coughing and wheezing, Reign still stares at me and I stare back.

At the taut lines of his face. Those pulsating, almost glowing bruises.

At his shuddering, wildly breathing big body.

The Bandit.

The predator who so blatantly attacked someone.

For me.

To protect me.

"I..."

I don't know what I was going to say and it doesn't even matter now. Because Reign turns back to Brad, who's still trying to catch his breath, slumped and heaving, and grabs the neck of his t-shirt. He shoves Brad back into the trunk, making my heart jump into my throat again, and rasps, "If you ever, *ever*, put your filthy fucking hands on her, I'll fucking kill you, you understand?"

When all Brad does is watch him fearfully, Reign shakes him, as though trying to jar loose the answer he wants to hear.

And he does because Brad jerks out a nod and squeaks, "Y-yes. I-I get it."

"Good." Another shake. "Now apologize to her."

"Reign, I don't think that's necessary," I chime in.

He gets up in Brad's face again. "Apologize!"

Frantically, Brad looks at me and whimpers. "I'm s-sorry. I-I'm fucking sorry, all right? For touching you. For p-propositioning you. For fucking e-everything."

"I-I forgive you." Then, to Reign, "Now let him go."

Finally, fucking *finally*, he does. And Brad's pushing at Reign who goes back easily and scrambling away.

I don't wait for Brad to disappear completely before turning back to this crazy and insane and strangely protective — *protective* — guy standing in front of me.

"What were you trying to do?" I ask, pushing on his shoulders. "Are you crazy? You could've really killed him, Reign. You could've —"

"Proposition," he says in a low voice, his stare as intense as ever.

"What?"

"What did he mean when he said he'd propositioned you?"

Oh shit.

I snatch my hand off his shoulder and move back, repeating, "What?"

Opting to play dumb is the only thing that I can think of.

Because it looks like he wants to go after Brad again.

Stupid Brad.

He takes a step toward me. "What was he talking about?"

"Nothing," I tell him, shaking my head. "He was talking about nothing. It's not important."

"It's not important," he says, dipping his chin toward me. "Or is it nothing?"

"It's both. Not important. Not anything," I say quickly, moving back.

And somehow I find myself in the same position as Brad.

Spine stuck to that tree with this hunk of a guy standing before me.

Only he doesn't have to put a single finger on my body to take my breath away.

He's doing that with his bloodshot eyes and his bruised face.

"Tell me."

His words are rough and raspy but still commanding.

And there's no doubt that if I don't tell him, he won't let it go.

It's better to just give him what he wants.

But I'm not doing that without taking some precautions first. So I go for his t-shirt again. I fist it at his ribs tightly. With *both* hands. Then, "I'll tell you. But you have to promise me that you won't lose your shit and go after him again."

His gaze flickers down to my hands on his body.

To my puny fists that, if we're being honest, won't do much to hold him.

But I have to do something. I have to make sure that he doesn't attack Brad again.

"Promise me, Reign," I prod.

He looks up. "No."

I pull at his t-shirt. "Reign, you have to promise me. You —"

"Because a promise is an oath and I'll break it."

"You —"

He licks his split lip. "Don't wanna break an oath to you."

I don't say anything after that.

And neither does he.

I guess there's no need.

There's no need for words when a rush goes through my body.

A hot rush.

So hot that my skin stings with it.

My body aches with it.

And my mind is flashing. With memories. With things of the past.

Usually, I fight it.

I fight when they surface, but right now I don't have the strength.

Right now, I let them come.

As I study the red flecks in his eyes. As I count his eyelashes.

And breathe in his summery, sunshine-y, watermelon-y scent.

"He meant actually propositioning me," I whisper to Reign. "When everything happened, when we... when Lucas broke up with me, the news spread everywhere. At the manor obviously, but also at school. And so... So guys would come up to me and ask me out, leave notes in my locker, that sort of thing. But not in a nice way. In a bad way, a mean way. Kind of like coming on to me because I was this... this slut who cheated on her boyfriend with his best friend and so they thought I was fair game."

I realize that by the time I've told him the sorry tale, he's gone rigid.

Even more so than before.

He's gone all heated and intense, his jaw clamped shut in a way that must be painful for him with all these bruises. His eyes go even bloodier.

"Reign?" I prod, trying to wake him up.

A pulse jumps on his cheek. "It doesn't end, does it?"

His low, threadbare voice makes my heart race. "What doesn't?"

"*This.*" A pause, then, "My fuck-up."

My fists tighten in his t-shirt. "Your what?"

He clenches his teeth something fierce, his eyes narrowing, his words muttered and low. "Lucas is all fucked up. He's this close to losing it. This close to losing everything that he's ever worked for. You're still at that shithole of a school. When you should be out there, ready to go to NYU. Ready to become a fucking writer or whatever the fuck you want to be. But you're not, are you? Because of me. And now I find out," he swallows painfully, smacking a hand on the tree, "that there are motherfuckers out there who dared to look at you. Who *fucking dared* to think that they could talk to you that way and there would be no consequences. And they *dared* because *I* fucked up. Because of what I did. Of all the lines I crossed, all the rules I broke and I —"

"Hey," I stop him then.

Not only by my words but also my hands.

That I remove from his abs and put on either side of his neck to grip him, to make him look at me, *really* look at me, to focus.

"You didn't do anything, Reign," I tell him when I know he's looking at me and *seeing* me. "You didn't do anything *alone*. I was there too. I did it too. The blame isn't just yours alone. It's mine as well. My blame is bigger and you know that." When it looks like he's going to say something, I squeeze his neck and keep going. "And I'm not getting ready to go to NYU because *I* screwed up. Because my grades weren't good enough. You had nothing to do with it. *Nothing.* And I ended up at St. Mary's in the first place because I broke the law. You didn't ask me to. Were you an asshole to me over that phone call? Yes. Have you always been an asshole to me? Hell yes. But that didn't mean that I had to do what I did. That didn't mean I had to retaliate in the way I did. I always knew there was a chance that it could have an impact on me, on my parents. God, I knew that, Reign. I fucking knew. But I still chose to do it. So it's not your fault. It's mine. And I... I'm sorry." Again, it looks like he's going to say something but I push through. "For what I did. For breaking into your room and then... smashing everything. Your soccer trophies, your furniture. All the photos, knickknacks. The things that must've mattered to you. Things that —"

"They didn't," he says, his mouth parted, his eyes wild.

And I press my fingers on his neck, digging my nails. "What?"

"Nothing mattered. Not one thing in that room mattered to me more than..."

My own lips part as I stare at him. As I wait for him to finish his sentence.

More than what?

What mattered to him?

But he doesn't say anything.

And I decide not to pry for some reason. "Well, I'm sorry nonetheless."

We stare at each other for a few moments and I realize that it's... peaceful.

Such a weird way to describe this moment.

That's filled with stormy breaths and intense stares. With so much heat radiating off his skin, so much sweat running down mine because of it. With my nails dug into his skin and his fingers clawing at the bark.

But it is what it is.

And what it is, is calming somehow.

Maybe because I've been carrying this around for a long, long time now.

What happened to me at the school, how people treated me; what I did to his room, how regretful I've been for that. How I put both my future and my parents' future in jeopardy.

I've wanted to purge this for so long. Only I didn't know that I was going to purge it to him — I had no intention of ever saying sorry to him; my ex-boyfriend's asshole ex-best friend — and that in doing so, I'd feel relief.

And because confessing things to him has brought me so much peace, I decide to tell him. "I blew it."

"What?"

"The apology." He frowns as I keep going, "I-I think I blew it. It was the worst apology ever. Like, ever. I mean, I didn't expect him to forgive me right away or you know, even be nice to me or anything like that but..."

His eyes are probing. "But what?"

"He left with another girl, Reign."

His biceps flex on either side of me, his eyes flashing with anger.

And I think... I *think* it's on my behalf.

With racing breaths and a strange lightness that he's on my side, that he can feel my pain, I spill the rest of the story. "He left with a girl and... and he knew what he was doing. He knew he was hurting me. He... I didn't make an impact on him. I didn't reach him like I wanted to. I didn't —"

"You did."

"No, I didn't. He barely talked to me. He barely looked at me, let alone talked to me."

"He did."

"No, he *didn't*, Reign," I insist. "You weren't there."

"He couldn't take his eyes off you."

"He... What?"

What did he say?

My heart thuds then. "H-how do you know?"

No answer is forthcoming.

But then I don't think I need one. I think I already know.

"Were you..." I swallow, rubbing my thumbs over the thick vein of his neck. "Watching me? W-with him."

Nothing.

Except a pulse on his jaw.

A tic.

And again, I don't need him to say it. I know it.

"Why?" I whisper.

His pulse is pounding under my fingers. My pulse is pounding too.

Other than that, he continues to hold his silence.

He continues to stare at me with glowing, flashing eyes.

"Because you were protecting me," I state.

And I state it without anger, without the outrage that I'd felt last night.

It felt like an insult. An intrusion.

Because it came from him, this protection.

But tonight, it doesn't.

Tonight, it feels... safe.

Maybe because he did protect me, from Brad.

Maybe because after what Lucas did tonight, completely sober and without influence, Reign was the first person I thought of. The first person I wanted to see.

"Took my eyes off you for ten goddamn seconds," he says finally, his voice pure gravel and jagged edges. "And the next thing I know my best friend isn't there anymore and that fucker's mauling you."

My heart clenches in my chest and I bite my lip. "Thank you."

His chest moves on a large breath.

"For saving me from Brad."

Another large breath.

I don't know why I say it then, but I feel like I have to. "I'm not *yours* to protect though."

And then, it looks like we're breathing, *existing* as one.

If my breaths are shaky, his are shuddering.

If my heart is racing inside my chest, I can feel his pulse going hundreds of miles a second.

I bet his blood feels as hot as mine. His skin definitely feels as hot as mine.

And when he inches even closer, bringing his mouth only a hairbreadth away from me, I bet he feels something in his tight gut like I do in my soft belly.

Something writhing and twisting.

Swirling and swooping.

"You are," he rasps.

I flinch. "What?"

Very hard.

There's no way he didn't notice that.

There's no way he *isn't* noticing how my fingers have become claws now and how I'm dragging them over his pulse, his smooth, hot skin. How I'm scratching him and how I can't stop.

Because look at what he's doing to me.

Look at what he not only just said — the most bizarre words ever — but also the way he's staring at me. At my face, all flushed and definitely pink; my trembling lips; the pulse at the base of my throat.

My dress.

God, the way that he stares at my dress, the parts that it covers and then the parts it doesn't.

My heaving chest, my shoulders, my arms.

My legs.

And it's all even more obscene than it was back there, back at St. Mary's, by the side of the road.

Because he isn't doing it to get a rise out of me.

There isn't a mocking twist in his lips or amusement in his eyes.

He wears only one expression in this moment: possessiveness.

Red hot and burning.

Like I'm really his. Like I've been his for some time now. Years.

Since the first moment he saw me. Since before that even.

And then, he explains to me how.

"You're my best friend's girl, aren't you? So you are. You are *mine*. To protect. To shield. To guard, to shelter and to keep safe," he pauses after rattling out all the synonyms, "from every motherfucker out there. From every goddamn motherfucker who thinks he can pounce on you now. Who thinks you're defenseless and alone and fair fucking game. Because you're not. You're under my fucking protection, you understand? So I'll watch you. I'll keep an eye on you and," his eyes drop to my mouth then, making it tingle and swell, "I'll choke the life out of anyone who thinks they can put their hands on you."

I think I fell asleep.

While riding on his bike.

My chest plastered to his muscular back. My arms wrapped around his sleek waist. My cheek pressed on his shoulder. The only way I know for sure that I'm waking up now is that I blink my eyes open when we reach St. Mary's, and realize that I have to untangle myself from him to get down.

But I don't think anyone can blame me for falling asleep.

In fact, it's a surprise that I haven't fallen asleep the two times before I've ridden with him.

He's just so warm, with summer stitched into his very skin.

And strong with all these corded muscles.

But I guess the first when I rode with him, I was still shocked that I was wrapped around him like that. And the second time — which was earlier tonight — I was too angry at him and nervous at what the night had in store for me.

And as disastrous as everything has turned out to be, this time around I managed to fall asleep because something has changed.

I can feel it.

Between him and me.

He feels safe now.

It's crazy and bizarre because only a couple of hours ago, even though we were working together, I was still so distrustful of him. But it feels like I've lived a lifetime in these short hours and now I've come out on the other side of it.

So standing by his bike, I eye his bruises again. "Did you deserve it?"

And then I wait.

With bated breath.

To see if he's lived a lifetime in these short hours like me or not.

He's also climbed off his bike and looking down at me, he says, "Yeah."

My eyes shoot up to his, at his raspy voice.

As if he's woken from slumber as well and I believe he has.

Because he did come out on the other side of it. Like me.

With my heart racing in my chest, I whisper, "What did you do?"

He takes a moment to answer. "Broke something."

I frown. "Broke what?"

"Something that mattered."

"What does that —"

"Here."

I know he did that deliberately. To put me off from questioning him.

And I'm so intrigued right now that I want to stay on it. I want to push him.

But I won't.

Because I feel like what we have right now, is fragile.

And super new.

I don't want to poke at it lest I burst it.

Besides, there are other things that demand my attention. Especially when I see what he means by 'here.'

It's between us, in the palm of his hand.

Looking up, I ask, "A phone?"

"Take it."

I look at it again before glancing back up. "You want me to... You want me to take this phone?"

"Yes."

I blink a couple of times. "*Why*?"

"Because you don't have one," he replies patiently.

"But I do," I tell him.

"At St. Mary's," he clarifies.

He's right about that. I don't have a phone at St. Mary's.

Personal technology of any kind is prohibited, including cell phones, laptops, iPads and whatnot. If needed, we use the school-issued, communal phones and computers.

But that still doesn't explain why he's giving me a phone.

He takes mercy on me though and says, "We're working together, right? Colleagues, if you will." I nod and he goes on, "So you need to be able to contact me and I, you. In case of emergencies."

"Oh."

"It's easy to hide." At this, I go speechless but he launches into a whole explanation. "Since you aren't allowed to have a phone at your piece of shit school, I got you a flip phone. It's also a piece of shit but it's small, compact and you can easily hide it. Probably in your chest of drawers or in the back of your closet. Under your mattress." He looks up then. "Just make sure to hide it in a place where you can get to it easily but no one else can. And always, *always* switch it off when you're not using it. And fucking always have it on silent. No vibrate either, do you understand? And do not, under any circumstances, carry it in your backpack or your pockets. Just put it in a safe place and leave it there."

For several seconds after he's finished instructing me on how to hide an illegal phone, I simply stare at him.

He was instructing, wasn't he?

In a sharp and a stern tone. Rattling off things to do and not do.

I mean, I probably would've figured it out on my own. Well, except the vibrate thing. I definitely would've left it on vibrate.

Oh, and I definitely, *definitely* would've carried it everywhere with me.

"Why not?" I ask.

"Why not what?"

"Carry it with me in my backpack."

He stares at me for a second, then, "Because you don't want anyone to find it on you."

"Right." I blink. "Because even if someone does find it in my room, which they won't because I will hide it nicely, I still have a chance of denying that it's mine. But I can't do that if it's found on me."

He nods, a short and stern nod, much like his pedantic instructions. "Take it."

I still don't. "H-how do you know?"

"Know what?"

"That I'm not allowed to have a phone." I swallow. "And that I have a dresser and a closet in my room."

Well, the latter could be just a fluke.

I mean, it's not uncommon to have this kind of stuff in your dorm room. But something tells me that that's not the reason why he knew.

His lips purse slightly. As if he doesn't like the question and doesn't want to answer it.

He even goes so far as to look away from me.

But I'm not letting this go. "Reign?"

He sighs, big, his chest expanding, his broad shoulders moving. "Asked around." Then, "After I read the manual."

"What?"

Again, it's clear from his closed-up features that he doesn't like this line of conversation. But tough luck, I'm not letting this go. I move closer to him and prod. "Reign, you r-read the St. Mary's manual?"

Another sigh, just as long and hard as the last one. "You gotta know the rules to break 'em, yeah?"

"A-and then, you asked around?"

"Yes. To make sure."

"To make sure what?"

"That you don't get caught." A second later, he adds, "Because you have a knack for it, don't you?"

I do.

I did get caught.

I was too much of a good girl to be careful last time. So he's teaching me how to break rules the right way and keeping me safe.

Protecting me.

"Are you going to take it or not?" he asks when all I do is stare at him, stunned and breathless.

"Yes," the reply comes flying out, and then I do.

I pick it up, this small, easy to hide, black flip phone and whisper, "Thank you. And it's not a piece of shit."

And then I smile.

A small, shaky smile.

Fragile as this new thing between us.

His gaze falls to my mouth and he stares at it.

The only pink thing on my body.

"Desert Rose," I whisper.

He looks up. "What?"

"My lipstick shade," I explain. "That's what it's called. Desert Rose."

His eyes flash. "You didn't wear lipstick. Back when you lived at the manor."

"I didn't," I tell him. "I wasn't into makeup and stuff."

"Just books and words."

I jerk out a nod. "Y-yes. But I... One of my friends here, she's great with makeup and stuff. So she taught me and..."

"And what?"

Clutching the phone to my chest, I shrug. "I thought I needed it. Tonight."

To look pretty for him.

For his ex-best friend.

"You didn't."

"What?"

His features tighten up and he commands. "It's late. Come on."

Much like earlier in the night, he starts walking then. But this time, he's going to the brick wall; I know it. Because he wants to help me climb over. Because he knows I don't know how to climb.

And unlike earlier in the night, I let him.

I don't argue. I don't fight.

All I do is feel thankful and safe.

CHAPTER EIGHTEEN

Before we moved to Bardstown, we had a difficult life.

While my parents always struggled to make ends meet, my dad's accident was a big blow to our family. I watched my mother pick up the slack with two — sometimes even three — jobs, without any complaints. I watched my dad being frustrated about not being able to help. And sometimes I watched them argue and fight about these things.

So I did everything that I could to make their life easier.

I did my chores on time. I did my homework on time. I went to school and came straight back. I hardly ever hung out with friends because I knew I'd have to help out at home. I knew I'd have to make dinner or do the dishes or laundry or whatnot.

And I always prided myself on that.

On being level-headed and good. On being able to take care of not only myself but also my parents when they needed it.

I mean, they took care of me, didn't they?

So it was only fair that I took care of them as well. Because that's what a family does. We take care of each other and we put them above our needs.

So then how did this happen?

How did it happen that my parents can barely look at me? Let alone talk to me.

I'm home for the weekend and we're all sitting at the dining table, eating dinner. It feels like those couple of years when my dad was laid up and everything in our house was somber and depressing.

There's very little conversation and each of us simply keeps our eyes on our plate. There's an occasional clink of silverware, squeak of the chair, clearing of a throat but not much else.

It's me.

I did that.

My actions from two years ago took whatever little joy my parents had and left them like this, all strained and stressed out. Sometimes I wonder if it's better when I'm not around. I wonder if my mom and dad at least talk to each other if not to me.

As it is, no one is talking to anyone right now.

And like always, I can't bear it.

I can't help but try to fix it. Try to fill it with something, *anything*.

So I glance at my mother and go, "This is very delicious, Mom."

She looks up — her eyes are as brown as mine; actually I'm a carbon copy of my mother, same coloring, same dirty blonde hair and a petite build — and gives me a nod. "Thanks."

"New recipe?" I swirl the fork in my spaghetti. "I feel like you did something different with the sauce."

And it's delicious as always.

My mother is a wizard in the kitchen, especially with putting something delicious together with just leftovers. And she'd always try to get me interested in cooking and her recipes. I'm not as good as her but I can cook. I also have a discerning palate, thanks to being my mom's guinea pig.

Which I think she remembers even though she has been mad at me for two years now. Because her eyes sparkle and a small but fond smile appears on her mouth. "I did, yes."

Encouraged, I smile too. "It's tart but not really. Like it's sweet too."

Her smile grows. "Is it?"

She'd always do that, test me and tease me, and when I'd get it right, she'd look at me all fondly and nod, saying that I was even better than she was at my age.

I nod, scooping up just the sauce with my spoon and tasting it. "It is. It's so good, Mom. What'd you do?"

She gets a twinkle in her eyes. "Worcestershire sauce and brown sugar."

"Stop, no. I can't even say it."

She chuckles and glances at my dad. "Neither can your dad."

Who has a smile of his own on his mustached face.

My dad looks like one of those eighties heroes, with sideburns and a thick mustache that curls slightly on the ends. Super dashing and super strong. I love his mustache. My mom does too and I know that's why he doesn't get rid of it.

My dad would do anything for my mom.

And it shows in his dark eyes when he looks at her. "Oh, I can."

"Say it then," my mom challenges.

My dad's smile grows as he forks more spaghetti in his mouth. "Can't talk with my mouth full."

"You just did."

He shakes his head, forks in more spaghetti and points to his mouth.

My mom throws the napkin at him. "Your dad's a liar."

And I'm so happy to see that.

To see them playing around with each other like they've always done.

God, please stay like this.

Please just be happy.

But of course not.

Because I ruin it with my thoughtless words, "Oh my God, one of my friends, Callie. Mom, she's such a good baker. Like, so so good. You have to try her cupcakes. And her cookies, I can't even. They're the..." I trail off when I notice the utter stillness in the room.

The utter stillness on their faces.

Shit.

I completely forgot.

It completely slipped my mind that they don't like to talk about St. Mary's. Or anything related to that place. My classes, my friends, how I live there, what I do. All the rules and regulations that I have to follow.

I think they just want to forget that I go to a reform school.

That I'm still going there. That I was stupid enough to not graduate on time.

But of course they can't.

So they simply avoid talking about it.

While he went ahead and read the manual, and asked around...

Don't, Echo. Don't think about him right now.

Not in front of your parents.

My face burning with embarrassment, I lower my eyes to the plate. "Sorry."

The room goes back to being silent and tense and filled with the stupid clink of silverware. And I'm so frustrated that I'm about to start crying, begging my parents to please, *please* forgive me for everything that I've done.

But then my mom speaks. "So we wanted to talk to you about something."

I snap my eyes up, my heart in my throat. "About what?"

My mom looks at my dad and he straightens up in his chair. I do too because this is it.

This is why they asked me to come home, isn't it?

My parents emailed me yesterday evening and said that they wanted me to come see them this weekend. It was sudden and unplanned; not something you do at St. Mary's and they know that. Still, I got my permission slip signed and took the bus to come home this Friday afternoon.

I have been waiting all evening for them to tell me why.

Although I have a feeling that I may already know the reason.

Given that the whole manor is abuzz with it.

Mom looks at me. "Your father and I discussed this and while we're both wary about telling you, we think it's the best course of action."

My palms grow sweaty and I put down my spoon. "Best course of action for what?"

"To get a handle on the situation," my dad says.

I look at both my mom and dad. "O-okay. What's going on?"

My mom's the one to answer me. "Lucas is back in town."

My breath gets caught up in my throat and all I can do is stare at my mother, mutely.

"His father is unwell," she tells me. "And he's back in town for that. They say it could be any day now that... his dad could pass away."

"How do you..."

"Someone at the manor," mom replies.

My parents really liked Lucas. And I was always very happy about that, my boyfriend and my parents getting along. So when we broke up, my parents were disappointed.

Especially disappointed about how I brought it on. How *my betrayal* brought it on.

I don't think they could grasp the concept of their good, responsible daughter doing something so reckless.

"But that's not why we wanted you to come home this weekend," my dad says and I grow alert.

My mom and dad look at each other again and I detect a movement under the table. They've got their hands joined; I know. They've done this a lot ever since everything, as if they've had to form their own team. Them versus me.

I don't blame them but that doesn't mean it doesn't hurt.

And just because everything hurts these days doesn't mean that I'm used to it.

"He's back too," my mom says.

I knew it.

I knew when I saw their email that this is exactly what they wanted to talk to me about.

Him.

Not Lucas but his asshole ex-best friend.

The guy I kissed on my sixteenth birthday and thereby blew everything to pieces. The guy that my parents have always hated, but more so after that kiss.

And whom my father tried to beat up that night.

God, I've never seen my dad that angry. That enraged and furious.

One second I was shocked that Lucas had seen me with his best friend, the next I was running after him, trying to stop him, talk to him, explain. And the second after *that*, my dad was upon Reign.

It was a mess.

A big giant mess.

My dad had Reign pinned against the wall, screaming in his face. My mom was trying to pull my dad back. I was crying, trying to pull my dad back also. And I know that he would've killed Reign, or at least broken a few bones in his body, if my mom hadn't sent Reign away. And that was the last time they both saw him before he left town and went back to New York.

So I knew that him coming back would bring up old wounds. Old anger, old hurt.

The only good thing is that he isn't here.

As in, *here* here, at the manor.

He's staying at a motel, something that I had no idea about until I came home this morning and heard a few guards talking about it. They all shut up when they saw me in the vicinity but I'd heard enough.

To wonder.

As in why would he be staying at a motel when he has a big mansion at his disposal.

Especially when he hasn't been back in two long years.

Not even for his dad's funeral.

But again, now is not the time to dwell on that.

Blushing, I bring both my hands down to my lap and thread my fingers together, drawing strength from my own self like my parents are drawing from each other.

Strength to stay calm. To not shiver and shake at simply the mention of him.

To not betray that I already know everything that they're telling me right now.

But most of all, I need the strength to tell them that they have nothing to worry about. That I won't repeat the same mistakes or do anything that might hurt them that way again.

That they can trust me.

They don't give me the chance though as my mother continues, "And I want you to promise us something."

"Promise you what?"

"That you will have nothing to do with him."

"What?"

My dad shifts in his seat, impatient. "We don't want you anywhere near that prick, do you hear me? *Anywhere* near him."

"Scott, relax," my mother says. Then turning to me, "Promise us, Echo. Promise that you won't have contact with him while he's here."

My heart is slamming in my chest.

Slamming and slamming as I say, "M-Mom, I told you. I've told you a million times, I have no interest in him. What happened..." My fingers lock themselves together even harder. "It was a mistake. I never intended or wanted to do anything with him. I'm not —"

"But it happened nonetheless," my dad growls. "It *happened* and it can happen again. And if it does —"

"Scott, lower your voice please," my mom says, trying to calm him down.

But I can see the anger on his face. On her face as well.

"No, I won't," he says to her. "He climbed through her window. Through her fucking window, Annie. While we were in the house. While we were downstairs. He had the goddamn audacity to come into my house and seduce my daughter. And my daughter was stupid enough to be seduced by him. *My daughter.*"

This has always been the running theory in my house.

That Reign was the one to seduce me and lead me astray.

Again, probably because they can't imagine their daughter doing something like this without coercion.

I think it's hard enough for them to contend with the fact that their daughter was making out up in her bedroom while they were downstairs watching TV, and with a boy who was *not* her boyfriend, *plus* that two days later, she vandalized the room of said boy and got arrested for it, that they can't compute anything else.

They can't compute that I did what I did of my own free will.

Kissing, vandalizing and ending up at a reform school, where I still go.

"I should've beaten the crap out of him two years ago," my dad continues, growling, "I should beat the crap out of him right now. For coming back. For setting foot —"

"But Dad," I cut him off. "He d-didn't... He didn't seduce me. I've told you that. I was —"

"Echo," my mom snaps. "No."

"But Mom —"

"No, not one word."

I bite the inside of my cheek to stop myself from talking.

From explaining to them — probably for the hundredth time — that he didn't coerce me or coax me. He didn't force himself on me or render me stupid with seduction.

"We don't want to talk about it," my mom says while Dad sits there huffing and puffing. "We don't want to hear about it. You've hurt us, Echo. You turned our lives upside down. After everything that we've done for you, after everything that your father and I gave you, this is how you repaid us. You repaid us by blowing everything to pieces. By being reckless and stupid and selfish. We could've lost our jobs, our livelihoods. You realize that, don't you? You could've cost us everything that we'd ever worked for. Especially when you know your dad's condition. We trusted you. We *depended* on you and you stabbed us in the back. Not to mention, you wrecked your own future. You not only lost a good and loving boyfriend, but also all your dreams about going to NYU."

She is right.

I did that.

I changed everyone's lives, not just my own. I did stab them in the back. I betrayed them when they trusted me to be good. For the first time ever, my parents had good jobs. They didn't have to break their backs to provide for me and I threatened all that with my stupid, reckless actions.

"So we don't want to hear anything from your mouth," my mom continues, "except one thing and one thing only. We want you to promise us that you will stay away from him, from that boy. You will have no contact with him whatsoever. No contact, Echo.

"You know how he is, don't you? You know how much of a troublemaker he is. He's always been a constant source of shame for the Davidson family, a constant source of disappointment. He didn't even show up for his father's funeral, Echo. His own father. Mr. Davidson didn't deserve that. He didn't deserve to be disrespected like that. He was a good man. And you know this better than anyone, don't you? He could've pressed charges back then but he didn't. He let you go. He still kept us on. We owe him, Echo. We owe him a lot. *Promise* us that you will be good. That you won't jeopardize everything that we've worked for, not again."

My eyes are brimming with tears but I don't let them fall.

This time I control them. I make them stay put.

I'm not going to act like a victim and cry for this. I don't deserve to cry for this.

Especially when I've already broken the promise that they want me to make.

When I've already *had contact* with him.

And I'm not going to stop.

I can't.

I have to make it right. I have to fix things.

Not only with Lucas but also with my parents.

Don't I?

I can't get into NYU or change the fact that I haven't graduated yet. But if I get back together with him, maybe my parents will finally forgive me. If I make everything like it used to be, then they will see that I'm still their good daughter and that they can depend on me.

So yeah, I'm going to fix things.

And he's helping me.

The guy they want me to stay away from. The guy they think seduced me.

He didn't.

He absolutely did not.

And maybe, just *maybe*, I can use this opportunity to finally convince them of that. To prove it to them. To make them see that not only did he *not* seduce me but he's not the evil, inhuman asshole that they think he is. That even *I* thought he was.

I know lying is bad but I only do it so I can show them that I'm good.

"I promise."

I want to do it.

I've been wanting to do it for the past two days.

Ever since he gave me this phone.

I've been toying with this idea of texting him but I've been stopping myself.

For many, many reasons.

The biggest one being the disaster from last time when we had any contact over the phone. Although I know I'm being irrational here. The circumstances are totally different. Before, we were enemies, staunch and forever. Now, not so much.

Now we're working together and we've turned over a new leaf.

Now he makes me feel safe.

Which brings me to the second reason: this phone is only for emergencies.

A work phone, if you will.

And we're not working right now. The other night, while coming back to campus, Reign told me the next opportunity to see Lucas would be sometime next week, which let me just point out that I'm so relieved about; after two very disastrous encounters with my ex-boyfriend, I need a break. I need to just stay away from him for a little while. So there's not even a need to switch the phone on.

However.

There's this big thing.

That my work phone has... reading apps.

Yup.

It has an app for ebooks, something that I love to pieces. *Pieces.*

I'm actually a fan of both, paperbacks and ebooks, and so I read on both. Which means I read two books at any given time.

But as much as I love paperbacks, I have to say that I love the idea of carrying around a library in my pocket even more. I love the idea of browsing through that library with only a touch of my fingers and that I can read well into the night even when everything is dark around me. I used to do that a lot: paperbacks during the day and around school, ebooks at night, lying down on my side with the phone propped up on the pillow.

So I should text him, right?

If not for anything else but to thank him at least. For giving me this phone with reading apps on it. Even though it's hard to read on the tiny screen, it's still the best thing I've ever gotten. Maybe he doesn't even know the kindness he's done me.

Up in my bedroom, propped up on my pillows, I switch on the phone and open the text app.

His number is the only one saved on here. Oh, and the name it's saved under is Bossman.

Yeah, hilarious.

Shaking my head, I type in:

> Hi.

Biting my lip, I hit send.

But then I panic. It's like, 12:01. Maybe he's sleeping.

So then I send:

> Are you sleeping?

Which freaks me out more because then I start to wonder if he knows who I am even. So I decide to say,

> This is Echo.

After that I just clench my eyes shut and drop my phone on my belly.

Great. Just great, Echo.

Why are you such a dork?

Of course he knows who I am. He bought me this phone. He put his own number into my phone. *Of course*, he'd put mine on his too. Under Servant Girl, I bet.

A few seconds later, as I'm writhing in my embarrassment, my belly buzzes.

Or the phone on my belly does.

I scramble to pick it up and with a slamming heart, I open his reply.

> **Bossman**
> I know.
>
> And yes.

I don't know what it means or proves that I immediately understand what *he* means. He *knows* that I'm Echo and *yes*, he's sleeping.

I can even hear him say that.

In his dry sarcastic tone wrapped up in his rough, deep timbre as he lies *awake* in his bed or wherever he is.

Frowning, I type:

> **Servant Girl**
> Ha. Very funny.

His reply comes instantly:

> **Bossman**
> What do you want?

This, I can hear too.

Rude and mean.

I breathe out sharply before typing,

> **Servant Girl**
> There's a thing called politeness.
>
> Have you heard of it, Reign?

> **Bossman**
> No, Echo.
>
> What is politeness?

> **Servant Girl**
> It means being nice to people.
>
> Also known as to be civil, courteous, respectful and well-mannered.

> **Bossman**
> Ah, I get it now.

> **Servant Girl**
> Get what?

> **Bossman**
> You're the mail-order English teacher that I ordered by mistake.

I snort.

As if.

> **Servant Girl**
> Please. You couldn't afford me, even if you wanted to. 😌

> **Bossman**
> Yeah, I was going for a stripper anyway.

I narrow my eyes at the phone.

Because I swear to God, I can hear this too. I can also picture his smirk and his amused eyes while he watches my displeased expression and pursed lips.

> **Servant Girl**
> Why are you always so crass? 😒

> **Bossman**
> Because you're always so easy.

> **Servant Girl**
> Can we please have a normal conversation for once? 🙏

> **Bossman**
> Sure. Let's have a normal conversation for once.
>
> So tell me.

> **Servant Girl**
> Tell you what?

> **Bossman**
> The color of your panties.

This time the phone drops on my belly on its own. As my hands shake and a big gasp escapes. I even sit up on the bed. The phone then slides down to my lap where I stare at it like it's a snake or something.

A dangerous thing.

Swallowing, I pick it up. And type,

> **Servant Girl**
> What? 😱

> **Bossman**
> You wearing any?

> **Servant Girl**
> WHAT? 😱😱

> **Bossman**
> I hope not.
>
> What about a bra? You got a bra on?

> **Servant Girl**
> Stop. 🙈

I swear to God, I hear him chuckle now.

Dirty and filthy.

Making me all heated and restless.

> **Bossman**
> Yeah?

> **Servant Girl**
> Yes.

> **Bossman**
> You're the one who texted me.

> **Servant Girl**
> To talk. Not get asked about my… underwear.

I imagine another chuckle.

Damn it.

I probably should have written 'panties' just to try to be bold in front of him. I couldn't though.

My fingers wouldn't type that word.

> **Bossman**
> Well, that's the only kind of talking I do over texts.

Does he mean sexting?

He does, doesn't he?

Asshole.

Sighing sharply, I type:

> **Servant Girl**
> In that case, I feel sorry for any girl who texts you.

> **Bossman**
> Don't. They all leave very satisfied by the end of it.

I feel like he dropped his voice and stretched out 'satisfied.'

> **Servant Girl**
> Yeah because that's what every girl wants: sexting with Reign Davidson. 😒

> **Bossman**
> That and take out the ing at the end. Because a lot of them want that too with Reign Davidson.

> **Servant Girl**
> How egotistical do you have to be to refer to yourself in the third person? 😒

> **Bossman**
> Very. But only because I have a big ego. An enormous ego. An ego of epic proportions.

> **Servant Girl**
> How does it ever fit into your small head then?

> **Bossman**
> Oh my head's fine, trust me. It is a struggle though, to fit it in my pants.

What does...

Oh God. *God*.

Yikes.

I cannot believe I walked into that. I cannot *believe*.

> **Bossman**
> You walked right into that one, didn't you?
>
> Poor Echo.

> **Servant Girl**
> Shut up. 😒

He is smirking. I know he is.

I *know*.

> **Bossman**
> Also sexting, huh. Didn't think you knew that word.

> **Servant Girl**
> I know lots of words, thank you very much.

> **Bossman**
> Yeah, you're a logophile. I remember.

I bite my lip and type,

> **Servant Girl**
> I wanted to thank you. 🙏

> **Bossman**
> For what?

> **Servant Girl**
> For the phone.

> **Bossman**
> You already did.

>> **Servant Girl**
>> Yes but I didn't know that this had reading apps on it.
>>
>> It's amazing! I love reading on my phone. I used to do it all the time, late at night, in the dark. I'd fall asleep like that. With the phone on my chest or my belly. It was the best feeling.
>>
>> So thank you. Again. For giving me that. I missed it. So much. Ever since I went to St. Mary's and this is just… amazing. There's no other word for it.
>>
>> Well, gift. That's another word for it. It's a gift. You probably didn't even know all this but yeah. Thanks!
>>
>> 😄 😄 😄 😄 😄 😄 😄

Maybe I said way too much than was necessary but I had to gush.

I had to.

He gave me the best thing anyone ever could have.

Actually, no one ever has before.

Lucas always hated my reading. Well, hate is a strong word. He used to… dislike it slightly and never took much interest in it. He was a sporty guy all around. He wasn't into books, which is fine. But he'd hate it when I got so engrossed in a book that I wouldn't pay attention to him.

So I wouldn't read much around him or talk about reading.

Plus the fact that I was going to go to NYU for literature and creative writing. That sort of put us on shaky ground as well.

But anyway.

> **Bossman**
> I did.

I blink at his reply.

>> **Servant Girl**
>> You did what?

> **Bossman**
> Know.

I stare at his message for a few seconds. Until it clicks.

Until I understand what he means and then I can't type fast enough.

> **Servant Girl**
> You knew that I read on my phone?

> **Bossman**
> Yes.

> Wasn't hard to guess. Since you read all the time.

I put my phone down for a second.

And breathe.

I simply breathe. And stare out of my window.

The drapes are closed so it's not as if I'm seeing anything. But if they weren't, I would.

Look directly at his window.

Across the green grounds of Davidson Manor.

That's where his bedroom is.

Not that he's here. On the property. But still.

Then I pick it back up and type again.

> **Servant Girl**
> Did you know that I could download books on it?

> **Bossman**
> I gave it to you, didn't I?

Yes, he did.

So it was obvious. That he knew.

Why didn't it occur to me? Why didn't I put two and two together?

Probably because this is happening too fast.

Everything is happening too fast. Everything is changing and shifting too fast.

He's going from the guy who made me sick with hate to the guy who… doesn't.

Another text pops up on my screen.

> **Bossman**
> It's a piece of shit phone but it's a piece of shit phone you can download books on. Thought you'd find it useful.

Useful?

I'd find it *useful*?

That's the word he's going with. After everything I said.

After everything I said he's brushing it off like it's nothing. Like it's...

> **Servant Girl**
> It's not a piece of shit. Don't call my phone a piece of shit! 😊 And it's more than useful. I love it!!!!
>
> !!!!!!!!!!!!!!!!
>
> !!!!!!!!!!!!!!!!!!!!!!

I would've sent him even more exclamation points but my fingers are too sweaty and trembly for that.

> **Bossman**
> You only keeping it on at night though? For reading.

I bite my lip because I can hear him again.

His voice all rough and low, raspy.

All of a sudden, I realize that that's his *caring* voice.

It's the voice he uses when he's being... nice.

Can't believe I'm figuring all this out only now. Six years *after* I met the guy.

> **Servant Girl**
> Yes.

> **Bossman**
> And it's silent the whole time?

> **Servant Girl**
> It is.

> **Bossman**
> And you absolutely do not carry it around with you?

> **Servant Girl**
> No, I don't. It stays in the back of my closet.

> **Bossman**
> Good.

I bite my lip harder.

As my cheeks, my whole body blushes with his 'good.'

His praise.

> **Servant Girl**
> Although I'm not at school right now.

> **Bossman**
> Where are you?

> **Servant Girl**
> Home.

> My parents wanted me to come visit for the weekend.

But you're not here.

And then because I can't stop myself, I type out,

> **Servant Girl**
> They know that Lucas is back. That you're back. And they,

I take a deep breath here before I resume typing,

> **Servant Girl**
> don't want me to have anything to do with you. They made me promise to stay away from you.

I send that and then begin another text.

Meanwhile, his pops up.

> **Bossman**
> Well, they're smart, aren't they?

I shake my head as I finish typing and hit send.

> **Servant Girl**
> They think you seduced me that night but we know that that's not what happened. They won't listen to me though. I've tried to explain it to them so many times. But I'm going to show them. I'm going to prove it to them that you didn't do anything. You didn't do anything alone. I'm going to fix it, Reign. I'm going to fix it all. What my parents think of you. Your friendship with Lucas. Everything.

> **Bossman**
> No.
>
> Fuck no.
>
> Haven't I already told you that? All you need to worry about right now is yourself. I don't need you to fix anything for me.
>
> Except maybe toning down a little of your drama. Because all I did was buy you a fucking phone with a bunch of books on it. You don't have to drench me in your thankful tears.

I don't even flinch at this.

At the barrage of his rude texts.

One, because I know — for sure — that he's deliberately doing that, to put me off. And good thing that he didn't call my phone a 'piece of shit' again. Or I *really* would've drenched him in tears. Just to annoy him.

And second, because something else comes to me in this moment.

Something about that night.

The night my dad pounced on Reign.

I remember everything about it, all the chaos, all the mess. But for some reason, it's only now that I'm realizing that all the commotion had come from everyone else but him.

My mom was screaming at my dad. *I* was screaming at my dad, and my dad was screaming at him.

But this rude guy on the other side of the phone, somewhere across town, didn't say a single word.

He was silent. And he was passive.

He took it all. Whatever my dad said to him. Whatever he did.

> **Servant Girl**
> Why didn't you do anything? That night.

> **Bossman**
> Do what?

>> **Servant Girl**
>> When my dad grabbed you. When he was threatening you. You didn't say a single thing. You just took it all. Why? You're the boss. You could've done anything. Why didn't you?

I wait for his reply.

But it never comes.

Seconds pass. Minutes. With no reply forthcoming.

As disappointing as his silence is, I don't need him to tell me why.

I already know.

And I can't believe it took me all this time to realize this. That he could've said something, done something. He could've been his usual asshole self that people always talk about, that *I* have always witnessed, and made my parents' life even more difficult.

But he didn't.

Because of his guilt.

Everything, *all of this*, is because of his guilt.

And it just makes me ache. And ache and fucking ache.

It makes me hurt.

For him.

It makes me want to run to my window and sneak out to go find him. Wherever he is.

Because he's not here, is he?

He's not across the green grounds. Something that I've always hated, our bedrooms on the same level, our windows so aligned with each other.

But not anymore, not in this moment.

In this moment, I want him here.

I want to tear open the drapes and look at his window. I want to know that he's up there, and not somewhere in town that I don't know. I get so desperate that I'm about to text him. I'm about to ask him about where he's staying, why is he not here where he should be.

When I notice a shadow on my window.

A dark silhouette.

Of a large body and broad shoulders.

And even before that shadow moves and I see an arm lifting and tapping on my window, I'm out of my bed. I'm already dashing over and tearing the drapes open.

To reveal him.

CHAPTER NINETEEN

He's here.
Here.
Here. Outside my window.

Just like he was that night. The night of my sixteenth birthday.

He's perched on the nearest branch, his muscular arms propped up on the frame, looking all casual and athletic.

Beautiful.

With his summer skin and reddish-brown eyes.

So much so that I freeze.

And he has to command, "Open the window."

"You're here."

He stares at me for a beat or two.

And when it looks like I'm still not going to act like a normal human being, he repeats, "Open the fucking window, Echo."

Echo.

That's my name, yes.

But that's not what he said that night. That's not what he called me.

He called me by his own name.

He hasn't called me that ever since he came back, and I was happy about it. Glad and thrilled and ecstatic. But in this moment, I wonder.

If he'll ever call me that again.

I shake the thought off though and reach for the window. I throw the latch and let him in.

He's just as graceful and athletic as he was two years ago as he climbs in. His leg lunging over, his arms flexing as they grip the windowsill and he pulls himself inside.

It takes him about two seconds to accomplish this but to me, it feels like two years or so.

When I get to watch it in slow motion.

Every dance, every twitch, each play and flex of his muscles.

God, he's a soccer player through and through.

All sleek muscles and artistic grace.

And I was wrong before when I said that he's just as graceful as he was two years ago.

He's not.

He's *more* graceful than before.

Larger too, dwarfing every single thing in my childhood bedroom.

Dwarfing me.

"You came," I say, as if I called.

I did.

Only not in so many words and not outwardly.

But he still heard me.

And I can't stop staring at him. At his face.

His bruises look less angry than they did two nights ago. They're still there and still as vicious but they don't look as alive as they did before. As throbbing and painful.

Thank God.

He runs his eyes over my face as well. "You were getting a little out of control."

"I wasn't."

I *so* was.

I still am.

My breaths are all choppy. And my eyes are wide like saucers and I'm definitely all flushed and pink.

"You were about to go all emo on me."

"It's called expressing emotions."

"You're not going to list a hundred different synonyms of it now, are you?"

"I —"

"Because I really didn't order an English teacher."

Yeah, he ordered a stripper.

The complete opposite of the English teacher, certified logophile that I am.

Blushing even more, I swallow. "You could've just replied to my text."

He shakes his head slowly. "Not a fan of texting."

"Or just called."

"Not a fan of calling either."

I wonder if like texts, he prefers phone sex over simple, friendly calling.

Knowing him, he probably does.

And I admit that I was being sarcastic in the texts before, but I know that that's what every girl wants: to be phone-sexed by Reign Davidson.

Who's now taking in my room.

As if getting reacquainted with it.

My bedroom hasn't changed much since he was here last. I'm just as averagely messy and a staunch lover of pink as I was before. And it's all there for him to see in my scattered textbooks and strewn-about clothes and pink pens.

He opens a notebook, flicks through the pages; picks up a bundle of study cards and holds them up to me, with a quirk of an eyebrow.

"Uh, it's for school," I reply, feeling slightly breathless at his arrogant expression. "I have exams in a few weeks. Finals."

And isn't that wonderful?

My time at St. Mary's is approaching its end and God, I could die with happiness.

"Good," he says and I know he means it.

It's there in his biting tone and pulsing jaw. He really hates that school for me.

I tamp down a rush of butterflies enough to say, "I mean, I won't be going to my dream school but I can't wait to get out of there."

Even though I'll be going to community college instead of NYU, I really can't.

I'm just looking forward to no more curfews and rules and uniforms and absolutely no classes with barred windows. I will also be moving back to the manor and commuting to classes from here.

Although that's slightly less appealing, given how my parents are, but still.

"You might."

"I might what?"

"Still go to your dream school."

"NYU?"

"That *is* your dream school, isn't it?"

"Yes, but remember I told you that I can't go?" I sigh. "They don't accept reform school students and I sure as hell don't have the money to go if they did accept me anyway."

He gives me an inscrutable look that I think is weird.

But before I can dwell on it, he breaks my gaze and looks over my shoulder.

"Still the only non-pink thing in your room," he murmurs, his eyes riveted on something.

I don't have to turn around to know exactly what he's staring at.

It's my diary.

It sits in the middle of my pink bed much like it did two years ago; I was writing in it before I decided to text him.

He brings his eyes back to me, all shiny and dark. "Still call it Bandit?"

I knew he was going to ask me that.

I knew it.

But still I wasn't prepared for the pounding of my heart at his question. And also embarrassment.

This strange pinch in my chest, because I don't.

I *don't* call my diary by that name, not anymore.

If he'd asked me this two days ago, I would've bragged about it. I would've happily told him that no, I'm not that stupid anymore. I am plenty stupid but not *that* stupid.

But now, tonight, I don't want him to know.

I don't want to tell him.

But somehow he already knows. "Nah, you wouldn't."

"Why not?"

His gaze is penetrating. "Because you probably figured it out."

I know what 'it' is but I still ask, "Figured what out?"

"That some bad things can't be reformed. Some bad things have no good in them. They stay bad forever."

I ache now.

Or rather I ache *more* than I already did.

Before he so suddenly came here.

And I can't help but ask, "Where are you staying?"

He frowns at the sudden change of subject.

"I know you aren't staying at the manor," I say.

"Why," he asks instead, "you planning to stalk me too?"

"Why are you staying at a motel?"

Despite my perpetual reluctance to bring up the past, I remember that I'd used to think this a lot. Way back when I'd first met him. I used to wonder why he wouldn't come home. I'd wait for him even. I'd...

No, Echo.

No.

Don't go there. Not that far in the past.

He props his hip against my desk then, watching me for a beat or two. "Not sure people would want me here."

His frank, matter-of-fact and *truthful* reply makes me even achier as I say, "This is the first time you've been here since that night, isn't it? You didn't even come for your... dad's funeral."

His expression shuts down now.

The beautiful, black and blue lines of his face close up like a drawbridge, and I have no hope of ever breaching his walls.

"I didn't," he says in a flat voice.

"Why not?"

"Didn't want to."

"He was your father."

"I'm aware."

"And you couldn't... put aside your differences for one day and be there for him? When he died."

"No," he replies.

"Why do you hate your dad?" I ask finally, point blank.

Because I need to know.

Because there are so many things I need to know about him now.

So many things that I don't understand.

Things that I've seen; things that he's put me through in the past. And then there are the things he's doing right now.

How do I reconcile them?

How do I reconcile him going from being my ex-boyfriend's asshole best friend to this guy who stands only a few feet away from me. Who burns with guilt and regret. Who saved me the other night. Who wants to protect me. Who gifted me a freaking library in the palm of my hands and knows more about St. Mary's than my own parents do.

"He was a good dad, wasn't he?" I ask him when all he does is remain silent. "He was a good man. A good employer, a *kind* employer. He didn't press charges against me when I... He could've though. But he didn't. He didn't fire my parents. We owe him a lot, your dad. Lots of people owe him. And when you didn't even show up for the funeral, they all talked. They've all been talking for years. They've been..."

It's not new information. None of what I've said is new or a mystery in any way.

But I want him to say something.

I want him to give me something *new*.

I want him to tell me that all those people are wrong.

Oh God, that's what I want, isn't it?

I want him to tell me that all those rumors, whatever people say and have always said is wrong. That maybe there's a reason for it. A big, giant reason as to why he is the way he is, apart from him just being an ungrateful asshole.

I used to wonder about this too, way back when. But then he taught me that there was nothing to wonder about.

And finally he does say something, but not what I want him to. "Well, if people are saying it, I'm sure they're right."

"No, they're not," I tell him staunchly, despite the past and everything. "People can be wrong. People can be wrong lots of times. People can exaggerate. They can tell stories. They misunderstand. Because maybe they don't know the real story. Maybe there's a lot that they don't know. And if they don't, then they need to. *I* need to. I need to know, Reign. So you have to tell me. You have to say something, give me something. You have to —"

"Pretty little drama queen, aren't you?"

I'm surprised that I stopped talking, given that his murmured words were a lot quieter than my own. They were a lot quieter than my heartbeats even.

My heart's going wild right now.

Ready to burst out of my chest. Ready to explode.

Or it was, until he pumped the brakes.

Now I'm panting, barely able to drag in enough breath as he continues on a drawl, looking all kinds of amused, "You're not going to pass out on me, are you?"

"E-excuse me?"

"Or worse," he continues, moving his eyes up and down my body. "Drench me in your sparkly pink tears."

"I —"

"Because I thought we just got past that."

"You —"

"I'm sure you're pretty as fuck when you cry but I have this one t-shirt and I'd rather you not ruin it with your girly snot."

"There's not... going to be any snot."

His lips twitch. "Because then I'll have to take it off, and I don't think you can handle that."

I blink.

And then think.

About him calling me pretty as fuck. Even when I'm dripping snot on him.

And then I think about that t-shirt he's wearing that I'm supposed to be dripping snot on.

It's a soft looking dark thing with a round neck.

It sits snugly across his broad shoulders, highlighting his arched and corded muscles.

And then I think about him taking it off.

How we got from my little outburst to this, I don't know. That's his sorcery I think, that he can make me jump through one emotion to the next so seamlessly.

But all I can think about right now is all the times I've seen him without his shirt on.

Playing soccer at school; working out on the manor grounds; running in the early morning on the streets.

All tanned and glistening, looking like the end of June even in the snow.

And disgustingly so that I'd always stare at him even though he made me hatesick.

Which means he's right.

I wouldn't be able to handle it if he took his t-shirt off and flashed me his very beautiful and sculpted, soccer god of a body. In my bedroom no less.

Oh my God, he's in my bedroom right now.

I mean, I knew that.

I just didn't think of the implications.

I guess I just... wanted to see him so badly that it didn't occur to me that he shouldn't be here in the first place. If we get caught *after* I've made the promise to never ever see him, my parents are only going to hate him even more.

"You can't be here," I blurt out, determined to protect him now.

Something about my words or maybe the way I've said them, all breathily and yet urgently, strikes a chord in him. Not the emotional kind. The kind that's made of one part mischief, two parts danger and three parts amusement.

"Yeah?" His eyes glitter. "Why not?"

"Because my parents are asleep just down the hall."

Wrong thing to say.

Because that just makes him even more interested. It makes him straighten up from the desk, as if he's getting ready to pounce. "So?"

I move back.

Again, the wrong thing to do.

Because somehow my good girl-ness triggers his bad boy-ness.

But I can't help it. I don't know how else to be.

That I feel something skating up and down my spine, something like thrill, is a fact I'm choosing to ignore. Because this shouldn't be thrilling. This is a big, *big* risk that he's taking and he needs to understand that and leave.

"So if my dad finds out that you're here, then —"

"He'll beat me up."

"Yes."

"Probably try to kill me too."

"He w-will."

"I'm not that easy to kill though."

"But you are."

"Yeah, how's that?"

"Because you'll let him. That's how."

I feel something clashing at my back. The bedpost.

Because all this time, he was inching closer and I was moving back.

A dance of a sort.

That my good girl-ness succumbs to when he is close.

"Like you did that night," I continue, studying his healing bruises that my dad is going to make worse if he finds out Reign's up here, in my bedroom. "Because don't think that I don't know. I know now. I *know* that you didn't stop my dad, didn't say a word even though you could've. Even though for all intents and purposes, you're my dad's boss too. And I also know that you did all that because you felt guilty. You felt that it was your fault, what happened. When it's crazy and not at all true. And you can say no a million times but I'm going to prove it. So you have to leave. Now."

It's like he can't hear me.

Or rather he can, he just doesn't care.

Because my second outburst of the night — God, why can't I calm down when he's close; why do I have like zero chill when it comes to this guy — makes him smile.

Not a smirk but an actual, genuine if small-ish smile.

He tilts his head to the side, his eyes alive and on me. "You know, you're breaking my heart right now."

"You don't... You don't have a heart. You're heartless."

Lies.

He's anything *but* heartless. I know that now.

He puts a hand on his chest. "Well, whatever it is, it's racing right now."

I swallow shakily, remembering his exact same words from the night of The Horny Bard. "I hope it's racing fast enough for a heart attack."

He chuckles and my belly flutters. "I come all this way for you and this is the welcome I get."

"I'm trying to save your life, you idiot. And I didn't call."

Another lie.

Probably bigger than my first one.

"I came anyway. And let's do this once again, I don't need you to save me."

"I —"

"Although you can't help it, can you?"

"Can't help what?"

"*This*. Being such a good girl."

"I-I am a good girl."

"I know. Always trying to fix things, save them."

"That's not —"

"It's a tragedy really."

"W-why?"

He lowers his voice. "Because good girls are not much fun."

"That's not... That's not true."

"No?"

"I'm plenty fun," I say lamely.

He hums, his eyes all kinds of alive. "Not as much fun as other St. Mary's girls."

"What?"

"But it is what it is, I guess." Then, stepping back, "Goodnight, Echo."

He takes another step back but my hand reaches out on its own and grabs him.

I'm not even going to think about how my fingers just latch on to him, his t-shirt at his waist.

Or that something inside of me slides into place.

Now that I'm touching him, his heat.

Instead I focus on what he just said. "*What?*"

He glances down at my puny grip like he always does, probably to emphasize exactly how puny and repeats my word, only calmly. "What?"

I frown up at him. "What do you mean I'm not as fun as other St. Mary's girls are."

Something flashes through his eyes, a challenge I think. "It *means* you're not as fun. Also known as boring, tedious, monotonous." Then, raking his gaze over my blushing cheeks, "Colorless."

I'm breathing heavily now. "I'm not... *colorless.*" Then, "And how would you know?"

"How would I know what?"

"If I am or not. How would you know *anything* about St. Mary's girls?"

He lets a few moments pass before he replies, "I've had a few encounters, if you will."

"What kind of encounters?"

"Hookups."

"What?"

"Over the years."

I twist my fingers in his t-shirt. "You've had hookups with a St. Mary's girl."

"Yeah."

"Who?"

"Why?"

"Just curious."

"Don't be."

"Just tell me," I insist. "I go to St. Mary's. It's my school. I have a right to know who."

What?

It's ridiculous, what I just said.

I have zero right to know. I don't even know *why* I want to know but I do.

"Is that so?" he rasps, not buying my bullshit.

I tug on his t-shirt. "Tell me who the girl was, Reign."

He doesn't.

Or at least not right away. First, he takes me in.

It's not as if he hasn't seen me ever since he arrived. He has. We've been standing in front of each other all this time, *looking*. But for some reason this is the first time I take into account as to how I look.

What I'm wearing.

Maybe because he looks at me in the way he did my room only a few minutes ago. Slowly and as if getting reacquainted. Which is why I realize that I'm ready for bed.

My hair's loosely braided with most of it scattered around my face. I'm wearing a light pink, off-the-shoulder sleep shirt that comes down to mid-thigh.

Just regular clothes.

But holy shit, how could I forget?

That I'm not wearing a bra.

Oh lord.

One, because I hate bras and given the size of my boobs, I always have to wear one. *Always*, without fail. And two, because as I said, I'm ready for bed and who wears a bra while sleeping?

And now that I remember it, my no-bra situation, I wonder if he's noticed.

God please don't let him have noticed.

How freaking embarrassing.

But then I'm not thinking about my no-bra situation or if he knows it because he closes that gap he'd created just now, and I move with him.

Until my spine is right where it was only seconds ago, stuck to the bedpost. Only this time I think he's much closer because I'm still touching him, tugging on his t-shirt.

He's close enough for me to do all the things that I never want to do.

But always can and do anyway.

Count his eyelashes. Study the red flecks in his eyes and the curve of his plump lips.

Fill my lungs with him.

I'm in the process of doing all that when he says, "Not a girl. *Girls*."

I stiffen. "How many?"

He's watching me all intensely, penetratingly and I know I should hide my feelings from him. But I don't even know what I'm feeling right now to be able to hide it.

Except that I don't like the sound of that. *Girls*.

At all.

"Well," he goes, "there was one at this bar. She snuck in with a bunch of people, I think. She wasn't old enough to be there. And then another one at this party. Again, I think she snuck in. Uninvited. And then, there was one that I found in the woods one night."

"What woods?" I ask. "The ones on the estate?"

"Yeah."

I bring my other hand up and grip his t-shirt, extremely angry now. "What was she doing on *this* estate?"

His words are casual but his gaze is all heavy and almost meaningful. "Taking a walk."

"Or trespassing, more like."

"Didn't ask. Didn't care."

Of course, he didn't.

Asshole.

"What did she look like?" I ask next.

"Dark hair. Blue eyes."

The complete opposite of you, Echo.

What, no. I don't care.

That's not what this is about. That's not why I'm asking.

Again, I'm not sure *why* I'm asking but that's definitely not why.

Definitely.

"And?" I prod.

"And what?"

"What else? What else did she look like?" Then, "Please don't tell me you didn't notice anything else about her, except for her *sparkling* dark hair and *magical* blue eyes."

My irritation is amusing to him. As always. "Yeah, magical's the word."

"I —"

"And I noticed," he murmurs.

"And what was it that you noticed, Reign?"

"Her skin, for one."

"What about it?"

"Creamy," he rasps, still staring into my eyes. "Pale as fuck. Like she was made of moondust."

Moondust.

Now that's some word.

It's a word that my logophile heart latches on to. It's a word that I know I'm going to file away in the back of my mind. To think about later.

So I can hate on it properly.

So I can hate on it so much that it makes me sick.

Still, I manage to ask, "And?"

"Her lips."

"Lips."

"Yeah. Lickable." He licks his own lips as if remembering hers. "Plump. Juicy like some sort of fruit."

"She sounds wonderful," I say tightly.

"She was," he agrees and I dig my nails in his t-shirt, hating it and wanting it off.

Because I want to get to his skin.

I want to scratch his skin.

Maybe I should have drenched him in my tears after all so he'd be bare-chested now and all available for me to scratch and draw blood.

"Although," he continues, moving closer to me, putting his hand up on the bedpost, above my head. "That wasn't the best part."

"What was the best part?"

He licks his lips again. "Her dress."

"Why, because it was skimpy?"

Because he'd notice that, wouldn't he?

"No," he rumbles. "That's the thing though, it wasn't. It covered almost every part of her."

"So then why?"

"Because even though it did cover her up," his voice drops low, "I could *see*."

"See what?"

"Everything."

My heart's racing now. "Like?"

"Like the line of her panties."

My breath hitches. And then explodes.

At the fact that he said *panties*.

Something that he'd typed in the texts. He said it exactly how I pictured it in my head.

Exactly.

Low, rough, deep.

And I swear to God, I feel my own panties coming alive, the elastic digging into my flesh, the fabric rubbing into my skin.

"I —"

"And her cute little belly button."

I suck in my own belly as I feel it.

My own belly button.

Although I don't think that's even possible, but there you have it.

"It looked so fragile. So fucking delicate and small. Like a swipe on her tight little tummy. Made my mouth fucking water."

I don't even *try* to say anything at this.

I know I wouldn't be able to.

"And the best thing," he dips his voice and leans in, "I could see her tits."

"What?" I squeak.

"Yeah, she wasn't wearing a bra, see. So I could see her perky fucking tits. All round and heavy and so fucking plump. Kinda like her mouth. You know, ripe and juicy. Fruity. Something you could sink your teeth in and just *suck*."

His 'suck' hits me in my chest, in my own breasts, and they grow heavier than before.

Heavier and fuller.

Swollen.

And I realize that I should never have asked him this question.

I should've let him leave.

Because I don't want to hear any more. I don't want to hear him talk about this wild girl he met in the woods one night.

Whose skin was made of moondust and whose lips reminded him of juicy fruits.

"Her nipples too, by the way," he goes on though, oblivious to the turmoil inside of me, "I could see them as well. The size of a quarter and so fucking hard. Like bullets. Just pink and rosy. Slightly darker than the dress she had on. Made me wonder how much harder they'd get, if I sucked on them. Much, *much* harder I bet. Much darker too, than the threadbare pink sleep shirt she was wearing." Then, "But I didn't want to scare her. She looked like she'd never had her nipples sucked before."

I'm breathing harder. A lot harder than before.

I'm also slightly dizzy.

Not to mention, my body is buzzing. My body is... singing.

That's the only word for it.

My belly is all tremble-y and my breasts are so heavy. So achingly and *painfully* heavy.

But that's nothing in the face of how achy and painful my nipples are. They're so hard that they *burn* with the pain. They're punching holes through my threadbare pink sleep shirt. They...

What?

Wait a second. Just *wait*.

Did he say threadbare pink sleep shirt?

He did, didn't he?

He...

My eyes go wide and a gasp escapes me.

He noticed. He freaking *noticed*.

Not to mention, he was lying, wasn't he?

"Y-you were... lying," I say my thoughts out loud.

His growl of assent is his only response and I snatch my hands back, ready to fold my arms across my chest and cover myself up, ready to push him away even.

But he doesn't let me.

Because he comes even closer, crowding me against the bedpost, hardly leaving any space between us for me to put my arms up as defenses. And when I look into his eyes, swallowing and blushing, I find that he isn't amused.

Like he usually is.

When I walk into one of his double entendres or dirty jokes.

His eyes are intense. Blazing.

They're more red than brown as he rasps, "My turn, yeah?"

"T-turn for what?"

"To know."

My breaths break. "There's nothing to —"

"Have you?"

"Have I what?"

Instead of answering, he lowers his eyes and even though I'm still staring up at him, I know what he's looking at. I *know* he's looking at them.

My tits, my nipples.

Because he's making them hurt.

He's making them burn even harder.

"Reign," I whisper as a plea, asking him to stop.

Thankfully, he lifts his eyes. "Had them sucked."

I can't believe he's asking me that.

I can't believe we're having this conversation. This... This filthy, inappropriate conversation, and I breathe out a puff of air, my belly tightening, aching much like my tits. "That's... That's none of your business. I can't... believe you'd ask me that."

"I think it is."

"It's n-not. It's…"

My words go poof in the face of what happens to his features next. His sharp features get even sharper, his jaw going tight and his cheekbones arching up. Even his flaming eyes sharpen.

They become… predatory.

Possessive.

It's like a fire, that possessiveness.

Like a hot star between us.

Between our wildly breathing, closeknit bodies.

"You're my best friend's girl," he rasps. "Aren't you?"

I am.

Yes.

Although, I'm ashamed to admit that out of all the reasons I thought that this conversation is inappropriate, being his best friend's girl wasn't something that made it to my list.

It should have though.

Because that's the biggest reason why.

I swallow. "Yes. And so you shouldn't ask —"

"And you've been separated for two years now."

"That's —"

"And so it *is* my business. My *right*. To know," he says, bites out really, his eyes narrowed.

It should sound ridiculous.

What he just said.

It did when *I* said it.

But somehow it doesn't. Not right now.

Not when my breaths are all squirmy and my nipples are sore.

And my skin is on fire because of *his* skin.

His possessiveness.

"To know if someone else has touched me?" I whisper.

"Yeah. Because I know he hasn't."

No, he hasn't.

Lucas hasn't touched me in that way. We never got to that part.

I wouldn't let him.

For some reason.

We'd kiss and touch each other over our clothes. But I wouldn't let him put his hand under. And he always respected that. He respected my boundaries.

His best friend — or rather ex-best friend — doesn't.

He obliterates my boundaries, my walls, to make space for himself.

And usually I fight back. I hold my own.

But in this moment, I'm a feather, light and fragile, and he's the hurricane, cruel and forceful.

"No, he hasn't," I whisper.

He licks his split lip. "So then I have a right to know if you're in the same condition that my best friend left you in."

There's so many things wrong here.

I'm not an object. I can be in any condition that I want to be in.

Besides, his best friend is definitely not in the same condition that *I* left him in.

So I should stop this.

But I can't.

Not when he — the hurricane — practically looks like his life depends on my answer — the feather. When it looks like he'll snuff out, his fire, the eye of his storm, if I don't let him blow me away.

If I don't let him crumple me into pieces.

"So you're asking for your friend then?" I ask, my skin coarse with goosebumps.

His jaw clenches. Hard. "Yeah."

I feel that force in my belly. "And if I told you that someone had?"

His jaw clenches again. Only *harder*. "Then you'd be signing his death sentence."

This time I feel that violence in my chest. "You'd k-kill someone just for touching me?"

I don't know why I ask that when I already know.

He not only told me but showed me with Brad the other night.

"For touching what belongs to my best friend," he tells me.

Which I do.

I do belong to his best friend.

He's the love of my life.

And so that's the intention I reply to him with, for his best friend, but why does it feel like I'm also telling this *to him*.

"No. No one has touched me."

His Adam's apple jerks with a thick swallow.

"I'm in the same condition as he left me in," I continue and his eyes flash. "For your best friend."

And then I step up to him.

I lick my lips, drawing his gaze down to my mouth as I say, "Now that you have your answer, I want you to wait here."

His eyes snap up and he frowns.

But he doesn't say a word and I have a feeling that he can't.

That me still being untouched for his best friend is somehow a big fucking relief for him. So big that he can't form words. He's slightly dizzy.

Good.

I don't want him to talk anyway.

"I'm going to go change into something appropriate. Something more suitable for company. Especially the company of my ex-boyfriend's *pervy* ex-best friend. And then when I come back out, we're going to watch a movie, you and me."

At this, he does speak. "What?"

I smile up at him. A small but confident smile. "Yeah, I'm thinking *Titanic*."

He looks horrified. "*What?*"

I smile wider. "Because I think I will drench you in my tears after all."

He draws back. "Fucking *what?*"

I step up to him again. "It's romance, Reign. I love romance. Romance makes me feel good. It makes me want to laugh and cry all at the same time. And since you're my ex-boyfriend's ex-best friend, it's your duty to sit here and wipe my tears and blow my nose when Jack dies in the end."

"No."

I shrug. "Sorry, bro code. I don't make the rules."

It's a testament of how shocked he is, how horrified he seems to be at the prospect of watching *Titanic* with me, that I'm able to maneuver and turn his big body toward the bed, and then push him onto it.

A feather turning the path of a hurricane.

He goes sprawling down on the mattress, but catches himself on his arms, his thighs spread wide, his eyes staring up at me, still astonished and slightly horrified.

"So you make yourself at home, all right? And I'll show you how *wild* a St. Mary's girl can be."

At my words, those eyes of his narrow and he finally gathers his sense enough to growl.

Ha.

That'll teach him to mess with me.

And tell me false tales and ask me inappropriate questions, and fucking call me a boring good girl.

As I'm turning around to go put on more clothes, I swear I hear him mutter, "Stupid fucking *Titanic*. The door was totally big enough for two."

CHAPTER TWENTY

Who: The Bubblegum
Where: The second-floor bedroom in the carriage house on the Davidson estate
When: 10:40 PM; one night after the movie night with Reign

Dear Bandit,
You covered me with a blanket.
When you left my bedroom the other night after watching not one but two movies.
Well, partially.
We started out with Titanic and as I'd told you, I did end up crying. On and off throughout the movie. And like a good ex-boyfriend's ex-best friend, you supplied me with tissues. But I guess at one point you got tired of passing me the tissues and actually offered me your t-shirt.
Not really actually.
As in you didn't take the t-shirt off and offer it to me, no.
You placed your large hand on the side of my head and made me lean on the tight globe of your shoulder. So I could cry on it and soak the fabric of your t-shirt after all.
You didn't say one word. Didn't even look at me. Simply kept your

eyes on the screen, your jaw tight, and herded my head toward your body with your warm and strong hand, and I automatically knew what to do. Curl up against you.

It was very shocking.

Actually the fact that it didn't feel shocking, me crying on your shoulder, was what shocked me the most. The fact that it felt so natural.

Watching a movie with you.

Anyway, when Jack had sunk to the bottom of the ocean despite the door being big enough, I loaded Pride and Prejudice on my laptop. You didn't say anything and I didn't take my head off your shoulder.

But of course, I nodded off in the middle of it and the next thing I knew it was morning. And I was under the covers, my head on my pillow rather than on your muscular, summer-scented shoulder. Which means you must've put it there, put me there before you left.

You put everything back.

Like it was before you'd come in.

And I know you enough now to know that you did it to protect me.

Because that's how you are.

Whether you like it or not.

And this is what I am: a good girl.

And whether you like it or not, I'll protect you too.

~Echo.

CHAPTER TWENTY-ONE

Three days later, I'm standing at the edge of yet another party.

Happening at the same place as the last party, in the woods. And it's probably attended by the same group of people. I think it goes without saying that I don't like parties. Not at all. I've never liked them even when I'd go to them with Lucas. But he was my boyfriend and I wanted to make him happy so I'd go. And the fact that this is like, my third party in only ten days or so, is making me hate them even more.

The only consolation is that he is here with me.

My ex-boyfriend's ex-best friend.

We stand at the edge of the commotion, surveying the scene.

Or rather he's surveying the scene, I'm lost in thoughts.

Thoughts of how this is the first time I'm seeing him after the movie night, and that I haven't even thanked him for putting my room and me to rights. Looking away from the party that I wasn't paying attention to anyway, I look up at him by my side.

"Thank you."

He snaps his eyes over at me, a thick frown between his brows.

His bruises have calmed down a bit more, which is good.

What is *better* is that he doesn't have any new ones.

Meaning he hasn't been in any fights lately. It's still a mystery to me as to why he was in the first one at all but I'm happy nonetheless.

"For the other night," I explain, when all he does is stare down at me like I've lost my mind. "For, uh, getting me under the covers. And you know, putting away my laptop and things before you left."

I don't see where the confusion is now that I've explained everything.

Or if it is, in fact, confusion that's making him frown at me still.

"I'm just saying," I go further. "Because I didn't. I hadn't, thanked you I mean." Then, "The next line is yours. And it's supposed to be 'you're welcome.'"

At this, he turns at me with a sharp sigh. "You listen to anything that I just said?"

"What?" Then it hits me. "Oh! Sorry. You were saying something."

He was.

Shit.

While surveying the scene, he *was* telling me something. And I'm ashamed to say that I didn't catch a single thing. I totally blanked him out.

I go to apologize but he mutters a curse before saying, "I want you to pay attention now, all right —"

"Okay. Sorry."

"I've got *someone*," he begins sharply, letting me know that my interruption wasn't appreciated *at all*, "babysitting him right now. Which means he's sober like he was before. But this time, he's also alone. And he's going to stay that way. I'll make sure of that. Do you understand what I'm saying to you?"

I nod.

Because I do understand. He's saying that he not only paid someone — again — to look after Lucas, he's also going to make sure that no girls arrive at the scene.

Isn't he?

"No one's going to bother you this time," he continues, proving me right, his features rippling with residual anger on my behalf, from the other night. "You're going to talk and he's going to have to listen. Even if I have to fucking tie him to a tree to make that happen." Then, muttering to himself, "Actually, maybe I should anyway. Things would've been a fuck of a lot easier if I had."

"How did you become friends, Lucas and you?"

Given that he's all business right now and he hated that I was distracted before, this wasn't a wise question to ask.

But as I've already said, there's so much to discover about him.

So much to learn, and I just can't contain myself now.

I have to know.

Everything.

Of course, that doesn't mean that he'll tell me.

But then he does. "On the school playground."

My eyes go wide at this morsel of information that he's thrown me.

"He was new and so some kids were picking on him," he finishes.

"And?"

"And so I picked on them back. As in, literally picked them up and threw them."

"Holy shit."

"I was a big kid." He shrugs. "It also kinda helped that they were already scared of me."

I don't think it's possible for my eyes to go any wider, but they do.

They totally do, because.

Because.

"You saved him," I whisper over the loud drumming of my heart.

His features scrunch up in something like disgust. "Fuck no. I was a bully too. Only my targets were other bullies who picked on someone smaller than them. But same difference."

I shake my head. "I think you totally saved him."

He sighs sharply. "Yeah, and my reward was a week-long suspension."

"Saved him."

"Because prior history of violence. Not the first time I'd *saved* someone like that."

"*Saved*," I insist. "*Him.*"

He closes his eyes as if he can't take it anymore. "Oh, Jesus."

"I changed my mind," I tell him.

His eyes snap open. "About what?"

"You're not the bandit."

"What?"

"You're Robin Hood."

He opens and closes his plush mouth, as if wanting to say something but not being able to. I guess he thinks I'm too ridiculous for words.

But it's okay.

I don't mind.

Because I know I'm not.

I'm very, very non-ridiculous when I say, "Of bullies. Because you're the bully who saves kids from other bullies. So you're the bully who bullies other bullies."

"Yeah, very poetic and a fucking mouthful," he bites out, displeased. "Can we please, for the *motherfucking* love of God, cut the drama now?"

"It *is* poetic," I say, nodding. "And a mouthful. So is 'ex-boyfriend's ex-best friend,' but that doesn't mean it isn't true. Also I can't cut the drama. I'm a writer."

His chest moves abruptly, on a sharp breath. "Look —"

"And maybe sometimes bad boys can't help it either. Saving people."

His eyes narrow and I smile.

Although he is right.

It's time to cut it and switch gears.

"Will you be watching me then?" I ask. "With him."

Immediately, his displeased looks goes away and he answers, "Yeah."

Like it never even occurred to him to not.

Not for a single second.

And it probably didn't.

"The whole time, right?"

I sound needy. I know that.

Under any other circumstances or with any other person, I'd be embarrassed.

But not with him.

Not when he jerks out a determined nod even faster than his earlier reply.

I nod too. "Okay, I guess I'll go now, and find him."

But before I go, I give him this, this one last thing.

That I instinctively know he wants.

"It's Watermelon Sugar."

His eyes drop to my mouth because he already knows what I'm talking about. That I'm telling him the name of my lipstick.

He keeps his gaze on it for a bit.

As if to memorize the shade of it, different from Desert Rose, which I wore the last time. This one's a brighter shade of pink with some red mixed in.

When he's done, he steps back.

Like he did the other night, putting himself in the background so I can focus on his best friend.

And I do.

I go in search of Lucas.

And as I walk, I tell my heart to stop beating for Reign when I'm going to see his best friend. I tell my mind to focus on the task at hand and not at the fact that he saved Lucas once upon a time.

By the time I see Lucas, I've managed to get all my thoughts under control.

Like Reign said, Lucas is alone except for this one guy with him, and they're both sort of huddled together at the edge of the party, in a secluded area. But when they see me coming, the guy leaves and Lucas stands there, his eyes pinned on me.

"Hi," I say, reaching him.

"You're here."

"I came to see you."

"Another apology?"

"No."

"Good."

"Last time it didn't go so well."

His lips twitch at my morose statement. "No, it didn't."

A very subtle movement but my heart leaps in my chest. "So I was wondering…" I wring my hands, debating how to best put it. "Uh, I'm probably, *definitely*, the last person you want to see right now but I was wondering if we could just… talk? I know you're going through a hard time and you don't… you don't have to talk about that if you don't want to. You probably don't want to and… We can talk about something else, anything, catch up?" God, that sounds awful, catch up, as if all we had been was distant friends and nothing more. "Or you know, whatever."

I wait for him to reject me.

This is even worse than the apology that I'd given him the other night.

I might as well turn around now and go back.

But as it happens, I don't have to because he says, "Okay."

"What?"

He roves his eyes over my features. "Let's talk."

My heart leaps in my chest again. "Oh, uh, okay." I smile hesitantly then. "Okay, I —"

"Nice dress," he interrupts me, his blue eyes flicking up and down my body.

"Thanks," I say, trying to feel relaxed now that we're talking. "It's your favorite color."

"And that's why you wore it."

The fact that he knows makes me blush.

It's not as if it was hard to guess though. That I wore this color for him or that my hair's framing my face because he likes it that way.

Which makes me realize something super obvious.

In the two years that I dated him, I wore blue a lot. I wore blue more than I wore pink, which is my favorite color. Even when I went out with my friends, I wore his favorite color. And I kept my hair loose even though I've always preferred braids.

I knew I did it all to make him happy. He was my boyfriend and I wanted to give him everything. So I wore the color he liked; I listened to the music he'd pick out; I didn't talk about NYU even though that's always been my dream school; or about what book I was reading at the time, because early on when we started dating he told me books put him to sleep and he preferred sports.

I never did anything that might bring conflict between us.

Except that night.

When I said no.

Why I'm thinking about this right now or why it feels like such a big revelation, I don't know, but I am and it does.

"And that's why you wore your hair like that," he says, tipping his chin up.

"I... I'm..."

"What do you want, Echo?"

His abrupt question makes me jump. "What?"

"You want something, don't you," he says, his eyes and his tone both inscrutable. "And before you say you want to apologize or catch up, I'm going to stop you and tell you that I don't believe you."

"I..."

He waits for me to answer but I'm too chickenshit to say anything. "You what?"

I know the answer to his question.

I've thought of nothing else but the answer to his question ever since he came back to town. But how do you put it into words? How do you say, *hey, I want you to stop screwing up your life and also forgive your best friend who's always been like a brother to you and so let's get back together,* in a nice and tactful way?

"Did you miss me, Echo?" he asks while I'm still silent and thinking.

And I grab that lifeline like I'm truly dying. "Yes. God, yes. I did."

He takes a step toward me. "Me too."

My heart is drumming in my chest with his nearness. "Y-you did?"

He keeps inching closer. "I did, yeah. I loved you, didn't I?"

Loved.

Past tense.

Because I threw away that love like it meant nothing. *I* made that happen and so I suppress the sting I feel at that, the sadness.

"I loved you too. So much," I tell him, trying to inject all the emotions that I'm feeling into my voice.

He stares into my eyes, his lips parted, his chest moving with slow but long breaths. "I think I have an idea."

"About what?"

His lips tip up but there's no humor in his smile. "Given how you constantly show up where I go, all dressed up and pretty. Given how desperate you look right now, to talk, to be there for me in my difficult time, there's only one thing that you could possibly want, isn't there?" Before I can say anything to that, he goes, "You want me."

He's hit the nail on the head and I flinch. "I..."

"Don't you?"

I blush so hard and my mouth trembles so much that I can't answer him. "I'm... I just..."

Then he goes ahead and runs a finger down my cheek. "Gotta say, it's nice to see you doing all the work this time."

I flinch again. "Lucas, I —"

"Besides," he keeps going like he doesn't want to hear what I have to say. "It's only fair, isn't it? Seeing how *I* did all the work the last time around. Chasing you, running after you. While all you did was string me along. All you did was keep me on the leash."

"I didn't... I *didn't* string you along."

"We probably have different definitions of stringing along then."

"I don't –"

"When I say stringing along, Echo, I mean," he grinds his jaw, "I didn't get to fuck you."

My eyes go wide at his severe, derogatory tone. "What?"

"For all the work I did for you, for all the hoops that I had to jump through, you didn't even have the decency to open those legs for me."

"Lucas, you —"

His eyes go harsh. "You didn't have the *decency* to give me what belonged to me. *By right*." He scoffs. "How selfish do you have to be though, that we went out for two fucking years and not once did you think about me. Not once did you think about what I must be going through."

My heart's slamming inside my chest.

Okay, so maybe two things.

There were two things that I ever said no to him on.

His ring on my sixteenth birthday and *this*.

Taking things further than kissing and making out.

And God, what an awful time to realize that the reason I was such a pliable girlfriend was *because* I wouldn't let him take things further. Because I made him wait and so I did everything to please him in other areas.

But this is *so* not the time for revelations and epiphanies.

I take a step toward him. "Lucas, it wasn't like that. It wasn't —"

"Since we're catching up, let me catch you up to the fact that it was for me though," he says, his eyes hard. "I could've done it, you know. I could've taken it from somewhere else. What I wasn't getting from you, and as naive as you were, you never would've been able to figure it out. And God's honest truth, I was tempted. I was so fucking tempted, *so many* fucking times."

"Lucas —"

"But I kept it in my pants. I fucking kept it *in*."

I flinch again. "I'm…"

"But you stabbed me in the back instead."

My mom had said the same thing and that same pain goes through my body when Lucas says it too.

Same pain. Same hurt.

Same shame.

"So things are going to change now," he continues.

"What?"

He stares at me for a few seconds. "You want me back and I'm willing to work with you. But I need something in return."

"In r-return?"

"Yes." He jerks his chin at me. "That thing between your legs."

"What?"

He smirks. "You open those legs for me and I'm yours."

I take a step back. "Lucas —"

"It shouldn't be hard though, right? You fucking kissed my best friend like the back-stabbing bitch you are. Knowing what it would do to our relationship, *knowing* that you were ruining everything. This should be a piece of cake for a slut like you."

Tears are streaming down my cheeks. "Lucas, please."

"You let me fuck you like the slut you are," he says, his voice low and derogatory. "And I'm all fucking yours, baby."

A tiny sob escapes me. "I'm so sorry, Lucas. I'm…"

"As pretty as your apology is, I'm not really interested in that," he says, coldly. "And if all you're going to do is cry in front of me, then I think we're done here. Because I'm itching for a fuck and you're killing my boner."

And then he's leaving.

He's walking away and I don't know what to do.

I don't know how to stop him. What to say to him to make him stop hating me.

What to do to fix everything.

And I just...

I just want Reign now.

And it's as if by magic, by this weird telepathy that we have, he appears in front of me.

Much like he did the other night when I wanted him to be close.

"What the..." he says, taking my tears in. "What the fuck happened?"

I stare up at his blurry face. "He..."

His jaw clenches. "What the fuck did he do? What *the fuck* did he say to you?"

"N-nothing. He..."

Breathing sharply, he shifts on his feet. "I'm gonna fucking kill him."

When it looks like he's going to go in search of Lucas and probably do the same thing to him that he did to Brad, I grab his t-shirt.

I fist the fabric and shake my head. "No, you won't."

He doesn't like that and it's clear on his furious face. "Echo, just fucking —"

"He hates me. He truly hates me."

And why wouldn't he?

I was a bad girlfriend. I never realized that up until now.

I mean, I knew what I'd done was bad.

But tonight, I got to see my relationship with Lucas in a different light. In a new, *awful* light. Where I never gave him all of myself. Where all I did was take, make him wait and wait and then stab him in the back.

Why would he want to get back together with me?

Why would he want to have *anything* to do with me?

"He doesn't."

"I never had a chance," I tell him, hiccupping. "I never had a chance to fix anything because I... broke everything so badly. He was so..."

"He was so *what*?"

Rivers of tears stream down my cheeks. "Angry. He was so mad, Reign. And I don't know what I could possibly do to get him to forgive me. To get him to stop. To get him back to *you*."

Because somehow, in this moment, that's the only thing that matters.

To save their friendship.

The one that began on that playground so many years ago.

A growl escapes him. "I told you, didn't I? You don't need to worry about me. You don't fucking need —"

I don't give him a chance to say whatever it is he was going to because I move in.

Without thought, I put my arms around his warm and strong body, and hug him.

I press my cheek on his hard but comforting chest and drench his t-shirt in my hot tears.

I don't expect him to do anything.

I don't expect him to hug me back. He probably thinks I'm being too dramatic right now. He probably doesn't even like it, even though he let me cry on him the other night.

But he does do something.

After several seconds of being all rigid and strained while breathing wildly, he lets his muscles relax a bit. And then in the most astonishing turn of events, he brings his arms up and wraps them around my body.

I finally drag a breath then.

A hiccuppy breath, laced with tears, but a breath nonetheless.

As I burrow in his chest.

As I hide myself in his body and he lets me. In fact he makes it happen himself when he tightens his hold and puts his large hand on the back of my head to press my cheek to his body even more.

And God, it feels so nice.

It feels like I could sleep like this, pressed up against his summer-like body.

Sniffling, I whisper, "Please take me home. I want to go home."

He doesn't say anything but I do feel him exhale a breath and nod, and I close my eyes in relief.

CHAPTER TWENTY-TWO

The Bandit

"You," I bark at the naked chick riding Lucas as soon as I barge into his bedroom, "get off him and get out."

I throw her clothes at her to make my point.

Well, I'm assuming they're her clothes because I picked 'em off the floor just now. But who the fuck knows with the revolving door that my best friend has got going on.

I don't really give a shit though.

As long as she does what I want her to.

But first she needs to stop screaming and flailing at the sight of me.

"Hey," I snap my fingers at her to make her shut up, "listen, can you shut the fuck up, okay? No one's gonna hurt you. Just leave."

Miraculously, she does listen to me and shuts up, even though her eyes are fearful. Then she grabs the clothes I've thrown at her and scurries out of the room, probably embarrassed.

She shouldn't be.

I'm not here for her and it's not as if I haven't seen a naked chick riding a dick before.

I have, and lately, it always seems to be my best friend's dick.

Who looks miffed that I interrupted his coitus.

He drags himself up on his bed, pulling his pants up to cover himself.

Good.

While I'm not opposed to squeezing his neck while his dick hangs in the wind, I do appreciate the courtesy of him getting his limp fucking organ out of my sight.

And in the next second, I'm pinning him against the wall.

When he opens his mouth to say something, I jam my wrist in his neck to shut him up.

"You made her cry."

I squeeze his neck with such violence that he starts making choking noises and scratching at my wrist.

But I'm stronger than him.

Always was and always will be.

And I'm made even stronger in this moment with my rage.

It outweighs my guilt in this moment; my usual MO these past two years.

"You made her *fucking cry*," I growl at him.

I still don't let him speak.

I still keep that tight hold on him.

"I told you to stop, remember? I fucking told you to pump the brakes on your assholery or you'd cross a line," I continue, seeing red. "Guess what, that line was tonight. And you fucking crossed it."

Somehow I find it within myself to loosen up my hold a little and let him breathe.

"Let go of me," he wheezes.

"*No*," I bite out. "Not until I make you understand something very important, you stubborn little fuck."

His eyes are furious and I bet mine are too.

But he doesn't know the level of rage that I have right now, the depths of it, the breadth, the height.

Because if he did, he'd lose that look and fucking cower at my feet.

"You're gonna lose her," I tell him. "Forever. For... fucking... ever." I can't help but squeeze his throat at every pause back there. "She's trying, do you understand that? She's fucking trying to make amends. She's fucking trying to tell you that she cares about you. That she still loves you and would do anything to get back together with you. It doesn't matter to her that you've become a useless piece of shit who's only capable of hurting her. She doesn't care about that. All she cares about is that she loves you and she made a mistake. Because you're so perfect, aren't you? So fucking perfect that you don't even realize what you're throwing away."

His breaths are sharp and deep and he's clenching his jaw so tightly that it looks like he may be doing himself some serious damage.

Good.

Great.

Saves me the trouble of breaking his fucking face.

"So you need to get over your jealousy and actually see what's in front of you. You need to get your head out of your stinking fucking ass and grovel. Do you understand? You fucking grovel at her feet like your life depends on it. You lick her feet, yeah? You lick the fucking ground that she walks on. You lick the fucking dirt. You treat her like the precious, priceless gift she is or I'm gonna kill you. I'm gonna choke the life out of you and I'm not even kidding. So get your shit together. Right the fuck now."

I keep holding his throat for a few more seconds.

Just to drive my point home.

Just to make sure that he got it.

When it looks like he does or at least I think that he does, I let him go.

I step back and watch him slump against the wall.

Then I bring out my phone and send him a text.

Sitting on the nightstand just by his side, his phone lights up and he frowns.

"That's her number," I tell him and he focuses back on me. "You're going to call her and you're going to say that you're sorry. And then you're going to fucking *promise* her that you won't ever do what you did tonight. And Lucas," I step up to him again, staring him in the eyes, "if you don't, I won't leave you standing like I'm doing tonight."

Then I turn around, intending to leave.

But I only make it to the door when he says, "Yeah, because you've always been so much stronger than me."

There's a bitterness in his tone that I haven't heard before and I turn around with my hand on the knob.

He's moved away from the wall now and is panting as he says, "I knew it."

"Knew what?"

"That you wanted her."

"What?"

He wipes his mouth with the back of his hand. "*Before* you ever told me."

I freeze then.

My fingers gripping the knob tightly. My heart slamming in my chest.

He chuckles at my outward reaction. "I know you thought that you were very subtle. But you weren't."

My grip on the doorknob tightens even more.

And he cocks his head to the side. "I've known since the first moment. Since the first night that I saw her in the woods. I could see how smitten you were with her. How fucking gone for her. I didn't blame you. There was something about her that just made her irresistible. She had that effect on me too. And I thought you'd come to me about it, tell me. Maybe even tell me to back off when I told you that I liked her. But you never did. You never fucking said a single thing. You never said that she was yours. Instead you went out of your way to be an asshole to her. To practically push her my way. Which was pretty funny when you think about it. All the times I had to tell you to back off, to behave." He chuckles again. "I admit I did it to amuse myself more than anything, and maybe that makes me a bad friend. Because while you were doing it all for our friendship, I was letting you. But I wanted her."

I'd expect his words to cause a roar in me.

A rush in my ears. A drumming in my chest.

But there's nothing.

All there is is a pin-drop silence as I listen to him.

As I absorb every single word that he's saying into my bloodstream.

"I wanted her like I've never wanted anything in my entire shitty life," he says, his eyes pinned on me, his eyes hard, *calculating*. "And my life was shitty. You know that, don't you? It always has been. And so I thought I was owed that. I *deserved* her for all the crap that I went through growing up. Not to mention, we both know that you aren't much of a catch anyway. Yeah, you're rich and handsome and all that fucking bullshit that every girl wants. But you're not exactly the kind of a guy a girl can take home to her parents now, are you? We both know that you aren't the kind of guy who could ever make a girl like Echo happy. You don't have it in you. You aren't made that way. I could though. I could make her happy. I could give her love and commitment and be the kind of boyfriend she deserves. So I wasn't going to give her up. I wasn't going to just hand her over to you when I knew I was so clearly the better choice. When you didn't even fight for her.

"So yeah, I *knew* from the beginning. How much you wanted her. And I took her anyway. And then she fell in love with me and for the first time in my godforsaken life, I had something good. I had something of my own. Even soccer wasn't mine. You remember that, don't you? How they'd bully me, my teammates. Because I was small. They didn't care about my talent. They didn't care that I could play as good as any of them. That I could outplay them even. They didn't care about any of that until *you* came around. Until you made it known that I was your friend. So yeah, I had nothing of my own, except her. Even though you pushed her toward me, I made her love me. *I* made her fall in love with me. I even got her parents to like me.

"But *then*, you had to go and take that away from me. You had to make it all about you, didn't you? You had to stab me in the fucking back because how could you not. Because that's who you are, aren't you? That's all you're capable of. Betraying people, screwing them over. Disappointing them."

I call her a drama queen.

But I don't think I'm being dramatic when I say that it feels like something has died inside of me.

I'm not being *fucking dramatic* when I say that I have grief.

Deep in my chest, my gut.

And that in the last however many minutes he was speaking, I've gone through all five stages.

Denial, anger, bargaining, depression, acceptance.

Denial that the thing I wanted to hide from him, the thing I tortured myself over, is something he already knew. And how is that possible?

He's lying. He has to be.

But unfortunately, he's not.

So then the *anger* that he knew while I was burning in my own hell. When I was longing and pining and *hating* myself for it, he was letting me.

Bargaining that I'd give up anything to go back, to not enter this room. To not stand here and listen to him say all the things that just killed our friendship.

Because he did.

He killed it.

Depression that the only friend that I ever had is dead now and there's no way that we can ever go back. No way that I'll ever get my best friend back.

Not that I ever thought that I could — not after my whole confession about something that he already knew — but still. Now even the tiniest hope has died.

And finally acceptance that whatever he just said is true.

I did push her toward him and I did it because of our friendship. Because I did think he deserved her. He deserved good things after the life he's had. And yes, I've more or less had the same life but he's a better man than I am.

He has more to offer than I ever did.

I'm definitely not the kind of guy a girl takes home to her parents. I never wanted to be and I never will be. I don't know anything about love, commitment and whatever the fuck they make movies about. The kind that she likes to watch and cry over. I never understood the passion and romance they write about in books. The kind that she likes to read and will write one day.

All I know is how to be a disappointment.

That's what I've trained myself to be and that's what I am.

Besides, all of this is bullshit anyway, isn't it?

Because she's in love with him. And she made the right choice, picking him.

So nothing has really changed.

Well, except the whole dead friendship part.

Standing at the door, my fingers grasping the knob so tightly, I go, "Great story. I specifically liked the part about how our years-long friendship is now flushed down the toilet."

"Hey, you did it first when you kissed my girlfriend."

"Yeah, but then didn't you already explain how she wouldn't have been your girlfriend if I hadn't pushed her toward you?" I look him in the eyes as I continue, "Because we both know if I'd gone for her, you wouldn't have stood a chance."

So maybe there's still a little anger left over from my fucking grieving process.

Hatred flashes through his eyes for a second before he says, "You know what, I think I'm gonna give her a call after all. And then I'm going to ask her to make a choice."

I changed my mind.

Maybe I will break his legs and leave him on the floor before I leave.

"Between you and me."

I want to say things but I won't give him the satisfaction.

He won't get a single thing from me after tonight.

So I hold my silence.

"And who do you think she's gonna pick? The love of her life or the guy who makes her sick with hate."

I take one final look at him and his smirking face before leaving.

When I reach my bike, I dial Ledger's number. He picks up even before the first ring is done. Meaning he's as hard up as me.

To fuck someone up.

Good.

I'm volunteering.

"Hey," he says, his voice alert.

"Meet me at Yo Mama's in twenty minutes."

"Fuck yes."

I know Homer won't like it, more bruises. He already almost lost his shit when I showed up looking like roadkill for my first day at his office, but he's just gonna have to suck it up.

I've got a dead body to bury.

CHAPTER TWENTY-THREE

Sitting huddled by the barred window of my dorm room, I write in my diary.

Or try to.

But no words will come and neither will sleep.

But then my phone lights up with a call and I get jarred awake.

As if from a trance.

Instead of the name 'Bossman' flashing like I expected, it's a number.

I have it memorized. I know who it belongs to.

And my heart starts beating so loud that I'm surprised that the 24/7 warden camped out at the front reception doesn't come barging into my room, checking to see what the ruckus is all about.

With shaking fingers, I accept the call and put the phone to my ear. "Lucas?"

"Hey," he greets me.

"What... You're calling me," I say.

"I figured I should."

"How did you... How did you get this number? No one has this number. No one even knows..."

Oh.

Someone does have this number.

Him.

He's the only person who has it and he gave it to Lucas. Didn't he?

He gave my number to Lucas to call.

And I don't have to wonder about his intentions; I already know.

He did it to help me. He did it to help Lucas.

To help bring us together.

"I've been calling you all day," Lucas says then.

"Uh, my phone..." I lick my lips. "I keep it switched off. We aren't allowed phones at St. Mary's."

He goes silent for a second before going, disinterestedly, "Right. Okay. Anyway."

And I have to admit that his disinterest in my affairs pricks me a little.

But it's okay.

There are other things to worry about than my ex-boyfriend not being interested in my reform school.

"Listen, about last night," Lucas begins. "I shouldn't have said those things. I took things too far."

I wrap my arm around my midriff and whisper, "You were angry."

He sighs. "I was."

I bite my lip. "Because of everything that happened."

"Yeah. I..." His voice drifts off and I dig my fingers in my waist, waiting for him to speak. Then, "You hurt me, Echo. What happened hurt me. And I've been angry at you ever since. I'm not sure what I'm angrier about though, the fact that you ran away when I gave you that ring or that only hours later I found you kissing my best friend."

I flinch.

"For the longest time," he continues, "I thought that those two were connected. That you said no because you were going behind my back. That all the hatred you felt for him, all the ways you told me he made you sick was a lie. You were screwing around with him and —"

"Lucas, no," I cut him off. "My running away, saying no to you, had *nothing* to do with him. It was me. It was my weird hang-up. I would never, *not ever*, go behind your back. Not with your best friend. Not with anyone. And I'm so sorry that you felt that way. That I *made* you feel that way. It was never my intention. If I could go back and undo all the damage that I've done, I'd do it in a heartbeat. I'd... I'd take back everything that I did. And Lucas, I... Everything that you said last night... It was true. I was a bad girlfriend. I made you wait. I made you... And then I said no when you proposed to me..."

And it still remains something that I haven't been able to figure out or fix.

I still feel trapped at the thought of saying yes.

And sometimes when I think about getting back together with him and him popping the question again, I freeze. I start to panic.

Not going to lie, I also start to panic when I think about having sex with him. Like he so clearly wanted yesterday.

How strange is that. How unfair to Lucas.

And that's on me.

That's *my* problem.

I look up at the dark ceiling and let out a breath. And with that, all my thoughts. "These past two years, they've been difficult. For me definitely. But also for you. I... I know that you've *changed*. I-I mean, I saw with my own eyes. All the partying and the girls. But I also know about... your classes, your grades. About soccer. You loved soccer, Lucas. You *love* soccer. Soccer is your life. You have so many plans. So many things that you want to do, that you always wanted to do when you got out of Bardstown. And you've worked so hard for it. Harder than most people. I can't... You can't throw that away. You can't throw something away that you've worked your entire life for. Because of what I did."

God, please let him listen.

This is important.

This is more important than anything else right now. He cannot ruin his life because of me. The guilt would eat me alive.

"So you've been talking to him," he says.

And I tense.

We haven't talked about him, have we?

We haven't touched on the topic of his ex-best friend. Not properly at least.

And definitely not about all the things that have changed now, between him and me.

All the new developments and discoveries that I've made.

"Is he your friend now?" Lucas asks then.

"Yes," I whisper.

And it's so strange that he is. That the guy who used to make me hatesick is someone I've come to rely upon.

But what's even stranger is that it feels like a lie. Calling him a friend.

He feels like so much more to me than just a friend.

Only I don't know what else I could call him, and if I knew that, I'd tell Lucas.

"Yeah?" Lucas's tone is hard. "Because from what I remember, you hated him. You couldn't stand the sight of him. You fucking vandalized his bedroom. Not that he didn't deserve it, but now you're telling me you're friends with him. The guy you *kissed* by mistake."

"I know what it sounds like," I tell him. "But it's not like that. The only reason we ever started talking was because we care about you. *He* cares about you. He regrets what happened. Like I did. He made a mistake like me and he's just trying to fix things. Me too and —"

"Did you mean it?" he cuts me off, not interested in discussing his ex-best friend with me. "What you said last night."

"What?"

"That you want to get back together."

My heart slams in my chest.

Slams and slams.

"Look, you're right," he says when all I do is breathe quicker than normal like a dork. "The last two years *have* been hard. You've seen most of it. And yeah, I love soccer. And I do realize that if I continue down this path, I might lose it forever. And so I'm willing to... do what you're trying to do. To fix things. I'm willing to give up parties, girls and everything else that goes with it, and focus on what's important. Soccer and you."

"Me?"

"Yeah. Because I did miss you. I didn't lie about that last night."

"Me too," I reply. "I didn't lie about that either."

A long sigh. "So I'm willing to go back to things as they were. Between us. I'm willing to forgive you."

He's willing to forgive me.

Two years.

Two long years I've waited to hear those words. I didn't even think that I'd ever hear them.

That and the fact that he'd take me back.

But before I can react to this statement he continues. "But I want you to stop talking to him."

"What?"

"If we're going to try things again, then I need you to cut all ties with him. You're going to have to shut down this friendship or whatever the fuck you've got going on with him."

"But —"

His sigh is sharp, impatient almost. "I told you, Echo, what you did fucked me up. And if there's any hope of us working out, he needs to go."

My breaths are frantic.

My heartbeats, my thoughts.

My words too, and I don't even know if he can understand me but still I keep going. "But h-he's your best friend. He's —"

"He's not," he replies in a final sort of voice. "We're not friends anymore and we won't ever be."

"Oh God, Lucas, you can't," I say urgently, coming up to my knees on the bed. "You can't let what happened ruin things between you two. You can't let *me* ruin things. You have to believe me when I tell you that it was a big giant mistake. He —"

"*Your* mistake, isn't it?"

"Yes. Mine. In fact, Lucas, listen —"

But he cuts me off again before I can confess the real reason why it was *my* mistake that night. "Because of which *my* life has changed. *My* life has become difficult. My life needs fucking fixing."

"God, yes. And —"

"So this is how you fix it."

My words have all dried up now and all I can do is pant and gasp.

"This is how you make amends. You let him go and you come back to me. I'm willing to forget that kiss, Echo. I'm willing to forget you said no to me. In fact, I'm willing to forget how screwed up our relationship was. How you strung me along. And you did that, didn't you? You called yourself a bad girlfriend."

"Yes."

"So this is how you become good. This is how you fix everything that you've done."

Seconds go by when all I can do is hug my waist, dig my nails into my flesh and keep my eyes pinned on the cracked floor of my dorm room, with the phone clutched to my ear.

I think my brain thinks that if I don't move or make a sound, nothing bad will happen.

The ground won't shift and the world won't fall apart.

Because that's what it feels like.

That the world is falling apart.

"But he saved you," I whisper as a tear skates down my cheek. "He saved you on that playground. All those years ago. He's a good friend, Lucas. Don't do this to him. Please."

As soft as my words were, his are just as loud and scoffing. "Yeah, he loves to tell that story, doesn't he? How he *saved* me." Then, "Listen, you don't need to feel so bad about him. He doesn't care about you, despite what you think. Despite whatever he's shown you. It's all a lie. Do you remember the Halloween party? Where he got me so drunk with all those girls on me."

I do remember it.

I remember being so enraged because of it. I remember hating Reign for it.

But now that I think about it, after everything that I've seen and after everything that he's done, I can't believe it.

I can't believe that Reign might have done something like that.

But then if Reign hadn't, why would Lucas say that he did?

Why would Lucas... lie?

That doesn't make sense. That...

"And do you remember how he never wanted us to be together? That's the guy you kissed and that's the guy you're defending. He's incapable of thinking about anyone other than himself. So you think about that and give me a call when you're ready."

"**H**ey, I need to talk to you both," I say to Jupiter and Poe as soon as I find them.

It's lunch break and they're sitting outside in the courtyard, on one of those concrete benches. In fact, the rest of the thin population of St. Mary's is here as well, scattered around the space. It's summer and the sun is out, and this is the only way we can soak some up, given we're trapped in this concrete prison of a reform school.

Jupiter throws a pencil at me when I sit down. "There you are."

"Yeah, I –"

"Do you want to get out of here or not?" she asks sternly.

Holding onto her floppy purple hat, Poe leans forward. "Or do you want to stay at St. Mary's for the rest of your life?"

I shake my head. "Listen, I —"

"No, you listen," Jupiter says angrily. "We have finals."

Poe brandishes a textbook in my face. "We need to study so we can get our lives back."

Right.

Finals next week.

I remember. I just don't care at the moment.

"I have a problem," I say when they calm down.

They both look at me for a second or two. Then, Jupiter goes, "I knew it."

Poe nods as well, blowing on her bangs. "Yup."

"Well, yes, I do have a problem and —"

"It's been two days," Jupiter interrupts me.

Poe shakes her head. "And you haven't said anything."

"I know. I —"

"We've been giving you time though," Jupiter tells me.

Poe slaps a hand on her textbook. "But that time is over now."

"Oh my God," I lean forward and look at them one by one. "I know. That's why I'm here. That's why I said I have a problem. Can you guys let me talk?"

"Right," Poe goes.

"Sorry," Jupiter mutters. Then, "How can we help?"

Ugh.

I love them.

They've been so supportive of me and my flimsy, barely thrown-together plans. They've listened to me, helped me, and I would've told them about my date/non-date with Lucas that happened two days ago. Like I've been telling them about all the developments and dates.

But I've just been so heartsick.

So sad and miserable.

But ever since Lucas's call last night, that sadness has been replaced by determination.

"I..." I swallow. "He said he was... ready to forgive me and try again."

I watch emotions go through their faces. Surprise for a second or two, followed by elation for me. Which lasts another second or two but is eventually replaced by confusion.

And then concern.

Probably because I don't look as elated as I should be.

"Okay," Poe goes, nodding.

"Yeah." Jupiter nods too. "Okay."

"It's just that... I personally thought that it was a good thing. Him forgiving you." Poe looks at Jupiter. "Right?"

Jupiter nods at Poe. "Yeah. It *is* a good thing. It is exactly what Echo's been working toward." She turns to me and repeats, "Right?"

"Yes," I whisper. "But."

"But?" Jupiter asks.

"But he wants me to..." I sigh. "Do something first."

Poe frowns. "Do what?"

"He wants me to stop talking," I worry the edge of Jupiter's textbook, "or having any sort of contact with... Reign. But I..."

They both give me time to put my thoughts together.

"I don't want to," I tell them. "I'm not going to."

My determined tone would've shocked them a few days ago. Like it did when I'd told them how I've been meeting up with Reign at night and how he's been helping me with Lucas.

But it doesn't.

They get it.

Because now they know. They know everything that I know about Reign.

About my ex-boyfriend's asshole ex-best friend.

Who as it turns out isn't that much of an asshole after all.

I mean, he is.

But not the kind who makes me sick with hate anymore. He's the kind that protects me, keeps me safe, makes me warm and laugh and yes, blush.

The kind that I'm not giving up.

It's not even a question. I knew it as soon as Lucas hung up the phone.

I'm not giving up Reign and it pisses me off that Lucas wants me to.

Why is he doing this?

It's *Reign*. It's his best friend. His brother.

I understand that given the situation, Lucas's trust is shaken. Of course it is. But if he can give me a chance, why can't he give Reign one too?

If the crime was committed by the both of us, then why am I getting forgiven and not him?

"Lucas isn't going to like that," Jupiter tells me.

I realize that.

I realize that this isn't the way to be a 'good' girlfriend. And after everything that I've done I probably should give Lucas whatever he wants.

But if not giving up Reign makes me a bad girlfriend then so be it.

I've only just found him. He's my friend — well, kinda; I mean he's more but still — and I don't give up on my friends.

"Well, he's going to have to deal," I say.

"But are *you* ready to deal with it?" Poe asks. "This is what you wanted."

"I did," I say, clenching my teeth. "But not like this."

They both look at me, probably trying to determine how serious I am.

But then, both Poe and Jupiter smile and high five each other.

"I'm so glad you said that," Jupiter says.

"Me too."

They both love Reign now. Especially Poe, after I told them how he gave me a phone with reading apps on it.

Because someone gave her something as well.

A sewing machine. A *purple* sewing machine.

Because Poe not only loves fashion but she loves to *make* fashion too. As in, make dresses.

And so someone — a man — who cares about her deeply gave her a sewing machine. He also happens to be her guardian turned school principal — yup, our principal; Principal Alaric Marshall.

She used to hate him too, actually.

Long story there, but now it looks like that hatred is gone and something else has taken its place. Something that makes my friend smile and blush more often.

Anyway, it just warms my heart to see that my friends like Reign. That like me, they finally see the truth.

"That's why I need your help," I tell them. "He's blocked my number."

"What, why?" Jupiter asks.

I shake my head, my heart squeezing in my chest. "Probably because Lucas said something to him."

If Lucas said something to me, I'm pretty sure he said something to *him*. I'm pretty sure it happened the night Reign convinced Lucas to give me a call. While I can't say exactly what went down, I know that it must've been horrible.

It must've been awful.

Because ever since Lucas's ultimatum, I've been trying to call Reign but I can't.

I can't call. I can't text.

Which means I'm blocked.

"I need to talk to him," I tell both my friends. "I need to tell him that I'm not doing it. That I'm not giving up on him. It's not happening."

Not only that, I'm going to *make* Lucas forgive Reign.

I know what he'll say.

I know he'll curse a bunch of times and tell me to not worry about it.

But I don't care. Like I don't care about Lucas's bogus ultimatum.

But first.

"I have to find him and I need your help to do that." I look at Poe. "He's friends with Callie's husband, right? Reed? Can you talk to her? Can you ask her if Reed knows where Reign is? He's staying at a motel. But I don't know which one and I need to find him."

Poe covers my hand. "Consider it done. I'm going to get you all the information you need to track him down."

CHAPTER TWENTY-FOUR

Ledger Thorne, with his long wavy hair and his glinting dark eyes, is a force of nature.

A dark, angry force of nature.

And his attention — more like aggression — is focused on another force of nature, Tempest Jackson.

If someone had told me that I'd be witnessing the fury of these two forces, say, this morning, I'd have said that they were crazy.

As it is, I'm thankful that both of them are here.

See, when Poe said that she was going to get me all the information to track Reign down, she didn't lie. She did bring me everything, plus a companion.

Turns out, Callie's husband Reed did know where Reign was and it wasn't at the motel. But at a gym called Yo Mama's So Fit, specializing in boxing. Apparently, he works out here almost every night, including tonight, and his workout buddy is Callie's brother, Ledger Thorne.

Callie's sister-in-law and my newly-made friend, Tempest, who lives in New York but frequently visits, overheard this and offered to help. Because this gym is located in a very secluded and poorly-lit part of Bardstown. She even came to pick me up at the usual spot in a shiny red sports car, which she drives like a maniac; I truly thought I was going to die tonight.

She is currently engaged in a showdown with Ledger, who was ordered by both Callie and Reed to look out for us. And now that I see her with him, I'm wondering if she decided to drive me over not only because of the unsafe surroundings but also because Ledger was going to be here.

Not that I'm complaining.

As I said, I'm super thankful that they decided to help me. Much like the night of The Horny Bard.

"What's your problem, asshole?" she asks, looking up at Ledger and standing with a cocked hip. "Let us in."

Ugh.

I totally feel her frustration.

So maybe I *am* complaining a little because apparently, there is a problem.

When we arrived here ten minutes ago, we noticed that the gym was closed. Before my heart could plummet though, we saw Ledger coming out of a back door, giving me a little hope that maybe the place isn't closed after all.

But instead of letting us go in, he's planted himself between us and that steel door, and I'm just about ready to start screaming with anger and irritation.

Listen, the fact that this is a '*boxing*' gym is already making me feel nauseated.

Because since when does Reign box?

He's a soccer player. He plays soccer. He kicks a muddy ball around a field. He even has a scholarship for that.

He's *not* a fighter.

That's why he had so many bruises on his face, isn't it?

So I need Ledger Thorne to move out of the way so I can go in and put a stop to whatever Reign thinks that he is doing. And yell at him and then demand answers.

"What are you doing here?" Ledger asks Tempest instead of doing what we want him to do.

"My brother told you, didn't he?" Tempest says, gritting her teeth. "I'm here with a friend. And she needs to see *your* friend. Who's in there."

"Your fucking brother told me that if he could've locked you up in a room, he would've. In a heart-fucking-beat. But since you know how to bust out, now somehow it's my fucking responsibility to babysit you." He motions at me with his jaw. "*And* your friend."

Admittedly, Reed did say that.

I heard it from Poe who heard it from Callie that Tempest's brother was frustrated beyond words. He didn't want either Tempest or me to go anywhere near that gym. But of course, we wouldn't listen. And if Callie and Reed's newly born daughter Halo had a fixed sleeping or feeding schedule, he would've accompanied us himself. As it was, it fell to Ledger to help us.

Tempest fists her hands. "You don't have to babysit me, okay? I'm not a child. So you're off the hook. Just —"

"The fuck I am," he snaps. "And the fuck you aren't."

Tempest sighs, glaring up at him. "Look, you want to be my brother's little lackey and do his bidding, that's on you. But if you think for one second —"

He steps closer, his eyes wild-looking now. "The fuck did you say to me?"

Tempest looks ready to rip him a new one too but I step in with my palms up. "Okay, let's settle down, both of you. Listen, Ledger," he snaps his eyes over to me and I barely suppress a flinch at how scary he looks despite my own ire, "I'm sorry for inconveniencing you tonight. And I'm really thankful that you're here to help us, *me*. You're here to help me when you probably don't know me but I'm —"

"I know you."

"Oh." I open and close my mouth for a second, taken aback. "Well, I still thank you. But if you —"

"You're the reason he's this close to losing it."

My heart drops. "What?"

"And the reason I'm allowing this to happen. Maybe you can talk some sense into him," he adds before turning back to Tempest. "*Or* I would've told your asshole brother where to stick it." Shifting on his feet and taking a deep breath, he says, "Now, I want you both to stay close to me, all right? This isn't a place for either of you. And no, I don't wanna hear any bullshit right now about what you can or can't do. This isn't about feminism or some shit. This is about safety and common fucking sense." He directs this comment to Tempest, who was in the process of saying something, probably arguing. "You both are under my protection tonight, and if I have to chase either one of you down, I'm not going to be happy."

"Aren't you always not happy, though?" Tempest quirks up her brows. "*Angry Thorn?*"

Ledger stares at her for a moment, blank face but taut features. "Yeah. Which means you don't want to make me even more *not happy*, all right, Firefly? Come on, let's go."

If I wasn't extremely anxious after Ledger's comment about Reign 'losing it,' I probably would've appreciated more that Tempest, for all her bluster, blushed really, really hard at 'Firefly.' And that Ledger's eyes glinted the most when she did. Not to mention, I definitely would've wondered about his anger issues and why people call him 'The Angry Thorn,' his soccer nickname.

But I have my own problems right now, and ignoring it all, I follow Ledger inside the building.

Which I realize is more or less the size of a high school gym.

Actually, it *may* have been a school gym once upon a time, with wooden bleachers surrounding the basketball-sized court. But now everything is turned into concrete, from the floors to the steps. And there are no hoops or the line thingies drawn on the floor that tell players where to throw the ball from.

There is a ring though.

Like a boxing ring.

And tons and tons of glaring lights focused on that ring.

So many lights that the rest of the space is in darkness.

And so that is where I decide to focus, on that ring, on what's happening inside it, under those spotlights.

There are two people, two men specifically.

They're both bare-chested and tall and towering. One of them has a broad body with thick muscles while the other one has a body that's more streamlined and sleek, built for speed.

That doesn't mean though that this sleeker guy doesn't have muscles or definition.

Oh, he's got definition.

His muscles are packed and more sharply carved. More finely honed.

Tight and ropey.

You can see the clear shape of them, the density.

You could study that body in an anatomy class. Draw diagrams based on it. Build science models and structures.

I watch them circle each other, their hands covered in a white gauze kind of a thing and put up in kind of like in a fighting stance. A second later though, there's no *kind of* about it because with those raised fists, they begin to fight.

And when that first fist flies and hits the jaw of the sleeker guy, I gasp.

As if waking up from a fog.

I know that jaw.

It's angular and square and perpetually covered in stubble. It's *his* jaw.

It's him. It's his streamlined body.

The one that I've seen several times in the past. At the manor, at the school, on the soccer field.

All smooth and summer-skinned.

So vital and alive.

That same body of his is now getting beaten up.

Oh my God.

Oh my *God*.

That other guy is killing him. He's *so totally* killing him and it happened so fast.

Like, that first punch flew and caught him in the jaw; then he rolled out a punch of his own that got the other guy just under his solar plexus. And after that there were a series of punches that the other guy threw that Reign was able to dodge and duck and leap away from, while getting a few punches of his own in. The bell rang, signaling the end of the round. And then rang again to signal the start of another one.

But *now*, now there's no leaping or ducking or whatever the fuck all these defensive moves are called.

Now there's only beating.

There's sweat and blood flying in the air, and bones and muscles smacking against each other. And then the bigger guy flips Reign and snakes his arms — both arms — around his neck and presses and presses.

Holy shit.

He's trying to choke Reign.

That's when I start running.

I start hearing noises, shouts and screams and cheers and jeers around me.

As if this is a show.

What is wrong with people?

Why isn't anyone stopping this? Why isn't anyone doing anything?

As it turns out, I can't do anything either. Because I come crashing against something. A metal fence kind of thing that runs all around the ring. And just when I decide that I'm going to fucking climb over it even though my climbing skills aren't anything to write home about, someone grabs my arm from behind.

It's Ledger.

I know he's saying something, clearly something related to me running away from him when he'd specifically told me and Tempest not to. But I don't care and I don't even hear him, my eyes glued to the horror that's happening in the ring.

Neither do I hear a couple of other guys, one of them with tattoos peeking out of the sleeves of his suit jacket, who arrive only moments later and are now engaged in a conversation with Ledger. I think that tattooed guy is someone important and I hear Ledger calling him Ark or something.

But whatever.

Ark can go suck it. Ledger too and all these other people who are trying to stop me.

Frustrated and angry and scared out of my mind, I call out, "Reign. *Reign!*"

I don't have a lot of hope that he'll hear me over the ruckus and I'm ready to call out even more loudly. I'm ready to bring down the roof, the walls, the fucking sky, for him.

But *Jesus Christ*, he does hear me.

Like always, my voice somehow reaches him and his gaze flies over at me.

The force of his reddish-brown eyes is such that I draw back slightly.

I start to struggle even harder in Ledger's hold now that he's looking at me with a confused frown.

Then his eyes shift.

They go to something above me, at which point his entire face changes. It goes all taut and angry and even deadly. And then with muscles and veins and emotions pulsing on his face, he jerks back and snaps out of the hold.

Oh, *thank God*.

In only a matter of seconds after that, Reign's pushing his opponent onto the ground and punching and smashing the guy's face on the concrete. And a few seconds *after that*, the guy's smacking his hand on the ground and yielding.

The bell rings and Reign's eyes come back to me and, panting, he stands up with a clear intention.

Of coming to me.

My breaths cease to exist when, taking the tape off and wiping his mouth, he begins to charge toward me.

Just hurry, please.

Without breaking eye contact, he jumps over the ring and lands with a kind of thud that I think vibrates the earth beneath my feet.

It definitely vibrates in my belly.

And then he's standing before me, his eyes dark and stormy, his body sweaty and blood-splattered, breathing wildly. Then, shifting his gaze over my shoulders, he spits, "Stop touching her."

That vibrates in my belly too.

His deep growl.

That I realize is intended for Ledger, who lets go of my arm instantly.

And raises his palms up in a gesture of peace for a second before flipping Reign off.

He doesn't care though.

Because he has other important things to do.

Like leaning over me.

My body arches up on its own, my hands grabbing hold of his shoulders, even though I have no idea of his intentions. I still don't understand what he means to do when his hands come to my waist and hold on.

Not until my feet are leaving the floor and a gasp is flying out of my mouth, do I get what he's trying to do.

He's trying to pick me up and throwing me over his shoulder, turning my world upside down.

Before he begins to walk.

Carrying me over his shoulder like a gladiator's victory prize.

I watch as we leave the fighting arena and go through a narrow hallway. We pass by doors on doors, all made of steel and gray-colored, until we stop at one and go inside. The moment he hits the lights, illuminating a row of dark gray lockers and a bunch of bunk beds, I'm being turned over again and put down on the ground.

Or rather made to sit down on something solid, probably made of wood, with my legs dangling. And he's face to face with me again. His undulating chest and his stormy eyes.

"Y-you picked me up and... and carried me," I whisper the obvious, my hands still gripping his biceps.

"Because you were trying to jump over that railing."

"I-I was trying to get to you. I was —"

"And you can't jump over anything for shit."

"That's not —"

"*What* are you doing here?" he asks angrily, various cuts and scrapes pulsing over his face.

My hands travel up and go to his jaw, trembling. "You're bleeding."

He grabs both my wrists, pulling them away from his face. "What *the fuck* are you doing here, Echo? How the... How did you even know I was here?"

"Your bruises were healing. They were getting better and fading and —"

His fingers around my wrists flex and tighten with irritation. "Who told you to find me here? Who was it? Was it that motherfucker out there? Was it Ledger? I'm gonna —"

"Do you understand what I'm saying to you?" I scream then, fisting my hands in his tight grip. "Do you *understand*? Your bruises were healing. Your bruises were fading. They were going away. You were getting better. You'd just stopped looking like you were hit by a wrecking ball and now you look as if you should be dead. You look as if you're *going* to be dead soon. And I want to know *why*. Why were you out there? What were you doing? Why were you fighting when you're a soccer player? When you're not a freaking fighter. *What is this*? What is this stupid fucking place where people were chanting while you were getting beaten up like it's the Hunger Games."

"Listen —"

"No," I scream again. "You listen. *You*! If you don't answer me right fucking now or if you make some stupid off-hand, sarcastic remark and try to boss me around or gross me out, I swear to fucking God, Reign Marcus Davidson, I will bring this whole place down. I will *burn* this whole place down. Burn it to the ground, okay? And then I'm going to cry and sob like the hysterical, dramatic girl that you think I am. So you answer me right now: What the fuck were you doing out there?"

I'd think that screaming like a banshee and getting all up in his face would probably calm me down a little bit. But I'm just as keyed up as I was when I was watching that awful fight out there. And it doesn't help that Reign keeps me waiting for a couple more seconds while he stares down at me with anger reflecting in his eyes, and grits his teeth.

Then, very, *very* reluctantly, he rumbles, "Fighting."

If he was trying to appease me, then he needs to do better than that. "I thought this was a gym."

"It is."

"What kind of a gym is this?"

"The kind that puts on occasional fights."

"Why were you fighting?"

"Because it's my summer job."

"Summer job?"

"A job you have over the summer."

I breathe out sharply. "Since *when* do you have a summer job?"

"Since I can't exactly have a job like this *and* play soccer."

"Don't get smart with me," I snap, lifting my chin. "Why do you need a job when you're filthy rich?"

This time around when he grits his teeth and works his bruised jaw back and forth, I feel like he's turning his teeth to dust.

Or ash maybe.

With the way his reddish-brown eyes are on fire.

"Because I'm not," he says finally.

"You're not *what*?"

"Filthy rich."

"What, you're —"

"My father," he says with a sharp breath, "wrote me out of his will before he died."

"What?"

His nostrils flare. "Which means he cancelled my Amex and took away the keys to his filthy rich coffers. And so now I have to work for it. Like the rest of the mere mortals. But with soccer and my classes, I can only do it over the summer. *Hence* a summer job."

"Why?" I ask, frowning. "Why would he do that?"

"Probably got tired of putting up with his asshole son."

"No, that's not an answer." I glare at him. "Tell me why he did that. And..." I lick my lips. "Is that why you didn't show up for the funeral? Because of the will. Because you were mad at him?"

"I didn't come to the funeral," he bites out, "because I *couldn't*."

"What does that mean?"

His fingers grow punishingly tight around my wrists. "It means that if I'd set foot on the Davidson property or anywhere near my family, I would've been arrested."

"A-arrested?"

"Yes. That was my father's last wish. To get a restraining order against me." Then, "His lawyer was very helpful in explaining all the terms over the call."

My breaths are very loud in this moment.

Very loud and very broken too I think.

Very strangled.

Just like my heart inside my chest.

My first instinct is to say that I can't believe it. That Howard Davidson, the generous and kind man that he was, would never have done something like this to his son. He loved his son. He did everything that he could to reform him while Reign did everything that *he* could to rebuff and reject and disappoint his family.

But that's not true, is it?

That's not true at all.

I'm beginning to see that.

"You can wipe that fucking look off your face," he tells me harshly. "I probably wouldn't have showed up, even without the restraining order."

He would have.

I know it.

I know it in my heart.

Even though I've *just* found out that I probably don't know anything about his father and their relationship — like, two seconds ago — and even though I've only known Reign, *really* known him, for about two weeks, I still can say with every certainty that he would have showed up for his dad's funeral.

Even if he'd done it begrudgingly.

And with anger.

Because there's a lot of that here. Anger.

Hidden depths. Hidden things that I've only recently started to suspect but wasn't sure about.

But instead of correcting him, I ask, "Why does no one know about this? About your father disowning you, taking out a restraining order against you?"

"Because that's how my father did things," he says. "In secret."

"I-in secret."

"Yes." A pulse jumps on his bloody cheek. "Because he loved to play the good guy. The big man that could never do anything wrong. That everybody loved."

They did love him, Mr. Howard Davidson.

And they hated his son.

Oh God.

"Is that…" I swallow. "Is that why you have a bike now?"

"Yes."

"And the motel. Is that why you're staying there instead of the manor?"

"Yes."

"Because your dad took out a restraining order on you," I say. "That's why you haven't been home in two years. Two years, two months and…"

Wait.

Just *wait*.

Is that a coincidence?

That everything in his life exploded almost *exactly* when it exploded in mine.

A chill runs through my body then.

Is it a coincidence?

"Interrogation's over now. You —"

"No," I tell him with determination, with dread. "Tell me if there's a connection."

"Echo —"

"Tell me if what I did is somehow connected to what your father did." I swallow brokenly. "To you."

"No."

It's a lie. It's a fucking lie.

I know it.

I dig my nails in his heated biceps. "Just tell me the truth. I just want to know the truth."

Please, please tell me.

I beg him with my eyes. With every breath I take.

With my whole body.

And I know when he gives in. His chest shudders with his own gusty breaths and his fingers loosen from around my wrists. "When I heard about what happened at the manor, about you being arrested, I..." He clenches his teeth, as if refusing to talk about it even now. But then, he goes on, "I wanted him to take back the charges. I wanted him to punish me instead. Because I was responsible for whatever you'd done. And so I offered myself up. And he accepted. Kicked me out of his will, disowned me, told me to stay the fuck away and all that crap."

His eyes flash and flicker with his fury, with memories. "I thought if he took it out on me, he'd forget about you. He'd forget whatever he'd planned for you. But I guess I underestimated him. I underestimated how much he *hated* me. Because he didn't leave you alone after all, did he? He sent you to St. Mary's. And he did that because he knew how much I didn't want him to. He did it because he knew how important it was to me that you remain," another clench of his teeth, "safe."

Safe.

He wanted to keep me *safe*. He wanted to protect me even back then.

So it was him then.

Not his father.

Like my parents thought. Like everyone else thought.

Like I thought.

It was him who kept me from ending up in juvenile detention, not the esteemed and generous Howard Davidson.

My mom even made me write him a letter, an apology letter, a grateful letter. For sparing me even though I acted so foolishly. For sparing my parents and letting them keep their jobs. And I wrote it happily too. I wrote it feeling guilty and grateful.

While the guilt part was legitimate, my gratefulness wasn't.

It shouldn't have gone to him.

It belonged to his son.

His second son, whom everyone thinks is a disappointment.

But he's not, is he?

He's the most wonderful guy I've ever met.

Most wonderful and layered and *complicated*.

"You... Y-you saved me." He tenses under my hands. "And he punished you because of it."

He leans over me then, braced on his arms, his hands splayed wide on the wooden structure — a table — that I'm sitting on, his body shifting.

At which point I realize that he's standing between my spread thighs.

And those spread thighs of mine are actually wrapped around his hips rather than lying passively on the table. Maybe it should feel inappropriate — and I'm sure it is for a myriad of reasons that I can't think of right now — but I don't care.

I tighten my thighs around his hips even more, my limbs sliding along his sweaty, dense muscles.

If he notices me rubbing up against him, he doesn't give me any indication.

His focus is on my face, on what he's about to tell me.

"First, if my father hadn't disowned me for this, he would've done it for something else. It was coming. Sooner or later. He probably chose that moment just for the hell of it. And second, I didn't save you. I *couldn't* save you. You still ended up at that school, didn't you? Because of me. Because my father wanted to punish me."

Then, scoffing, "Actually, knowing my father, he never would've pressed charges against you anyway. As I said, he loved playing the big man. The man everyone thought was so giving and generous. He probably would've let you go on his own, called a few reporters to give a big interview about being forgiving and whatever the fuck. He did it all because I interfered, because I let him know how much it *mattered* to me. I should've thought it through though. I should've..." He swallows thickly. "It was just that..."

There *was* an interview about his father in the local newspaper.

About his generosity and kindness.

So in a twisted way, it all worked out for him in the end and I hate that so much.

I fucking hate his father.

"It was just what?" I prod him.

I watch the play of emotions on his bruised and battered face.

The anger, the frustration, the *regret* as he rasps, "I couldn't take that chance. I couldn't risk it. I couldn't *risk* my father punishing you for something that wasn't really your fault." Then, "So however you wanna look at it, it was me who sent you there. *My* actions."

A lump forms in my throat then.

A big and jagged lump.

I shake my head. "No, you saved me from going somewhere worse. You protected me. Even back then."

Even when he hated me.

He doesn't like that however. That I'm giving him credit.

So he growls, "No, I didn't. I —"

I would've gladly argued with him all night till I'm blue in the face, but I don't want to do that. Not right now.

I want to soothe him.

Talk to him. Somehow make him feel better.

So I interrupt him. "So your father has always been like this then?"

But that's not all. I don't just interrupt him with my words. I also do it with actions.

I rub my palms over the globes of his shoulders, my thumbs gently pressing on his tight muscles, and his eyes turn liquid. And molten.

As if he's liking it, my impromptu and inexperienced massage.

"Yes," he rasps.

I knead the spot where his neck meets his shoulder. "But only with you?"

"Yes."

"N-not with Homer or…"

"No. Homer's the good son. The obedient son. The kind of son my father always wanted."

"And what were you?"

"The opposite. Bad. Disappointing. A rebel." His lips quirk up in a small, humorless smirk. "I was the kind of son he didn't want, didn't know what to do with, so he had all his fun with me."

"What… What kind of fun?"

He stares into my eyes, stares and stares and it feels like I'm this close to getting lost in them. "The kind where you sometimes end up with a split lip or a broken nose." Then, licking the tiny drop of blood off his lip, he continues, "So as you can see, I *am* a fighter. Not just a soccer player."

"He..." My fingers clutch him tightly, *protectively*, as my heart thuds. "He h-hit you?"

"Sometimes, yeah. When other things didn't work."

"What other things?"

"Things like locking me up in my room. Taking away my toys and all that crap."

"Reign, that's —"

"Every time he punished me, I did something worse to retaliate. And then, he'd punish me harder so I'd turn around and do even worse things, and so it went on and on. Until he gave up when I got older. I guess I grew taller than him, stronger. He knew he couldn't take me, couldn't hit me, couldn't lock me up or scare me. So he sent me away to Connecticut."

That boarding school.

That everyone said he was sent to because his father didn't know what else to do.

His *father*, the mean, evil bully. Who picked on Reign, someone smaller than himself.

That's where it comes from, doesn't it?

Reign's protective instincts. His urge to save people.

My Robin Hood.

I tighten my hold around his body. "I think your father was a horrible, horrible man."

His lips twitch. "I thought that *you* thought that my father was a wonderful, wonderful man."

"I didn't know the truth."

"And now that you do," he rumbles tightly, "I don't need you to pity me."

Tears sting my eyes then.

But somehow I blink them away. I swallow them down.

I can't break down just now. I can't start sobbing and crying when he's talking to me, when he's telling me things. I can't make it about myself when this is about him.

About this broken and bruised boy.

Both on the inside and out.

That I don't pity at all but am in awe of. For surviving all that. For surviving *and* growing up to be someone who is capable of caring about others. Who understands the meaning of friendship and loyalty and protection.

My broken, beautiful, wonderful Bandit.

"I don't pity you," I tell him, my fingers resuming the kneading of his muscles. "Not after the way I saw you fight out there."

He pulls a face, which with his numerous bruises must be very painful but he doesn't let it show. "That guy was a moron."

"He was bigger than you."

"He was a fucking idiot."

"Who was beating up on you."

"I was letting him."

"Why?"

"Because I was supposed to lose."

"You were... What?" I frown. "*Supposed* to?"

His chest moves again, on a big breath, and he grits his teeth.

As if he just remembered it himself. That he was supposed to lose.

What does that even mean?

"Yes, *supposed* to." He mutters a curse and stares at me belligerently. "Which you completely blew for me, by the way. With all the screaming as if I was dying and your world was ending."

"You *were* dying," I insist, upset. "He was strangling you."

"I was making it look believable, *Jesus*. I was gonna tap out in a second." He shakes his head before continuing, "You cost me ten fucking grand with your drama and pink girly tears."

Ignoring his rude remarks, I inch closer to him, my frown thickening. "Wait a minute, is that why you were supposed to lose? Because you were getting *paid* for it."

His jaw tics. "Yes."

"But that's... Is that legal?"

His jaw tics some more. "Yes." Then, "And no."

"What does that —"

"Not every fight's fixed. This one was. Something that I was looking forward to for fucking days."

"Oh God, why?"

"Because it means more money."

"And?"

"What *and*?"

"I feel like there's an 'and' in there."

He's getting annoyed by my questions now. I can tell.

He's reaching his limit.

But he does reply, "And I deserve it. Getting beaten up."

And then I just blink, my lips parted but barely breathing.

Because he thinks getting pummeled almost to death is what he should get for what he did.

For kissing me. For betraying Lucas. For having me sent to St. Mary's.

He deserves it for the sins that he's committed for two years, two months and however many days ago that I can't remember. And the reason *he* does is because he burns with it every second of every day.

If he was like me and kept a diary, I bet he'd be marking days in it.

Days and days of guilt and fire and war inside of him.

And so I have to tell him now.

I have to tell him that I choose him. That I will *never ever* give up on him.

That I will not let him suffer like this.

"You done?" he asks, his eyes intent and unforgivable.

I let my body loose, my fingers grasping his neck like an anchor, ready for him. "Yes."

"You gonna answer my questions now?"

"Uh-huh."

"Good."

CHAPTER TWENTY-FIVE

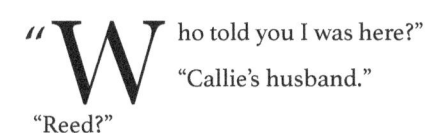

"Who told you I was here?"

"Callie's husband."

"Reed?"

"Yes." I nod and launch into the whole explanation. "Callie's my friend. Well, she's recently become my friend. And I asked Poe, my other friend — who's also recently become my friend — for her help to find you. And that she should ask Callie to ask Reed about where you —"

"Why?" he asks, impatient.

"Because I thought Reed would know where you —"

"*Jesus*," he growls. "*Why* did you want to find me?"

Oh right, that.

"Because I wanted to talk to you," I whisper, "and you blocked my number."

His eyes narrow. "And that didn't clue you in that I *didn't* wanna talk to you?"

"Well, yeah," I say, biting my lip.

He watches me bite my lip with almost a glare. "But you decided to stalk me anyway."

I let my tingling lip go. "I wasn't stalking. This *isn't* stalking."

"Yeah, no. This is pretty much stalking 101."

"So, fine. *Okay*. I was stalking. But only because I wanted to tell you things."

"What things?"

Letting out a deep breath, I look into his angry but beautiful dark eyes. "That we're friends."

"What?"

"You and me." I swallow. "We're friends now."

He stares at me for a beat or two. "How's that?"

"Because we've made progress."

"Progress."

"Yes." I nod. "In the p-past few days."

Again, he studies me for a few seconds. "What kind of progress?"

"Well," I clear my throat, blushing under his intense gaze. "For one, we don't make each other sick with hate anymore."

"We don't."

I blush harder. "No. And you've been helping me. With my problem. And protecting me and keeping an eye on me. And we saw that movie together the other night. Plus we text and I know you call it a work phone but sometimes I just text you to talk to you and I think —"

"Yeah, you do."

I dig my fingers in his neck. "I know you hate texting."

"Yes."

"But sometimes…" My heart's racing really fast now. "Sometimes I just want to talk to you."

His jaw tics as he stares and stares at me.

"And now you've blocked my number."

Even though I've only essentially had this phone for a little over a week and it was only last weekend when I started texting him just for the hell of it, it still felt like a loss.

Not being able to contact him.

Because I do it just to say hi to him.

Or tell him about the book that I downloaded. That never would've been possible if not for him. Or that I stayed up all night to read it.

That's what friends do, don't they?

They talk to each other. They text and call.

And while I know that he doesn't feel like a friend or only like a friend, I don't know what else to call it.

When Reign doesn't answer me, I say, "And so I came here because I wanted to ask you to unblock it and ask why you blocked it in the first place. And I have to tell you that —"

My words cut off when he pulls my head back.

Yanks it back, actually, with his hand in my hair.

Actually his hand is in my braid. It's wrapped around my braid.

So *tightly* that my neck is all craned up and stretched and even though I've never been in a position like this, where I'm so thoroughly taken over and dominated, I don't feel scared.

Nothing about his angry eyes or his rough hands is scary to me.

It's all thrilling. And exhilarating and euphoric.

"Your boyfriend know that you're here?" he rumbles, his tone biting. "*Being my friend.*"

I swallow and he watches the play of the delicate muscles in my throat like some kind of a predator. "He —"

"Because I don't think he's gonna like it very much. You," his fingers tug on my hair, "with *me.*"

I flex my thighs around his slim hips and fist *his* hair in response. "*Ex*-boyfriend." His brows snap together and I explain, "You said boyfriend. He's not. He's still my ex."

His frown thickens even more before he mutters, "Jesus. He didn't call, did he?"

"He did. The very next night."

"He apologize?"

I nod, or try to.

But his grip in my hair stops me, *thrills* me anew.

"Yes." Then, "You asked him to, didn't you?"

"I shouldn't have had to."

And this is the guy I'm supposed to cut ties with.

Insanity.

If Lucas thinks I'm giving Reign up, he's fucking *insane*.

"So then," he continues, studying my features, "why the fuck is he still your ex?"

"Because I choose you."

He blanches.

He literally pales at my words and his hold on my hair loosens. "What?"

"The night he called," I say, keeping a tight hold of him still. "He said that... he'd forgive me. And that he'd take me back, but I have to... I have to cut ties with you." I bring my fingers to his bruised and bloody face then and grasp it gently. "But I'm not going to. I'm *not* going to cut ties with you. I choose you, okay? I'm not sure why Lucas is doing this. Why he's ready to forgive me but not you. But I'm going to fix it."

"No," he clips.

"I knew you'd say that. I *knew* it. But I'm not backing down," I tell him. "I won't back down. You're my friend and I'm not giving up on you. I won't. Plus I've just realized something."

"What?"

"That we're even." When he frowns in confusion, I say, "I know you think you deserve all the bad things. But I want you to think about something. I want you to think about the fact that we're even, you and me."

"Even."

"Yes. You think you provoked me. Into doing what I did that night. Years of torment and then that phone call which made me sneak in and vandalize your room. Fine. So let's say you did provoke me, but it was still *me* who did that. If you don't want to put the blame on me then that's okay. But it makes us even. You being a giant asshole to me for years and me destroying your childhood bedroom. There. Even."

Exactly.

We're even. We're both culpable.

And I'm done letting him count days and months and years of regret.

"That's fucking ridiculous."

"It's fucking genius and you know that. Plus," I raise my eyebrows, "you saved me from going to jail."

"I —"

"And you can say different till the end of time but I won't believe it. I will still write you thank you notes. I will still create limericks for you. And serenade you with a boombox about how grateful I am." When it looks like he's going to say something else, I jump in quickly. "And as for the other thing, about Lucas not forgiving you, I have the solution for that as well."

"What *fucking* solution?"

His words are all growled now. "I'm going to tell him."

"Tell him what?"

"That it was me. That *I* was the one who kissed you first."

I did.

I remember it vividly. I remember it as if in slow motion.

The very moment *I* leaned forward and put my mouth on him. And kissed him.

I also remember him going still.

As if in shock.

While I was the one moving my lips over his, tasting his plush mouth like I'd never get enough.

And I kept going until he broke.

Until he started to kiss me back, and then there was no stopping me and him.

Not until everything blew apart.

So yeah, I was the one.

Who did it. Who started it.

And that's why I always thought — especially after that phone call and how he refused to help me — that he must've told Lucas everything. That he must've put the blame on me because it did belong to me, and preserved his friendship.

But he didn't.

He kept my secret.

It reminds me of the first time we'd met. When I'd lied to him and he protected me by keeping my secret.

He's somehow always protected me, hasn't he?

So no, I'm not giving him up.

And I'm getting him his best friend back.

"I'm going to tell Lucas that it was me. *I* made the first move. And if he wants to be mad about that then he can be mad about that. But he can't just forgive me and not you. He has to forgive us *both*. He has to take both of us back, not just me. It's not fair to you. It's not fair after everything that you've been through and after everything that you've done for him."

I know that a kiss is a kiss, and that Reign did kiss me back after his initial non-participation.

But it doesn't change the fact that I was the one who started it.

And while I've kept it a secret all this time, I think I need to let it out. I decided it right after his phone call. Exactly the moment when I decided that I'm not giving up Reign; although there was no decision involved there, but still.

Lucas needs to know everything and he needs to forgive his best friend. And again, if that makes me a bad girlfriend then so be it. I'll find other ways to be good.

"You did, didn't you?" he says in a low voice.

My nod is jerky, ashamed. "Yes."

"Why?"

"What?"

In response, he puts his hands on me.

On my waist and holds on. Like he did when he carried me over like spoils of war. And I'm not going to lie, I love it. I also love how he's shifting between my spread thighs, adjusting our positions so we're even more locked together.

Good.

I wind my arms around his neck too, even more firmly and tightly, and hold on.

I don't want him going anywhere.

He *can't* go anywhere.

"Why did you make the first move?"

His softly rasped question makes me come out of my happy daze and blink. "What, what do you mean?"

Keeping his eyes intent and steady, he says, "You hated me back then, didn't you?"

"Yes."

"So then," he licks his split lip, "why did you come on to me?"

I swallow. "I... It was... It was a mistake."

His fingers on my waist tighten for a few seconds, almost fisting my dress. "Was it?"

"Yes," I say. "Y-you know that already. I made a mistake. We both did."

Hasn't that been established already?

A mistake. We both made it.

So I don't know why we're talking about this now.

But apparently we are because he continues, now with his hands moving up and down my waist, "Interesting mistake though, isn't it? Kissing your boyfriend's best friend."

His large, warm hands go from my ribs down to my waist, spanning my entire torso, his thumbs meeting in the middle of my tight tummy.

It's distracting.

It's hard to focus on what he's saying, what he's asking me when he's stroking my entire belly like this.

So intimately.

More intimately than I can bear.

So I try to get away from him.

I try to unlock my ankles from his back and slide my arms away from his neck. But he doesn't let me. He gathers me close, with both his hands going down to my thighs and hiking them up along his sleek waist.

Before leaning over me again and murmuring, "A mistake is something like forgetting an anniversary, for example. Or forgetting your boyfriend's birthday. Getting your girlfriend a rose instead of a fucking daisy, which happens to be her favorite flower. That's a mistake."

"It was," I tell him, my fingers digging into his bare shoulders. "I told you a million times that it was. I made a mistake. I don't know why we're talking about this. I don't know —"

"We're *talking* about this," he squeezes my waist, making me arch my spine, "because kissing your boyfriend's best friend isn't a mistake."

"That's —"

"Kissing your boyfriend's best friend is a secret forbidden wish."

I shake my head. "N-not for me."

His reddish-brown eyes are penetrating, *knowing*. "No?"

While mine are frantic and wide. "No. I never thought about you in that way. I never thought... I didn't even want anything to do with you. I *don't* want anything to do with you, not like that."

Oh God.

Oh my God.

I'm panicking. I'm *panicking*.

Because his dark eyes look predatory.

Animalistic.

That glint. That *smirk*.

Why is he smirking?

Why is he roving his eyes all over my face, my parted and trembling mouth?

Before moving down to my body. And I do too.

I can't resist it.

I can't resist staring at what he's staring at.

And it arrests my breaths, my thoughts for a few seconds, how we are.

How my dress is all hiked up, baring more of my thighs than I usually do. And whatever is bared is hugging his sleek, sweaty waist.

And how intimate we look like this.

How our bodies are so in contrast with each other.

I'm so pale and creamy. And he's so summery and olive-toned.

How my thighs are all fleshy and soft. And how there are freaking cuts on his obliques, a ladder in his abs. That V going down to his boxing shorts.

And then I flick my eyes up and up and realize that I was right.

Out there I mean.

People could study his body for science.

Even bruised and black and blue, he looks... epic.

He looks so cut and sleek and strong and, wait...

There's a tattoo.

On his chest. Left side of it.

Numbers.

Random-looking. That I can't make heads or tails of. But I know that these neat-looking digits weren't there before. Not when he still lived at the manor.

"I think you do," he murmurs.

My eyes fly up, horrified. "I-I do what?"

"Want something to do with me," he reminds me of our conversation before I got so thoroughly distracted.

I resume pushing him away. "I don't. I —"

"I *think*," he rasps, staying put despite my efforts, "that you have a thing for me."

"What?" I shriek almost.

"And I have a thing for you too."

I freeze then.

I totally absolutely freeze.

My nails stop where they are, lodged into his skin, mashing over the vein on the side of his neck. My eyes stay locked with his. My spine stays bowed and my lips stay parted, gasping breaths.

His smirk is gone now.

So is his cocky, arrogant look.

Instead, his features are all intense. His eyes are liquid.

The bruises on his face make him look both dangerous and fragile.

Like he's capable of crushing me, but I'm capable of crushing him too.

"What?" I whisper.

He takes my face in with his molten eyes. "I kissed you back, didn't I? Why did you think I did that?"

"I don't... I didn't..."

Think.

I didn't think why. Not for him and not for me.

I've pushed it down, pushed it aside, the kiss.

Because there's nothing to think about anyway.

He's my ex-boyfriend's ex-best friend.

And I'm his ex-best friend's ex-girlfriend.

But before I can tell him that, he goes, "I did that. Because I wanted to. Because I have a thing. For you."

"B-but that's..."

"A very big thing."

"You're lying."

He's lying.

Isn't he?

He has to be.

It doesn't make sense. It's bizarre. It's absurd.

It's like his protecting thing from a few days ago.

Except this is even more of a fiction than him trying to protect me.

Me.

The servant girl.

It doesn't...

"I wish."

"You..." I can barely think, let alone make words. "You were always so..."

"Horrible to you."

"Yes." Then, to prove my point, I repeat, "*Yes!*"

Horrible. Awful. Hateful.

His lips turn up in a small, *sad* smile. "Part of my charm. And partly a consequence of wanting your best friend's girl when you shouldn't."

My whole body winces.

My muscles spasm. My heart spasms.

As I look into his eyes, shocked, disbelieving, so confused. "I don't... I don't understand this."

Things flicker in his eyes, great big waves of emotions. "Neither do I."

"Since *when*?"

"That first night."

The first...

"The... The night of the f-firecrackers?"

"Yeah."

I barely remember that night.

I barely remember anything except one thing.

One *blaring* thing.

"But that was..." I lick my rapidly drying lips. "That was *before* Lucas."

"I know."

"You l-liked me before Lucas."

"I did."

I take a few moments to gather myself. I would've liked more though. I would've liked hours and days and probably weeks to pull myself together.

But I don't have that kind of time.

I want to know.

I want to know *everything*.

"If you liked me before... Lucas, then why didn't you... Y-you never said anything. You never..." And then I just go back to repeating everything because it doesn't make sense to me. "You were so horrible to me. I thought you hated me. I thought you hated me with him. I thought..."

Oh God, he didn't.

He didn't hate me with his best friend. Or rather not for the reasons I always thought.

I think he hated me with him because he... had a thing for me.

Holy shit.

Holy fucking shit.

CHAPTER TWENTY-SIX

He can see it.

On my face.

That I'm finally getting it. I'm finally *comprehending* what he's telling me.

"I never said anything," he says, his eyes grave, his features grave as well like this is the most important thing in his life, the most important truth. "Because he liked you too. Because he was my best friend. I never said anything, treated you like shit, because I wanted you to choose him."

"C-choose him."

"Yes. Because he was a better choice."

My heart contracts at this.

Contracts. And constricts. *Chokes.*

At the pain in his voice. Frustration. *Anger.*

"So I just watched," he rasps.

I squeeze him with my limbs, my chest heaving. "W-watched?"

His hands go back to stroking.

Going up and down the sides of my body, from my ribs to the base of my belly, as he rumbles, "All the time."

And I can't help but ask, "In school?"

"Uh-huh. At the cafeteria. The library. The soccer games. *Especially* the soccer games. You always came to the soccer games."

"For Lucas," I whisper.

"Yeah, for him," he says, his words slightly clipped. "You'd sit right at the front with a bunch of your friends. You'd cheer for every goal he made. Every fucking pass. Every dribble. Even though you had zero interest in the game."

He's right.

I never took to soccer. Even though it was my boyfriend's life.

But like a good girlfriend, I always went to support him and never ever let it show that I was bored to death at his games.

"Soccer is boring."

His lips twitch. "To you, yeah." Then, "Because when something is interesting to you, your eyes shine. They become all dark and wide. You laugh without having to remember that you should. Your cheeks are flushed. Your..." he licks his split lip, "whole body lights up."

He's right. I *think*.

I mean, I've never actually noticed these things about me but *he* did.

Because he watched me.

He *watched* me.

He had a thing for me.

My ex-boyfriend's ex-best friend.

"I... H-he liked me being there," I tell him.

"Yeah, I know that too. He wouldn't shut up about it," he says, his thumb pressing on my tummy on the downward glide, making my already broken breaths even choppier. "About how his girlfriend was right there, in the front row, watching him play." He squints his eyes, as if lost in memories. "Sometimes I thought he was trying to make me jealous."

"He w-wouldn't."

"*I* would."

"Make him jealous?"

"Fuck yeah." He licks his lips again and I bite mine, watching him do it. "If you were mine, Echo, if you were there to watch me, I'd make *him* and every motherfucker out there jealous out of their minds. And so sometimes I wondered."

"Wondered what?"

"If you ever did. Watch me."

"I did," I blurt out, my nails digging into his skin.

"Yeah?"

"I did watch you play. Always."

I was there to support Lucas, not ogle his best friend, but I did.

I noticed every goal he made, every pass, every dribble, and then hated myself for doing it.

"I don't know anything about soccer," I go on, "but I always thought you were... magnificent."

"Magnificent."

"Yes. The way you," I look for a word, "*moved*. The way you glided across the field. Like the wind. Like something wild and free. Unstoppable."

He isn't named the Daredevil for nothing.

He was always reckless and fast. A risktaker.

It both angered and impressed his coaches and commentators. They talked about it often enough. He'd do things — run impossibly fast, flip backward in the air, send the ball flying through the stadium — like no one else.

Not even Lucas.

Even though Lucas was the captain, it was always Reign that they talked about. It was always him that they praised for making the impossible possible.

"And then every time he kissed you in front of me," he says roughly, his fingers grazing close, *so very close*, to my breasts, "I wanted to break his fucking face."

"You d-didn't," I gasp out, holding on to him harder.

"And then of course, you'd be crying over him because that's who you are but I wouldn't care. I'd still do what I've always wanted to do."

"Do what?"

"Throw you over my shoulder and take you away."

Like he did tonight after his fight.

And the fact that he wanted to do it *always*, makes me breathlessly ask, "Where?"

"Somewhere away from him. Somewhere I could wipe your pretty tears off and make you kiss me the way you kissed him."

We're so close now due to his maneuverings.

That every frantic, hiccuppy breath I take, my chest drags against his.

My tits drag against his tattoo.

"That's not…" I shake my head. "That's not nice."

"Yeah, I figured." He chuckles softly. "And if you don't like that, you're not going to like what I tell you next."

"What?"

"That every time you glared at me," he lowers his voice, a mischievous glint in his eyes, "I'd get hard."

I shudder. "You'd…"

"Every time you got angry because I said something offensive, or you acted like you couldn't stand the sight of me, I'd be hunting down an empty classroom or a secluded spot where I could rub one out." Another lick of his lips and oh my God, I'm going to reach up and bite it if he doesn't stop that. "*Every. Fucking. Time.* I probably hold the world record or some shit for jerking off in a high school classroom."

I want to laugh.

I *want* to.

But I can't. I can't do anything except sputter out a few words. "I'm… I didn't… That's…"

Making him chuckle.

And his chuckle is even worse than him licking his lips — which is not a surprise but still — that a quickening starts up in my belly as he goes on, "But that's nothing compared to what I'd do when your boyfriend would tell me."

"Tell you what?"

He leans closer then and my tits aren't just grazing his chest, they're all mashed against it. They're all flattened against his hard, *hard*, chest.

So much so that his mysterious tattoo might be mine.

His heat might be mine.

His heartbeats too.

And as if that wasn't enough, this sudden and overwhelming contact between us, he goes ahead and flicks the side of my breasts. His rough thumb finally, *finally* making contact with my plump flesh, and my thighs jerk and ride higher along his tight obliques.

"That you still hadn't given it up."

"Given what..."

Oh.

Oh! He means...

He means my virginity.

The thing he was asking about the other night. For his best friend.

"It's..." I go, sounding all outraged or wanting to at least. "It was none of your business."

He chuckles again, his hands going even more restless on my body. "No, it wasn't. It was more than my business."

"What?"

"It was my fucking obsession."

He's stroking me harder now. Squeezing my belly, massaging my sides, pressing into my breasts.

I'd tell him to stop.

Only I'm doing the same thing. I'm rubbing my palms over his shoulders, stroking his biceps, the sides of his neck, tugging at his hair.

"And so I'd ask him," he swallows, "if he'd taken your cherry yet."

"You..."

"I'd try to be sneaky about it, you know," he continues. "I'd try to provoke him at practice, give him shit about his passes. Tell him to loosen up, get laid and then he'd get mad and tell me that he couldn't. Because his tight innocent girlfriend wouldn't put out. Or when we'd get drunk, I'd try to get him to talk. I'd share my escapades just so he'd share his. And he never had anything."

"That's..." I pull at his hair, looking for a word, "sneaky."

"Yeah, I know. I said that."

I dig my heels in the small of his back. "You're an asshole."

"An obsessive asshole," he corrects me. "Who'd then beat off in his room, standing by his window."

"Window?"

"Because I could see yours through mine."

Wait, what?

He'd...

"You'd... do *that* while staring at my window?"

Another chuckle. "Yes, Echo, I'd do *that*, standing at my window while watching yours. Sometimes I'd even see you. Fluttering around in your room, your honey-blonde hair in your good girl braid and your tight little body in your pink pajamas. Sometimes you'd sit in your bed and read. And smell your hair. *Jesus Christ*, I'd lose it when you did that. Smelled the tail of your braid, curled it in your tiny fingers. I'd fucking blow all over my windowpane."

I go to say something but I feel a tug in my hair and I realize that he's pulling at my braid again. He's wrapping it around his hand once again, but this time more gently. This time, he wants to feel it. He wants to rub his thumb over the tail.

And he wants to watch himself do it.

"I knew it," he murmurs.

"Knew what?"

"That it'd be soft." Another tug. "Like silk. Velvet. I fucking knew. And I fucking imagined."

"Imagined what?"

He looks up. "Fucking your hair."

I jerk. "What?"

"Yeah, I don't think I've ever imagined fucking someone's hair. Except yours. It's just..." He tugs again, almost viciously. "Something about it. All honey-colored and thick and rich and soft. So fucking sweet."

He brings my braid up to his nose and smells it, making me jerk again.

His eyes are closed and he growls softly, taking a whiff.

"Y-you have a hair fetish," I tell him. "It's g-gross."

It's not gross.

Not at all.

What it is is arousing. Oh my God, it's arousing.

I don't think I've felt this way before.

This... hot and squirmy. And aroused.

Well, except for that one kiss we'd shared. Which I'm not going to think about.

I don't want to think about that kiss.

Still snorting my smell, he says, "No, I've got an Echo fetish."

My breath hitches. "Reign, I think we shouldn't talk about this. I-I have a boyfriend."

He opens his eyes. "*Ex*-boyfriend."

"Reign —"

"And while I'd fuck my fist, watching you smell your hair, *thinking* that I'm fucking your braid, I'd imagine that you were saving it for me."

My heart slams inside my chest, really, really loudly.

Or maybe it's his heart.

Thundering inside his chest and reverberating inside mine because we're basically one body right now.

"I wasn't," I tell him, quickly, urgently, fearfully, knowing *exactly* what he means.

"I'd imagine how it would feel to take what's mine."

"It's *not* yours."

It's not.

It's not.

It's *not*.

It never was. It never will be.

But the place between my thighs doesn't seem to care. The place between my thighs is buzzing. It's alive and pulsating. And I don't know how to make it stop.

And what he says next doesn't help either.

"You'd be tight, I knew that." Letting go of my braid then, he spans my torso, squeezing it as a whole, as if proving a point. "I *know* that."

My spine arches. "No, I'm —"

"Knowing my luck, you'd probably be sewn shut."

"That's —"

"Knowing my luck, Echo, you'd probably start crying at the first sight of my dick."

I scratch his neck. "I will not start crying."

"You're a crybaby," he tells me. "You'll cry."

"I *will not*."

"You'd probably start bawling at how big it is."

"It can't be that big."

"How thick and angry."

"Why would it be angry?"

He squeezes my ribs again, making me gasp as he says with clenched teeth, "Because of you. Because of how tight your pussy is. How tight and small, two sizes too small for my dick. And how it wants to get in. It wants to fucking pound its way into your tight pussy hole but can't. It has to be patient."

I'm squirming something fierce now.

At his generous use of the p-word.

Somehow, I still am able to say, all primly, "Patience is a v-virtue."

He barks out a chuckle, this one humorless. "Yeah, doesn't feel like one though." Then, another squeeze of my body. "But I'll try, Echo. For you. You know why?"

"Why?"

"Because if I don't, I'll make you bleed." Then, "Well, you'll bleed anyway but still."

"You don't... You don't know that."

"I do. I do know, Echo. Knowing my godforsaken luck, you'll cry *and* you'll bleed." Then, "Because of me."

And God, he looks so regretful at that.

So torn with remorse that I want to tell him that it's okay.

It's fine.

So I'll cry and I'll bleed, so what? It happens to almost every girl when it's her first time. I've read enough books to know that. I've heard enough stories.

"It's okay," I say, still grasping his neck, his pulse pounding beneath my hands. "A lot of girls bleed and —"

"No, it's not," he says, his jaw ticking. "It's not okay but I will make it so. I will make it okay, baby."

I suck my belly in, trembling again.

This time harder than all the other times before because of his endearment.

"How?"

He brings his hands up then, cupping my cheeks.

So softly, so tenderly.

That I want to weep.

"First, I'll clean you up," he says, his thumb rubbing over the apple of my cheek. "With the softest of cloths. Made of silk or fur or something. I'll find one. And then I'll run you a bath. With bath oils and whatever the fuck girls like. And if that doesn't work, I'll ice your pussy, baby. I'll ice it and then I'll lick it. I'll suck it into my mouth to make the sting go away."

"Reign, please…"

"And if nothing works at all," he continues, pressing his fingers into my face, "I'll fucking drink it down."

"What?"

He brings his lips super close to mine.

Super duper close.

As close as you can get without touching and I hate that.

I want to touch.

I want him to touch my mouth with his.

But all he does is whisper, "I'll drink it all down. Your tears, your virgin blood, your pussy juice. I'll fucking bathe in it, whatever you give me, you understand?"

My mouth falls open at what he's saying.

And I swear, I *swear*, I taste his blood on my tongue.

As if in solidarity.

"I'll do anything. If you were mine, I'd do *any-fucking-thing* to make it all better. If you let me put it in, I'll do anything to make it all okay."

The guttural need slashing his face takes my breath away.

It makes me grab onto his wrist and whisper, "Will you…"

He goes all alert when I chicken out from actually saying the words. "Will I what?"

I swallow, dig my nails into his wrist, blush something crazy.

He notices it, the flush on my cheeks, and his eyes go all… liquid again.

All shiny and tender.

And he whispers, "What is it, baby?"

God, what is he *doing*?

I'm not his baby. I'm not his anything.

I'm not…

And yet, I ask, "Will you wear a condom?"

I don't know why I asked that. Why it entered my brain.

But it did.

As if all of this is actually happening. As if this is real.

It isn't.

It's all make-believe. It's all his imagination.

He swallows. "You want that? You want me to wear a rubber."

"Yes." I nod, my heart pounding inside my chest. "You have to. I'm not... I'm not on the pill and..."

"And what?"

"Y-you've been with... other girls."

There it is. That's why.

That is why it entered my brain.

Because of other girls. Because of his... escapades, as he put it.

And God, I'm jealous.

I'm so so jealous.

I'm burning with jealousy. Like I was that night.

When he talked about those St. Mary's girls, even though that was all make-believe too.

Staring into my eyes with his penetrating gaze, he says, "I'm clean. We get tested. For the team."

"Okay."

"And I haven't..."

"Haven't what?"

"I haven't been with anyone in a long time."

My heart starts to race because somehow I know how long. But I still ask, "How long?"

He stares into my eyes. "Two years, two months and twenty-five days. Well, kinda even longer than that but yeah."

Oh God.

He hasn't... not since the kiss. Not since he kissed me and...

"And before that I've never, *not ever*, done it bareback, Echo. I've never fucked a girl skin to skin. Never wanted to. Not only because it's fucking stupid to do that but also..."

"Also what?"

He goes silent then. So very silent. And a light frown emerges between his brows as if thinking. Then, "I guess, I... Whenever I imagined all the things that I imagined about you, I'd imagine being skin to skin. No barriers. Nothing between us. Not one thing. Not even a thin piece of latex. And even though I knew that I'd never get to be with you, I still held out a stupid fucking hope. I still thought... what if? And so I... I guess I was preparing myself. I was saving that for you." He scoffs softly then, lost in thought. "Not that it's an achievement or something, *saving* that. But yeah, I did. Like you were saving it for me."

"I wasn't," I whisper softly, without any inflection or force.

"Real smart though, Echo," he says, ignoring me again. "That you asked that. Real fucking smart. Because you can trust me to never ever hurt you that way, but you can't trust me with the other thing."

"What other thing?"

His eyes turn possessive then. So, so possessive as he says, "The pill thing."

"What?"

"Years, I watched you with him," he says, his features so raw and sharp. "Years, I watched you be his. *Years*, Echo. You didn't think that if I got you, if I got anywhere near those creamy as fuck thighs, I wouldn't send you back to him with your tight little pink pussy full of my cum, did you?"

A breath gushes out of me then.

My stomach hollows out.

And my pussy pulses even harder.

"You wouldn't. You..."

"Yeah," he whispers, his fingers holding me all possessively, like a predator clutching its prey. "I would. I fucking would. I'd stuff you full of my cum and send you back to him, with me dripping down your milky thighs. I'd fucking send you back with my cream pie in your pussy, Echo. I'd even come all over your tight little tummy and your juicy tits, hose down all your good and ripe parts with my cum and then rub it all in, just so you smell like me when you go to your *ex-fucking-boyfriend*. And if you aren't on the pill, then..." He shrugs. "That's the best goodbye gift ever, isn't it? His girlfriend carrying a little secret in her belly. His best friend's baby."

It takes me a few seconds to gather my strength.

To gather my scattered, fuzzy thoughts enough to say, "No, you wouldn't do that."

He chuckles again.

But this isn't dirty. This is mean. This is mocking.

Much like his words. "Wouldn't I?"

"No, you wouldn't," I tell him firmly, looking into his eyes. "You'd never do that. You're not like that. I know you want me to think that. But you're not. You're trying to scare me. You're trying to stop me from going to Lucas, from telling him about —"

"Well, I already did."

"What?"

His jaw clenches then.

The bruises pulse on his face. And they pulse so violently that any illusion I had of him appearing fragile because of them dissolves.

"You're so worried about him forgiving me when he's ready to forgive you, aren't you?" he begins, his hands still framing my face but that tenderness and warmth is missing. "Well, he's ready to forgive you and not me because he knows."

"Knows what?"

"About my obsession with his girlfriend."

My mouth parts.

That's the only reaction I can give him right now.

To the information that feels the most shocking.

That Lucas *knows*.

"He knows that I want what belongs to him. He knows that I want *you* and that's why he doesn't want you anywhere near me." Then, "But imagine what would happen if I told him that his girlfriend wants me back."

"I —"

"I read your diary."

I thought I knew what it meant to feel afraid. You'd go all tight and rigid.

But I didn't know that sometimes you go all limp too. I didn't know that your body could go all weak, as if sinking. And it's happening to me right now.

My hands fall away from his wrist and the frown between my brows slackens.

"That night. When I was up in your bedroom, I read your diary. I read all the things that you'd written. About that night. About that kiss. About how you still dream about it. How randomly, out of the blue, you taste me. On your tongue."

I'm barely breathing now.

Barely.

As he continues, "Watermelons, yeah?"

I jerk then.

He makes me.

As if he knew I was near death and so he's injecting me with life.

He's injecting me with hate.

"Gotta say though, you're one fantastic writer, Echo. You were born to write. Too bad your diary is full of your ex-boyfriend's best friend. Well, ex-best friend. But you get the picture, don't you?"

My throat is all dried up.

All scratchy and raw.

"You..."

"You could go ahead and tell him who made the first move, if you like. To be a good girl. To fix things. And maybe you will. Maybe everything will be fine. But then I don't know how you will fix the things that break if I tell him what *I* know. What I have is much more damaging, isn't it? He may be able to forgive you for kissing his then-best friend, but I highly doubt he'd be so generous about you... *waxing* poetic about that kiss in your diary for years."

"Why are you..." I blink, my head shaking, "Why are you doing this?"

His breath is sharp and his fingers are still cradling my face. "Because you keep forgetting I'm an asshole. You keep forgetting that you hate me. That I make you hatesick. I told you we can't be friends, remember? Years ago. This is why. Because I'm a selfish motherfucking asshole and just so you don't forget in the future and annoy the living shit out of me, I'm going to give you an ultimatum too. The kind that you will remember for the rest of your life."

"W-what?"

"If you want me to keep your secret, then I want what I'm owed."

"What does... What does that mean?"

"It means," his mouth curls up in a cold smirk. "That I want my payment."

"What?"

"I know you think I'm some kind of a good guy. That I helped you or saved you or whatever the fuck you're thinking, out of the goodness of my heart, but," he says, still tenderly cradling my cheeks and staring down at me, "I don't have much of a heart, remember? I'm heartless. So I want something in return. I want the thing that you haven't given to anyone else. Not even him. The guy you love. Your ex-fucking-boyfriend. Because you're saving it for me."

I know what he's saying.

I *know*.

But I still can't make sense of it. I still can't make sense of what he's doing.

"You give me that tight little cherry that you're so dearly holding on to, and I'll keep your secret. I'll let you *keep* what you think I gave you, your ex-boyfriend."

CHAPTER TWENTY-SEVEN

The Bandit

I didn't mean to read her diary. That's the first thing.

I, for one, know how private it is. How intimate.

All I wanted to do was touch it.

Touch the one thing that has connected us since the beginning.

Or rather *had* connected us, since I don't allow myself to write anymore.

And then touching led to opening. That led to flipping through the yellow pages. But even then I had no intention of reading any of her words.

Until I accidentally flipped open an old entry and stumbled upon 'watermelon.'

I don't know why that fascinated me so much, that word. That word written in the same sentence as 'kiss.'

Look, I have wondered about that kiss. About why she would do it when she hated me. And the only logical explanation is that she was distraught after what had happened that night. After the whole proposal disaster. And since she had a crush on me way back when, she took solace in my arms.

Another thing: Yes, I know about her crush. When we had first met. Why else would I have had to push her toward Lucas? I knew she had a thing for me — misguidedly — so I crushed it.

That she still thinks about that kiss though was a revelation. But then as I said to Lucas the other night, it doesn't mean anything. A two-minute kiss doesn't negate her love for Lucas.

But anyway, when I did read that word in her diary, there was no stopping me. I read that line and then another, and another and the next thing I knew I'd read the whole paragraph.

But then my self-disgust became too much for me to go on and so I shut it and put it back in its place.

Despite all that though, despite my horrendous invasion of privacy, I had no intention of ever bringing it up.

Ever *using* it against her.

But I had to.

That's the second thing. That I *had* to.

I didn't want to blackmail her but she left me no choice.

I did have a feeling that she'd pull something like this. That she might object to Lucas's so-called ultimatum. It's the good girl in her. Wanting to save everyone, fix everything. So I figured I'd block her number and help out my dead best friend one last time. I figured if I ignored her for a few days, she'd give up and be with who she's supposed to be with.

But of course not. She had to come find me.

She had to fucking *stalk me*.

And so I had to improvise.

I had to fucking scare her somehow. Scare her away for good.

Scare her back to the fucking love of her life.

"You still alive?"

My brother's voice wakes me up.

Because of course that's what I need right now. The third degree from my noble big brother.

I eye him across the conference room table. "Unfortunately."

Always put together and polished, he eyes me back, his face a mask of disapproval. "There are better ways to kill yourself."

I lick my split lip, loving the sting. "What can I say, I like to torture myself."

"Is that what you do? At that gym of yours."

I stare at him for a few beats before saying, "For the millionth time, it's a boxing gym. I'd love to tell you that we sit around and braid each other's hair and talk about our next knitting project. But that would be a lie and I'm not a liar. Goes against my principles."

I shoot him a mock smile.

My big brother stares at me flatly. "Apart from the fact that it makes a very bad impression on our partners, sitting across from a street thug while discussing land permits and other hotel-related needs, I'd like to remind you that I have a black belt in karate. I've also been trained in jujitsu and mixed martial arts and I never looked like that."

I throw him a shrug. "Don't know if you've heard, but word around the water cooler is that I'm a fuck-up." I point at my bruised face. "That's where that comes from."

Homer clenches his jaw in further disapproval. "I can very easily find out what's going on at that gym. You're aware of that, aren't you? I'm giving you a chance to come clean."

"About what?"

"If you're mixed up in something bad." He looks over my face again. "Something dangerous."

"And if I am?"

He breathes out sharply. "Then I put a stop to it."

The only bad thing that's going on is that I'm throwing fights, and I'm fucking good at it. Despite that though, I messed up on my last, pissing a lot of people off. Including my boss, Ark Reinhardt. Since this was my first offense, my only punishment was a clipped one-sentence warning and two more fights on my schedule this week. To make up for the lost money.

Ark is very good at taking care of his fighters and keeping his business legit and on the up side. Meaning even if my brother sets his cronies on him, they probably won't be able to find much.

But I don't want him to.

I don't want him to interfere in my business, or to look like that.

Like he's doing me some kind of favor. Like he's swooping down to be my hero.

I don't need any fucking heroes.

I became my own hero and everyone's villain a very long time ago.

"Why, so you can appease your guilt? For not coming to my rescue when I really needed you." I clench my teeth. "I didn't. And I don't now. I'm not your charity project. You wanna get one, you go to the shelter and adopt a fucking puppy, all right?"

I know I've pissed him off.

But even his anger is all polished and controlled, with hardly a flicker on his carefully blank face. Then, throwing me a curt nod, "As you wish. But I want you to know that I'm here, if you need me."

"I won't," I tell him. "And ditto. On better ways to kill yourself."

"Excuse me?"

In response, I tip my chin to the files spread out on the table.

It's fucking seven o'clock and we're still at the office, prepping for a meeting tomorrow. Apparently it's for some big project in Indonesia, because why shouldn't we have a hotel halfway across the world and why shouldn't my brother bring me in on a project like that in order to 'train me.'

A project that's slowly killing me.

It's only been a couple of weeks since I started working here and I have to admit, I don't know how my brother and all these people who work here nine to five haven't killed themselves out of sheer boredom. Or the fact they all have to wear a fucking tie.

Not me though. I'm very firm about that.

But to each their own.

Homer sighs and shuts the file in front of him. "I guess we could call it a night."

I shut the file too, springing up to my feet. "Yeah, you guess fucking right."

I'm fucking starving.

I need a cheeseburger — no, two cheeseburgers — and a large order of fries. And then I'm gonna soak myself in an ice-cold bath so I can at least stand up for my fight later tonight. Best thing about throwing fights, I don't have to do much. But I do like to put in some effort.

I'm almost out the door when my brother stops me. "Are you free next Saturday?"

I turn. "Are you asking me out on a date again?"

He sighs sharply.

This isn't the first time he's asked me to go do something with him. We've been working late most nights and he's always ready with his dinner invitations and whatnot. And again, it pisses me the fuck off that he's trying so hard.

Trying to be my fucking friend when I've told him a thousand times that he doesn't need to be.

"I'd like to invite you to play soccer with me," he says then.

"What?"

"We have a little club," he says, clearing his throat as if bashful. "Just some old school friends and teammates. We play two weekends a month and," he clears his throat again, "everybody would love to meet you."

I know about his little soccer club.

They meet up at the Bardstown country club twice a month to throw the ball around recreationally. My brother was the one who started it, probably back when I was a freshman in high school.

And the only reason I know about it is because I remember feeling... jealous.

Of the fact that my brother would go play with his school friends rather than with me.

I know. I *know*, stupid.

My brother and I couldn't — *can't* — stand each other, let alone play soccer together.

And then there's the little fact that I don't even like soccer.

But I felt what I felt, and his invitation takes me back to when I was fourteen years old and irrationally wanted my big brother to invite me.

Shoving my hands down into my pockets, I ask tightly, "And why would they love to meet me?"

He does the same thing with his hands and I wonder if that's where I get it from, this habit. If so, I'd very much like to break it but as it is, my hands are fisted and I don't wanna show how this conversation is affecting me.

"They know how good of a soccer player you are," he says. "And they'd love to play with you."

"And how do they know about my soccer playing skills?"

"I might've mentioned something."

"And how would *you* know anything about what kind of a player I am?"

He stares at me a beat before shifting on his feet and sighing. "I've seen you play. Only on video, unfortunately, but it's very apparent that you're good. You're very good, Reign. You have a natural talent. A natural grace and athleticism. People can't be taught that, what you have."

My fists tighten. "I'm touched but —"

"I know I've never said this and I probably should have, but," he cuts me off and stares at me all gravely, "you're a much better player than I ever was. And I know that you'll do great things with it when you get picked next year and —"

I bark out a laugh, cutting *him* off this time.

Cutting off whatever the fuck he's trying to do.

"What is this, how to be a big brother in ten days?" I scoff. "Not sure if there are any more ways to say it, but I don't need a big brother. Okay, *big brother*? I don't need you to compliment me on my soccer skills or fucking watch me play. Or tell me how bright my future is. Especially when the only reason I even started playing was because I was forced to. And I was forced to play because of you. That it turned out to be my ticket out of here is fate's cruel irony. But if you think I wanna 'get picked' or go pro or whatever, then you're not as smart as our wonderfully dead father had thought."

He frowns then.

Probably a first outward reaction from him. "I have to say... I'm slightly confused. I thought you were entering the drafts."

"Not sure why you would think that, but no. I'm not." Then, "I don't like soccer. In fact I hate soccer. And I have no intention of playing it beyond college."

"Reign, I'm sure you don't mean that," my brother says. "I wasn't lying when I said you're a natural at this. You can't let your talent go to waste. It's wrong. You —"

"I can, actually," I quip. "See, I don't care about doing the right thing. Which means I'm not going to play the game that you love for the rest of my life just because I'm good at it."

"Reign —"

"Okay, this is starting to piss me off, all right?"

He shuts his mouth thankfully, even though his eyes scream anger.

Whatever.

It's not my job to make him feel better.

"This isn't what I agreed to. You do what I asked you to do and in exchange, I work with you at the office. You don't need to invite me to your exclusive soccer club or advise me on what to do with my future. We don't need to *bond* or have a heart-to-heart. We never did before and we're not going to start now. So," I sigh, "I decline your invitation. And next time you wanna invite someone on a date, how about your fiancée? She'd be thrilled to go with you."

That makes him even more pissed off and I'm happy.

At least now he's at my level.

With that, I turn around and leave the conference room.

Fucking asshole.

I thought Homer was like my father but I was wrong. He's worse.

At least with my father, I always knew where I stood. I always knew what I was meant to feel. Hate him as much as he hated me because he was a monster through and through.

My big brother, however, is a different kind of devil.

He wants to be my friend. He wants to mend fences. He wants to be my fucking brother.

Jesus fucking Christ.

Please spare me from all the good fucking people and their good *fucking* intentions.

I have no interest in being saved or being the kind of brother Homer wants. I wouldn't even know where to begin to let go of my anger and stop hating him.

I was always going to leave once I finished it.

The task of getting her back together with him.

And now that my brother has delivered on his promise — he texted me this morning to let me know that it was done — there's not even that holding me here. I wanted to give him the courtesy of staying until we wrapped up this project in a few weeks. But if he's going to insist on killing me with kindness, maybe I should leave him high and dry.

It'll serve him right.

It will fucking serve her right too.

CHAPTER TWENTY-EIGHT

Who: The Bubblegum
Where: Dorm room at St. Mary's School for Troubled Teenagers
When: 11:23 PM; one day after Reign confesses his crush on Echo

Dear Bandit,
For years, I wondered.
I wondered why you gave me that anklet.
I know now.
For years, I also wondered why I didn't throw it away. Why I kept it in my nightstand. Why every time I opened it, I'd strain to hear the tiny chime of the bells on it.
Now I think I know that as well.
~Echo

CHAPTER TWENTY-NINE

I'm officially a high school graduate.

For a week now, actually.

I never thought that something that was always so sure in my life, graduating high school, would become a thing to hang in the balance, but it did. And now I'm just glad that it's over. That I'm out of that school with barred windows and tall brick walls.

Plus we got to have a last blast, a graduation party that all the girls at St. Mary's, including me, organized. It was fun despite the minor hiccups, which have to do with Poe and how she went missing from the party for a few hours. But long story short, everything is fine now and I'm going to miss my friends badly.

It's a good thing that we all live so close by though. In the week since finals and moving out of the dorm and back into our parents' houses, we've already met up as a group once. We went to this amazing carnival over the weekend, all the girls and their respective boyfriends and husbands, and it was super fun.

Okay, I'm lying.

It wasn't a fun weekend.

I mean, it was good to see all my friends and hang out with their partners, but I don't think I had as much fun as everyone else. I also don't think I'm as glad as everyone else about graduating and moving on with my life.

Because I only recently realized that I haven't moved on.

I'm still stuck.

In the same place that I was two years ago.

I'm still stuck on the night I turned sixteen.

So it's only fair that tonight, in an attempt to move on, I wear the dress I wore that night.

A pink summer dress with a sweetheart neckline and ribbony strips that I've tied on my shoulders in a butterfly knot. I also do my hair the same way, in a loose braid, and tie that with a pink hair tie. I do my nails, also pink, and wear pink sandals.

The only thing I change from that night is putting on pink lipstick, since I wasn't into makeup and all back then.

Lastly, I tell my parents that I'm going to my friend Jupiter's house for a sleepover. Since they don't like any of my St. Mary's friends, they aren't very happy about it. They didn't even like me going to the carnival. But since we're coming off of me finally graduating, they're at least allowing me to see my friends.

But of course, I'm not going to her house.

Well, not right away at least.

And I do feel bad about lying to them but I have to do this.

I have to go to the place first where I'll get to move on. And that's where Jupiter takes me when she comes to pick me up at my house.

"You sure you wanna do this?" she asks me as I get ready to get out of her car.

The interior of the car is dark but I can still make out the concern on her face. "Yes, I'm sure."

"I feel like this has disaster written all over it."

"Yeah," I agree with her. "But this is the only way."

"Is it though?" She frowns. "Because you don't have to do anything. You could just... forget about it."

"I could," I agree again, clutching my overnight bag. "But clearly I have a very good memory. And if I try to forget about it again, I might end up doing something even more disastrous than what I did last time."

She grimaces. "Okay. Call me when you're done."

My heart skips a beat at 'done.'

Which is crazy because that's all I've thought about.

Being *done*.

Getting it over with.

Moving on.

"Yeah, I will," I say, smiling slightly. "Thanks."

I'm ready to get out again when she blurts out, "I feel like as your best friend, I should give you some pointers."

I shoot her a look. "You can't."

"I could try. I could —"

"Have you done it before?"

She purses her lips. "No." I raise my eyebrows at her and she grumbles, "But I've seen it before. I've read about it. I know the theory of it."

"So do I. But unfortunately, this isn't a group discussion. We won't be talking about it. We'd be doing it."

Another shiver runs down the length of my body at 'doing it.'

"Fine. Whatever. Just thought I could help."

Feeling bad now, I reach out to hug her. "You are." I squeeze her frame tightly. "Just come get me when I text you and we'll spend the entire rest of the night watching movies."

And hopefully, I will feel like a new person.

A *moved on* person.

She squeezes me back. "Okay. Good luck."

Finally, I get out of the car and let out a shaky breath, reading a neon sign: Bardstown Motel.

It's a typical L-shaped motel with a black metal railing and rooms facing the parking lot, and the highway beyond. I make my way through parked trucks and cars, looking for the room number that I want. From both Poe and Callie, I know that the reason for which — whom — I came here is staying in room eleven and is in for the night. Poe asked Callie, and Callie asked Reed, who asked Ledger. I could potentially have asked Ledger myself; I even got his phone number from Callie. But I didn't want to seem too stalker-ish and so I went the more respectful route.

And here I am.

Before I lose my courage, I raise my hand and knock at the gray door.

It's probably me and my jangled nerves but I think my knock kinda reverberated through the entire parking lot.

It's okay though. It's fine.

But then I hear footsteps drawing close.

And I swear they reverberate through the whole parking lot as well.

And pulse in my body, low in my belly, making me press a palm on it.

Finally comes the click of the door, which I think goes even beyond the parking lot and my body and reaches the whole town. Making me think that the whole of Bardstown knows that I'm here.

Standing in front of him.

My ex-boyfriend's ex-best friend, wearing his favorite color.

And I know it's his favorite color now.

I *know*.

I also know that he's shocked to see me.

He's frowning and his lips are slightly parted.

And probably adding to his surprise is me, saying, "Hi."

He doesn't say anything.

Which is just as well. I don't want to stand out here and have a conversation with him where I feel so exposed so I add, "Can I come in?"

His frown only grows. "What —"

I don't give him time to respond and simply bulldoze my way in. And the fact that he's shocked works in my favor because he steps back and lets me.

His room is what I'd imagine a typical motel room to look like. Gray walls, gray sheets on a queen-sized bed and gray drapes on the windows. A dresser on one side of the bed, and a couple of chairs on the other. Plus a closet and a door left ajar, leading to the bathroom.

Back when he used to live at the manor, I never went into his bedroom. Except for when I went to his bedroom to vandalize it. And even though his room was right across from mine, and our windows looked into each other's spaces, I always made sure to never ever look.

And now that I know *why* I never looked, I look at everything in here.

I notice that he has his clothes draped over the chairs, and his shoes strewn about right next to them. There are a few boxes of pizza on the table, along with a few soda cans. A duffel bag right next to the closet, and his keys and a black leather wallet on the dresser.

He's sort of like me in the mess department.

Not really surprising given we have other things in common as well.

"What the fuck —"

I spin around at his voice. "Are these your office clothes?"

He snaps his mouth shut and I'm not going to lie, I'm loving that.

He loves interrupting me, doesn't he? So now it's his turn.

Although I *am* curious to know as well.

In all the time I've known him, I don't think I've ever seen him with a button-down shirt. He usually wears a t-shirt or a soccer jersey or one of those loose workout vests. The latter ones I've always hated the most because they're very sexy, exposing his bulging biceps and sleek and cut obliques. But now that I'm seeing him in a dress shirt, I have to say that maybe a shirt is what I hate the most.

Because the way the cotton fabric clings to his broad shoulders and his chest is beyond sexy.

It's criminal.

His top few buttons are open, exposing a large patch of his clavicles and that sculpted chest, and his sleeves are folded up to his elbows, showing off his corded forearms. Not to mention, the light color highlights how summery his skin is.

How even though he's wearing something as civilized and respectable as a dress shirt, he's anything but.

But then again, no one could ever mistake him for a young boardroom mogul.

Not with his face still black and blue.

He's actually gotten a few new bruises as well; we're gonna talk about that in a second.

When I'm done looking him over, I go back to his face.

And yup, he's still frowning.

Although his confusion has cleared and it looks like he's waiting for my cues — *good* — with his hands shoved down in his pockets and his reddish-brown eyes pinned on me.

I raise my eyebrows. "Well? Are they? Because that's all anyone can talk about at the manor. You working with your brother."

It's true.

It's a very hot topic these days.

Something moves across his features then. "You graduated."

And I realize that that something is admiration. Happiness even.

On my behalf.

The fact that I didn't even have to remind him about my finals and that he deduced it from my offhand comment about the manor, makes me want to smack him.

For what he did two weeks ago.

For how cruel he was when we always seem to be so in tune with each other.

As it is, all I do is lift my chin and say, "Yes, I did."

His lips curl up into a small smile. "You're free."

I shake my head. "Not yet."

That's why I'm here, aren't I?

To be set free.

His frown is back. This one's even more ferocious than the last one. "What does that —"

"Where's your tie though?" I cut him off again.

He exhales an annoyed breath, his chest undulating in his shirt.

It's hard for him.

Having me run the conversation.

Tough luck though. This is my show tonight and he doesn't have a choice.

"Don't like 'em," he replies, his reddish-brown eyes displeased and pinned on me.

"Right. Because you like to make your own rules."

"I also like it when people call before coming over."

"You blocked my number, remember?"

"And yet you don't seem to get the hint."

I drop my overnight bag on the floor. "Which is why I've decided to move in. I figured you wouldn't be able to avoid me if we lived together."

His eyes fly down to the little pink bag on the floor — I specifically chose the girliest little bag in my closet — before flying back up to my face.

And oh my God, his expression is priceless.

Even more priceless is his shocked, "The fuck?"

I wasn't going to laugh but at the speed he went all pale, I allow myself a small smile. "I'm not here to cramp your style. So relax, would you, Bossman?"

His eyes flash and that arrogant expression is back on his face.

Pair that with his office clothes, and I realize that he looks every inch the Bossman tonight, albeit with criminal tendencies.

The second son of the Davidsons, wealthy and coming from old money.

But that's not true, is it?

Thanks to his asshole dad.

"So then why are you here," his lips turn up in a small, mocking smile, "*Servant Girl*?"

His low tone hits me in my belly and knocks the breath out of me for a second but I forge ahead. "I want to know if this is how you did it."

"Did what?"

"Got me into NYU."

Oh yeah, did I mention, I got into NYU.

My dream school.

That I thought was out of my reach potentially forever.

Not only because I couldn't graduate on time but also because there was no way that I could afford it without a scholarship. But turns out, I not only got in — thanks to the generosity of one Homer Davidson, who convinced my parents to apply on my behalf *and* got me accepted even though it was too late to even apply — but now I don't even need a scholarship to go. Because recently, we came into a lot of money.

Again courtesy of Homer Davidson.

He said that it was a reward for my parents' hard work and a graduation present for me. He said that my future shouldn't have to suffer for one mistake that I made two years ago. That he had full faith that I'd learned my lesson and that I'd go on to do great things.

Which means I leave for NYU in four weeks.

Or so my parents think.

Reign's face has gone completely blank. "Don't know what you're talking about."

"You do," I tell him, looking into his eyes. "You know all about what I'm talking about. You're the only one who knew about my NYU plans and the only one who had the means to do anything about it. Oh, and let's not forget about your legendary guilt. About everything. Because apparently, the whole world revolves around you *and* sits on your shoulders. Despite me very recently telling you differently."

"I —"

"You put all of that together," I raise my chin, interrupting him yet again and oh my God, it's the best feeling in the world. "And add it to the fact that everyone knows how much you hated your father and his company — for good reason — but you're working there anyway, makes me think that there's a connection between the two. So we can argue about it all night if you want, or you could just tell me the truth."

I know I'm not wrong.

I *know* there's a connection.

Just like there was a connection between me vandalizing his room and him getting disowned.

I hear his long breath all the way over here, across the room where I'm standing. Then, "Fine. You cracked the code. Congratulations."

Shit.

I was afraid of that.

"And he..." I suppress the rousing dread, "asked you to work with him?"

He gives me a curt nod. "For a year."

"What?"

This is not good.

This is a freaking disaster.

I don't want him to work in a place where he doesn't want to. Now that I know the truth about his dad, who knows how his brother is. Who knows what kind of a man he's grown up to be and if Reign is safe with him. I mean, I know he's physically safe but what about emotionally and...

"My brother's okay," he says, breaking into my thoughts.

It doesn't escape my notice that yet again, we're so in tune that he knows what I'm thinking. And yes, it does make me want to punch him again. But I have other problems that need my attention more.

"Y-you sure?"

Sighing, he nods. "He's not like... him. Not in the ways that you're thinking. He's annoying though, but not..."

"Evil?"

"No."

"You promise?"

His jaw clenches.

I know if he promises that what he's telling me is true, I can trust it.

Because a promise is an oath.

And it's very tied up in our history.

A lot of things are tied up in our history but let's focus on this first.

Nodding curtly again, he says, "Yeah. So relax, would you, Servant Girl?"

My relief is so great that I don't even care that he threw my own words back at me. "So you're going to work with him for a whole year then?"

"No."

And just like that I feel bad for his brother. Because now that Reign's gotten what he wants, he's going to go back on the deal, isn't he?

I shake my head at him. "I thought you didn't break promises."

He stares at me a beat before saying, "Only the ones I make to you."

I give myself a second to let the tidal wave of emotion sweep through me. Sweep through every part of my body, leaving goosebumps and broken breaths in its wake.

Then, "I want you to take your money back."

"What?"

A deep breath. "I don't want your money. So please ask your brother to take it back."

I know it's been hard for him to go at my pace in this conversation.

But now it's *really* hard.

Now it's costing him with the way his bruises have come alive and his jaw is ticking. "No."

"It's very generous but I don't think it's appropriate," I tell him.

"It's not my problem what you think."

"I don't think," I take a deep breath, "my boyfriend would like it very much if another guy paid for my education."

Low blow; I'm aware of that.

But in his words, not my problem.

Not my problem that he flinches. And that his eyes grow both harsh and slightly agonized at my comment.

Not your problem, Echo.

Not after what he did.

"Well," he mashes his teeth, "your *boyfriend* is just gonna have to live with the fact that my dick's bigger than his. Always has been. Since I was the one who's always been paying for your fucking education. I'm the one who has paid for the roof over your head, the clothes on your body and the food in your belly. Or my family has. Same difference. He's lived with you being my Servant Girl for years now, he can survive a little longer."

God, he makes me so mad.

He makes me *crazy*.

This is exactly what he'd said the night he came to my room through my window. The night of my sixteenth birthday, where I'm still stuck. Back then I thought it was his usual arrogance but now I know different.

Now I know it was his... obsession.

"You can use that money, Reign," I tell him. "It's your money. It's rightfully yours. Please take it back so you don't have to almost kill yourself in the ring every other week."

If anything, my insistence has made him even angrier. Not that I expected anything less from him, but still. And I really don't want to take the next step but I will, if he makes me.

Which he does.

"You really think that's gonna make me stop? Taking the money back."

I sigh because it isn't.

Money isn't really the motivating factor here.

I wish it was. And that's why I had to try that first.

"Is that why you came here?" he asks then, shifting on his feet. "Because after what happened last time, pissing me off isn't really a smart choice."

"Why, because you know my secret and you could ruin me?"

"Very easily."

"Fine." I shift on my feet too. "You leave me no choice then. If you don't quit, I'm going to tell everyone."

"Tell everyone what?"

"About your fights. About how some of them are fixed. Because you're not the only one who knows things, are you?"

He remains silent. But his eyes promise mayhem.

Not that I care.

"I'm not kidding. And I think you know that."

Which is why a vein emerges and beats on his temple.

Then sighing, I say, "I can't watch what you're doing to yourself. I can't stand it. And I won't. I will absolutely not stand for it. Now I've tried explaining it to you multiple times that you need to stop punishing yourself, but you don't listen to me. So this is how things are going to go down: you're going to stop or I will tell everyone *everything*. I will tell on you and then I will go all hysterical and dramatic on your ass. And you know that I can do it. You know I'm very much capable of that. So you're going to stop. I don't care how. I don't even care if you want to or not. All I care about is that you —"

"Okay."

"What?"

"Okay," he repeats, his eyes and features grave. "I'll stop."

I frown suspiciously. "You will?"

"Yeah."

"Just like that?"

"Just like that."

My suspicion still isn't gone. "And you promise?"

He lets a second pass by and then he nods. "I promise."

Oh, thank God.

Thank fucking God.

"Thank you," I say then. "For both. For promising to stop and... for NYU."

For a few seconds all he does is stare at me. Then, shrugging tightly, "It was nothing."

He's wrong. It was everything.

Like so many other things that he's done.

This bruised and battered guy. Who does the tenderest of things in the cruelest of ways.

My Bandit.

"I have questions," I say, moving on to the next thing on my agenda.

The other important reason why I came here tonight.

With an overnight bag.

He senses the shift in our conversation, quite possibly the shift that will finally reveal the reason to him as to why I came. And he goes even more alert than before as he asks, "About?"

"How much," I swallow, fisting my hands, "did you read?"

Of my diary.

No matter his answer, it's not going to change that he read it. That he violated my privacy in such a gross fashion. He violated my trust. He *violated*.

Transgressed, overstepped, contravened.

But still, I'd like to know.

I'd like to know how much of my heart, my very soul, did he get to look at.

And I'm thankful when swallowing thickly, he gives me a straight answer. "A paragraph."

That doesn't tell me anything.

My paragraphs can go from one line to the whole page. I'm chaotic that way. And again, one word is one too many, but still I have to know. I have to know exactly how much, how many.

"How long was it, the paragraph?"

Another swallow. "Three lines."

"And that's it?"

"Yeah."

"Did you do it to... Did you do it for fun?"

"No."

"To hurt me then?"

"Fuck no."

"Then why?'

I spend the next few seconds in agonizing wait as he simply watches me. Then, "To feel..."

God.

"To feel *what*, Reign?"

Another swallow, as if his throat is rapidly going dry and scratchy. "To feel close to you."

Good thing there's a wall behind me, or is it the lone dresser in his room?

I can't tell.

All I know is that I'm very glad that I have something to lean on. Because my knees have gone weak. My knees are trembling. They're knocking against each other.

And I wish I could simply collapse.

I wish I could... touch him.

Gosh, I want to touch him. So, *so* badly.

And now that I know why it's very hard to stop myself.

But I feel like if I do, he might break. He's so tightly wound in this moment.

So tightly coiled, as though revealing this one vulnerable thing about himself might ruin him.

It might ruin me too.

So I wait and ask, "You know it was wrong, though, don't you?"

"Yeah."

"You hurt me. Even though you didn't want to."

"I know."

"You used it *against* me, Reign. You used my deepest, darkest thoughts against me."

His chest shudders with a breath. "I know and I..."

"You what?"

And then I do break him.

Without laying a single finger on him, I watch him crack.

I watch him shift on his feet.

I watch him yank his hands out of his pockets and rake his fingers through his spiky hair. He even tugs on a few strands as he replies, "And I regret it, all right? I fucking regret using it against you. I fucking regret ever touching your diary. Touching something..." His features ripple with disgust, self-recrimination as he takes a couple of steps toward me and then back. "I regret touching something so precious and pure. But I... Like an asshole, I couldn't stop myself and then you were... you wouldn't listen. You *wouldn't*..."

Finally, he sighs, his shoulders rolling up and down, and stares into my eyes, his own swimming with torment. "What I said that night was bullshit. That fucking ultimatum crap. I did it to scare you. I did it so you'd run and you'd run straight into his arms where you belong. But here you fucking are. *Again*. Here you are, being a good fucking girl, trying to save me. I don't need you to fucking save me, all right? What I need from you is to go. Go run off to your boyfriend and live your happily ever after. What I *need* from you, Echo, is to stop coming after me. With your big brown eyes and your goddamn pink dresses. I don't even know why you're wearing pink tonight or why your lips shine like that. Like, what is that shit? Why's your pouty mouth glittering like a fucking target, like something that I can't look away from. I don't know and I don't fucking care. All I care about is that you leave me the fuck alone. Because if you don't, I'm going to do worse things to you than just reading your fucking diary. Do you understand?"

I do.

I understand that he was trying to scare me that day. I mean, he's the guy who's kept my secrets, big and small, over the years. I always knew that he's never going to out me.

That's why I want to smack him and punch him for trying to push me away like that.

I also understand that he's in pain. That I'm making him hurt.

Probably like he hurt me when he read my diary. Probably more than even his bruises. Because I've seen him handle them well.

But this... *this*, he isn't handling well.

Me being here in my pink dress and my pink lipstick.

His ex-best friend's ex-girlfriend. That he's wanted for so long and hated himself for it.

So I finally tell him why I came here.

"I can't," I say, shaking my head. "Not yet."

"Why the fuck not?"

"Because you were right."

"What?"

"I do have a thing for you."

I thought that if I finally confessed that I have a crush on him, I would be struck down by lightning. Or at least the ground would open up and I'd fall into it.

Both very dramatic things but given the situation, quite ordinary.

Especially when I take into account that I've had this crush for six years now. As long as him.

That's what he told me, didn't he?

That he's had a thing for me since that first night.

Well, me too.

Only I'd blocked it out. I'd shoved it down so, so deep that I almost forgot about it.

But my heart didn't, did it?

That's why I kissed him.

That's why I made that first move.

"I've been thinking about it," I tell him. "Ever since the night of your fight. Ever since you told me about your... crush. It was like you flipped a switch or something and now I can't stop remembering. It's crazy, I know. It's crazy that I didn't remember something so *important*. But I guess I was just... so hurt. So deeply hurt, every time you'd be an asshole to me. Every time you'd do something mean, it'd sting so bad that I just pushed it deep, deep down inside of me."

While only moments ago he was all raw nerves and jagged emotions, he's completely still now.

Completely frozen.

As if my words have cast a spell on him.

"I forgot how crazy I was about you," I say, studying his beautiful face, his tall body and doing it without guilt for once. "I'd think about you constantly. After that first night, I mean. After how you lit up the whole sky, turning night into day. I thought that was the best birthday ever, meeting you in the woods. And stupid, dramatic girl that I was, I looked for you on my next birthday too. I'd found out that you were back and I went looking for you. But instead... I found the love of my life."

I take a pause here, gather my breaths, my thoughts, my fucking heart.

Because it's the truth.

It hurt me to think about the past and so every time I'd remember something, I'd push it down.

I tell myself to not go there.

I tell myself to look forward. To focus on the present.

To not *remember*.

And over time I got good at it, I guess. In forgetting.

"And you'd think that falling in love with your best friend would make my crush on you go away. Starting a relationship with him would stop it. But it didn't. I may have pushed it deep down inside of me and forgotten about it, but my heart didn't. My soul remembered. So yeah, kissing you wasn't a mistake. Well, not in the way that I've been assuming. It was my secret forbidden wish. But..." I sigh long and hard. "That doesn't change the fact that I still love Lucas."

Who is a better choice.

But is he?

I know Reign thinks that. I know Lucas loved me and he was a good boyfriend to me. I know my parents loved him as well.

I also know that if Reign hadn't pushed me toward him, I never would've gone for Lucas.

I *know* that now.

I was crazy about Reign. Crazy to the point of destruction. *Crazy* to the point where I would've stood up against the whole world for him. I would've stood up against my parents for him.

And he would've broken my heart anyway.

Because that's who he is, isn't he?

I've seen him. He goes from girl to girl just like that. And yes, he hasn't been with anyone in two years, that doesn't change the fact that he'll one day go back to being the playboy that he used to be.

And that's why Reign is the wrong choice for me.

I would've given him my heart and he would've broken it into a million pieces.

But that's not important.

What would have happened has nothing to do with what *did* happen.

I did fall in love with his best friend. I did choose him and now he's ready to forgive my betrayal.

He's ready to give me another chance.

And I've decided to take it.

"I've decided to cut ties with you," I tell Reign. "If that is what Lucas needs then I'm going to give it to him."

Finally I see a movement on his frame.

A pulse on his jaw. A flicker in his eyelid. His limp hands forming fists.

"But I need to move on first," I continue. "From you."

More pulses. More flickers.

His fists tightening even more.

"I need to go to Lucas with a pure heart. I can't... I can't go to him with you in my heart too. My crush should've ended but it didn't. And I feel so guilty about that. So guilty for wanting you. So guilty that we have this connection. This crazy... *chemistry*. We're so in tune with each other. We...

"I know you feel guilty too. For everything. Which means we both need to move on. We both need to clear our consciences. We both need to end it. I want you out of my system and I need to get out of yours. I can't live with this pain, this guilt, this crush that I have on you, and I'm not going to let you live with it either."

Exactly.

Ending this is the only way forward.

It's the only way he can be free. I could force him not to hurt himself. I could explain things to him, but nothing would cure his guilt except purging it out of his system.

And the same holds true for me as well.

I can't be a good girlfriend to Lucas — the kind he deserves; the kind who doesn't make him wait like I did — unless I purge his ex-best friend out of my system.

I open and close my fists and before I can lose my courage, I raise my very jittery hands and untie the ribbons that are holding my pink dress up. One flick of my hand each and my dress comes undone, falling with a soft rustle and a rush of air, pooling around my feet.

Leaving me all naked.

Then, I whisper, "I want you to take my virginity."

CHAPTER THIRTY

His eyes are wide. I've never seen them this wide before. I've also never seen them this dark.

This fraught with things.

So many things that I can't even begin to understand or untangle. I'm wondering though if one of those things could be something that should make me blush.

Because as it is, I'm not blushing.

No, wait. I am.

What I mean is that even though I *am* blushing, I have no desire to cover myself up. I have no desire to hide myself from those big reddish-brown eyes that look more red than brown, more blazing than perhaps the sleeping sun.

However, I will say that even though I'm not very sure of what he's thinking, I bet one of those things might be that I'm too dramatic. That my whole dress pooling at my feet routine was a little too movie-like.

Honestly, I don't think so.

I think it was perfect. To symbolize this moment.

This crazy, insane, *twisted* moment.

Of me giving it up to him.

That one thing that I've never wanted to give to anyone, not even the guy I love.

But I don't see any other way.

I don't see how we can ever move on from each other, if we don't do this. If we don't say goodbye to each other in this way. Last time our crush led to a kiss — only — but if we don't get rid of this infatuation, who knows what more we'd end up doing.

How much more guilt we'd have to face.

So yeah, we both need this.

Curling my bare toes into the scratchy gray carpet — I kicked off my sandals about a minute or two ago while he was staring at me like I'm from another planet — I say, "Reign?"

Nothing.

He's still staring at me, my face to be specific.

Not my naked body.

I swallow. "Say something."

He blinks.

At least he's alive.

I take a step toward him and he jolts. His hand thrusts out as he says, "Don't."

"Don't what?"

He backs up, his body crashing into the door. "Just... Just stay where you are."

"Why?"

"Because..."

"Because what?"

"Jesus. Fuck." Then, "*Because* I fucking said so."

There's nothing funny about this situation. Or at least, there shouldn't be.

I'm naked — *naked* — in front of a guy for the first time in my life, asking him to take my virginity. That's serious. But the way he looks so... scared makes me smile a little and take a step toward him. "You do know that you're not actually the boss of me, don't you? I mean, I was just kidding when I called you Bossman back there."

He presses himself even more against the door, his chest starting to heave. "And you do know..."

Again, he trails off and I prod, moving forward. "I know what?"

He clenches his eyes shut. He even presses a fist into them for a second as if he's so pained. "Can you fucking stop walking toward me? I can't *fucking* think right now."

I shouldn't take so much pleasure in his agitation. Or that he can't seem to throw his usual dry comebacks at me. But I do.

I'm taking all the pleasure that I can. For making him uncomfortable.

For being so wild for him.

He likes wild girls, doesn't he?

So here I am.

Still smiling and still slowly, very slowly, approaching him, I say, "It's called Glitter Glitter Baby."

"What?"

"My lipstick."

Glaring, his gaze flicks down to my mouth for a second. "Why is it shiny?"

"Because it's gloss."

"What the fuck is gloss?"

"It's a kind of texture that's shiny."

Glancing down at it again, he licks his lips, muttering. "Whatever."

God, he's such a guy sometimes.

"Do you want to taste it?" I ask next.

His eyes fly back up to mine and his fists curl at his sides. "What the fuck?"

"I put it on for you."

"Jesus Christ."

"I also wore my pink dress for you."

"So then, for the love of God, please put it back on."

"It's the same one I wore the night you kissed me."

"I know."

"Oh, you do?"

He frowns, grimaces too. "Yes, Echo, I know. I also know what you wore on your twelfth birthday, your thirteenth birthday, your fourteenth and your fifteenth. That's not the fucking point."

That has the power to give me pause and halt me in my tracks.

It does.

I know he has an uncanny ability to remember things but this is crazy, even for him. Especially when he wasn't even there for a couple of my birthdays.

"You weren't even..." I clear my throat, managing to keep moving forward. "You were in New York for my fifteenth birthday."

I specifically remember Lucas telling me that Reign had gone off to New York that weekend to party with some of their teammates. While Lucas had decided to stay back and celebrate my birthday. So there was no way Reign could've seen me.

"No, I wasn't."

"B-but he —"

"I wanted to be," he cuts me off in a rough voice. "I had made plans to be in New York but I couldn't. I came back."

"Why?"

A grimace. "I had to... I had to see."

"See what?"

"What you were wearing," he replies, in an even rougher, edgier voice, his reddish-brown eyes penetrating. "If you were wearing pink like you always do. So I drove back from New York, kept tabs on you through Lucas and stood outside your window because by the time I'd made it back, he told me that he'd just dropped you off."

That also has the power to stop me, but there are only a few more steps.

Few more steps and I'll be there.

Where my Bandit is.

So I push myself. "You stood outside my window?"

A muscle on his cheek pulses. "Yes."

"On the off chance that you'd see me."

"Yes."

This is somehow even wilder than him doing *that* while watching my window.

I bite my lip. "What was I wearing?"

He stares at my mouth almost violently. Then, "A light pink dress. It had... dark pink flowers on it and poofy sleeves."

"They were roses," I tell him, my heart racing in my chest, my body buzzing that I'm so, so close to him now, *so close*. "And they're called cap sleeves."

He leans forward then, his face all agitated and angry. "I don't fucking care what kind of flowers they were. It's not gonna matter what kind of flowers they were. When you get here. When you get to where I can fucking touch you. I told you if you keep coming after me, I'm going to do worse things. I *told* you that, *just ten minutes ago*. So if you don't listen to me, I'm going to call your bluff. Because it's a bluff, isn't it? Some kind of revenge for what I did that night. I get that. I understand revenge. I *respect* revenge. But if you think I'm going to be noble and *not* touch you, if you think I'm *not* going to put my hands on you, on your creamy skin, and do exactly what you're daring me to do, then you're fucking stupid. You're fucking stupid, Echo, if you think I'm gonna let you walk out of here without taking what you're so carelessly tossing at me. So stop before you get here."

I don't. I get there.

I get where he can put his hands on me.

His breaths are such that they crash against my creamy skin. They crash and gust and make my goosebumps come alive. They make my nipples come alive too, my tits, my belly.

That place between my legs.

Everything bursts with life, and that's saying something because my bare body was already swollen and brimming with about a thousand lives ever since I took my clothes off.

"My name is not Echo," I whisper and his eyes flare. "It's Bubblegum. You gave me that name, remember? That first night. Because you said I was too pink. Which I now know is your favorite color. Because it's *my* favorite color, and because that's why you're always commenting on my dresses." Then, "Oh, and I could've been a Strawberry. But you hate strawberries, so I'm Bubblegum."

His breaths are even noisier now. Even gustier.

His chest rising and falling so wildly, chaotically. And even though he's the one who's clothed, if I focus, I bet I can see all the way through to his heart underneath. Thundering and pounding and battering inside his rib cage.

"And the next time when we met, I told you that I'd given you a name too." His flinch is followed by a growl, low but a soft one. "So here I am where you can put your hands on me. What are you going to do about it, *Bandit*?"

Tick tock, the time passes.

He growls again. He glares at me. He clenches his jaw.

It feels like years.

But I guess it's only a couple of seconds later that he does something about it.

It's only a couple of seconds later that he puts his hands on me and I'm done for.

I die. And go to heaven.

It has to be heaven.

Because not only does he put his hands on me — both of them on my face — he also puts his mouth on my mouth.

Which means this time, *he* makes the first move.

Although we can argue that I made the first move when I took my clothes off. And then I kept coming at him. But he was the one who did the actual touching and…

Echo. Gosh, who even cares right now?

Right.

I'm an idiot.

Who cares who made the first move as long as someone did. As long as the result is the same: a kiss.

Our second.

Or maybe the continuation of the first. Because it's not a gentle kiss by any means. Or a slow one.

He's not trying to ease me into it. He's not trying to give me time to adjust, no.

This kiss is a full-fledged feast.

A full-fledged binge of mouths and tongues and teeth.

And watermelon and summer.

Because he still tastes like that. He still tastes like my favorite fruit and feels like my favorite season.

I'd laugh with joy, if I could.

I'd thank God, if I could as well, for making him fit me like my favorite dress.

But I can't because I'm busy right now.

I'm super busy with eating him up, with sticking my tongue down his throat while I suck on his, with smacking my teeth against him. With bowing my spine for him when he comes at me, his hard chest pressing into my soft one, and tilting my face at the angle he makes me, so he can go deeper.

I'm busy, busy, *busy* exploring him.

His harsh terrains against my soft planes.

My bare curves against his clothed ones.

My nipples dragging over his cotton shirt, bumping into his buttons. My upper tummy pressing against his belt buckle. My thighs scraping against his dress pants.

And then there are my hands.

Stroking his shoulders, massaging his neck, tugging on his hair.

And scratching.

I'm scratching everything that I can get my hands on.

I don't know why I always end up doing that, scratching him like I'm a cat in heat. But he seems to love it. He seems to love it so much that he growls into my mouth. Then his own hands, that were focused on keeping me all still while he drinks from my mouth, move.

And do the same.

His rough, warm hands in my hair, around my neck, down my sides.

Coming back up to pinch the side of my tits.

At which point I moan.

I even scream I think, in his mouth, when his fingers make contact with my heavy breasts. And when he growls in response, I shift restlessly against him because I want more.

Because I want him to do that again, growl like an animal and squeeze my tits.

I want him to squeeze my pussy even.

Like, I want him to stick his hand between my thighs and do what he's doing to my breasts right now, rub and stroke and work it with his rough, fighter fingers.

I want him to work my pussy.

I want him to fuck my pussy too.

And oh my God, have I mentioned in all of this, that he's so hot?

That his mouth is so warm and heated and a ball of fire. His body is too and I'm sweating and shivering and going all flushed and breathless.

I'm going all crazy.

My thoughts are all broken up and I'm thinking things in half-sentences and completely out of order to make any sense out of them.

Plus I'm so wet.

Down there I mean.

I'm all sticky and creamy and feverish.

And *wet*.

Did I mention wet? And...

Suddenly, I'm not thinking anything as air rushes into my lungs as an unwelcome intruder. Because he's broken the kiss. He's also picked me up in his arms and I'm so dazed that I don't even remember my feet leaving the ground and my thighs coming up to wrap themselves around his slim hips.

"What..." I pant into his mouth.

He pants too, his eyes dark and burning. "I warned you."

I lick his lips, shamelessly. "Don't... Don't stop."

I feel my waist being squeezed and my hair being tugged at, making me realize that he's got both his arms around me. Staring into my drugged eyes, he growls, "You sure about this?"

Which in turn makes me realize where *my* hands are — buried in his hair — and so I pull at his strands. "I'm gonna die if you don't kiss me."

He chuckles, which is more or less simply a puff of air, his chest moving. "Listen, I —"

I pull his hair even harder and undulate against him. "Fucking kiss me, Bandit, or I swear I'll kill you before I die. And —"

He kisses me.

Good.

Probably because he got scared. Which is even better, because I wasn't lying.

I'm aware, in a very vague way, that we're moving.

That he's begun to walk while still kissing me and sucking on my lip, nipping and biting. Something that I realize that I love. Him taking little bites out of my lips, making them sting in such a delicious way.

Hurting my mouth while making love to it.

But again, my happiness is short-lived.

Because he once again breaks the kiss. Plus I realize that I'm not even in his arms anymore.

That I'm lying on the bed and he's hovering over me.

I frown. "W-what —"

He shushes me with a hard kiss and a bite, before he crawls away from my body and springs back to his feet, and restless, I come up on my elbows to see what he's doing.

And when I see it, I immediately realize that breaking the kiss was the right idea.

I was being stupid. Selfish.

Because while I have seen him multiple times without his clothes on — well, without his shirt, but still — he hasn't seen *me* yet.

He hadn't seen me up until this point.

Up until this point, he had kept his eyes on my face only. He hadn't gone down.

He is now though.

Now he's looking at every part of me. From my disheveled braid to my flushed cheeks. My rapidly breathing chest and my jiggling tits. My hard, berry-colored nipples. My clavicles. My ribs, the curve of my belly. My thighs and calves.

The shiny thing around my ankle.

His gift.

From long ago.

His eyes fly back to me when he sees it.

Biting my lip, I tell him, "I thought you'd like it. Me wearing your gift for you."

His Adam's apple jumps and his eyes both flare and go up in flames.

Which means he likes it.

I wonder if he likes the other things though.

My naked body, for example.

I know that I'm pale. I know that I don't have very many muscles to speak of. I have zero upper body strength, as evidenced by my lack of climbing skills. I'm basically a regular pale and soft bookworm.

And maybe, given that he's a muscle god and an athlete, I should be embarrassed. I should probably ask him to turn out the lights. But not only has that ship sailed when I got naked in front of him, but also I think asking him to plunge me in shadows would be cruel.

It would be so, *so* unbearably cruel to him.

Because he's eating me up with his eyes. He's devouring me with them. Much like he was devouring me with his mouth and his hands.

And just like when he was kissing me, his body is all heated right now.

I can feel it from here.

The heat radiating out of his skin. The *need*.

Raw and sexual and animalistic.

So that his whole frame is vibrating.

His whole towering body is taut and shaking and shuddering with his breaths.

Fisting the sheets, I call out, "Reign?"

His eyes shoot back to mine. "You're…"

I wrinkle my nose. "Too pink?"

A puff of breath escapes him. "Fucking beautiful."

I blush. "Yeah?"

He swallows again. "Even more than I imagined."

I swallow too. "And you imagined a lot."

"Yeah."

The lump in my throat grows bigger. "M-me too."

God, it's such a relief to admit that. Such a relief to not fight with myself. To not push these things down. And I'm glad I told him. *So* glad.

Because I see emotions passing through his features.

Shock. Wonder. Disbelief. *Relief*.

That he's not the only one.

He's not.

He's so not alone in his pain.

"You did, huh?" he rasps, his fingers fisting.

"Yes. You're the… You're the first guy I ever thought was sexy." I smile shyly at him. "I didn't even know the meaning of sexy before that."

Another puff of breath, this time accompanied with an arrogant tilt of his lips. "And I didn't know the meaning of beautiful. Until I saw you in those woods that night."

Oh God.

Oh my *fucking* God.

I fist the sheets tighter. "Reign —"

"You weren't kidding," he gulps again. "About what you want me to do."

I shake my head. "No."

"Because I didn't wanna look," he says, roving his eyes over my body once again. "At you."

"Why not?"

"Until I looked, I could pretend..." He licks his lips. "I could pretend that it wasn't real. That it wasn't you that I was touching. Although who the fuck was I kidding, it was you. No one... has ever felt like you but I... Maybe, just *maybe*, I could survive this, you understand? If I didn't *look*. But now I have. Now I have seen you. Now I'm..." Another swallow. "Seeing you and you're... the most beautiful thing I've ever seen. You're made of moondust and sugar and... If you back down now, I'll —"

"I won't."

I will never ever back down.

Not when he looks like this. All overcome.

Not when he's *talking* like this.

When has he ever talked like this? When has he ever been... dramatic?

Because he was being that back there, wasn't he?

Only to me, it sounded perfect.

So, so perfect.

His chest shakes again. "So you're really *mine*."

Now it's my turn to shake.

Time for my breaths to hitch and my throat to well up with emotions. And words.

Well, just one word: Yes.

I'm really his.

His. His. His.

But somehow my brain kicks in and I whisper, "F-for tonight."

And it's like I broke something. Something precious.

Not only inside my own chest but inside his as well.

And whatever it was, it *hurts*.

Especially when all the emotions that were flickering on his face vanish, leaving behind sharp things.

Sharp peaks of his cheekbones, sharp hollows, sharp jut of his stubbled jaw.

I don't like it.

I don't like it at all. It only makes me hurt more and I blurt out, "It's b-because we're both in pain. And we're suffering and I-I think… I just want it to end. I want us to move on and —"

And then he takes his shirt off and my words go poof.

He rips it off really, snagging it at the back and yanking it off his body. And then…

Then there are just muscles.

Miles and miles of them. Tanned and summery and rippling.

All jam-packed and sleek. Dense.

So beautiful.

And yeah, sexy. Such a work of art. So much so that even the black and blue bruises, the numerous cuts and scrapes, do nothing to take away from the allure of his body.

They do twist my heart though. At how brutal they look. How painful.

And all because of the two years' worth of torment. Maybe even from before that.

For wanting what doesn't belong to him.

His best friend's girl.

I flick my eyes up and focus on his rippling chest. "You didn't have that before."

I'm referring to his tattoo.

A series of numbers, in a plain script, on the left side of his chest. Tonight I get a good look at them: 1510.234 3023.456 When I first noticed his tattoo, two weeks ago, I couldn't understand what it's supposed to be. And tonight, after reading and re-reading the numbers, I still don't.

"No, I didn't."

I look up, into his eyes. "What is it?"

"Something that matters."

Confused, I frown. "What does that —"

Suddenly my words halt and then simply dissolve on my tongue like sugar because he bends down, his sculpted abs curling. Which is fine, or would be fine, if he hadn't also gripped my ankles at the same time. Both of them, and in a very firm hold. And then keeping his eyes on me, he kisses one.

The one with the anklet, making me suck my belly in and bite my lip.

At his both tender and possessive gesture.

And then he gets on the bed.

He gets between my legs, that he widens.

Widens and widens and keeps going until my heart is in my throat and my eyes are big as saucers.

His smirk is back.

It's small but no less potent.

You'd think that it would dampen the fire in his eyes, the fire that's making them look all dark and glinting, but it doesn't. Somehow that arrogant smirk on his split lip and the intent look in his eyes go together.

They work super well and make him look larger than life.

They make him look like a force of nature.

The force that's parting my legs and I don't know... I don't know why or what he's doing and...

"R-Reign —"

He shakes his head. "No talking."

My belly clenches at his rough command. "But what —"

"You're mine, aren't you?"

"Just for —"

"Yeah, tonight." He squeezes my ankle. "Heard you the first time."

"I —"

"So now you listen to me," he says, flexing his grip. "You're done. Talking and making demands. You wanna take the pain away, don't you?"

I nod eagerly. "Yes."

"You wanna move on. You wanna end the fucking suffering, yeah?"

"Y-yes."

His jaw tics. "So then tonight, I make the rules, understand?"

"You hate r-rules."

"Not the ones that I make."

"But —"

"Tonight, my word is law. My *rules* are your fucking promise. Your oath. You know why?"

"B-because you're my boss?"

His eyes glint with arrogance. "Yeah. But also, I'm your Bandit and you're my Bubblegum."

My elbows slip and I almost go back down on the bed.

I almost fall.

With shivers. And tremblings. With relief.

That he finally, finally called me by his name. He finally called me what I've been wanting him to.

Even though I kept denying it.

I kept fighting with myself.

"So I want you to shut the fuck up and let me do what I want," he continues, his gaze sharpening. "Okay, *Bubblegum*?"

I hiccup out a breath. "Uh-huh."

He licks his lips like a predator who's getting ready to go in for the kill. "Good girl."

His raspy praise makes my tummy clench.

Or maybe it could be the fact that in the very next moment, he falls on me.

Exactly like a predator too.

Although falls on me is a wrong statement.

He mostly falls on the bed.

Goes flat on his abdomen as he resumes parting my legs until I'm almost doing a split. And then with his rough, scrape-y hands on my thighs, he... stares.

At my pussy.

And the fact that I'm on display for him like that makes me arch my hips and bite my lip again.

It makes me blush something fierce.

For the past two weeks, I've imagined this moment several times. Me going to his motel; me confessing my crush to him; and then me telling him what we need to do to purge it.

I always knew that there was going to be a kiss.

And then, of course, sex.

But every time I got to the sex part, I could never ever imagine it clearly. And it's not as if I haven't read any books or seen any movies. I have and I also masturbate like a normal girl. So I couldn't figure out why.

I can now.

It's because I never could've imagined *this*.

I never could've imagined lying on his motel bed, with him between my thighs.

Or that he'd be lying on his stomach and I'd be looking down at his dark head, his rippling shoulders, his upper back morphing into muscled hills.

As braced on his elbows, he... *gazes*.

At the place between my thighs.

With such focus and concentration and God, *devotion*.

And I was already so wet from his biting kisses.

I was so drenched and sloppy, but now under his scrutiny, I become wetter.

I feel a drop of my juice sliding out of my hole and he growls.

It's so deep that the bed rumbles with it.

And I love that so much that I arch my hips even harder, feeling a couple more drops leaking out. As if I'm a glass full of lust and my juices are running over. And then I jump because he rubs his thumb there, right at my hole, right at the center of my pussy.

"I knew it," he rasps.

"Knew what?" I whisper, looking down at his thoughtful frown.

He keeps staring at my pussy, *examining* it. "That you'd be this tight."

I jump again because his words are accompanied by a push of his thumb in my hole.

Only a slight push though.

As if testing the waters.

"I-I... Guys l-like that, don't they?"

His eyes jump up to mine. "You don't need to worry about what guys like."

"I —"

His hand on my thigh flexes. "No. *Mine*, remember?"

I swallow at his possessive tone. "D-do you like it?"

He goes back to looking at my pussy, his thumb circling over my hole. "Yeah." Then, "Which means it's not a good thing for you."

I know.

Because it will hurt.

But I'm not going to be a crybaby. Even if I want to. So, so badly.

Because *I've* asked him to do this.

So I say, "I won't cry."

Still circling my hole, he looks up again. "You will."

I will. I know.

"I won't bleed."

His jaw clenches. "That'll happen too."

I know that too.

Because it's not as if it's in my hands. It's not in his either.

But it's okay. It's okay.

I will survive.

"Do you have a condom?"

His eyes are burning. "Yeah."

I lick my lips. "Will you wear it?"

He licks his lips too. "You want me to wear it?"

I nod. "Y-yes. I'm not... I'm not on the pill, remember?"

For several seconds, he circles and circles his thumb around my hole. While staring and staring at me. As if casting a spell or something. Rubbing my pussy to make magic.

And he does make magic.

Because the more he circles my hole, the harder he stares at me, the more restless I get.

The more I leak.

And throb.

Oh yeah, I'm throbbing. In all of this, I forgot about the throbbing. The pulsing.

The clenching of not only my hole but also my clit.

God, my clit.

That he hasn't even touched yet.

"That still doesn't mean I have to wear it," he says finally.

It takes me a second to understand what he means. My lips part when I do. "But —"

"Because..." He throws me a lopsided smirk. "I could always pull out."

My breaths hitch. "But that's not —"

"I could always," he continues, in such a conversational tone, his thumb going around and around, "blow on your soft, creamy belly."

"Reign —"

"Right here."

"Where?"

He moves his hand from my thigh and brings it up. He strokes my creamy belly before tapping his thumb on the spot. "On your tight little belly button."

"On my..."

He dips his thumb in it, like he's doing with my pussy. "Yeah. I could come right here. Fill this little button up with my load. Although," he squints his eyes as if debating his choices, "if I get to do you bareback, I'm gonna come so much, I could paint almost your whole fucking body with my wad. So then maybe..."

"Maybe what?"

"I should come on your tits."

I squirm as he keeps stroking my belly and my core. "My t-tits?"

"Uh-huh." He looks at them next. "I could blow on your milky tits. Hose down your bubblegum pink nipples with my spunk and then when I'm done, I could use my cum as grease."

"G-grease for what?"

He looks into my eyes. "To fuck your tits."

My eyes go wide. "F-fuck my..."

"Yeah." He nods, giving me a flat look. "If I blow my load on your sexy fucking tits, Bubblegum, the tits that I've been jerking off to for years, the tits that I see in my fucking dreams, you better believe it that I'm gonna fuck them. I'm gonna *have to* fuck them."

I squirm again or maybe I never stopped. "I... You..."

I hear rustling as if he's getting closer to my pussy. "I'm gonna have to rub my load all over your tits like some animal. To make your skin all shiny, just like your lips right now. And then I'm gonna have to plump them up real good. Make them all juicy and ripe for fucking like I would your snatch. And when I'm done, I'm gonna gather them in my rough hands and make a valley. You know what that valley is gonna be for?"

I'm feeling his words in my pussy.

I'm feeling his warm breath on there too.

But I can't figure out why. I can't figure out what's happening except my belly feels really tight. My nipples are rock hard and my tits are tingling.

And on top of that, my eyes won't stay open.

My eyes have closed *and* I've fallen down on the bed now, unable to hold myself, so lethargic and drowsy. And so fucking weak with lust.

Licking my lips, I whisper, "F-for what?"

"For my dick," he says and I think I feel his thumb going in and out again. "I'm gonna make a nice tight valley for my fat fucking dick to slide in. Real tight, yeah? And then I'm gonna ride your tits, Bubblegum. I'm gonna fucking ride them and rock into them and beat them up. Again, just like I would your sloppy fucking snatch. I'm gonna go up and down your creamy and dreamy tits and just because I'm a motherfucker, I'm gonna bump into your jaw. Into your lips."

"Why?"

"Because I'm greedy, see." He presses his hand on my lower belly now, massaging my pelvis as the fingers of his other hand practically swim in my drenched, leaking core. "Because fucking your virgin pussy and blowing my load on your tits is not enough for me. Even fucking your tits isn't enough."

"So then what is?"

"Making you lick it."

"L-lick what?"

"My dick."

I jerk again, fisting the sheets tighter. "W-what?"

"Yeah. I'm gonna knock at your mouth every time I go up your tits so you open it and give me a lick."

"But I've never done that before."

"No?"

"No."

He hums, his voice rough and deep, so much like his fingers on my body. "It would really help me out though."

"It would?"

"Uh-huh. It would make me come faster and give you a pearl necklace."

"What's a..." My head lolls side to side. "What's a pearl necklace?"

"A pearl necklace, Bubblegum," he explains patiently while playing with my pussy and oh my God, with my clit. I feel it. I *feel* it, "is when a very, very good girl like you licks the dick of a very, very bad boy like me. Even though she's never licked a dick before. Even though her mouth is a virgin just like her pink pussy. She still does it. To make him happy. To take away his pain. She licks it whenever he wants her to."

"Really?"

"Yeah." He rolls my bundle of nerves between his fingers as he keeps going. "Sometimes she also sucks on it because she's such a good girl, see. She also lets him put it in her mouth. She lets him slide his big dick in her sweet little mouth and lets him fuck it like her pussy and her tits. And when she does that, when she lets that bad boy fuck her good girl mouth, he rewards her. He has to. She's been such a good girl. So he comes all over her neck and makes her pretty jewelry with his pearly white cum."

At this point, all I can do is slide my legs up and down.

All I can do is rock my hips, and hope. And wish and pray.

That I become his good girl. I pray that I'm good enough that he gives me a pearl necklace too.

"I-I want that," I tell him.

"Yeah? You want me to give you a pearl necklace, baby?"

"Yes. Please. I want to be your good girl."

In fact I don't think I've ever wanted anything else in my life.

Not good grades. Not an A on an assignment.

Not even my parents' praise and trust.

"So then you gotta let me fuck you bareback," he tells me.

I squirm and shudder. "Oh but... but I can't. I—"

"Come on, Bubblegum," he cajoles. "I'll make it so good."

I shake my head. "N-no."

"I'll make you feel so good, baby."

"But I..."

"I'll fuck you so hard and deep."

"R-Reign —"

"I'll fuck you so fucking hard, Bubblegum. Just let me in without a rubber."

"I-I..." I lick my lips. "Okay. Okay."

And then I explode.

My restless limbs, my sweaty fists, my heavy pelvis and tingling tits.

Everything falls to pieces and yet comes together in a crescendo.

Because he puts his mouth on me.

I know it. *That*, I know for sure.

Even though my eyes are clenched shut and I'm delirious, half crazy in lust, I still know that he just took a big swipe of my core, curling his hot tongue over my juices, my clit, and making me come just like that.

Making me gush.

God, I'm gushing. I'm *literally* gushing.

I feel juices pour out of me in a mad rush and I hear his gulping, slurping noises. Followed by his growls and satisfied hums. As if whatever I'm giving him tastes so good.

It definitely *feels* so good.

Making me moan and arch. Making me undulate not only my hips but my entire body as I come and come and flow into his mouth and think that I'll never stop.

And I realize that this was the magic he was weaving.

He was hypnotizing me with his rough voice and dirty words.

So I could relax and go all loose.

I'm proven right when, once my seemingly never-ending climax is done, I feel him springing back up to his feet. By the time I blink my eyes open, he's already divested himself of his pants and is now in the process of rolling down the rubber, the thing he just convinced me to not have him wear.

My heart thuds at the first sight of his cock.

It's a partial sight though because he's turned on his side and his hands are covering most of it. Which I know he's also doing on purpose so I don't get scared.

And so I let him.

I let him protect me from everything bad and scary, even his thick hard cock, and move my eyes to take the rest of him in. His muscled thighs, sprinkled with dark hair; the tight globes of his ass and holy God, how is it that he's so beautiful?

How is it that his ass looks better than mine?

All tight and round and *bitable*.

Scratchable, too.

But then everything about him makes me want to scratch, scratch, *scratch*.

A second later, my thoughts break because he's on the bed again and he's crawling over me. He's settling himself between my thighs and I notice that his lips are all glossy and swollen. From my pussy I think, and I love it.

I also love that he's slowly covering me with his body like a warm, summery shadow.

And then his dick — the thing he was distracting me from — settles on my belly and here he is.

Over me and braced on his elbows.

He licks his lips as he stares down at me and I realize that it's not only his mouth that's glossy, it's also his jaw.

"I... Is that..."

"You," he rumbles, his eyes blazing. "Yeah, you drenched my fucking mouth, Bubblegum."

"D-drenched?"

His shining lips twitch. "And my jaw *and* my throat."

I squirm beneath him, feeling his dick rubbing on my stomach. "I-I'm not..."

"It's called squirting."

My eyes widen. "It is not."

"You squirted."

"I did not."

I did. I so did.

Because the way I came tonight was different than all the other times I've made myself come. I'm still coming actually. My pussy is still fluttering and twitching and I can feel my juices running down my core, smeared on my thighs.

"I guess, me doing you raw and fucking your tits really gets you going, huh," he teases.

I grip his obliques and scratch. "It does not."

He chuckles, leaning closer. "It almost made me blow in my fucking pants."

"It did not," I breathe out, amazed.

Oh God, what's wrong with my vocabulary?

Where are all the words?

"Yeah, you were so hot, coming like that."

"Is that... Is that normal?"

"You wanna be normal, baby?"

I think about it. Then shake my head. "No."

"Yeah? Then what do you wanna be?"

That's easy.

Quite possibly, the easiest thing I've ever had to answer.

"Your good girl," I whisper.

I watch emotions pass through his features, making him swallow.

Before he comes down to give me a hard, biting kiss again.

This time I think it's a reward.

For giving him the right answer. For wanting to be his.

Just for tonight though, Echo.

I know, I know. But I don't want to think about that right now.

Breaking the kiss, he whispers, "Ready?"

Yeah, I am now.

I'm so totally and absolutely ready.

I nod. "Yes. And thank you."

He frowns.

"For... For taking my fear away."

He exhales a large breath, his muscles grazing my body, his cock, all hard and hot, as he replies, gruffly, "It's gonna be okay."

I know.

He's going to make it so.

I nod again.

He reaches down and adjusts my thighs around his hips, sliding our skin together, putting his dick right where my hole is, nudging at it.

Then, "Put your hands on my shoulders."

I do it.

"Don't let go."

"Okay."

"No matter what."

"Okay."

Then, his eyes staring into mine, he does it. He pushes in.

No, wait. He pushes *all the way* in.

And all I can think about is that I knew it. I knew that this would hurt. I knew that I'd feel the stretch, the burn, the sting, the fucking pain I always read about. I also knew that I'd tear up. That my tears would run down my eyes and soak my hair, the sheets below.

And I'd bleed.

I always, *always* knew that.

But I didn't know that there would be someone who'd go through the same pain as me.

Not physically maybe, but emotionally.

Someone whose eyes would cloud over just like mine, and whose body would become just as tight.

Someone who'd lick my tears then.

Who'd run his tongue along the sides of my cheeks, my eyes, and drink them down. Who'd soothe me with sweet hums and kisses all over my face and my throat.

Who'd *wait*.

For my body to adjust to his size.

To his girth and his invasion.

Until that initial pain turns into restless pleasure.

But most of all, I didn't know that that someone would be him.

My Bandit.

The guy I'd met in the woods all those years ago.

But then, he's also the guy who turned night into day, isn't he? And if he could do that, if he could light up the night like that, why wouldn't he be able to turn the pain of losing my virginity into something so pleasurable?

Now as I watch him above me, his features sharp and beautiful, his eyes intense and pinned on me, as he slides in and out of my body, I realize that it couldn't have been anyone else.

It had to be him.

My first.

No one else would've made sense. My virginity belonged to him and him only.

And then, he comes down at me.

He curls his strong athletic body and dips down, putting his mouth on my tit. He takes a nipple into his mouth and then I'm not thinking anything at all.

I'm not *capable* of thinking. I can only feel.

His warm breaths, his hot mouth. His hard sucks on my nipple. His hands in my hair, pulling and tugging.

His dick in my pussy.

Pumping and pounding and gathering speed.

So much speed that I'm rocking with it. That I'm pulling at his hair too. I'm scratching his shoulders, his back. I'm digging my nails into his ass.

I'm moving with him.

And it's easy too, to move.

Our bodies are practically sliding against each other. Because we're so hot and sweaty. We're so drenched and misty. We're on fire, his summer skin and my moondust body, and it's so good.

It's so *so* good.

Even the ache in my belly feels good.

The soreness, the tightness. The fucking quickening.

Everything feels swollen and stretched just like my pussy and it only gets worse — and better — when he comes for my mouth. When he mauls my mouth just like he was mauling my tit only a second ago, and then we're kissing and moaning and gasping, and just like last time, I explode.

Everything falls apart and comes together.

But this time, I'm much more aware of it. I'm much more awake for my orgasm.

For my pussy to gush again and drench his dick.

That actually feels bigger now.

So much bigger than it did only two seconds ago.

And then he's breaking the kiss, my Bandit, and his smooth strokes are getting jarring and haphazard as he braces himself on his hands this time, detaching himself from my body.

Only so he can arch and jerk.

Throw his head back as all the muscles in his torso tighten and ripple.

And he comes, growling.

Howling even.

He comes and comes and comes, thrusting inside of me, smacking against my body, jiggling it with his strength. The power of his climax.

His beautiful, erotic climax.

His beautiful, erotic body with every muscle and vein standing in relief.

I don't think I've ever seen anything more beautiful than his orgasm. I don't think I've ever seen anything more beautiful than him *period*.

And so I have to hug him. I have to press my body against his so I reach up and get him.

I wind my arms around his neck and bring him back down.

Thankfully, he gets the message because he winds his arms around mine, tucking his face in my neck.

And then I wait.

With his cock still throbbing inside of me and his arms around my body, for this connection between us to break.

I wait for relief to come.

I wait and wait.

But the only thing that comes is my tears.

CHAPTER THIRTY-ONE

The Bandit

I miss writing in my diary.

It's not something I think about often. Because it's not something that I liked to do in the first place.

But I have to admit that I miss it.

And tonight I miss it with an ache that I haven't felt in the two fucking years since I quit.

If I still wrote, I'd probably write about her hair.

How it's spread out on my pillow. How the moonlight catches on it and makes it look like it's spun from gold and sugar. Everything about her is made of sugar, by the way. Which I'm not gonna get into right now because I'm waxing poetic about her hair, but still.

Anyway, I'd write about how I kept playing with it tonight, as she lay in my arms, all spent and pink from her epic orgasm.

Another slight detour here: Jesus Christ but my Bubblegum's a squirter.

Who the fuck knew?

Who the fuck knew that I was holding a goddamn miracle in my hands.

Plus she's tasty too. Her pussy juice is like ambrosia.

Back to her hair though.

So I kept playing with it and then she looked at me with pretty sleepy eyes and untied her ribbon. So I could really, actually get at it. So I could untie her braid and run my fingers through the silk-like strands, make a fist out of them, rub them on my mouth, my nose.

Fucking rub them all over my body.

I'd write about how I did all that and she let me.

With a sweet, drowsy smile.

Then, I'd write about her dress.

Pink and flowery with those ribbon-y straps. That she wore tonight.

Fuck me, but those ribbon-like straps do something to me. They do something to my already perverse head. Actually, all her dresses do something to my dirty, horny mind but those ribbon straps take the cake.

And then I'd write about how I made her sleep naked.

She wanted to put on her clothes, not the pink dress but the one that she'd brought with her.

In her pink little girly overnight bag.

A white dress; I saw.

I bet it was probably one of her jacked-up reasons. About white being the color of peace.

Because she came here to find it, didn't she?

She came here to end the fucking suffering. The pain. To end this connection between us.

Stupid girl. Brave girl.

Coming to me like that.

Sleeping in my bed like that. All innocent and trusting.

While I sit in my chair and watch her.

While I imagine violating her body in a thousand different ways.

In all the ways that I've thought about over the years.

So many, *many* ways that it gets me hard again.

Not that I wasn't before.

I've been oscillating between a semi and a full hard-on from the minute after we finished.

And since I'm her Bandit, big and bad, I palm my cock and start jacking off.

I start fucking my fist as I watch her sleeping body. Her flickering eyelids, her parted mouth. Her chest rising and falling gently. Delicately. Beautifully. That shining anklet on her leg.

My beautiful brave girl.

Only she isn't my girl, is she?

But that doesn't stop me from jacking off to her until I come all over my stomach with a low grunt.

And then I wait.

Like I've been waiting for hours and hours, again from the minute after we finished.

For all the things that she said would happen if I took her cherry.

All the laundry fucking list of things she'd promised would come to pass.

I wait and wait.

But nothing happens.

Except the clock strikes midnight, alerting me that my time's up.

She's his now.

CHAPTER THIRTY-TWO

I couldn't sleep at all last night.

I kept writing in my diary until the sun came up.

Although if anyone asked me what I wrote, I wouldn't be able to tell them. I wouldn't be able to tell them when I stopped writing either. Or what I did all day.

Up until this moment.

When I'm sitting in my best friend's car, parked at the edge of the woods.

Where yet another party is in full swing.

My parents think that I'm still at my sleepover with Jupiter and I kinda am. Only like last night, I'm taking a slight detour.

"You sure about this?"

Just like last night, Jupiter's face is hidden in the dark interior of her car. But I can clearly see her concern. "You know, you asked me the same thing last night."

"I know." She sighs. "But I'm asking again."

Because she's a good friend. She's the best friend a girl could ask for.

I'm lucky to have her.

So lucky that I might start crying right here, right now. I might crumple under this pressure in my chest. But I don't want to.

Because it's a happy day.

It's the day of my freedom, my independence.

It's the day I go back to the boy I fell in love with when I was only fourteen.

"I'm sure," I tell her, my voice catching in my throat.

Which I guess she notices. "Because you don't sound sure. You haven't sounded sure all day. You haven't *looked* sure all day either. In fact, you haven't looked okay all day."

I don't remember what I did all day so I'm going to have to take her word for it.

Even so, I reassure her. "I'm okay."

Now, if only my voice would stop catching in my throat. If only my chest would stop hurting.

If only. If only. If only.

"No, you're not."

"Jupiter —"

"You miss him."

There I go again, wanting to cry. Wanting to bawl and cave under this pressure.

And this time, it's harder to hold back my tears.

This time, it's harder to remind myself that it's a happy day.

"You do, don't you?" she asks in a gentle voice.

I swallow thickly. "I..."

"And it hasn't even been twenty-four hours yet."

No, it hasn't been.

It's only been eighteen hours and thirteen minutes since... since everything.

Since that gray motel room. Those gray sheets.

That messy room.

That now seems... cozy. Homey even.

In a way that nothing has felt in the past two years. Or six years even.

Not even my own pink bedroom.

"Listen." Jupiter leans toward me. "It's okay if you miss him. It's okay if you don't want to do this anymore. If you've changed your mind after what happened between you two last night. It's *okay*, Echo."

"I... It's n-not. It's... I-I have to do this. I..."

"Why?"

"Because..." I wring my hands in my lap, barely able to breathe now. "*Because* Lucas is depending on me. He's... His life. His career. Everything that he's worked for. It's all hanging in balance. Because of *me*. Because I betrayed him. And so it's up to me, don't you see? It's up to me to fix it. Plus everything is falling apart for him right now with his dad being sick. I can't let him down. I can't..."

Not to mention, *my* parents.

This is my chance to win back their trust. To redeem myself in their eyes.

To go back to being their good girl.

"Yeah, see, I thought you'd say something else," she says.

"What?"

"I thought you'd say that you love him."

"Of course I do. Of course I..."

"If you do, Echo, then why wasn't that on your list of things?"

My heart is racing now. My palms are sweaty and shaky.

Much sweatier and shakier than they were only a minute ago.

My breaths are practically fogging the window right now as I say, "N-no, I... It's... I have to do this, Jupiter, okay? I have to make it all okay. Because I never... I never wanted to come between them. I never wanted to break their friendship. Be the reason why two best friends lose each other, and now they have. Their bond is broken and Lucas is all angry. And *he*..."

He is all regretful and in pain.

He's tortured.

About wanting me. About the kiss.

And that's why I went to him last night. To fix it all.

To make him and myself move on.

To purge this guilt from him and to turn myself into a good girlfriend for my ex-boyfriend.

And now that we have — we have, haven't we? — I have to go back to Lucas.

Because I still haven't lost hope. Even after Reign told me that Lucas knows. This teeny-tiny hope that they can be friends again. That I can somehow bring them back to each other.

Look, Reign's always been alone, all right?

He's always been misunderstood and judged by people. And I will be damned if he's judged by Lucas too.

And while fixing Lucas's downward spiral and winning back my parents' trust are important to me, I know that *this* is why I have to go to Lucas. I know Reign would've stopped me last night if I'd told him. So I didn't.

That this is the main reason.

For Reign.

I'm going to give Lucas what he wants so I can somehow convince him to forgive Reign.

Oh, and also love.

I love Lucas.

Do you?

"Echo." Jupiter grabs both my hands in my lap and squeezes them. "It's not your responsibility, honey, all right? To fix things. To fix Lucas's career or his broken heart or his friendship with Reign. You can't make everything okay. Not when it comes at the price of your own happiness. Your own heart. It's not fair to you. You have to think about yourself. You have to think about what *you* want."

But I *can't* think about what I want.

I can't be selfish.

You can't be selfish in love. In love, you do things for other people. You sacrifice. You be good.

But God, I don't want to be good.

For once, I just want to be myself.

No. Stop.

"I..." I close my eyes for a second to focus. "I think I'm gonna go now."

I can see that she doesn't want to but after a moment, she does let go of my hands. "Okay. Fine. Just, uh, just call me, okay? I'll come get you." Then, "Unless your ex-boyfriend is as possessive and domineering as his best friend. Which I don't see happening, but still."

My heart skips a beat. Several beats actually.

Thinking about how Jupiter is right.

My ex-boyfriend *isn't* as possessive and domineering as his ex-best friend is.

Or was last night.

He wouldn't let me call Jupiter for a ride. Said that there was no way he'd let someone else take me wherever the fuck it is that I want to go. Not after what… happened. So he'd dropped me off at Jupiter's himself last night.

Eighteen hours and seventeen minutes ago, as of now.

With shaking legs, I climb out of her car and begin walking.

Toward the party.

Toward Lucas.

I wish I wasn't doing this at a party, but this is where Lucas said he'd be. When I called him yesterday and said that I wanted to meet him; before going to the motel.

It was the first time we were talking. Since he gave me the ultimatum two weeks ago.

Since then, there had been radio silence between us. I never called and he had no reason to talk to me until I made up my mind.

But now I have.

As I approach closer and closer to the party though, to the loud music and the high laughter, to the happy crowd and the love of my life, my heart is racing.

My mind is racing too.

My body is shaking and sweating. It feels like I'm walking toward something disastrous. I'm walking toward something that I may never come back from.

Because I'm walking so far, *far* away…

From *him*.

But then, I'm doing it for his friendship.

I'm doing it for him.

For him. For him. *For him*…

And then suddenly I come to a halt. Because I remember something.

Well, I remember everything now — from the past I mean — but now I remember it in a different way.

I remember all the other things I did for him.

All the other things I did — I felt — *because* of him.

The first time I thought Lucas was nice to me in those woods, on the night of my thirteenth birthday.

The first time I kissed Lucas.

The reason I said yes to going out with Lucas in the first place.

All these thoughts run in my head like a movie reel.

Followed by *these* memories:

I thought Lucas was nice to me that night because *he* was mean to me.

I kissed Lucas because I wanted to prove something to *him*.

I said yes to a date with Lucas because I knew that *he* wouldn't like it.

I *knew* that.

I wrote it in my diary even.

In my fucking diary.

That he read. And he could tell. From only three lines, he could tell that I had a crush on him.

Imagine if he read all of them. Imagine if *I* read all of them.

All of my diaries.

Six years' worth.

Six fucking years' worth of pages. And every single one is full of him.

Every single page is how he makes me feel.

How much I hate him. How sick he makes me.

I could name them my Hatesick Diaries.

Oh God.

Oh God.

Oh my *God*.

And then, again in flashes, my own written words come to me.

Every time he'd do something to hurt me, I'd write about how I sought comfort in Lucas. Every time he made me cry with his insults, I'd write about how Lucas is the best boyfriend ever for wiping my tears off. Every time he'd stare at me with his cold eyes, I'd write about how thankful I was that Lucas has kind eyes so he can make me forget his reddish-brown ones.

Not to mention, my own parents like Lucas because of how much they hated Reign. How they'd always compare the two and tell me how lucky I was that someone like Lucas was my boyfriend and not Reign.

And now, *in this moment,* I'm going back to Lucas because of him.

I'm going back because I want to give Reign his best friend back.

That's what I wrote in my diary last night. I *remember* now.

And the fact that he thinks that Lucas is the right choice for me. He said that, didn't he?

He said that that was where I belonged. With Lucas.

In fact he's not only said it, he's showed it to me.

And I wrote all of that.

I listed all the things he's done, all the ways he's pushed me toward Lucas since the very first night we'd met.

If you love him, then why wasn't it on your list of things...

Because I don't.

I do not love Lucas. I'm going back to him for his ex-best friend — and a variety of other reasons — but not for him.

No, no, no.

That's not true, right?

It can't be true.

It can't...

I do love Lucas. I *do*...

Standing here, in the dark woods, with a party raging on only a short distance away, I pant.

I pant and pant and feel dizzy.

How have I never realized this before?

Every single action in my relationship with Lucas was an equal and opposite reaction to his ex-best friend.

My love for Lucas was born out of my hate for *him*.

It was born out of how much *he* made me feel.

It was born out of *our* connection. The crush that I'd buried deep inside of me and wanted to kill.

There's no killing it.

It's in my soul now. It's always been there and it always will be.

It will...

I jump when I feel a grip on my arm and I'm spun around, only to stare at the familiar eyes.

Reddish-brown and glinting.

A familiar face, sharp and bruised from his fights, and beautiful.

My Bandit.

"Reign," I breathe out.

The canopy of trees covers us in darkness but as always, I can still see when his nostrils flare. I can still see when he works his jaw back and forth, breathing loudly and noisily.

With a hint of a growl.

My own breaths are noisy as well.

But oh my God, they're also easy and peaceful.

So much easier and more peaceful than they've been ever since he dropped me off at Jupiter's last night.

"What —"

He spins around then, cutting me off, and starts to walk. He starts to drag me behind him, taking me somewhere. And so just like that, out of the blue, I'm being pulled away from the party, from the boy that I loved, or thought I did.

And Jesus Christ, the relief is so big.

That I let him.

I let him drag me away, take me wherever he wants to.

Only I think the problem is that I'm not fast enough for him. That I can't match his long and lunging strides. So he stops and swivels to face me again but before I go crashing against him, he bends down and picks me up.

He throws me over his shoulders like I weigh nothing at all.

And maybe to him, I don't.

Maybe to him I'm featherlight and made of moondust.

Like to me, he's safe and his strong body is made of my favorite season.

So I don't even make a sound except maybe a few gasps and low moans when my tummy hits his strong shoulder and his corded arms wrap around the backs of my bare thighs. And then he's walking again and I grip his t-shirt, burying my nose in the small of his back, and closing my eyes.

God.

He's here. Somehow he's here.

Somehow I'm in his arms again. I can smell him again, feel his heat. Feel how vital and alive he is as his chest goes up and down against me.

A couple of minutes later, he comes to a halt and puts me down.

Settling his arms on the scratchy trunk, he crowds me against a tree and going all loose, I arch up, thrusting my body even closer. Breathing heavily, he sweeps his eyes all over my face, over my craned neck and my bowed body. And while he's doing that, I do my own sweep.

I drink him in with my eyes.

Even though it's only been eighteen hours and forty-one minutes since I last saw him, I missed him.

God, I missed him so much.

"How did you..." I whisper, my fingers still clutching onto his t-shirt. "How did you know I was here?"

His eyes come back to my face and his features tighten up and flicker with violence. "Because he's here."

"I'm... Reign, I —"

He leans closer, his biceps straining on either side of me. "It didn't work."

"What?"

"Your stupid fucking plan," he says, his teeth clenched, "*didn't* work."

My lips part on a choppy breath. "Reign, l-listen —"

"No, I'm done listening. I'm *done*," he says, his eyes brimming with mayhem. "I saw you first. Back then. I *found* you first. And then I waited a whole fucking year to see you again. I waited a whole fucking year to see the girl I saw in the woods that one night. And then, I waited and waited and fucking *waited* four years to kiss her. Even though she was my Servant Girl. She worked for my fucking family and so for all intents and purposes, *I* had the right. Me. To do whatever the fuck I wanted with her. But instead of exercising that right, I watched her. For those four years. I *watched* her be in love with my best friend and hated myself for it. I hated *her* for it. I hated and hated so much that it made me sick. *She* made me sick. But here's the kicker, see. She wasn't done. She wasn't done making me sick, so then two years later after she kissed me, after she came on to me herself, she came to me again. She said that she wanted me to take her cherry. Because she had a plan. A very stupid fucking plan of curing my sickness. Of curing hers too, by the way. So she could fix everything. So she could stop the suffering, the pain. So she could go back to my asshole of a best friend. But..."

My heart is gripped in a vise.

A vise that's choking me.

Making it hard for it to beat. Making it hard to breathe.

"Reign, please listen to me. I —"

"But it failed," he says in a guttural, abraded voice. "Not only did it fail epically, it actually made everything worse. I'm sicker now. Than I was before. I'm crazier. More insane, more obsessed. I'm fucking possessed, do you understand? And it hurts." He thumps a hand on his chest. "*Here*. It fucking hurts, Echo. Even more than it did before. So now," he licks his lips, "*I* have a plan."

I twist my fists in his t-shirt. "What plan?"

"I *plan*," he explains, his eyes narrowed, "on taking what I want. On *taking* what rightfully belongs to me. What should've been mine in the first place."

What should've been his.

Me.

I should've been his; he's right.

He doesn't even know how right he is. I haven't even told him yet.

All the things that I discovered. Only a few moments ago.

My heart in my throat, I whisper, "Me."

"Yeah, *you*," he confirms, his voice sanded down to a whisper too, scratchy and low. "Because you know that if I hadn't backed down, Lucas wouldn't have stood a chance. If I hadn't pushed you to him, your fucking boyfriend wouldn't be making ultimatums. I let him have you. I *let him* keep you. As a gift. But I'm taking it back because it's my turn now. It's my fucking turn to have what I want. And I've paid my dues, haven't I? I've fucking paid them and then some and now I'm done. I'm done feeling guilty for what I want. I'm done feeling guilty for watching you, for that kiss, for wanting something that doesn't belong to me. Because as it turns out, you do, don't you?"

I swallow and breathe and fall apart and come together in a single moment. "Y-yes."

His chest pushes out aggressively as he growls, "And not just for one night either."

"No."

"Yeah," he rasps. "You're mine, Echo. You're fucking mine until I decide to give you back."

"What?"

He comes even closer, his chest pressing into me with every breath he takes, every word he speaks. "That's why you came here, yeah? To go back to him. To go back to your ex-boyfriend with your pure loving heart. And you can. But not before I'm cured. Not before you've soothed this ache in me. This hurt. There needs to be some justice, Echo. Some fucking compensation for all the ways you've consumed me. Not to mention, for coming up with the stupidest plan in the history of mankind. So you can go back to him and fix everything like the good girl you are when you've paid your dues to me. When you've fixed me. When you've fixed my sickness. You always wanted to fix me, didn't you? Well, here's your golden fucking chance."

For the past month, I've been consumed by my need to save Lucas. To fix things for him. It's only tonight — a few moments ago — that I've realized that that need had nothing to do with love. It was my guilt. This heavy, suffocating guilt of having a hand in his downward spiral.

I feel an immediate need to soothe *him* as well, this guy in front of me.

I feel this immediate, *urgent* need to make things better for him.

To pay my dues for making him ache. For making him *watch*.

But this is different.

Oh God, this is *so* different.

Yes, I'm guilty for not realizing my feelings sooner. For making him and myself think that I was in love with his best friend when I never was.

I never fell in love with Lucas because I was in hate with Reign.

But this urge to fix things for him comes not from a suffocating, choking feeling of guilt but from something that feels so good and warm and freeing.

Something that feels like summer and watermelon and lemonade.

Something that makes me want to wrap my arms around him and never ever let go.

Something like lo —

No, don't think that right now, Echo. When everything is still in upheaval.

So there's only one answer that I can give him.

That I *want to* give him.

That I give him with all my rapidly beating heart and throbbing soul.

"Okay," I whisper.

His chest is still pressing into mine, his breaths still gusty. "What?"

I open my fists and slide my hands higher.

I go up to his chest and massage it, already slipping into my role of a good girl.

His good girl.

Because I'm *his*.

I always was.

"I'll fix you," I whisper again, digging my fingers into his steel-forged muscles.

His chest shudders.

His heart thunders beneath my palms.

"I'll pay my dues."

His mouth parts as his fevered gaze goes back and forth between my eyes. Then, "So you're mine."

Last night I had a qualifier on his statement, and it cut me so deeply to say it. Because it was such a lie. Tonight though, I can tell him the truth.

And smiling, I do. "I'm yours."

But then he puts his own qualifier and I flinch. "Until I give you back."

It's okay though. It's fine.

I'll think about all that later.

Right now, I need to focus on this.

On finally realizing all the new things that I've just found buried inside my heart.

On him.

So I keep my smile in place even as tears sting my eyes. "Until you give me back."

And then I make the first move.

For our third kiss.

CHAPTER THIRTY-THREE

We're kissing each other.

We're devouring each other.

As if we won't get to do this again.

As if *we were afraid* that we won't get to do this again.

Which is the truth, isn't it?

Last night was a one-time thing.

But thank God, *thank God*, he came back.

Thank God, he came back in time. Thank God, *I* realized things in time.

Thank fucking God, he's lifting me in his arms now. He's getting between my thighs. He's pressing his body, his pelvis into mine.

Oh Jesus, yes.

And it's like I've finally come awake.

All day I've been in this foggy state, the edges of the world dulled out and unclear.

Everything is clear now though.

With him between my legs, filling that empty space, I'm aware of everything around me.

The scratchy bark behind my back. The hot summer air. The dark night. The fact that he's rubbing me right there. He's rocking and gyrating against me right where my clit is.

And holy God, there's his dick.

I can feel it through the layers and layers of our clothing.

And it feels big. *Huge.*

As big as it was last night, stretching me out, invading me, and I want that again. I so want it.

I moan into his mouth, pulling at his hair.

"Thought I was too late," he says hoarsely. "Thought you'd gone back to him."

I shake my head, panting against his lips. "N-no. I couldn't. I —"

He presses open-mouthed kisses along the column of my throat. "I would've taken you from him. Would've torn you away from his arms, if I had to. Fucking kidnapped you."

I tilt my neck to the side, giving him all the access, giving him all my skin, my veins to suck on. "I would've gone with you. I would've gone wherever you wanted."

"I would've fucking killed him," he continues. "I would've fucking killed anybody who tried to stop me. I —"

"Shh," I whisper, rocking against him, humping that tent in his pants. "I'm here. I'm right here. I'm with you."

He growls.

Hard and deep.

As he licks and sucks and bites. "I'm *not* letting you go."

"I'm not going anywhere."

He growls again and tugs at the straps of my dress, the neck of it. I arch my back to unzip my dress in the back and help him out. He yanks at it, along with my bra, baring my breast, and then latches onto a nipple.

I almost cry out and dance in his arms as he sucks and sucks and sucks.

As if drinking from me.

Sucking on his medicine.

Slurping on what will make him better, and so I thread my fingers through his rich, dark hair and press his face into my tits. Willing him to drink more. Willing him to take everything from me, all the relief, all the ambrosia.

In between sucks though, he asks, "You feel okay?"

I press on the back of his head to direct his mouth to my tit. "W-what?"

He gives my nipple a deep, deep suck. "In your pussy."

I pant, my nipple sore from his suckling, yet not sore enough. "Y-yes."

"You took it, baby?" Another deep, *deep* suck. "The pills."

Last night before he dropped me off, he gave me an Advil. For the pain. Which I thought was useful because I did feel soreness where there shouldn't have been. But then, he also told me to take another one today just to be safe.

This, I thought was excessive and I let him know it.

But like the bossy control freak that he is — which let me just say is so surprising when it comes to him and his bad boy ways, but it turns out he's a control freak when it comes to me — he put his foot down, and since I was so heartsore at saying goodbye to him, I agreed.

And I took one. Well, two. Because he asked me to take two.

Which is the only thing I remember doing throughout the day.

"Uh-huh," I reply, moaning. "I did."

"Two?"

"Yes," I say impatiently.

He bites my nipple slightly and rewards me with a, "Good girl."

I arch my back some more, preening under his praise. But to my acute disappointment, he stops sucking.

Panting, I ask, "What happened? What..."

He groans and drops his head on my chest. "Fuck."

I tug on his hair. "What's wrong?"

He rolls his head, his breaths puffing on my heated skin. "Shit. Fuck. *Fuck*."

"Reign, talk to me," I insist, cupping his stubbled jaw, making him look up

His eyes are all pained and dilated. "Don't have it."

"Don't have what?"

"The condom."

"What?"

His jaw moves beneath my fingers. "Don't have it on me. I didn't..."

Oh no.

Shit. Stupid condom.

I know I said that he needed to wear a condom last night. But the thing is that...

My thoughts come to a halt when he goes to move away from me and automatically, I cling harder onto him. Automatically, I wind my arms around his neck and my thighs around his hips, and hold on.

I'm not letting him go.

There's no way.

I just found him.

We just found each other.

"W-what are you doing?"

A sigh escapes him, his eyes slowly losing their lust-drunk look. "Taking you home."

"What, why?"

"Because you need to get away from me."

I squeeze my limbs around him. "I do not need to get away from you."

Another sigh and a shake of his head. "Was being greedy anyway."

"You —"

"You just lost your cherry last night," he continues. "Can't fuck you yet."

"Why not?"

"Because you need your rest."

"I do not," I tell him, squeezing him again. "What I need is your dick."

"Echo —"

"And what *you* need is my pussy," I say, writhing against his dick that's still hard and I think throbbing as well, to make my point.

His nostrils flare. "No."

I frown, incredulous. "You don't mean that. You can't mean that. We have to have sex."

A tiny hint of amusement shines through in his hard eyes. "No, we don't *have* to have sex. Come on."

He tries to move away again, and of course I don't let him go.

I grab his face in my hands and make him look at me. "Listen, you don't need a condom, Reign. You —"

"Yes, I do."

"No, you don't," I insist. "Because —"

"*Because*," he cuts me off, squeezing me now, flexing his arms around my tiny body, "you've lost your fucking mind and forgotten what I told you. You've *forgotten* that if given the chance, I'd do everything in my power to get you fucking pregnant. Every fucking thing in my power to make my sick and twisted fantasy come true."

"What, what fantasy?"

He goes silent then.

His nostrils flaring, his eyes flickering with something.

"Reign." I lick my lips. "What fantasy?"

"It's nothing."

"No, tell me. You have... *fantasies* about getting me... pregnant?"

The p word makes me shiver. It also makes me ragingly horny.

I know we've talked about this before. But that was just... talk, right?

He never said anything about his fantasies or whatever.

"You want to know about my fantasies?" he asks.

"Yes."

"All six years' worth of them? Six years' worth of dreams and thoughts I had. Dreams and thoughts that kept me sane. While I *watched* you with him."

My heart is pounding now.

It's racing and twisting inside my chest.

At the need in his voice. The guttural, rough pain that he's suffered. And just like the night he confessed his crush on me, I want to know.

I want to know everything that he dreamed of, that he thought about.

That he fantasized about.

And then I want to do it all. For him. With him.

Not because of the guilt but because of that something else I don't want to think about right now.

Because I have a feeling that his dreams might be similar to mine. His dreams might be the ones that I'd love seeing behind my closed eyelids now that my eyes are opened to everything that's in my heart.

"Tell me," I whisper.

He gives a low chuckle, a puff of a breath.

And usually his chuckles are dirty and erotic but this one's pure torture. "Why?"

"Because from tonight, whenever I close my eyes, I want to see them too. Those dreams. I want to see *you*."

I already did though.

But it's not something that he needs to know right now. It's not something that we need to go into.

Especially when his bruised face pulses with a deep, heavy emotion and his Adam's apple bobs with a jerky swallow.

And I think he will.

I think he will give me his dreams, but first he wants to look at me. He wants to sweep his eyes over my features. Which is fine.

He can take his time.

I certainly took mine, didn't I? To realize everything.

So I can be patient. I can let him torment me and torture me like I did him.

As he stares at my disheveled dress.

My bare tits, my glistening nipples.

My bare legs even. Because my dress has hiked up and it's riding very high up my thighs, almost to where my panties are.

Something that I hadn't realized up until now.

Something that I probably should be embarrassed about.

Even though we're hidden behind a tree and there's darkness around, we're still out in the open. We're still entwined around each other and if anyone walks by, it might look like we're doing something... illicit.

Something that should be done behind closed doors.

But I don't care.

I've kept my feelings so well hidden up until now, I don't want to hide them anymore.

I don't want to cover them up again. I don't want to cover how I am with him, so different, so shameless, so full of happiness and peace.

So *his*.

Finally, *finally* he palms a tit in his rough hand and says, "Fucking your tits."

I arch into his ministrations. "Oh, I knew about that."

He chuckles softly. "Yeah, that's a pretty popular one with me. Right up there, in my top five."

"You have a top five."

"I have a top ten," he corrects me. "But we'll go with five for now."

Biting my lip, I go, "What else?"

At this, he moves his hungry eyes away from my tits and goes to my braid. It's half loosened and draped over my shoulder, the tail brushing his torso.

He picks it up and wraps it around his wrist like he did the night of his fight. He takes a whiff, a snort and rubs it on his lips. And I think that this is the hottest thing that I've ever seen; I thought the same thing that night as well.

That nothing in this world is hotter, sexier than Reign Davidson smelling my hair, slathering my scent all over his beautiful face. And I fist his t-shirt at his shoulders, squirming against him.

Which makes him open his eyes, all dark and dilated.

Then, "Fucking your hair. But you already knew that too."

I hiccup. "B-but I don't know how you'd do that."

Which makes him chuckle again. This one's tortured as well as he says, "Well, I'm good at improvising. But I think I'd start with rubbing my dick in it. In your honey-blonde hair. Making it all wet and messy with my pre-cum." He tugs on my braid, watching his dusky hand around my strands. "And then I'd take a fistful of it and wrap it around my thick meat. And then I'd hump it. I'd hump your hair like I hump my fist thinking about it. And then I'd blow in five fucking seconds."

I swallow. "F-five seconds?"

"Yeah." He looks up. "If I get to fuck your hair, Bubblegum, I'm coming all over it in less than five seconds."

"But it takes me a really long time t-to tie my braids."

"Yeah, that's what I'm counting on," he says, his eyes both intense and amused. "I'm counting on the fact that it takes my good girl at least a fucking hour to do her hair. Because that'll make it even more fun for me to mess it up."

I frown when I feel him tug my braid again.

I also moan, all horny, at the prospect of him ruining my hair.

"That's just mean," I tell him.

Which makes him chuckle again. "Well, what if I told you it's good for your hair?"

"You fucking it?"

His mouth pulls up in a lopsided smirk. "Yeah, and coming all over it."

"I —"

He leans over and whispers against my mouth, "And for your skin."

"Your cum is good for my skin?"

"Uh-huh," he rasps, kissing my mouth softly. "My cum is going to make you all pink and pretty. Shiny as fuck. So you should let me come on your face every single day. Twice a day."

"You're m-making that up."

He hums, smirking against my lips. "Maybe. But you should let me do it anyway."

"Is that in your top five?"

"To give you a facial? Fuck yeah."

"Is that what it's called?"

"Yeah. It's like a reward, see."

"L-like the pearl necklace."

He kisses my lips softly. "Yeah, exactly like that."

I kiss him back. "What else?"

Kissing me again, he goes on, "Wanna tie you up."

"Y-you do?"

"Yeah."

"With ropes?"

"Yeah." Another kiss. "But mostly my belt. I've got a nice black leather belt. Soft and supple. Tight."

My heart is racing again. "I've never... I've never been tied up before."

"Yeah, I know, Bubblegum," he says. "Didn't think you had."

"Is it…" I swallow, "Is it going to hurt?"

At this, his chuckle is definitely dirty and erotic and makes me whimper. "My poor little crybaby."

"I'm not," I grumble even though I so am.

"No, it won't hurt," he tells me, kissing and kissing, giving me his tongue now. "Not the tying up part."

"So then, which part?"

"The part that comes after I've got you all tied up in my bed."

"What will you do?"

In response, he gives me his tongue to suck on.

Like candy maybe. Like an anesthetic.

A drug to keep me all sedated and calm.

A potion to keep me docile and obedient. So I don't freak out when he tells me what he has to tell me. So I don't scream too much when he strikes.

And knowing all that, I still suck on it and suck on it.

Because I want to be struck. I want to be obedient.

I want to be under his influence and be his good girl.

"You already know, don't you?" he coos. "You know what I'll do to you when I tie you up."

My lips slip against his when I whisper, "I-I think so."

"Yeah, because that's my number one fantasy."

"To get me pregnant."

"Yeah, baby. Dreaming about tying you up in my bed and breeding you is how I've lived my life for years now. So much so that I don't even think it's my obsession anymore. I don't even think it's a sickness."

I jerk against him. "T-then what is it?"

"It's my fucking religion." I squirm again as he keeps going, "Thinking about cutting all your clothes off is how I pray now. Thinking about tearing your pretty pink dresses is how I breathe. It's how I fucking exist. And you're going to wear pink for me, Bubblegum. You better believe it."

"Because pink is your favorite color."

"Yeah." Then his eyes go hard. "And because I fucking hate blue."

He tugs at my dress to emphasize his point, because I'm wearing blue.

And because he knows why.

And then and there, I promise to never wear blue again. To always wear my favorite color for him. Because that's why it's his favorite too.

"I won't."

"Fuck yeah, you won't," he rasps, rubbing our lips together. "You'll wear pink and even though I fucking love you in pink, I'll still take a knife to it. I'll still cut it off so I can get to the real prize. My real favorite color. The color of your soft-as-fuck moondust skin."

My skin breaks out in goosebumps then.

At this possessive tone. His growly tone.

"And then what?" I ask.

He breathes out sharply. "And then, I'll spread your legs and feed you my cock. I'll feed it to your pussy and keep going until I'm right where I wanna be. Right at the spot that I dream about."

"What spot?"

"Your womb."

"My w-womb."

"Yeah, baby." He kisses me softly, wetly. "I'll wedge my dick right up in your womb and then I'll fuck it. I'll fuck your womb and that might hurt, okay?"

My belly clenches. "It might?"

"Yeah. If I fuck you so deep and so hard, it might hurt your tummy. It might make you cry."

"I won't though," I tell him bravely. "I won't cry."

He kisses me again. "You will. But it's okay. Because like last night, I'll lick it all up. I'll make it all better for my Bubblegum."

"I know you will," I whisper, kissing him back.

"Good," he praises. "So then, I'll fuck your womb. I'll fuck it and fuck it, all the while thinking and thinking about your belly swelling up."

I pant now, unable to drag in enough air.

As he spins his erotic tale. As he tells me his favorite dream.

Licking his lips, he continues, "I'll fuck it while thinking about your womb growing and expanding. Becoming bigger and bigger. But then that's not the only part of you that'll be bigger."

"What else?"

He presses a hard kiss. "Your tits will grow too."

My tits tingle at his words. "Oh yeah."

And his eyes go back to my naked breasts. "They'll become big and heavy. Creamy." He palms them again, both at the same time. "Milky."

Speechless, I arch into him, offering him more.

"Jesus Christ, the day you start to drip from here," he worries my nipples, "I'll be done. It'll be game over for me."

"I'm..."

He worries and worries my nipples, watching them with fevered, manic eyes. "I'll fucking worship at the altar of them. I will. I will latch onto them, I swear to God, and never ever let go. I'll drink from them from sunup to sundown."

I gasp, all shy and hot.

Very strangely horny. Even so, the good girl in me protests. "But R-Reign, that's... No."

"You serious, right now?" he asks, disbelieving, still watching my tits, still playing with them but with a frown now. "You're seriously going to keep me from your milky tits."

"I... I'm..."

"Because I'll die," he growls, plumping up my flesh.

"Y-you're just being dramatic."

At this, he does look up. "Fuck no. Wanting to drink from my girl's tits who's going to have my fucking baby is not drama. It's just how things are. It's just how I'm going to show her that I'm grateful. I'm so fucking grateful, Bubblegum, to you. For making me the happiest that I've ever been in my life."

And then, I break down and say, "Okay. Okay."

Because how can I not?

How can I take this away from him?

I'm not cruel. I'm not that kind of a good girl.

What I am is *his* good girl.

So he can drink from my tits if he wants to.

"Yeah?" he asks in a rough, barely-there voice. "You'll let me suckle your tits then?"

"Oh God, yes. Yes."

"Even when they get all sore and hurt-y."

"Y-yeah. Because you'll make them better."

"Fuck yeah, I will." He rewards me again with a kiss. "I'll make it all better for you, I promise. And you know I don't break promises to you."

"No, you don't."

"So yeah, if you let me feed from your pregnant tits, I'll cover you in diamonds and drape you in velvet. I'll fuck your pussy over and over, and feed you my cum."

I'm so tightly wound up in the web of his dreams that I don't know up from down. But then that's what he did last night too. Wrapped me around his filthy tales and made me feel so horny and hot and safe.

So I say, "But I'm already... I'm already pregnant, you don't need to... you don't..."

"Listen to me very carefully, Bubblegum, okay?" He goes serious, his eyes all lusty and grave. "If I get you pregnant, if I breed your cunt like I want to, you better be prepared for me to fuck you twenty-four fucking seven, yeah? I'll fuck your pregnant pussy. I'll feed from your pregnant tits and I'll fucking come all over your tight pregnant belly when I'm not flooding your hot little snatch, okay? So let's close that discussion right here."

"Oh God, Reign. Please stop. I can't —"

"But," he says, interrupting me. "None of that can happen until I actually come inside you. Until I actually blow my load. And I've just started to fuck you, haven't I? I've only just started. And we have a long road ahead of us."

"So then, do it," I tell him, all impatient. "Come inside me."

"Well, even if I do, we don't know if it'll work. We don't know if I'll get you pregnant just by fucking you once."

I twist his t-shirt. "So then fuck me twice."

"Yeah?"

"Yes."

"Okay. I'll fuck you twice. And thrice. And then four times." He places a soothing kiss on my lips. "I'll fuck you as many times as it takes to breed you, okay? Because I have a job to do, don't I? I haven't tied you up to my bed just for shits and giggles. There's a purpose, isn't there?"

"Uh-huh."

"And what's the purpose, baby?"

"To b-breed me."

"Yeah," he whispers happily. "To breed you like my good little servant girl."

My belly is clenching rhythmically now.

With every word he says.

As if my body is out of my control.

Just like his body. Which is moving now.

Rocking into mine just as rhythmically as my womb.

Because he's lost in his dreams as much as I am.

"What happens when I'm pregnant?"

His whole body shudders at this.

Shakes.

"Then, I fucking beat my chest in victory," he says hoarsely. "I fucking howl in victory. Roar to the goddamn sky that I won. That I get to keep you now. Because that's what this is all about, isn't it, Echo? I wanna tie you to my bed and fuck you over and over. Even when you tell me to stop. Even when you tell me that I'm hurting your pussy now, hurting your little tummy, wrecking your womb with how much I've fucked it and trashed it and come in it. All *this* to breed you like my good little servant girl. So I don't have to watch. So I don't have to stand on the sidelines and watch him be with you. *Play* with you. Play with *my* Bubblegum. Especially when she's mine. She was *mine* right from the beginning. From the first sight. But I had to give her away. I had to *share*. I had to *watch* someone else play with you, my doll."

He gives me a hard kiss then.

A hard and a harsh kiss as my heart twists and twists in my chest.

"That's why. That's how twisted I am, that I dream about ruining your life just so I could win against my best friend. Just so I could take you from him, steal you away. So no, we're not having sex tonight. Not without a rubber and —"

I press a hand on his mouth then.

And with shivery breaths, I go to his ear and finally whisper, "You won't need a condom, Reign. Because I'm on the pill."

He jerks.

A big, shuddering movement. That I feel in my bones.

As if a bomb went off.

And I realize that maybe it did.

Maybe that's why everything gets so silent.

So far we've been breathing and panting, whimpering and moaning. But now, we don't make a sound. Now he stares at me, his face and eyes sharp, his lips barely moving when he goes, "You are."

"Yes."

"When?"

"About t-two weeks ago."

He doesn't have to think back to calculate what it means. He already knows. "The night of the fight."

I nod and his hand goes up to my neck. The back of it where he grips me tightly, squeezing it.

My heart skips a beat at his predatory action, possessive action. "I went to the sick room, t-the clinic at the school and saw the doctor the next day. She wrote me a prescription."

"So you lied."

"Last night."

"Why, because you didn't trust me to wear a condom?"

"I trusted you," I tell him truthfully.

"So then why?"

Yeah, why.

Because I wanted to keep a distance from him. Because yesterday I thought that I was his but only for one night. And so even though I went to the clinic to get on the pill — *for him* by the way; I went right after the night of the fight, right after he confessed his crush on me and told me that he wanted to fuck me bareback so yeah, it was for him — I still kept it a secret.

To keep it all business.

Gosh, I'm an idiot, aren't I?

I've been an idiot for six years now.

For not recognizing the truth.

For not seeing who he is to me.

"Because I didn't know that I was yours."

His face hardens. "And why are you telling me now?"

I comb my fingers through his spiky hair. I trace them over his peaked and bruised features, his summer skin marked by fading bruises. I bury them in his stubble and whisper, "Because I know now. I know that I'm yours. I'm *your* good little servant girl. Because I should've been yours since the beginning. Because you don't have to watch, not anymore. You can play. Only you get to play with me now. You get to make all your dreams come true. All six years' worth of lovely dreams and wonderful fantasies."

Still, the silence dominates for a few moments.

Still, he watches me immobile and frozen.

Until he doesn't.

Until he comes for my mouth and claims it in a kiss again. And then we're devouring each other like we were only a few minutes ago. We're writhing and pulling at each other's hair and each other's clothes. And then he puts me down, and spins me around. He pushes me toward the tree and I go, only because I'm all limp and loose.

Only because I'm his.

So I let him arrange me.

I let him put my arms around the tree, and set my cheek on it. I let him yank on my hips and widen my legs.

Finally, he flips up my dress and bares my ass to his reddish-brown eyes. What he sees makes him squeeze my cheeks and smack them.

Just like that.

Without any warning. Without any preamble.

If I wasn't so out of it, I would've screamed at the shock. At the abrupt crack.

As it is, all I do is whimper and watch him, blinking, hugging my tree for support.

"Fuck me," he mutters as if to himself, twisting my panties. "Pink with little hearts. I'm going to burn for this, aren't I?"

"N-no."

"I am. Because every time a guy like me," he looks up, smacking my ass again, "fucks a girl like you, an angel cries in heaven."

I would've said something to that if I could.

But the shock of his palm renders me speechless. Oh, and I feel him sliding my panties down my bare thighs. He makes me step out of them and picks them up.

Smelling them.

Like he did my braid.

Licking the crotch too before he pockets them and unzips his pants.

My eyes go down to where his fingers are working, waiting for the first sight of his cock. But he leans down over me, drapes his chest on my spine and kisses my cheek softly, hiding his dick from my sight again.

Probably to protect me.

"Because *every time*," he yanks me back, "a Bandit raw dogs his Bubblegum's pussy, the fucking God cries in heaven. So good for you, baby. Good for you that you kept it from me. That you denied me the pleasure of fucking you raw."

I want to tell him no again.

That I wasn't good. I was bad to keep it from him.

I also want to ask him what is raw dog.

But I can't.

All I can do is gasp and moan. Because he chooses that very moment to enter me.

All bare and raw.

So I guess that's what it means, raw dog.

Doing it without a condom.

And oh my God, is there any other way to do it?

Is there any other way to get fucked but stuck to a tree like I am, with your back arched and your dress all twisted up, and your guy — this hot and big and sexy guy who's been obsessed with you for six years — giving it to you from behind?

No, I don't think there is.

I also don't think he was telling the truth just now.

When he said that I denied him the pleasure of fucking me raw.

Because I not only denied him, I also denied myself the pleasure and I'm so glad that I don't have to anymore. I'm also glad that he has me trapped between him and the tree, one hand holding my hip for purchase and other squeezing my breast. I'm glad that he's breathing right next to my mouth, grunting and moaning right alongside with me so I can revel in his ecstasy.

So I can revel in his euphoria at pumping into me bare.

And God, he definitely looks euphoric.

His eyes are closed, his mouth's parted, his chest is shuddering at my back, and I can't help but want to touch him. I can't help but want to feel his happiness with my fingers.

So I do.

I somehow manage to stop scratching the bark and go to his face.

I manage to grip it with my fingers.

At which point, he wakes up.

He opens his dark, dark, *so very dark* and dilated eyes, and looks at me. And the moment he does, I come.

It's so strange.

That I come just from eye contact.

Just by witnessing the depths of his obsession, his possession, but I do.

I come on his cock and if I was more experienced or if I was with someone else, I'd be embarrassed that I came by his tenth stroke probably. Tenth very deep and hard stroke but as it is, I'm not.

As it is, I'm writhing and arching under him.

My pussy is fluttering and contracting over his length.

And Jesus, he groans again.

He also speeds up his thrusting. So much so that now every time he bottoms out, his hips smack into my ass. His jean-covered thighs hit my bare ones. And his fingers tighten up and squeeze me.

My own fingers are still on his face, his hard jaw, his jutted-out cheekbones.

And so when he comes, I feel it everywhere.

I feel it in my fingers when his jaw goes slack, at my back when his chest vibrates with his deep groan.

And in my pussy *and* my womb.

Where he comes.

He comes right where he told me he would. Right where he wanted to.

Deep and high in my womb.

I feel him throbbing there. And for a second I think that if I put a hand on my belly, I might feel him there too. His thick cock making an impression, pulsing just under my skin, filling me and filling me.

And so I feel a strange sadness.

That his dream won't be able to come true.

Because I'm on the pill.

But it's okay. At least I gave him this. And he seems to like it. His eyes are closed and his lips are parted, and he's jerking and shuddering over my body.

Much like his cock inside of me.

When his climax is done, he opens his eyes and whispers, "Mine."

My pussy clenches over his length again and I whisper back, "Yours."

CHAPTER THIRTY-FOUR

He's playing with my hair.

I feel the strands being tugged at my scalp and turn my face to look at him.

Lying on the grass under the stars, his eyes are closed and his mouth's relaxed. His chest goes up and down so gently that he might as well be sleeping.

But he's not.

The fingers of his outstretched arm — which is also acting like my pillow — are working.

Sifting through my wayward strands, curling them, pulling them lightly.

Like he was doing last night.

So I do what I did last night as well.

I open my braid for him.

So he has more room to play with. So his fingers can frolic and dance all over my hair.

"You have a hair fetish," I whisper, glancing up at him.

He opens his eyes, his lips quirking up lazily. "I have an Echo fetish."

My heart skips a beat, both at his words and at his voice that sounds just as lazy as that lopsided smile on his face.

I turn on my side, feeling his biceps flex beneath my cheek.

Putting a hand on his face, I say, "You look so pretty."

I know pretty isn't a boy word per se. But he looks so beautiful like this, all relaxed and drowsy. His eyes shiny and his mouth all plump and wet from our kisses earlier.

He licks that plump mouth of his. "And you look so fuck-struck."

What?

"What is fuck-struck?"

"A girl who's struck by fucking. Also known as sex-struck or sex-drunk or just plain starry-eyed."

"First, that's so not a word. And second, I am so not."

"First, I just made it a word. And second, you are because we both know my dick makes magic."

"If your dick makes magic, Bandit, then my pussy is a spellcaster because you've never looked this relaxed before."

He hums, turning on his side and toward me, his other hand settling on my waist. "That she is, Bubblegum."

I stick my tongue out at him and he chuckles.

And I realize that other than being dirty and filthy, his chuckles can make me smile too.

They can fill me with happiness as well.

Then, sighing and taking in his pretty face, I whisper, "I'm so glad you won't be fighting anymore."

"Me too. Getting blackmailed is fun."

"You blackmailed me first."

"Yeah, because getting stalked's fun too."

I narrow my eyes at him. "Hey, you stalked me first."

His eyes rove over my features. "Yeah, I guess I did."

I bring my hand up to his hair and curl his strands like he's curling mine. "How did you know about this place?"

Because it's a beautiful place.

It has thick, carpet-like green grass, thick woods on one side and a shimmering lake on the other. Plus the sky looks really pretty from here, all starry and moon-eyed.

After we finished at the party that I never made it to, I told Reign that I didn't want to go back home yet. I wasn't ready to leave him, wasn't ready for our night to end. So I told him to take me someplace on his bike.

And he brought me here.

To this beautiful lake and the kind of woods I actually like, all peaceful and quiet.

"Used to come here a lot," he says. "Back when..."

He stops and clenches his jaw and I know.

What he's trying to say.

So I finish the sentence for him. "Back when your dad used to be mean to you?"

He throws me a short nod and I lean in to give him a peck on his lips.

As kind of a reward for telling me.

I already know that it's not easy for him, to talk about things. When you've kept so many secrets all your life — his dad's abuse, his crush on me and God knows how many other things — it's not easy to share.

But I'm glad he's trying.

"When I was little," he says, his eyes carrying a faraway look, "I couldn't run away. I'd be trapped wherever he chose to put me. In my room, in a closet. In the basement. But then I grew up. I could... get out of things, places. Windows. So I'd run away. I'd go to," he swallows, "Lucas's house sometimes. Sometimes I'd steal my dad's cars and drive around. One day, I found this place and it was so... peaceful. So pretty. I didn't wanna leave."

If I blink, I know my tears would fall.

I know they're sitting right there, on the edge.

So I don't.

I don't want to cry in front of him right now. I don't want to make it about me, make it so that he has to console me. Because I know he would.

Although I do say, "You're the most amazing guy I've ever met."

"What?"

I lean closer to him. "The most amazing and wonderful and strong guy I've ever met, Reign Marcus Davidson."

He studies me for a few moments before saying, "And you're the most dramatic, girly and fucking emo girl I've ever met, Echo Ann Adler."

I shake my head and insist, "I know you don't like to hear that but you are. You're so strong, Reign. You persevered. Also known as you persisted; you carried on; you hung in there; you hammered away; you were tenacious and look at you now."

"Look at me what?"

"You live in New York," I say in a duh tone. "You're in college. You have a soccer scholarship. You're going to be drafted next year. You're going to be such an amazing player. You *are* such an amazing player, Reign. So amazing that one day you'll go to the European league. You —"

"I'm not."

"You are. I have all the faith in you. You're going to be —"

"I'm not entering the draft."

I wait for him to say something more, add to what he just so casually threw out there.

But when he doesn't, I go, "What?"

While I'm freaking out over here, he again very casually shrugs. "I'm not interested in getting picked."

"How can you not be interested in getting picked?"

"Because I'm not," he says, still all relaxed. "Because I don't wanna play soccer."

"Are you insane?" I fist his hair. "What are you talking about? You want to play soccer. You're so good at soccer."

I think by the time I finish my voice is so loud that it's echoing all through the woods. And the sigh he makes in response is just as loud.

And impatient.

"No, I don't."

"But —"

"I knew," he begins with a voice that's tight now, hard, "my dad wouldn't have paid for my education, not that I cared about one, but still. He would've made up some excuse, put it on me to save face so I knew that it was the only way I could've gotten out of town. The only way to go to the same college as my best friend. I never had any plans of playing soccer."

"But you..." my own voice small and unsure, "you love soccer."

Scoffing, he continues, "No, I fucking don't. I hate soccer. Always have, always will. It's yet another thing that my father forced me to do because my brother was so good at it. Yet another way to control me, mold me into something that I'm not."

My tears threaten to fall again.

And this time it's harder to make them stop because a lump grows in my throat as well. Making me ache and ache for him.

Ache for this broken boy.

This broken rebellious bad boy.

I wish I could say something to him. I wish I could somehow make whatever he went through go away. Go back in time and erase all the hurt, all the damage done to him by his father. By all the people who misunderstood him.

By me.

What was I thinking? Why didn't I see it before?

Why didn't I look beyond the surface, beyond his meanness and cruelty, and see who he is underneath?

Why did I let him push me toward his best friend?

"I'm... I... I hate this," I say finally, such inadequate words. "I don't like this. I don't like this for you. I —"

He sighs, his fingers fisting my dress at my waist. "It doesn't matter, all right? I don't plan on sticking around for the draft and all that bullshit anyway."

"What?"

His expression shutters then and I hate this even more.

I hate it to my core.

That he's shutting me out. That there's something he's not telling me.

And I have a feeling that something is going to be the information that I'm really not going to like.

"Reign," I prod, bringing my hand down to his face. "Tell me."

His jaw tics for a few more seconds before he says, "I'm not staying."

"What does... What does that mean?"

"It means," he says, sighing, "that I'm not sticking around to work with my brother for a year and I'm not sticking around for college or the draft. I'm leaving."

Fear seizes my breaths. "W-when? Where?"

Again, his shoulders move up and down casually, like this isn't the most disastrous thing I've ever heard. "I don't know where. Away from here. Far fucking away."

I press his cheek. "That's not an answer. That doesn't tell me anything. That's barely anything, Reign. That's —"

"It's the only answer I have," he cuts me off. "And as for when..."

He pauses here and oh my God, I know.

I *fucking* know when.

I fucking know what he's going to say and I don't want him to say it.

I do not want him to say another word.

But before I can stop him, he continues, "When this is over." He tightens his fist in my dress, pulling at the fabric as he adds, his teeth clenched, "When you go back to him."

I know I should take a second here.

I should pause myself and frame my response correctly and tactfully.

Because I know it's important.

But I'm freaking out. I'm losing my mind and so the words simply slip out. "What if I don't want to go back to him?"

He stiffens beside me.

I feel his muscles turn to stone. His biceps stop flexing beneath my cheek and his chest stops breathing. Even his stomach plastered against mine grows all solid and dense.

Only thing moving on his reposed body is his eyes that grow blazing as they search my expression.

"This because of what just happened?" he asks, his words all low and growly. "Between us."

Again, I should choose my words carefully but I don't. "What if it is?"

He breathes then.

Long and hard, his inhale ending in a low growl and a heavy shake of his frame.

Then, almost ripping my dress with his hand, he goes, "Then I'd say that we're already over."

"What?"

He gets up all in my face, his hot breaths misting my skin. "Then I'd say, Echo, that you're stupider than I thought. And last night I thought you were plenty stupid. You were plenty fucking stupid and naive when you took your clothes off for me and tossed me a fucking bone. Without knowing how much I've wanted to rip into it, into *you*."

"Reign —"

"Because if you choose *this*, *me*, whatever the fuck I did to you back there, the way I fucking used you to ease the pain in my dick, over going back to the guy who loves you, who has loved you for fucking years, then I might as well leave now and never ever come back."

This time my tears spill and I don't — can't — stop them at all. "N-no, Reign, please —"

He comes over me then.

He rolls me over on my back and hovers over me, looms both like a threat and my salvation. Framing my face in his rough hands, he says gutturally, "Do you understand what's happening between us? Do you understand that this is just fucking? This is just sex. Okay, Echo? I'm just fucking you. I'm using you to cure myself. To get you out of my system so I can move on. The very thing you wanted to do yesterday. Do you realize that?"

I hiccup out a breath, as my tears keep pouring. "Y-yes."

He comes down to lick them. "Then you have to go back to him. You have to go back to the life you'd planned for yourself, yeah? NYU, Lucas. New York, becoming a big-shot writer. You *have* to go back."

I sob. "I —"

He starts to kiss me then, small tender kisses all over my wet cheeks. "You can't let this, whatever we're doing here, ruin it for you, understand? You can't let *me* ruin your life, Echo. That's the whole point. That's why I did what I did back then, pushed you to him. That's why I've done what I've done all these years. You *can't* let me. Tell me you understand that. Tell me or I —"

I wind my arms around him then and hold him to me. "I do. I-I do."

He stares down at me, his lips wet from my tears. "Yeah?"

"Yes." I hiccup again, trying to calm myself down, calm my sobs.

"I've regretted a lot of things in my life when it comes to you, Echo. But don't make me regret this," he says. "Don't fucking make me regret coming after you."

"I won't. I *won't*," I whisper thickly. "Just don't l-leave me."

His chest shudders as he wipes the trails of tears with his fingers. "I won't. Not as long as you understand that I'm not the guy for you. I'm the wrong fucking guy."

Miraculously I've stopped crying and I squeeze my arms around him. "I do. I understand."

He searches my face for a few seconds before murmuring, "Good girl."

And the crazy girl that I am, I preen under his praise even as my heart is breaking. I kiss him back when he comes to claim my mouth. I open my thighs for him when he nudges my legs apart. I let him push my dress up and shove my panties aside as I arch under him before going for his own clothes. I arch for him when he thrusts his dick inside and starts to fuck me under the stars.

But I wasn't lying when I said that I understand.

I do.

I understand that he's the wrong guy for me. I understand that he's just using me and that he has no interest in sticking around. That he'll leave as soon as he's done with me.

I already knew that if I gave my heart to him, he'd only break it.

But there's something else I understand now as well.

I understand that sometimes the wrong guy is the right guy for you. Sometimes the wrong guy is the one you see in your dreams. You write about him. You write about all the things he makes you feel. All the ways he hurts you and makes you cry.

And then you write about all the ways he makes you laugh. All the ways he makes you blush and fly. All the ways he makes you feel safe and protected.

Sometimes the wrong guy is a part of your soul.

He's made of whatever it is that your soul is made of.

And so you have to choose him.

You have to choose him because it's not a choice.

It's not a competition. It's destiny.

It's fate.

It's written not only in your hatesick diaries but in the sky. That he turned bright on the night you met.

Not his ex-best friend.

Never ever his ex-best friend.

Not to mention, I understand that I can't tell any of this to him. Because he'll leave. Because he thinks I should be with the right guy and not the guy I want to be with.

And I can't let him.

I've only just found him. I'm not going to let him go.

So I lie under him as he fucks me like a boy obsessed, and I fuck him back as a girl obsessed too.

A girl with a secret.

And it is that I'm never ever letting him go. Even when he leaves, he'll stay in my heart.

Because he isn't the only one who's sick.

I am too.

CHAPTER THIRTY-FIVE

Who: The Bubblegum
Where: Jupiter's bedroom
When: 4:01 AM; the night when Echo becomes Reign's

Dear Bandit,
I am sick.
I've been sick for six years now. But it's not the kind of sickness I thought I had.
I'm not sick with hate.
I'm sick with the opposite of hate.
Anti-hate.
I'm sick with love.
~Echo.

CHAPTER THIRTY-SIX

I don't regret the kiss.

It took me two years, three months and however many days to finally recognize that fact.

That kissing itself isn't the thing that I regret.

I regret *how* it happened. I regret how it hurt the people important to me.

Especially my ex-boyfriend.

Because he never should've been that.

My boyfriend, I mean.

I never should have said yes to going out with him. I never should've made him — and myself — think that I loved him.

When I loved someone else.

I love him, don't I?

I love the guy who once upon a time made me sick with hate. Only it wasn't hate. It was love.

Love all black and blue like his beautiful face. Love dipped in poisoned watermelon and sour lemonade.

Love wrapped up in cruel hot summer and cold mean smirks.

So I love him.

I love Reign Marcus Davidson.

My ex-boyfriend's ex-best friend.

My big bad *wonderful* Bandit.

But never knew it.

That is the thing to regret here: that I never understood my own feelings and thereby hurt so many people. *That* is the thing I need to fix. *That* is the thing I should be guilty about.

Which means I need to tell Lucas.

And apologize for the right thing this time.

Although no, I'm not going to tell him that I'm in love with the guy he completely hates now. Or that I've always been in love with him.

Because first, I don't want to hurt Lucas more than I already have.

And second, I don't want to kill all chances of reconciliation between the two of them. I'm already risking it by not going back to Lucas after his ultimatum. I don't want to harm their chances any further.

Only as soon as I come to this decision — of telling Lucas — I find out that the tragedy that we knew was just around the corner has come to pass: Lucas's dad passes away. It happens the very next day from when I was supposed to meet him at that party and the funeral is two days later. Which I attend with a myriad of feelings.

Sadness for Lucas that he lost his father; even though there wasn't any love lost between them. Nervousness at seeing him because I still haven't given an answer to his ultimatum and maybe I can't now, given the changed circumstances.

But most of all what I feel is dread.

Because I know if I'm at the funeral with my parents, *he's* going to be there too.

And he is.

Wearing black like the rest of them: a black dress shirt, black dress pants and a black suit jacket.

Among the sea of black, he still stands out though.

His colorful bruises, his spiky hair.

Those broad shoulders and that tall body.

Probably because even though he's wearing a suit like all the men here, it does nothing to tame his dangerous, bandit vibes. Not to mention, the sun hits him differently than it does the world, recognizing his summer skin and fiery eyes.

Or maybe he hits *me* differently than the rest of the world.

Because he's the guy I'm in love with.

He's the guy I finally understand that I see with rose-colored glasses and a red pulpy heart.

So it's very hard to take my eyes off him.

To not seek him out in the crowd as they bury Lucas's father in a polished oak casket.

I try to be respectful though.

To all the people involved. To Lucas, to my parents.

But mostly I try to be respectful to *him*.

He's spent years watching me moon over his best friend, be his best friend's girlfriend. And even though I have zero intentions of ever returning to Lucas, he doesn't know that and so I'll be damned if he has to go through it again, even for a single second.

Not to mention, I'll be damned if he sees love in my eyes and regrets finally acting on his feelings and coming for me.

Although he's not making it very easy.

Not only because of his dashing suit but also because while I'm trying to be a good girl for him, he doesn't have to do the same for me.

He doesn't have to be good.

He doesn't have to look away from me or not stare at me from across the space.

Everywhere I've gone today, his reddish-brown eyes have followed me.

I've felt them on the back of my neck, running up and down my spine, caressing my body, my face, my dress.

My braid; the thing that he's obsessed with.

So when during the reception, Lucas actually seeks me out at his house, I don't like it.

At all.

He says that he wants to talk to me in private and when I go to protest, my parents insist. And before I know it, I find myself following Lucas through his large living room and into this long hallway that leads to rooms in the back.

And every step I take, I feel *him*.

I feel his eyes growing even more fiery, more heated. I bet his body is all tight right about now, shaking in the way it does when all his muscles go extra taut and strained. His bruises must be pulsing along with his stubbled jaw.

I wish I could turn around and tell him that it's okay.

But I can't.

So cringing and fidgeting, I enter Lucas's father's study as directed.

"Hi," I greet him, not knowing what else to say.

Wearing black like the rest of them, plus a tie — unlike *him* — Lucas stands at the door, leaning against it, his blue eyes pinned on me. He's as grim-faced as he was at the burial and my heart goes out to him.

"I'm sorry for your dad," I whisper, rubbing my hands on my thighs.

He shrugs finally, his shoulders appearing broader in the jacket. "We all knew it was coming."

"But still, it can't be easy."

"Well, he's gone now and I don't want to talk about it."

"Okay. I understand that."

For a few seconds after that, he simply stares at me.

There's a reason he brought me here, and while I'm slightly nervous about it — because I think I know that reason — I'm going to be patient and have him come out with it when he wants to.

"You didn't show up at the party."

I knew it.

I wanted to call the very next day and meet up with him. But then we heard the news and I didn't think it was the right time to talk about this stuff. To compound his already complicated grief.

But I guess, if he wants to talk about it, then we should.

"I was going to but…"

"But what?" he asks impatiently.

I take a deep breath and say, "But I realized something."

"What?"

"That I never apologized for the right thing."

He frowns, shifting on his feet. "What the fuck is that supposed to mean?"

I take a moment to look at him then.

His blond hair and blue eyes. His fair skin.

His tall body.

He's changed; I can see that.

And not in his looks, which have matured, but also in his demeanor. In the way that he carries himself. He looks closed off now, tight and rigid. Maybe jaded and cynical.

Angry.

That's my doing.

For betraying him.

I wonder if I hadn't kissed his best friend, would he still look like that? If we'd stayed together, would he still have looked... unhappy?

And I think that he would have.

Even if he was happy when we were together — which I don't really think he was — he would've grown unhappy eventually. He would've grown discontented. He would've grown angry and jaded and cynical.

It would have happened one day.

With or without the kiss.

Because I never would've been able to make him happy long-term.

I never would've been able to give him all the things that he deserves.

I still would have said no to his proposal.

"You were right," I say finally, looking him in the eyes. "About what you said that night."

He frowns. "What?"

"That I was a bad girlfriend," I explain, and his frown thickens. "I *was* a bad girlfriend to you. I didn't know that before. I didn't realize it. I didn't realize what I was doing to you. Or maybe I did, I don't know. All I know is that I never gave myself to you, fully, *completely* like a girlfriend should. And so I tried to compensate for it. I tried to wear your favorite color, listen to the kind of music that you liked. I tried to wear my hair the way you thought looked pretty. I tried to watch sports with you. I tried to take interest in things that you liked. I *tried*. And while back then I didn't know why I did all that, I know now. I know that I'm not right for you. I know that I'm not the kind of girl who'll make you happy, Lucas. Who'll give you all the things that you want, all the things that you deserve. And I'm so sorry about that. I'm so sorry that it took me years to realize that. Years to realize that I'm not the girl for you.

"And God, I put you through so much grief. I put you through so much pain. I betrayed you. I broke your trust. I rejected your proposal. I sent you down this awful, horrible path and... What I said before still stands, Lucas. You'll never know how much I regret putting you through this, but please know that I don't deserve this. I'm not worth ruining your life over. So please, don't do it."

Again, silence reigns for a while.

Again, he holds my gaze for what feels like hours.

Then, "So you picked him."

I flinch then.

Not only because he is right — although not in the way that he's thinking; I picked him six years ago and didn't know it — but because what I just said has nothing to do with Reign.

It's about me and him.

And how wrong we are for each other.

"Lucas, that's not —"

"Even after what I told you. Even after how you broke me the first time."

"Lucas —"

He steps forward. "I told you that I'd quit it all. For you. I told you that I'd focus on what's important. On what matters, and knowing that, knowing how you fucked me up, you still picked him."

"Lucas, it's not about that. It has nothing to do with him. It's about —"

"Then, pick me."

"Lucas —"

He takes another few steps forward, his eyes harsh. "If it's not about him, if you haven't picked him, then come back to me."

"But Lucas, I'm not right for you. We're not right for each other. I never loved you the way —"

Another few steps forward and then he's right here.

He's grabbing my arm before I can even think about moving back.

"Do you think I care about that right now?" he bites out, his grip flexing, tightening around me.

"What?"

"I don't. I don't fucking care if you loved me or not. You can learn to love me. Because even when you didn't love me, we still managed to have a great time together, didn't we?" His hold tightens even more. "You were trying. So I can try now. I can fucking try to like what you like. Books, right? You like fucking books. I can read books. I can like them."

I shake my head. "Lucas, no. It shouldn't be this way. Trying is good to an extent but —"

"Fuck that. *Fuck* what it should be. We made memories. We made plans. We could have that again. We could be fucking together again."

My eyes tear up at his grip. "No, Lucas. We can't be. We never should've been."

Which tightens yet again, to the point of real pain now. "Do you have any idea what you're doing? Any idea how this will affect me?"

I twist in his grasp. "Lucas, please. Let me go."

He leans closer, digging his large, strong fingers in my arm. "I just lost my father, Echo, and you didn't even have the decency to wait. You didn't even have the decency to pretend."

"Lucas, please," I implore, struggling. "You're hurting me. You —"

"Yeah, what the fuck about my hurt? What *the fuck*," he shakes me, his eyes manic now, "about what you put me through?"

"And I'm sorry for that. I'm sorry that I —"

"Sorry doesn't make up for it, does it?" he snaps, biting out, coming so close to me that I'm afraid now.

I'm afraid that he might do something.

Something drastic.

"Lucas, please, I —"

And just like that, he leaves me and steps back.

And gosh, I can breathe again.

I take big gulps of air, my arm smarting with pain, my eyes stinging with tears.

Lucas looks at me for a second or two, still angry. But at least that manic look is gone from his eyes.

Then, "Well, fuck you, Echo. For wasting my time. For stringing me along and then dumping me. Without actually giving me the goods that I'd been working for."

My heart twists. "Lucas —"

"And fuck you for picking him. It's always him, isn't it? He has to be the fucking center of attention."

I shake my head. "No. It's not about him."

He narrows his eyes. "It is though, isn't it? Somehow it's always about him."

"It's —"

He sighs then. "Well, tell him that I'm coming for him. Tell him to watch his back."

My heart jumps in fear again but before I can ask him what he means by that, he turns around and strides out of the room.

And I stand there, panting and sore in the arm.

But only for a few seconds.

After that I'm running out of there.

I have to get out of here, go find him.

Make sure that he's okay.

I have no idea what Lucas meant by his threat but I have to make sure that he's safe.

Not to mention, I have to make sure that he hasn't completely lost his mind. I don't know how much time has passed since Lucas took me to this study but Reign must be freaking out.

And so I have to put him at ease. Reassure him that I'm still his.

Halfway down the hallway though, I come to a jarring halt.

When I see him standing before me.

Only a few feet away.

His eyes are fierce and his chest is rising and falling like there's a storm inside of him.

A violent, electric storm.

A storm that I knew must be brewing.

It needs me. *He* needs me.

And from this intense connection between us, from this strange and wonderful telepathy, he knows that I will give it to him. Whatever he needs to calm himself down.

So he opens a door right by his side.

I've been in Lucas's house enough times to know that it's a door that leads to a bathroom and when he disappears inside, I follow him. I enter the dark space and he shuts the door behind me.

He crowds me against the wood, his body, all hard and straining, trapping me, pinning me in place.

Only then, when he has me in his grips, does he hit the switch and flood the space with bright lights.

My eyes lock with his.

The eyes that I've seen in my dreams ever since I was twelve.

"Reign," I whisper, gripping his suit jacket, breathing hard against him.

In response, he growls, deep and low in his chest, that echoes in mine.

And comes for my mouth.

CHAPTER THIRTY-SEVEN

He comes for my breath.

For my heart that's beating in the back of my throat, on the tip of my tongue that he's sucking on. That he's kissing on.

He's trying to drink me. Swallow me down his throat. Tear me into sweet little pieces and eat me.

I want to tell him to slow down.

To not eat me too much, too fast or he's going to get even sicker.

But who am I kidding?

I'm doing the same thing.

I'm eating him up too much and too fast. Drinking from his lips, soaking him up on my tongue.

Because he's not the only one who's sick here, is he?

"He took you," he rasps, his one hand in my hair messing up my braid, and the other on my waist, pulling at my dress.

I grip his hair too, pull on his suit jacket. "No, he didn't. He just —"

He kisses me then, stealing my words. "He took you in a room."

"J-just to talk."

"He locked the fucking door."

"He did?"

"Yeah. Fucking asshole," he growls, his fingers pinching and tugging.

"H-how do you know?"

"I checked."

"Reign!" I say, exasperatedly.

"What, you didn't think I'd leave you alone with him, did you? He made you cry the last time you were alone with him."

"But that still doesn't mean that you could follow me. You followed me, didn't you? You *followed* me."

"Yeah, I fucking followed you. Like that's news. I always follow you. I always stalk you. I stalk the fucking shit out of you and you know that."

God, this guy.

I clench my eyes shut for a second and just make a fist out of his hair.

Then, "My parents are here, do you realize that? My parents are right *here*, Reign. What if they saw you follow me? They already hate you. They're —"

"Fuck your parents," he says, leaning closer to me. "I'm not leaving you alone with him."

I don't think this is the time to remind him that he's the one who wants me to go back to Lucas.

He's the one who thinks Lucas is the right choice for me.

Shaking my head at him, I say, "I was fine. I promise. We just talked. He didn't do anything."

Not completely true but whatever.

"Unless you wanted to be alone with him," he says, completely ignoring me, his voice low but abraded.

"What?"

And then that storm inside of him escalates.

This madness that's thrumming under his dense muscles and solid body jacks up.

"You finally realized it, didn't you? You finally fucking *realized*."

I grip him tighter. "Realized what?"

He licks his split lip. "That you miss him so much that you can't be away from him anymore."

"What, no. Reign —"

"That you can't be mine because you're *his*."

"Reign, no!" I almost shout, despite knowing that the whole world is outside, including my parents.

But like him, I don't care about my parents anymore.

Fuck my parents. Fuck everyone.

I only care about him.

I only care about this crazy guy who's saying such crazy things.

Jealous things.

"I had to watch you," he rasps.

"Oh God, Reign, listen —"

"Didn't think I'd survive it this time," he says, his voice pure gravel. "Didn't think I'd be able to take it. I was... I need to go out there and kill him. I need to —"

"No, you need to stay here. With me."

"And make you watch."

"Reign, no."

He leans closer. "I can do that, you know. I'd fucking love to do that. I'd fucking *love* to just rip his head off and throw it at your feet. And then," he pauses as his hand on my waist slides up and pulls at my braid, stretching my neck back. "Then I'd love to fuck you, Echo. I'd love to fuck you right next to his dead body. *On* the dead body of the guy you're supposed to be with. The guy I've killed *just because* you're supposed to be with him and not me."

I don't know what to do here.

I don't know if I should tell him that I'm not.

That instead of breaking all ties with him, I broke all ties with my ex-boyfriend. I broke them and I'm never ever going back. I'm never ever leaving him, my Bandit.

Who'll leave me first.

Who'll leave me right now if I tell him.

That I don't love Lucas. I love him.

But he doesn't give me a chance to do anything at all as he keeps going, lost in his jealousy. "Actually, I should've killed him the first time you kissed him. Should've killed him because he got your mouth first."

I cradle his scratched and scraped cheeks. "I never kissed him the way I kiss you."

It's the truth.

The kind that I can give him.

And I'm glad about that. That I can give him at least this much.

"Yeah? And what way is that?"

With love.

Pure and unadulterated, *sick* love.

"T-the way that says I'm going to die if I don't get your mouth."

He chuckles harshly, pulling harder at my braid. "You're fucking drama, aren't you?" A hard kiss. "My pretty fucking drama queen."

"Yes, yours," I whisper.

"What else, what else did he do to you?"

"What?"

His chest is crashing against mine, pressing into my tits. Which he then grabs with his other hand. "He touch you here?"

I swallow, my breast perking up in his hand even as regret washes over me. "R-Reign."

"Tell me. He used to be super tight-lipped about it all. When I'd ask him. All I ever got out of him was that he never fucked you. But I want to know now. I need to fucking know. He ever put his filthy fucking hands on your milky tits?"

"Y-yes. O-over my clothes."

He squeezes it then, my tit. Hard, very hard.

In a gesture of possession.

"Over your clothes. What a fucking pussy."

"R-Reign —"

"Bet he didn't touch it like that, huh," he rasps over my mouth. "Bet it was all soft and proper. Bet he was a real gentleman when he mauled these pretty fucking tits. Over your motherfucking clothes."

He goes ahead and smacks it then.

He slaps my breast, making me jerk and moan.

Making me all horny and helpless.

Making himself all horny and helpless too.

Because he groans and presses another kiss on my mouth like he can't get enough. "Did he make it *here*?"

By *here*, he means my pussy.

He shows me that.

He thrusts his pelvis into me, jams his muscular thigh between my legs and rubs on it.

And the horny girl I am, I hump on it.

I hump my swollen, charged-up pussy on his thigh like I can't get enough.

But he hates that.

He hates that I haven't answered him yet, and so to punish me he lets go of my tit and goes for my waist. He grabs it and makes me stop, leaves me all hungry and starving.

"Answer me," he growls, his violent words now spilling down my throat like lemonade. "Did he ever get to touch your pink pussy?"

"O-once." His brows snap together and I hasten to explain, "Over my clothes. We were... We were making out and he just... put his hand down there but I stopped him. I-I told him that I couldn't —"

"Never heard that story," he says all casual like, softly. "And good thing too, isn't it, baby?"

"Reign, please."

"Tell me why."

"Reign —"

"Tell me why, Echo. Tell me what I would've done, if I'd heard that story before."

"You would've..." I bite my lip and he comes for it, biting it himself, making me moan again. "You would've killed him."

My answer amuses him, his lips twitching. "I was thinking more along the lines of cutting his arm off and throwing it in the trash for touching you *down fucking there*. But this works too. This is even better." A soft kiss now. "Good girl."

And it makes me so fucking horny and needy and oh my God, so crazy in love with him that I whine, "Please Reign. It doesn't matter now. It doesn't *matter*. You have me. You got me. You got my pussy first and —"

"You told him your name."

"What?"

"That first night you met him. He asked you your name and you gave it to him. Just like that."

"The night when you gave me the anklet?"

"Fuck yeah," he growls, his jaw ticking, his fingers wreaking havoc on my dress, my braid. "You fucking gave him your name like it belonged to him. But not to me."

"Not to you?"

He licks his lips again, his eyes all wild. "Yeah. You made me *wait*. You made me fucking wait till the end. You wouldn't tell me what your name was and I was fucking dying inside. It was ruining me, wrecking me by the second, that you wouldn't. That I didn't know the name of the pink little Bubblegum who took my breath away."

Oh.

Oh *God*.

I remember that. I remember that he kept asking and asking and I kept refusing to tell him.

I didn't tell him until the end.

And yes, I do remember that I gave my name to Lucas easily.

But not because it belonged to Lucas, like he thinks, no. But because giving it to Reign felt like giving it away. Handing it over. Putting it in his possession.

Putting *myself* in his possession.

Forever.

And that scared me.

Everything about him scared me back then. All the feelings that he invoked in me, right from the first moment. All these emotions. These butterflies and goosebumps.

This intense pull that wouldn't let me walk away from him.

From that mysterious boy who wore a black hoodie in summer and came out of nowhere.

That boy who's grown into the man I love.

Protective and possessive and *jealous*. And so so adorable to me.

So then there's only one thing to do.

To make up for what I did. For all the fears I had.

I kiss him.

I kiss him and kiss him, sedate him with my mouth. Like he has done in the past with me.

Making me forget where I am and what's coming.

And when he's all loose, I push him back and come down on my knees.

All before he can even figure out what happened.

When my hands go up to his belt though, he jerks. "What the —"

I look up at him, still working on his belt. "I was scared."

"What?"

"To give you my name. To give you even a little piece of me because I knew that if I did it would belong to you. Forever." His face flickers with a possessive look that steals my breath but I keep going, "But I'm not scared anymore. I'm fearless. And free. And yours."

Aren't I?

I am free now. I am fearless.

I've left everything behind. I've cut all the ties that were keeping me from him.

And just like the other night when he came for me, I feel relieved and at peace.

I feel like this is where I belong.

At his feet, on my knees.

Loving him.

I feel his abs going tight under his black dress shirt. "Echo —"

"I was worried," I tell him, un-looping his belt, opening the button of his dress pants. "When he took me. I knew you'd be in pain. I knew that you'd be going crazy over here. And so I'm making you feel better."

He puts a shaking hand on my chin, making me look up. "You sure he didn't do something?"

His concerned, protective tone makes me want to tell him. That Lucas got scary for a second or two, and threatened him. But if I did, he'd go ballistic on my behalf.

So I'm not going to tell him.

I'm also not going to tell him that I may have irrevocably broken their friendship. That no matter how hard I tried, Lucas was adamant on believing that it was his fault.

Instead, I focus on the task.

I've unzipped his pants by now, revealing his dark gray underwear and that huge bulge. "No, he didn't."

"He mention the ultimatum?"

"Yes."

"Fucking asshole."

I rub the bulge with my hands. "It's okay. I handled it."

He jerks under my ministrations before gripping my chin tightly, "What'd you tell him?"

I look up in his eyes and whisper, "That I'm not his."

"Not yet."

I swallow down *'not ever'* and give him what he wants. "Not yet."

He breathes deep, his whole body moving with it. "Good."

I'm not sure how I do it, but I manage to stay strong, and not break down with the absolute misery and hopelessness of the situation. My hands go to the waistband of his pants and underwear, aiming to push them down and finally reveal what he keeps hidden to protect me.

Because as I said, I'm not scared anymore.

Not of a single thing in this world now.

But he puts his hands on mine and goes, "What do you think you're doing?"

I blink up at him. "Giving you a blowjob."

His abs twitch and hollow out under his shirt. "Why?"

"I told you. To make you feel better."

His grip on me flexes. "And you think a twice-fucked, still practically a virgin girl crying over my dick is gonna make me feel better."

"I won't cry."

His grip tightens even more as he dips his chin and says, "No, you won't. You'll fucking sob at my feet in about two point five seconds."

"I'm not scared anymore."

He leans down slightly, his eyes all fired up and lusty. "I don't have the goddamn patience to teach you right now, Echo, all right? Or to console you like some sort of a good guy when you do end up drenching my monster with both your tears and your spit. So you take your cock-sucking mouth away from me or I'm gonna push past it and fucking choke you with the thing you're so eager to suck on, okay?" He straightens up then. "I don't need a good girl making me feel better right now."

"Then I won't be."

"You won't be what?"

"A good girl."

"What?"

I swallow, inching closer to him, my tits grazing his thighs. "I'll be the girl you want. The kind of girl you have a thing for. A wild girl. That's what you told me, remember? So I'll be that. I'll be whatever you want me to be. Because I'm yours. You made me yours. You came for me and I'm not going anywhere until you let me make you feel better. I'm not going anywhere until I fix this, your sickness."

He takes me in, his gaze sweeping over my face. I hope I look eager to him.

I hope I look all kinds of hungry and ready to service him.

"A wild girl," he rasps.

I nod, pressing my tits on his legs. "Yes."

"You know another word for that, for wild girls?"

"Tell me."

He bends down again, but this time he comes very close to my upturned face, his hand reaching out and grabbing the back of my neck, pulling me up further.

"A slut," he whispers and licks my mouth, making me want to lick his. "A wanton." He licks me again and this time, I do manage to catch his tongue with mine. "A harlot," another lick of our tongues, "a strumpet, a fucking whore," a lick and a suck. "You wanna be my fucking whore, Echo?"

"Yes."

His eyes go mean and glint. "You know what whores do, don't you?"

"Yes."

"What?"

"They suck dicks for a reward." I lick his mouth again. "Which means I already am your whore. Because I want it. I want my reward. I want you to give me a pearl necklace."

His features move and ripple with things.

His throat too.

But before I can decipher them, he kisses me again, growling and grunting all possessively. Then, "Fine. You win. You get to suck my dick. But let's see if you can earn that reward."

And then, he straightens up.

His eyes challenging.

As he leaves me to do my job and earn my reward.

And when I actually get to see his dick a second later, I know I'm going to.

I know that because it's hard, his dick. And long.

It goes up to his belly button, or it would if it was standing upright. As it is, it can't. And that's because in addition to being super duper hard and long, his cock is also super duper thick.

It's practically being pulled down by its own weight.

His dick is a monster.

He was right about that.

A beautiful, delicious, so fucking tempting monster.

He was also right that I was going to cry.

But not with fear but with joy.

And now that I have seen it, his dick is exactly the kind of dick a guy like him would have. Not that I have any experience in it, but still.

A big bad dick for a big bad Bandit.

Who's torn off his suit jacket and thrown it on the floor, along with pulling his shirt tails up his impressively ridged torso, so he could see what I'm doing down below.

Which reminds me that I should be doing something rather than just staring at it like I'm in love.

So I reach out and grab hold of it and get to work.

I put the head in my mouth and gosh, it tastes like watermelon.

With a hint of musk and salt.

And then I definitely know that my prize is in the bag because who can resist a dick that tastes like their favorite fruit. Who can *not* go all crazy over it, licking and sucking and slobbering.

Slaving over it, worshipping it like a whore.

Like some kind of a greedy, shameless slut.

A slut with great instincts though.

Something very surprising about myself but then not really.

I'm sucking his dick, aren't I?

I'm sucking the dick of the guy I'm in love with.

The guy I'm both a good girl and a whore for.

So of course I know what to do.

Of course I know that I should twist the base with my small, soft hands. And that I should suck on his knobby head. I should wet him as much as I can and lick that vein on the underside of his cock with gusto.

And with everything that I'm doing, he groans.

He tightens up. He jerks.

His thighs are flexing rhythmically. His abs are flexing rhythmically too.

His hands are fisted by his sides but I somehow know that he wants to open them and put them on me.

And then it happens.

When I take him deep inside, not really deep though since I'm a novice still but I try to get him at least to the back of my mouth, those fists of his unfurl and his hands fly to my head. His fingers curl themselves around my braid and then it's his turn.

To fuck my mouth like I'm his personal whore.

His personal toy.

And aren't I?

He had to share me before but now I'm his. He can play with me all he likes.

He can tug my mouth up and down his rod, making me gag sometimes, making me tear up sometimes too. And I happily let him.

I happily cry for him and drown him in my spit.

I happily moan for him.

Which is what I'm doing, moaning for him, when he jerks.

His thick cock becomes even thicker and tastier and all throbby, and I know this is it.

This is when I get my reward.

And he doesn't disappoint.

He whips his dick out and in time too, to come all over my chin and my throat.

Making me all pretty and decorating me with his hot, musky cum.

And then along with giving me a pearl necklace, he gives me one made of his fingers as well.

He bends down and grabs my throat. He makes me look him in his eyes, all dark and dilated reddish-brown eyes, as he squeezes my neck while rubbing that cum into my skin.

As if marking me.

Rewarding me even more. Giving me extra credit for being such a good whore.

Panting and with my mouth swollen, I whisper, "Thank you."

"My good girl," he mutters, squeezing my throat again. "My gorgeous fucking whore."

Before I can say anything to that, he's pulling me up and kissing me. He's thrusting his tongue inside of me. And I bet he can taste himself but I don't think that he cares. He just wants to kiss me.

But that's not all.

He wants to do more. He wants to play more.

So he spins me around, pushes me against the door, dropping down on his knees. And since I'm so dazed and drunk on his cum, I can't comprehend what he's doing. Why he's on the floor behind me and his hands are up on my hips, pushing my panties down. Why he's flipping my dress up and putting his mouth there.

On my pussy.

When he gives me the first lick, I realize though.

He wants to do what I just did to him.

He wants to eat my pussy. And he wants to do it from behind.

Not only that, he wants to do it from under my dress, which he lets fall all over him. As he widens my legs and grabs hold of my ass, opening me up and taking another deep, long lick.

Growling.

Which makes me reach my hand back and grab hold of his head, or rather my dress where his head is hidden. And then he's licking me and eating me up and sucking on my clit. I feel his head moving under my dress, up and down, side to side, and I'm so close.

I'm embarrassingly close.

And I would've come.

I would've gushed straight down his throat if someone hadn't knocked at the door. If someone hadn't...

What?

Someone has knocked at the fucking door.

Someone is *knocking* at the fucking door.

Right where my cheek is.

"Echo? You in there?"

My hand flies away then.

From where I was holding Reign's head, and I smack it over my mouth, my eyes wide open. My body shivering both with arousal and fear.

Lucas.

It's *Lucas*.

"Echo," he goes again, knocking at the door. "If you're in there, let me know. Your parents are worried. They... You didn't make it back and if you're —"

"I'm here."

What?

Oh my God.

Oh my fucking God.

Why did I say that? Why did I make a sound?

"Echo?" Another knock. "You okay? What... What's going on?"

I try to move back from the door.

I try to straighten up but I find that I can't.

That's because he won't let me go.

Plus now I can see him.

Now I can see his eyes, his dark and wet mouth, his disheveled hair from being under there.

Under my dress and between my thighs.

He's still holding on to my ass, his hands so strong and capable that I can't dislodge them. I can't push him away. With my heart thundering in my chest, I shake my head and mouth, *let me go*.

His response is to shake his head.

Once and very slowly.

Followed by going in and licking me.

Right in front of my eyes. While *looking* into mine, he goes in and licks me.

And like the whore that I am, I can barely suppress a moan.

"Echo? Answer me. What the fuck's happening? What —"

"I-I'm okay. I just need a little... time," I say, grimacing, pressing my lips together.

Because he doesn't stop.

The guy on his knees behind me.

He doesn't stop with just one lick, he goes for it all.

Like he was doing before Lucas showed up at the door.

He's eating me out with the same enthusiasm and abandon as before. Only now I get to see his head moving. I get to see his hands flexing on my ass. I get to fist his hair and arch up against him.

But of course that doesn't mean that this nightmare isn't happening.

That doesn't mean that my ex-boyfriend isn't standing right on the other side of the door.

And he sounds concerned.

"Are you... Are you crying? Tell me what's happening, Echo. You sound weird."

"No... I-I'm okay," I manage to say. "I'm... I'm just... Can I talk to you like in a second or two? I'll be right out —"

"No, I'm not going anywhere. I need to know you're okay. That you're actually fine. Please, sweetheart."

Oh God, don't call me that.

As expected, Lucas's 'sweetheart' doesn't go down well with his ex-best friend. His hands on my ass tighten up to the point of pain and he growls in my pussy, nipping my clit with his teeth, pushing me that much closer to my climax.

And it's going to be a big one.

I know it.

The fact that this is all happening, that he's eating me out with a witness on the other side of the door, is making me all the more shameless and horny.

And I need to stop it.

I need to stop my orgasm.

So in a burst of what could be the most disastrous thing in the world, I push my dress down and cover him up and open the door.

But only a few inches.

Only so I can peek through and show him that I'm okay.

Lucas's brows snap together at the sight of me.

God only knows what I look like right now.

Apparently a train wreck with my flushed cheeks and disheveled hair, and it's evident in his tone. "Jesus, sweetheart, you okay?"

Again, I know Reign isn't going to like it.

And he doesn't.

But I guess this second 'sweetheart' *really* didn't sit well with him because in addition to squeezing my ass really painfully and biting on my clit, he also does something else.

Something that I never even imagined he would or *anyone* would.

Lick me… *there*.

On my other hole.

And holy God, it's a miracle that all I do is grip the door really tightly and curl my toes in my black Mary Janes as I say, "I'm fine, Lucas. I'm… I just need a minute after the study, okay? Can you please understand that? I know you mean well and my parents mean well too. But I just need some time alone. Please."

And with that, I close the door with a snap, barely coming out of that alive.

I want to spin around and give it to Reign then. Lay into him. What was he thinking? What was he trying to do? We could've been caught. *He* could've been caught, and then my parents would've hated him even more.

But I can barely manage to take a relieved breath after Lucas, let alone put together a string of angry sentences, when he pushes me over the edge, the guy who's down there, tormenting me, licking my pussy like he owns it. Without a care in the world.

That guy growls into my core and sucks my clit so hard that I come.

And I realize that he really wasn't sucking on me until then.

He really wasn't trying to make me come when his ex-best friend was here. He was merely toying with me, showing me who I belong to.

Showing me that I'm his.

At least for now.

So as I gush into his mouth, I forget being angry at him.

And then he's emerging from behind me and pressing his wildly breathing chest on my spine. I arch up against him as he settles himself, his still uncovered and hard dick against the crease of my ass.

"You think he bought that?" he rasps in my ear.

I open my drowsy eyes, close my drooling mouth and reply, "I-I'm..."

He licks the side of my face like he always likes to do. "You think he really bought it that his *sweetheart* wanted to be alone?"

I reach back and put my hand on his face. "I don't..."

"Or do you think he knew?" He doesn't give me a chance to say anything as he goes on, rocking his hips, rubbing his dick up and down the crease of my ass. "I think he did."

I rock back, my chest pressing into the door, my nipples hard and sore. "No."

"In fact, I bet he took one look at you, at your bee-stung lips and he knew."

"H-how?"

"Because, baby, your bee-stung lips don't look bee-stung anymore."

"What?"

"They look dick-stung."

I jerk. "That's not... That's not a word."

He hums, licking me again, still rolling his hips. "Yeah, it is. It's a thing that happens when a girl like you with a bee-stung mouth sucks on a dick like a whore. Like she's sucking it to earn her reward. And so she sucks that dick so good, *so fucking good*, that her mouth swells up. It becomes all red and puffy. All soft and shiny and pouty. It becomes even more bitable, as if stung by a monster fucking dick. And we all know who's asshole enough to make her do that when her whole family is here."

"N-no," I whisper, threading my fingers in his hair, resting my head on his strong shoulders.

He kisses my forehead. "We all know who's asshole enough to eat her pussy when she's talking to her ex-boyfriend, don't we?"

I loll my head side to side. "You're not —"

"And maybe right this second he's telling your parents. He's telling your daddy that you're in here. And you're not alone like you told him. You're with me."

"No, he's not."

"And of course when your dad hears that, he's going to come running, isn't he? He's going to come running to save you from me. Save you from the bad boy who seduced his good little girl two years ago."

My heart races in my chest and I fist his hair. "No, you didn't, Reign. You didn't..."

He rubs his stubble against my cheek. "He's probably thinking that I'm seducing you right this second. That I'm probably forcing myself on you. He's probably thinking that since a Bandit like me doesn't have a shot in hell with a Bubblegum like you, that my only option," he lowers his voice, "is to rape her pink little snatch and ruin her fucking life, ruin her for every other guy out there."

I scratch him then.

His neck I think, or his cheek, as I writhe against him.

And moan, "You didn't. You did not. You never will. I don't care what people think. What *you* think. You're good. You're mine. And I'm yours. I'm *your* Bubblegum."

His hands on my body turn even more possessive and violent. "Yeah, you are, aren't you? You are mine. You're my cute little Bubblegum and only I get to play with you."

"Oh God, yes."

"Your body is *my* playground now. My fucking temple, isn't it?"

"Yes, yours."

"Your sweet little snatch is my wonderland," he keeps going, his fingers tugging and pinching, making it hurt, making me even hornier. "I get to eat it. I get to fuck it. I get to lick it until it explodes in my mouth and fills me with the medicine I need, don't I?"

"God, Reign. Yes."

"And your tits." He squeezes them then, pulling at my nipples. "They're my medicine too, aren't they?"

"Uh-huh."

"And I don't care what's going on out there. I don't care if the world's burning or going to pieces. When I need my medicine, I need it. When I need your tits,

I need them. I drink from them like I drink from your pussy. Whenever I fucking want."

"Always."

He pinches my nipples through my dress again. "And you know what else?"

"What?"

"Your asshole is mine too."

"Reign —"

"It's mine to fuck. Mine to eat. Mine to lick."

"It's... I..."

"You go tell your daddy that, okay? *And* your ex-fucking-boyfriend. Tell him that his sweetheart's asshole is mine too. I need it for my condition. I need it for how sick I am, how obsessed with her. And it tastes like fucking candy. And when I fuck it, and he better believe it that I *will* fuck his sweetheart in her asshole, it's gonna feel like candy too."

With those words, he pushes inside of me.

And I'm so wet and horny that my pussy welcomes him with practically open arms. My pussy molds around his thick length and I swear he feels thicker this time than any others. Probably because I've seen him now. I've seen the dick he uses to make me go all crazy and messy. The dick he uses to dissolve me into the ether and make me flow like a river over him.

And right about now, it's also making me see stars.

Right from the beginning. Right from the first stroke.

His dick, his thrusts, his growls, his entire fucking body has me clenching and clenching around his thick rod. I'm already coming and he fucks me through my orgasm like a man possessed. He fucks my fluttering pussy, my sloppy, gushy pussy, without giving me even a second of relief.

Because he's sick, see.

He needs his medicine. He wants to bathe in his medicine.

He needs it, he needs me, to make him all better.

And he fucks me and fucks me against the door until he comes inside my pussy. And then he fucks me on the counter and then he fucks me on the floor until I'm all loose and loopy. Until he's really flooded my womb with his load and I'm walking back to my parents with a swollen belly and him running down my thighs.

CHAPTER THIRTY-EIGHT

Servant Girl/Bubblegum
Hi.

Are you sleeping?

I can't sleep.

I know you don't like texting but talk to me.

Bossman/Bandit:
You know the only kind of texting I do like, don't you?

Servant Girl/Bubblegum
Fine.

Pink nightie.

Bossman/Bandit
And?

Servant Girl/Bubblegum
With lace around the neck.

Bossman/Bandit
Just around the neck?

Servant Girl/Bubblegum
Along the bottom too. And on the sleeves.

Bossman/Bandit
Poofy sleeves?

Servant Girl/Bubblegum
They're called cap sleeves, Reign.

Bossman/Bandit
Don't give a fuck what they're called.

Servant Girl/Bubblegum
Of course you don't. You're a wild, testosterone-y animal. 😈

Bossman/Bandit
And you're a good girl swimming in estrogen and pink glitter.

Servant Girl/Bubblegum
Still yours though.

Bossman/Bandit
Fuck yeah, still mine.

What else?

Servant Girl/Bubblegum
Pink panties.

Bossman/Bandit
With little hearts?

Servant Girl/Bubblegum
No. These have cute little polka dots and lacy bows.

Bossman/Bandit
Fuck. Me.

Servant Girl/Bubblegum
I don't care what you say, Bandit, but I think you're a little too obsessed with my panties. 😊

Bossman/Bandit
I'm a little too obsessed with everything about you, Bubblegum, but we're not talking about me.

Servant Girl/Bubblegum
Why not? I think we should talk about you. Tell me what you're wearing.

Bossman/Bandit
Nothing.

Servant Girl/Bubblegum
Shut up.

Are you really wearing nothing? 😊 😊 😊

Bossman/Bandit
Why, that turn you on?

Servant Girl/Bubblegum
No, not really.

I think I'm okay.

Bossman/Bandit
You're such a fucking liar, Bubblegum.

Servant Girl/Bubblegum
And you're such a fucking show off, Bandit. 😊

Bossman/Bandit
Call it what you want. I know that I ring all your bells.

Servant Girl/Bubblegum
Not all of them. Maybe like, three of them.

Bossman/Bandit
Baby, I make music on your fucking body and you know it.

Servant Girl/Bubblegum
Fine. Whatever. 😊

Tell me what your tattoo is.

Bossman/Bandit
No.

Servant Girl/Bubblegum
Is it a birthday?

Bossman/Bandit
No.

Servant Girl/Bubblegum
A phone number.

Bossman/Bandit
No.

Servant Girl/Bubblegum
A date?

Bossman/Bandit
Yes.

Servant Girl/Bubblegum
Oh my God! Really? 😭😭😭

Bossman/Bandit
No.

Servant Girl/Bubblegum
Ugh. You're the worst.

Bossman/Bandit
I know.

Servant Girl/Bubblegum
I miss you. 😔

Bossman/Bandit
Dropped you off two hours ago, Bubblegum.

Servant Girl/Bubblegum
So? I can't miss you if you dropped me off two hours ago? Well, tough luck, dude, I do.

Bossman/Bandit
Dude?

Servant Girl/Bubblegum
And let me tell you that it wouldn't kill you to tell me that you miss me too. 😔😔

Bossman/Bandit
We don't know that.

Servant Girl/Bubblegum
I think we should test that theory.

Bossman/Bandit
And I think you should go to sleep.

Ugh.

Asshole.

No, not an asshole. Just a very, *very* stubborn boy.

That I'm in love with.

Who in the next fifteen to twenty minutes is going to come to me. To my window. Because he always does. Whenever I text him.

That's why I do it.

That's why these days I keep the drapes open and a night light on as well. So I can see him the moment he appears. So I can jump out of my bed and run over to him. So he can kiss me and I can kiss him back, and then we can do the things that we always end up doing when our mouths touch.

And then I see it.

The branch just outside my window shakes and strains. A shadow moves, and even before he appears at the window, I'm springing out of my bed and running over. I'm throwing the window open and he's climbing inside, bringing with him the scent of summer midnights and cool breeze.

His heated and sexy body, that I climb over the second his feet hit the floor.

And his large hands that grip my ass, pulling me toward him.

Finally I meet heaven.

Because his mouth is on mine, kissing, nipping, sucking.

Fucking.

"You came," I breathe out in between kisses.

"Really fucking hate texting," he mutters, kneading my ass.

"No, you came because I called."

"Stop talking."

"And because you missed me."

In response, he bites my lower lip and gives it a deep suck, growling.

"And look, it didn't kill you. It never does."

"Be my good girl and shut the fuck up, okay?"

And just like that I do.

Because he's right. I'm his good girl and we have more important things to do.

Like kissing and tugging at each other's clothes. Like him ruining my braid and me getting my hand under his t-shirt to touch his mysterious tattoo.

I love to touch it, just for the record.

I love to also kiss it and lick it and then bombard him with questions about what it means. He hasn't told me so far but I'm going to figure it out one day. I'm smart and intelligent and determined.

Also horny.

So very horny.

That when he tumbles with me into bed, I automatically open my thighs so he can settle between them. So he can push my nightie up and pull my panties down.

Panting, he stops to look at them.

I wasn't lying when I said that he's obsessed with my panties.

He's obsessed with how feminine and delicate they are. All lacy and pink.

How they always have little hearts or dots or kittens and little flowers.

He's obsessed with how they smell too and like always, he brings them to his nose to take a whiff. To take a lick too. Right on the crotch, right where my pussy sits cradled, making a mess of them. Because let's face it, all I ever do these days is think about him and so my panties are always wet and sticky.

And he loves to lick it up.

To taste me.

He also loves to make me taste myself.

So when he's done snorting my panties like a drug, he brings them to my nose. He makes me smell my musk before nudging my lips open. And staring into his fiery eyes, I do it. I peek my tongue out and lick the fabric and his nostrils flare.

Then, he pushes them in.

He pushes my panties in through my lips, filling my mouth with them. "You know why I'm doing this, don't you?"

I nod, biting on the damp fabric, squirming under him, rubbing my bare pussy up and down his still jean-covered dick.

"Because we don't want anyone to hear."

I shake my head firmly, because we don't.

He comes down to plant a kiss on my filled-up mouth. "We don't want your daddy to hear that you're not alone. That there's a bandit in your room." Still planting soft kisses all over my face and my stretched mouth, he goes down to work on his jeans and take his dick out — *Oh, thank God* — as he rasps, "Who's going to pound his little girl's pussy. Who's going to make his little girl squirt all over his big Bandit dick. While he floods her cunt, hoping and praying that her tiny birth control pill doesn't work. Because you know I'm hoping for that, don't you? I'm so fucking hoping, Bubblegum."

I moan.

And whine.

Because he makes me crazy with his body, his words. Because that's all I can do anyway.

Slowly, he pushes inside and I arch up, digging my nails into his biceps. "And because it's not as if I'm gonna stop, is it? Fucking daddy's little girl. Even if he comes running into her room and stands over this girly, pinky bed with a gun to my head. I'm still gonna keep fucking her. I'm still gonna blow my load inside of her while I make her come. Because she's not daddy's good little girl anymore, is she? She's my good little girl now. My good little whore. And then it's just gonna be awkward for you. Getting fucked and maybe even bred in front of your daddy. So you hold on to those panties, all right? Don't make a sound and let me hit that pussy."

And he does.

He hits it like he hasn't in days.

When he only had it, had me, two hours ago. By the lake. Where he took me to on his bike.

But then that's how he is.

That's how I am and that's how things are with us.

We can't keep our hands off each other. We can't be apart for more than a few hours. We start to get sick. We start to crave and go crazy.

Ever since the funeral a week ago, we've met every single day. And every single day it's the same thing.

He comes for me when everyone's asleep.

He texts me to be ready and stands outside my window while I do. I always wear a pink dress and pink lipstick, plus his anklet. He helps me climb down from the window because he knows how much I suck at climbing. And then we take off on his bike. We usually ride for a couple of hours before always stopping at the lake. Where we do what we did that night, lie on the cool thick grass and stare at the stars.

We also talk.

God, do we talk.

Well, I do most of the talking, which is not a surprise, but he does respond. He doesn't clam up or digress or try to distract me when I ask him questions. Or rather he does it maybe twenty to thirty percent of the time, which is definitely an improvement from before.

I ask him about his childhood, his dad, his mom, his big brother. I ask him about the rumors that I used to hear at the manor and he dispels almost all of them. Because almost all of them are either exaggerated or had another layer to the story.

Like the rumors about him stealing his dad's cars; he'd do it to get away from his dad's abuse when he didn't have a vehicle of his own. Or him getting caught while selling pot, because he was trying to earn money so he didn't have to depend on his dad.

I'm not saying that he's a saint.

I'm just saying that he's not all sinner.

I also talk about my stuff a lot. I talk about my dreams, my books. The books that I'm reading, the books that I want to read, the books that I want to write. And I love it. I love that he listens to all the plots and the arcs of the stories. He listens and he has his own commentary to give. As in, how stupid the heroine is to chase the killer herself, or how judgmental and dumb small-town people can be.

And what a fucking relief it is.

To talk about all the things that I love without feeling guilty. Feeling as if I'm doing something wrong, something bad. Because the other person doesn't like it.

I also tell him about my parents. How it was growing up in Brooklyn. About their struggles with money; my dad's accident; how I've always tried to be a good girl for them and how they're still mad at me for what I did. Even though me getting into NYU has helped a little, my one slip-up from two years ago is still fresh in their minds and so they still don't trust me.

And the way he reacts is... unexpected.

"So what, do they expect you to be a good girl for the rest of your life? That's dumb. And too much fucking pressure," he grumbles, lying on the grass with me draped over his warm chest, shaking his head one day. "You're allowed to fuck up. You're allowed to be who you are without feeling guilty about it. Without feeling judged or that you're bad."

I didn't think of that.

I mean, I've thought of that for other people but never for myself. I always thought that this is how you're supposed to be. You're supposed to be good and perfect for the people you love. You're supposed to sacrifice for them. You're supposed to keep them happy.

And if you don't, you are bad.

You make one mistake and you're bad.

But maybe I'm not.

Maybe I'm just... me.

And I'm allowed to be me. I'm allowed to be wild and free without feeling guilty. Without always being worried about if I'm doing everything right. Without all the pressure and compromise on my happiness.

Jupiter said the same thing, didn't she? She said I should think about myself.

And I didn't get it at the time.

I do now, I think.

Because of him.

I raise myself up on my elbows and look at him, speechless.

He's got his head resting on his elbow, his biceps bunched up, and he frowns up at me. "What?"

"You're a genius." I go down and kiss a fading bruise. "You're a freaking genius."

His lips twitch. "Is that right?"

I kiss another fading bruise. "Yeah. You are. You so are. Genius." A kiss. "Brainiac." Another kiss. "Intellectual." Yet another kiss. "Mastermind. Alpha geek."

His hand shoots up and grabs the back of my neck, pulling me closer. "Not a geek."

I grin then. "Aww, are you shy, Reign Davidson? Is it going to mess with your street cred? It's okay." I kiss the tip of his nose. "I won't tell anyone how much of a geek you are. Plus I said *alpha* geek. Alpha. So I think you're going to be okay. I mean —"

He shuts me up with a growling kiss.

And then he puts me on top and teaches me how to ride his dick.

While he sucks on my tits and makes me moan to the sky.

Anyway, after all that, all the bike rides and amazing talks by the lake and all the sex, he brings me back home. He helps me climb up the tree and leaves me back where he takes me from, my bedroom. And then I try to go to sleep and I can't. So I read on the phone he gave me — I do have an iPad now and tons and tons of paperbacks but his phone is the only one I read on — until I break down and text him.

And then he comes for me again.

He fucks me in my childhood bed and cuddles with me. Sometimes we end up watching a movie but we never finish it because halfway through it — maybe even before that — we end up kissing each other again. We end up making out and then more often than not, he isn't satisfied just by kissing my lips, he needs to kiss me somewhere else too.

Down there.

I always let him, of course, but sometimes I make demands of my own.

Sometimes I'll beg him to give me his dick so I can kiss and suck on something too. So we've devised a strategy for that. Or rather he has. When he's eating me out, if I get hungry too, he'll spin me upside down and put me on top. With my mouth on his dick and his mouth on my pussy, a sixty-nine. That I'd always read about but never experienced.

It's intense.

So freaking intense.

But not more intense than when he refuses to indulge me.

When sometimes he absolutely refuses to give me his big bad Bandit dick while eating me out. Those times he will wring a crazy orgasm out of me and then when I'm still reeling, still loose and gasping, he'll emerge from between my thighs, mouth dark and wet and dripping from my juices, straddle my chest. He will either fuck my tits or just stick his dick in my gasping mouth.

During those times, he goes crazy.

He fucks my mouth like he fucks my pussy, thrusting and pounding and plowing in my mouth, his balls hitting me on the chin, his scent choking me in the best of ways. He grabs the headboard and rolls his hips in a rhythm that reminds me of a dancer or the athlete that he so is.

And when I'm all dripping with my own saliva and tears of joy, both in my eyes and my once-again horny pussy, he comes with a pained groan. Sometimes down my throat, sometimes on the tip of my tongue. Other times on my face, my neck, my tits.

Or his favorite, my hair.

Whenever he comes in my hair, he makes sure to clean me up. He takes me to my shower, lovingly washes my hair and the rest of my tired and sated body. Well, not sated because all that fucking my mouth gets me going all over again so we fuck in the shower too.

And then, *then* we go to sleep.

Needless to say, I love movie nights.

Anyway, when I wake up in the morning, I always find my bed empty. Which I understand of course. He can't be caught sleeping in my bed in the morning.

But that doesn't mean that it doesn't hurt.

Or the fact that he won't just stay with me in my bedroom the first time around, when he brings me back from the ride. Why do I have to text him, tell him I miss him — without him ever telling me the same — before he comes for me again.

It's because this is just sex for him.

He's only using me. This isn't something permanent and I belong with someone else.

And even though I feel differently, I'm not allowed to talk about it.

Because I'm his good girl. And because if I do, he'll leave.

But I do write about it in my diary.

Which, now if I read it, I'd call the lovesick diaries.

I write how even though he's gone in the mornings, he doesn't really leave me. He's still there, the texture of his skin lingering on my fingers from all the touching I do; the shape of his muscled shoulders is imprinted on my thighs from all the times he goes down on me; the taste of his lips flutters on mine from all the kissing we do.

Not to mention, his dick in my pussy.

So deep and high in it that I feel him in my tummy.

And I touch my tummy every chance I get.

I also check my phone every chance I get.

Because for a guy who hates texting, he likes to text me a lot. Throughout the day in fact. And you'd think that they're all dirty texts but they're not. Some of them are just random texts about what he's doing at the time. Like reading a file for his brother that makes him want to kill himself. Or a photo of his brother looking like a million-dollar man at a very boring meeting.

And other times he likes to give me commands and yes, they are dirty.

Like eating my lunch without my panties. Or asking me to go up into my room while I'm cooking dinner for everyone and make myself come. And then send him proof of my wet fingers. And then sometimes he asks for photos of my braid, my pink dresses, my pink-painted toes.

And then he'll call me randomly just to hear my voice.

Or just to hear me breathe even.

I save all his texts, all the pictures that I ask him to send in exchange for all the pictures he asks. A photo of his big strong hands, the buttons of the shirt that he's wearing, what he's eating for lunch, his hair. I even make him wear a tie one day and have him send me a picture of that, and he makes me send him a picture of my bare tits in exchange for putting him through the torture.

Anyway, it feels like a relationship, doesn't it?

It feels like something a girlfriend would do for a boyfriend and vice-versa.

Although my previous relationship was nothing like this.

I wasn't always glued to my phone, checking and waiting for another text to come through. I wasn't always walking around with a heightened sense of awareness of my own body, my own breaths, my heartbeats, a desperate fucking ache in my chest.

And I definitely wasn't into giving surprises.

Which I do, at his gym.

The same one where I found him fighting.

He doesn't fight anymore but he does go there regularly, every day in fact, to work out after work.

And while I know nothing about working out and all, I do know that it takes a tremendous amount of energy, so I bring him this shake that I whipped up. And I have to say he looks totally surprised.

Not only by me but also by the shake.

"You made that," he rumbles, panting, staring at the mug I'm holding out.

It's hard to talk right now, or even think, because he's gloriously naked. Well, half naked. At some point during the workout he must've torn off his gym t-shirt, which is now lying discarded on the floor where he was bench pressing horrible-looking weights when I'd walked in.

So for a few seconds, all I can do is watch his tightened muscles, rippling and twitching with his rapid breaths.

Oh, and sweat.

So much of it, dripping down, pooling everywhere.

Then, gathering myself, "Uh, yes."

"For me," he says, his voice even more rumbly and his eyes more intense than before.

"Yes." I swallow, still holding it out.

In response, he simply stares at me, his mouth parted, his body still feeling the aftereffects of his workout but slowly coming down from it.

I bring the mug to my chest and hug it, blushing.

Maybe I overdid it.

Maybe I shouldn't have come here.

Maybe he thinks I'm stupid and too dramatic and girly.

"My mom, as you know, is a cook, right? And you also know that she teaches me things. And I saw this really amazing recipe for a dark chocolate peppermint protein shake on Pinterest. Because I know you work out a lot. And I know you've never said if you like chocolate or peppermint but I thought who doesn't like chocolate or peppermint and so I made you some. Because you need it. For, uh, energy and to be able to bench press whatever it is you're bench pressing and —"

He steps forward then, stopping me.

Thank God.

He also takes the shake from me, opens the lid and gulps it all down in one go. Like, really in one go. He also keeps watching me while he does it, his Adam's apple going up and down and when he's done, he caps the lid, wipes his mouth with the back of his hand, and comes at me.

He presses a kiss on my mouth. "Two sixty-five."

I blink my eyes open. "W-what?"

"That's what I bench press."

My mouth falls open. "Oh wow. That's —"

He comes for another kiss. "Thanks."

"For what?"

"For making the most delicious thing that I've ever tasted."

"Oh... I..." I swallow. "You're welcome. It's —"

He doesn't give me the time to say my next words because he grabs my hand and begins to drag me somewhere. I have to speed-walk to be able to keep up with him, my sandals clacking on the concrete floor, the only feminine noise I realize, in this very male-dominated space. With grunts and growls and weights hitting the floor.

Soon, he's pushing through an iron door to reveal a room with bunk beds and lockers and more benches. The same one from the night of the fight.

"Out," he growls at someone who I didn't even notice was lounging in one of the beds. "Now."

Maybe it's Reign's voice or the sight of me all breathless that makes it happen but the guy — also shirtless and oh my God with so many bruises that I cringe — shuffles out and then it's just me and him.

"Who was that?" I ask Reign, who's in the process of putting the mug aside and picking me up.

He sits me down, not on the table like he did before, but on one of the benches, and kneels between my thighs. "Just a guy."

I put my hands on his sweaty shoulders. "W-what was wrong with him?"

"He fights." Then, licking his lips, "And apparently he doesn't have a pink little drama queen to blackmail him into stopping."

"Oh, I…" He pushes my dress up my thighs and I put my hand on his. "What are you doing?"

"Eating the other most delicious thing you make for me." Then, "Well, your pussy makes that but I'm not about to discriminate."

"Oh."

His lips twitch and he claims my mouth in a short kiss, ending it with a lick.

"What's this one called?" he murmurs, tipping his chin at my lips.

My lipstick.

He's asking about the name of the pretty pink shade.

Something else he's obsessed about because he's always asking me that.

"D-dangerous Woman."

He chuckles and I feel it in my pussy, who's already making the most delicious thing for him. "You a dangerous woman, Bubblegum?"

I bite my lip. "I am."

He chuckles again. "Well, I agree." His hands resume their task of pushing my dress up my thighs, baring my skin. "Look what you do for me."

"What?"

"Spreading your legs like that and letting me eat you out." He licks my mouth again. "Even though I haven't locked the door and anyone could walk in."

"R-Reign —"

"And look what you make me do for you." He reaches where he wants to, at the apex of my thighs, revealing my pink panties. "Bringing me down on my knees like this. Making me push my face between your creamy thighs so I can lick that pink little drama queen pussy like a rabid fucking dog for all the world to see."

And with that, he does it.

He slides my panties to the side and shoves his face between my bare thighs to get at me. And lap my cream up like an animal for all the world to see.

Which like him, I don't care about after my initial — also weak — reservation.

I guess because I don't really have to be perfect all the time. Not with him. Never with him.

With him, I can finally be myself. I can be wild.

Plus I don't think he'll let anyone see anything anyway.

He's super territorial that way.

And I'm proven right because somebody does come into the room.

It happens when he's done eating my pussy and licking all that cream. After he's shoved down his gray workout pants along with the bodice of my dress, and he's inside of me, filling my pink little drama queen pussy with his cock.

At this point, someone comes into the room but before I can even notice it, he hides me. He puts his big hand on the back of my head and shoves my face into his deliciously sweaty chest. He makes himself bigger and larger so as to hide me with his body, and turns around to snap at whoever it is that entered to *'get the fuck out.'*

I have zero clue though as to who it was because he never stops fucking me and while I'm burrowed and hidden in his chest, I get busy licking his tattoo.

So yeah, he protects me like I knew he would.

Like I'm really his queen.

Like a boyfriend protects his girlfriend.

But we're not that.

We're so totally not boyfriend-girlfriend, because this is just sex.

Even though I'd like to point out that we've met each other's friends, hung out with them even, like a real couple.

It's not news that we have friends in common. I mean, my whole stalking operation, first at The Horny Bard, and then at Yo Mama's So Fit, was successful precisely because we have common links.

And one of those friends, Callie, who lives with her husband Reed in this pretty glass house in Wuthering Garden, usually hosts a soccer game over the weekend once a month or so. Since I'm one of the St. Mary's girls now — along with Callie herself, Poe, Wyn, also Jupiter and Tempest; their other friend Salem's a St. Mary's girl too but she's in California right now with her pro-soccer player boyfriend Arrow so she can't go — they invite me as well.

Oh, and since Reign is here for the summer and he knows a bunch of the guys involved — Reed and Ledger and even Callie's other brothers, Stellan and Shepard — he is invited as well.

So we go together.

And hang out with the whole gang.

Plus Principal Marshall is there.

Or rather Alaric.

Because he's Poe's boyfriend now.

And I'm so glad about that.

While all the boys play soccer in the backyard, all the girls along with Callie's little girl Halo gather around on these cute little picnic blankets and talk. Also, steal glances at all the guys. And why wouldn't they? These are some really, really sexy men.

Plus they're all very athletic.

They run. They swerve. They dodge. They dribble and kick. They head the ball. They even flip and land on their feet with a laugh. Like that's so normal. Like everyone should just flip in the air all the time and high five each other.

"Soccer players, huh," Callie says, bumping my shoulder, staring at her husband, Reed, who's just gotten the ball and is dribbling it with such finesse that it could only be magic.

"I know."

Seriously though, soccer players with their sleek, streamlined bodies *have* to be the sexiest.

Soccer is art.

Or maybe soccer players are.

"And I didn't even know that my man could play," Poe sighs, staring at her boyfriend, who gets the ball from Reed and is now trying to pass it to a striker on their team probably.

I agree with Poe. Alaric is a history professor AKA total academic geek. So yeah, it was a surprise for us too. But apparently, there is nothing that he can't do.

"Well, I already knew." Wyn shrugs, watching her man, Conrad, who's managed to steal the ball from Alaric and is now trying to make his own pass. "My man's the coach and I totally suck at soccer."

I high five her.

Conrad *is* the coach. He used to coach high school soccer — he even coached us at St. Mary's for a little bit — but now he has a new job, coaching the pro soccer team for New York. Alongside his younger brother Stellan, the assistant coach, and Ledger and Shepard, both players on the team.

Usually they live in New York, Shep, Stellan and Ledger, but they're here for the weekend.

Anyway, while we're all perving over and praising soccer players, Tempest has other ideas.

She has Halo in her lap as she glares at one guy in particular, Ledger Thorne with his crazy hair and angry eyes. Who, before Reed got the ball, had scored a goal.

"I, for one, am super over soccer," she says, her chin lifted.

Is it me or was that really loud? And did Ledger hear it?

He definitely did shoot a glance our way.

Callie glares at her. "Hey, my husband's a soccer player. Who also happens to be your brother. We met at a soccer game, remember?"

"Whatever," Pest grumbles. "But just for the record, I don't like soccer players. I don't like how they're always so obsessed with their practice and routine and exercising and scoring and dribbling and running laps around the field. I think athletes, in general, are very superficial and hotheaded. There's zero depth in them. Zero layers." She holds her finger then. "Rockstars, on the other hand, I'll take. All that angst and poetry. Yum." Then, she kisses Halo's cute curly head. "Right, Halo? You and me, we're going to find ourselves an artist. Art's where it's at, really."

Wyn high fives with Tempest at this.

But I don't think that comment was for Wyn or any of us really.

It was definitely for Ledger. Who *definitely* heard her and, in response to her comment, kicks the ball so hard that it almost takes down the goalpost when it hits the net.

And then there's Jupiter.

My feisty, talkative best friend who hasn't said a word in all this.

So I move closer to her and whisper, "Hey."

She shoots me a startled glance. "Hey."

"I think you should tell her," I say.

Jupiter's eyes go wide because she knows what I'm talking about. And who: Callie.

"No."

"I know you're afraid of coming clean to her. But she's the nicest ever. She'll —"

She breathes sharply. "No."

"But —"

"No. End of discussion."

I give her a look. "So what, you're just going to sit here and stare."

"I'm not staring."

"You are."

"Echo."

"So you didn't catch that goal he made?" I ask, raising my eyebrows. "Oh, and you totally didn't gasp and jump when he slipped and fell a few minutes ago."

She swallows. "It doesn't matter. It's gross. And he has a girlfriend."

My heart twists for my best friend. "That's why you need to tell her. You need people on your side. And she will be, trust me. She'll understand. And it's not your fault. Not the gross thing, which I don't even think is gross at all. *And* also not the second," I drop my voice even lower, "that despite all of that, you like her brother anyway."

Her emerald eyes cloud over. "I can't."

"So you're never going to tell her who you are."

"No."

"But Jupiter, I think that's a mistake. I think —"

She covers my hand and squeezes. "Just drop it. Please."

I do then.

Because I don't want to compound her misery. It's plenty miserable loving someone without them knowing, without them even acknowledging your presence. It's even more miserable loving them when you know you're not supposed to for so many reasons out of your control. And even though I think Jupiter should do what I'm telling her to do, I will support her no matter what.

By the way, the guy we're talking about here is Shepard Thorne, one of Callie's brothers. And I so wish that he didn't already have a girlfriend and that he'd take notice of my pretty best friend. Despite her thinking that it's gross.

It's not and he doesn't.

All throughout the game, and it breaks my heart.

Anyway, if not for my best friend's misery, it's one of the best days of my summer so far.

Even when all my friends interrogate me about what's happening with me and my own soccer player. Who by the way is the best player among all the guys here. He even scores the winning goal, making me so elated for him and sad that he won't be playing professionally.

My friends flood me with questions.

I probably shouldn't have told them everything from start to finish, but ever since we all got our phones back, after graduating from St. Mary's, we're all continuously chatting and texting and calling each other. So these girls know every bit of my story now, all the good, bad and embarrassing parts.

Except the part that I love him.

They don't know that. No one knows that. Only my Bandit; the diary called Bandit.

Because I don't think I could bear to tell them that the guy who thinks this is just sex, is also the guy I'm in love with.

It will make everything harder.

I'll cry when I tell them. They'll be sympathetic. They'll tell me to tell him. To confess.

And then it'll be much harder for me to be his good girl.

It'll be much harder for me to keep this secret.

Much harder than it already is.

Because every single time that I text him 'I miss you,' I want to say 'I love you.'

Every single time he calls me his good girl, I want to say 'I love you.'

Every single time he touches me or kisses me or fucks me, I want to say 'I love you.'

I love you. I love you. I love you.

I've loved him for a thousand years. And I will love him for a thousand more.

I will love him till the end of time.

Because he's the guy I'm supposed to be with.

He's the right guy for me.

Him.

My Reign. My Bandit.

CHAPTER THIRTY-NINE

The Bandit

I know it's coming.

The end.

When I'll have to give her up.

In a couple of weeks, she'll move to New York for college and I'll have to let her go.

To him.

I'll have to...

Fuck.

Even the thought makes me wanna break this beer bottle in my hand. It makes me wanna crush it between my fingers, and I could do it too. With the rage that bubbles up inside of me every time I think about it.

This irrational... *something.*

I don't have a name for it.

For what happens to me whenever I think about giving her up and letting him have her.

It feels very similar to every bone breaking in my body, every muscle aching after a long day of practice, after a grueling fight. And every breath only adding to the trauma.

But I will let her go.

I will.

It's the right thing to do, and while I'm not the one to do the right fucking thing, I'm going to do it.

For her.

I'll do fucking anything for her.

So yeah, my time is running out.

Which means this is fucking pointless.

Sitting here, at The Horny Bard.

Plus she just texted me a photo of the book she's reading tonight — *Jane Eyre* — with her sweet smile. Because I wanted to see her and she never denies me anything. Although she does sass me a lot and her selfie was accompanied by a message.

> **Servant Girl/Bubblegum**
> I don't care what you say, Bandit, but I think you're a little too obsessed with my smile. 😊

> **Bossman/Bandit**
> I'm a little too obsessed with everything about you, Bubblegum. Now give me a kiss.

And she does. A selfie of her blowing me a kiss with her puckered pink mouth followed by another text.

> **Servant Girl/Bubblegum**
> Enjoy your night out! 🍻🥃🍸🍹

But I digress, which I often do when I think about her.

So where was I?

Yeah, wasting the limited time I have with her with a night out with my fucking friends.

We've claimed our regular spot, a corner with a bunch of soft leather couches and all the privacy that we need. Back in high school, we used to come here a lot to troll for easy pussy. And since we were all soccer players, well known in town, all we needed was a fake ID and a cocky smile.

By we, tonight at least I mean me, Ledger, Reed, Shep, Stellan, and well, my brother, Homer.

Because along with being sassy, my Bubblegum is also very nagging and bossy.

A typical fucking girl.

She's somehow got it in her head that I should be friends with my brother.

Just because she accidentally read a couple of texts on my phone from Homer about inviting me out to play with his club again. That she looked at my phone isn't a problem for me. She can look at whatever the fuck she wants; I've got nothing to hide.

She's the first person to know everything about me.

Very fucking weird and surreal.

But anyway, what I do have a problem with is that ever since she saw those texts, she wouldn't let it go. She kept nagging me and asking me and telling me that I should give my brother a chance. That I should try to mend the fences.

"Look, your dad's gone, thank fucking God for that. He was the problem in your relationship," she told me one night last week. "He was the poison and he's not here anymore. Which means you have an opportunity to fix your relationship now. Your brother really wants to get to know you, Reign. In fact, I think he came up with this whole work-for-me-for-a-year idea, just so you guys could get closer together. Just go to the game. One game. Do it. You'll like it. And if you don't like it, don't go back, okay? But I think you should. Don't let your dad win, Reign. He was a horrible man. Don't let him punish you and your brother. Fix it."

So of course I said some things.

About her 'fix it' behavior. About her good girl complex.

Which means she said some things too. About me being stubborn and an idiot.

And so we had a fight of sorts, which ended in her crying and me licking up those tears, and finally giving in.

Because I can't do it.

I can't see her cry; it makes my chest hurt.

I wasn't going to play soccer with Homer though, the game I hate because of him; I have my limits. So I invited him here. On my turf, among my friends.

And fuck me, but there was this happiness on his face.

When I'd issued the invitation.

I did it on very short notice too. A couple of hours ago, just when we were leaving work — which still blows by the way — thinking he might have plans. He did. But he cancelled them to meet me here. He's not even wearing his usual clothes, a three-piece suit with a handkerchief. He's got a dress shirt on and dress pants; not really bar clothes but definitely a change for him.

But the biggest kicker is that we're not having that bad of a time.

Homer specifically.

Probably because he's not as much of a newcomer as I'd like him to be. He's sort of friends with Stellan and Shep, or used to be back in high school. They're about the same age and played soccer against each other. While they'd lost touch after that, they seem to be reconnecting well.

"No more, all right," Shep goes. "I love my fucking niece. I love her to pieces. But if I have to see one more fucking picture of her pooping, I'm gonna lose it, Jackson."

"Fuck you, you dickhead," Reed grumbles, flicking through yet another photo of his baby girl, Halo. "She wasn't pooping in that picture. She was playing with a poop toy. And even if she was, it wouldn't be gross. Because my baby girl poops glitter and farts unicorns."

"Oh, Jesus Christ." Shep throws his hands up. "Please someone make this moron stop. He's killing my hard-on."

Reed flips him the bird before showing off yet another picture of Halo, his thousandth probably, since we sat down.

Ledger shakes his head, taking a pull of his beer. "It's not as if you can do anything about it. You've got a fucking girlfriend, remember?"

"Who do you think my hard-on is for, genius?" Shep throws back.

"Okay, *genius*," Ledger mocks. "Unless you know how to magically teleport her here from New fuckin' York, you still can't do anything about it."

Shep shoots his younger brother a look. "I can. It's called a telephone."

"I believe the correct term is phone sex," Reed puts in before jerking his chin at Ledger. "Which means you're gonna need some earplugs tonight."

It's Shep's turn to flip Reed the bird.

Through all this, my eyes inevitably go over to Stellan, Shep's twin.

According to Ledger, who's the biggest gossip ever, there's some tension between the twins. Regarding Shep's girlfriend, Isadora. Apparently, Stellan wants her too. Not that Shep knows, or so Ledger tells me. I'm not privy to a lot of details but all I can say is that if it's true, that was a low blow on Ledger's part.

For bringing something like that up in front of Stellan.

Who's keeping his eyes on Reed's phone, staring at his niece's pictures like his life depends on it.

I lean toward Ledger. "Nice job, asshat."

"Just trying to get him to snap out of it. Because it ain't happening. Shep's fucking crazy about his girl. Besides, what's he thinking, going after his twin's girl? That's the biggest fucking violation of the bro code and…" He glances at me, at my ticking jaw. "Well, *you* know what he's thinking."

"Shut the fuck up or I'll make you."

He smirks. "That's not very nice. I was gonna say sorry but now I'm not going to."

I clench my jaw. "That's because you're a fucking moron. And why don't you worry about snapping out of *your* funk, huh?"

He takes another pull of his beer. "Fuck you, I'm fine."

"Sure, you are."

He isn't.

Ledger's in a bad mood; he's always in a bad mood but since the soccer game last week at his sister's house, his mood's been blacker than usual. It's Tempest. He gets that way after seeing her. He hates everything; he kicks at things; he rages and then he calms down.

Whatever.

All I want right now is to get out of here.

Which I do when my own brother starts talking smack about me.

Well, not smack but it might as well be. Because he speaks as if he knows me. As if he knows anything about me and my life and my fucking soccer skills.

"Of course, he's much better than me," he says to Shep. "And I wish I could take credit for it, but it's all him."

I choose that moment to spring up from my seat. "I'm gonna take off."

The only face I focus on while saying that is my brother's and it tightens up. I see a flicker of disappointment and for some reason, it makes me hesitate. It makes me think that if things were different, if we were like Ledger and Stellan and Shep, if we were closer, I'd…

But what the fuck?

Since when do I hesitate when I disappoint people? Since when does that make me feel disappointed myself?

All the more reason to get the fuck out of here and have Homer stay away from me.

So I make my way across the bar, dodging the crowd, trying not to bump into people.

But unfortunately I do.

Crash into someone.

The last someone that I wanted to tonight.

The last guy of our group.

This is the first time I'm seeing him since his dad's funeral. That I admit I went to very, very reluctantly. Which is saying something, because when I came back to Bardstown, my only goal was to be there for my best friend. Even though he didn't want me to be. Even though he hated my fucking guts and has hated me for two long years.

But now I realize that it may have been longer.

It may have been since the first time we met.

I jerk my chin at him. "Hey."

He doesn't return my greeting though, his eyes growing harsh.

I glance down at the drink he's holding in his hand. "Beer. Kinda light for you, isn't it?"

"I'm building up to it. The hard stuff."

"Didn't think you needed any building up to. After two years of speed drinking, you must be more vodka than water right about now."

"You'd know, wouldn't you?" he sneers almost. "Since you've been my babysitter for two years."

Actually I'm realizing that I've been his baby-fucking-sitter for much longer now.

See, I've had time to think about it.

All the years of friendship. All the years of brotherhood.

Turns out, it was only one-sided and I was too stupid to see it.

I've been too fucking blind.

The thing that I thought was friendship was more of a co-dependency. Of him on me and vice versa.

He needed someone to save him from his shitty, pathetic life. And I needed someone to... need me. To want me for who I was because of *my* shitty, pathetic life.

Wasn't it?

I saved him from those bullies, and he saved me from feeling like a perpetual disappointment.

And then I kept saving him.

I saved him every time I didn't share about my abuse because I didn't want to take away from his. I'm not much of a sharing type anyway, and he made it even easier by keeping it all about him and his pathetic life.

I even saved him from feeling rejected when I gave up the soccer captainship. Oh, and never told him about the coach offering it to me first. Because I always thought that whatever I learned about soccer, I learned it from him and I didn't even like the game anyway.

So it was his.

I even gave him the girl, and it burns me — *fucking burns me* — that he's the right choice for her. That he can give her everything that I can't. He can love her when I don't even know the fucking meaning of the word.

When all I ever seem to do is either attack her with my body or make her cry with my cruel words. And when I'm not doing that, I daydream about doing it. About vandalizing her, mauling her, fucking possessing her. Absorbing her in my body so she doesn't know where she begins and I end.

It's sick.

Unhealthy. Selfish. Disappointing.

"I have been, yeah. I'll come by to pick up my check soon," I quip, feeling angry, more at myself for being such a perpetual disappointment and inadequate. "Now if you'll excuse me —"

"Does she know?"

"What?"

His anger is full-fledged now, flickering not only through his eyes but also his whole taut body. "You being here. Does *she* know?"

I'm not gonna lie, my heart fucking clenches up at his words.

At the tone of his words.

Taunting.

Knowing.

"Because I don't think she's going to like it. You trolling for pussy while hitting hers."

"What the fuck'd you say to me?"

He chuckles. "Are you saying that you came here to fucking meditate?"

I take a step closer to him. "I'm *saying* don't fucking talk about her like that."

Another chuckle, this one harder. "Wonder what she'd say if I told her."

"There's nothing to fucking tell."

"That her new boyfriend is on the prowl. On his old hunting grounds no less."

What the fuck is he talking about?

How the fuck does he *know*?

About me and her.

To be clear, I don't fucking care if he does know. That I'm with her. In fact, nothing would bring me more pleasure than rubbing it in his ugly fucking face. That the girl he loves is with me. After years of hiding my feelings and feeling fucking guilty about them, I'd love nothing more than to shout it off the rooftops and scream it in his face.

But as I said, he's the right choice.

Which means she'll go back to him.

To the guy she loves. Still.

The guy she wants to fix everything for.

Fuck. Fuck. *Fucking* fuck.

I'm only borrowing her. Only selfishly keeping her with me until I work her out of my system.

Like she's some kind of an object. Some kind of a plaything.

You're disgusting, aren't you, you fucking asshole.

So whether I like it or not, I'm going to have to keep it a secret, her and me. From her ex-boyfriend who wanted her to cut ties with me, and for good reason. Because I'll be damned if he makes her cry again and on account of me no less.

"I don't know what you're talking about," I say, words tasting like ash in my mouth, my fingers tingling with the need to squeeze his neck.

"You're an asshole, you know that," he scoffs.

"I'm aware."

"At least have the fucking decency to treat me with respect."

"Can't." I shake my head. "Got no respect for you."

"She *told* me, you asshole."

"Told you what?"

"That she picked you."

"What?"

He grinds his teeth, anger flashing through his features. "I offered her my heart. I offered her everything that she ever wanted and she told me to go fuck myself. She told me that she never loved me. That she was lying. All these years, she was fucking lying. And so she was ending it and picking you."

I can't breathe.

I can't fucking get any air.

I can't...

"But hey," he says, stepping even closer to me, "here's a word of advice: don't get too comfy. You never know when she'll do the thing she did to me, to you. And given how she's blowing up my phone with texts, that day might be coming sooner than you expected. Once a cheater, always a cheater, isn't it?"

I do it then.

I give my tingling fingers relief and fucking punch him in the throat.

When he goes sprawling on the ground, I bend down and growl, "Don't fucking talk about my girl like that."

And then leaving him there, I'm running.

I'm fucking running for my life.

I'm running to the girl who lied to me.

She fucking lied.

CHAPTER FORTY

I did a bad thing.
I'll be the first to admit that.
I did a very girlfriend thing.

Although I'm not a girlfriend and when I was one, I'd never done something like that. But then again, I hadn't done half the things that I have now that I'm a non-girlfriend girlfriend.

But anyway.

I withheld sex.

Or threatened to.

I told my non-boyfriend boyfriend that I won't sleep with him until he goes out with his big brother. And then I felt so awful about it that I started crying.

And then I slept with him anyway.

But the good news is that he did go out with his brother.

I would've been happier though if he'd gone out to play soccer. Which he hates.

Or rather *claims* to hate.

I say claims because I don't think he hates soccer. At least, not the game itself. I think what he hates is that it was something he was forced to do. Because of his big brother. And that it's still his big brother's favorite sport. And since he hates everything related to his abusive asshole dad, like he should, he lumps soccer in as well.

But I'm going to tell him.

I've decided.

I'm going to tell him that he doesn't hate soccer. He hates what it represents.

And then I'm going to tell him that I love him.

I know. I *know* I shouldn't.

This information is even more disastrous than the soccer thing. Plus I'm his good girl and so I should keep my mouth shut and I should let it lie.

But I can't.

Because letting it lie is actually *lying*.

And while it was okay in the beginning, to not tell him, to not reveal that I've cut all ties from my ex-boyfriend, it's not anymore. I can't lie to him anymore. I can't keep it inside.

He needs to know.

I *want him* to know.

And if it makes me a bad girl, then so be it.

Because he's the one who taught me to be myself. And loving him is a part of me.

As to when I'll do all this, I don't know. I think I need a plan, a proper moment to make the big reveal. Like I did with my virginity thing.

Which is what I'm thinking about, instead of reading my book, when I see him.

At the window.

Smiling like crazy, I throw my book away and jump out of the bed to let him in. And as soon as his feet land on my bedroom floor, I bombard him with questions.

"How was it? Was it good? Did you have fun?" I hop up and down, hopefully keeping it down because my parents are sleeping just down the hall. "Please tell me you had fun. Because I think you had fun. Well, I *hope* you had fun. I really want you to have had fun. Because I *really* want you to go out with him again. I think this could be like a regular thing for you. Like brother-bonding time. And —"

"Why?"

"What?"

"Why do you want this to be a regular thing?" he asks.

Which is fine.

It's not as if his question is out of the ordinary.

Although I will say that it's slightly weird. I mean, why wouldn't I want this to be a regular thing for him? I want good things for him. I want him to have a good relationship with his brother. Who from what I've come to gather is trying really hard to make amends. He's trying really hard to be friends with his younger brother whom he — inadvertently — abandoned while growing up.

But that's not the issue here.

The issue is his tone and the look on his face.

It's flat.

Blank. Or very carefully crafted to appear so.

I haven't seen him do this in weeks now. Not since he came to get me in the woods.

So it gives me pause, his demeanor.

Still, I push through. "Uh, because he's your brother. And I think he cares about you. And I think you care about him too. And I know what you're going to say now. I know you're going to deny it. But you do. And that's because you didn't leave. You wanted to quit working for your brother but you didn't. You're actually doing the work. You brought in your work the other day, when you came to see me, remember? Those files and stuff that you'd brought with you."

He did.

A few days ago, Reign came in with a bunch of files.

I'd thought we'd go out like we usually do but he said he needed to read up on it and write a report — his words were, "a motherfucking report" — and so we'd stayed in. He said that the only way he could ever read these boring files — "coma-inducing piece of shit files" — was if I was there with him and if he got to look at my pretty face.

So that's what we did.

He looked at my pretty face, along with occasionally — okay, frequently — kissing me and making me do things, like inch my nightie up to show him my panties; take my panties off so he could smell them and spin them around his large, dusky finger. While he wrote his report.

And while *I* was reading, when he'd let me.

It was the most fun I'd had reading.

Plus it led to the most mind-blowing sex ever.

"You hated writing that report. But that's even better," I point out. "Because even though you hated it, you were still doing it for your brother. That's called being a good brother. That's what family does for each other."

Finally, he gives me a reaction.

A twitch in his brows. "Why though?"

"Why what?"

"Why do you care?"

"Because I... do."

Another reaction.

Him moving toward me. Taking a small step but somehow it feels big.

Somehow it feels threatening.

And that doesn't make sense.

"That's not an answer, is it?" he says, his eyes flickering with something that I don't understand.

I'm not proud of it but I do take a step back then.

Again, it's the tone. It's his demeanor.

"Reign, I —"

"How about I ask you something else?"

"What?"

"Something that you may have an answer for."

"Reign, what's going on? What are you —"

"Did you?" he asks, taking another step forward.

And I hate it but I move back. "Did I what?"

For several seconds, he simply stares at me. He simply roves his reddish-brown eyes all over my face, my body, my pink nightie, my loosened braid.

And it's not as if he hasn't done this before.

It's not as if he hasn't looked me over a million times since I've known him. But he's never done it how he's doing it right now.

He's never done it with raw, unadulterated hatred.

And that's saying something because for the longest time I thought he hated me. For the longest time I thought his gazes were cruel and cold.

They weren't.

Not until tonight.

"Reign, what's —"

"Did you text?"

"What?"

His eyes grow even harsher. "Him. Did you text him?"

"Text w-who?"

"Your boyfriend."

And then I know.

I know why he's looking at me like that. And what's happening here.

Because he knows.

I think he knows everything. Every *single* thing.

Despite it being completely inadvisable, I go, "*Ex*-boyfriend."

His fists clench and he takes another step forward.

This time, however, I hold my ground.

Even though this last step was the most threatening and dangerous of all the others that came before.

"Did you or did you not," he says, his words biting, "text him?"

"I —"

"Did you or did you not blow up his fucking phone with texts?"

"Reign, I —"

"Did you or did you not go behind my fucking back and blow up his *fucking* phone with texts, Echo?"

I raise my hand. "Reign, listen —"

"Did you," he leans down then, his eyes fiery, "or did you not, Echo?" He doesn't give me time to say anything at all and keeps going, "Go behind my fucking back when you knew you were mine. When I specifically told you that you were mine. When you fucking promised me that *you were mine*. Did you do that or —"

"I did," I say hastily.

And the breath he takes at that is so loud and so heavy that it sounds like a growl.

I jerk closer to him. "But only because I'm yours."

Another growly breath.

"B-because I wanted…"

"Wanted what?"

His words are growls too. And they clench my heart.

They fucking clench my soul.

Because I know how this is going to sound. How *awful* this is going to sound.

How the truth will come out.

All my lies catching up to me.

But then from the looks of it, they already have, so.

I fist my hands and whisper, "I wanted to fix it."

His body flinches.

With a storm, I think.

And I wish I could wrap him in my arms right now and make this raging storm go away. Like I did back at that funeral. But I guess I brought this upon myself and him with my lying and hiding things.

"On the day of the funeral," I begin, my heart in my throat, "when Lucas took me to his dad's study. I… He wanted to talk about the ultimatum. He wanted to know about my decision. And I told him. I told him that I couldn't…" I take a deep breath. "Go back to him. I told him it would be wrong to go back to him. That I wasn't the girl who could make him happy. Who could give him all the things he deserved. So I… I cut ties with him. A-and he assumed it was because of you. He thought I was p-picking you and he said some things in anger. He threatened you, and I… texted him a few days ago — two texts; I wasn't blowing up his phone or anything — to just… talk to him. To see where his head was at and if I could somehow convince him to… not be angry at you. Because I was the one who rejected him, not you. So yeah, to fix it."

Like a good girl.

I wanted to fix this for Reign. I wanted to look for hope.

That one day they might become friends again.

That's why I texted my ex-boyfriend behind his back, the guy I love. That I've always loved.

I knew at the time what I was doing was wrong. I'm not an expert in relationships — God, I'm not, and neither am I an expert in love — but I do know that you shouldn't have secrets when you are in love.

That when you're in love, you should be able to tell them who you are, what you are.

You should be able to tell them all your deep dark secrets.

All your deep dark desires and dreams and fantasies.

When you are in love, you should be each other's diaries.

Lovesick, lovestruck, lovestung.

And my ex-boyfriend wasn't. That in itself should've been a clue, but yeah.

I know this now because of him.

Because of my Bandit.

And when I came clean to him about my feelings, I was going to tell him about this as well.

So maybe it's okay that he knows now.

That he knows everything.

His jaw is so tightly shut at the moment, so tightly clenched that I want to cradle it in my hand and trace it lovingly. Like a girlfriend does.

Because I am his girlfriend.

Whether he likes it or not.

He doesn't, in fact, like it. Because he unhinges his jaw and asks, "Why?"

I understand this as well.

His volley of 'why' from before. What he wants to know.

"Because I did."

His brows snap together.

"Pick you. Over him." And then I just let it out. "And that's because I'm sick. I'm sick in love with you."

I guess what they say is right.

That there's a peace in being yourself.

And I've been feeling that over the last few weeks. Ever since I found out that I loved him. That I've loved him all along.

Since then I've been feeling happier, lighter, more one with myself.

But not like this.

Not like how amazing I feel right now.

How euphoric, ecstatic and rapturous.

And also devastated and destroyed and demolished.

Because my rapture has come at the cost of his hatred. His fury. His blazing anger.

All of which I can see on his face right now.

His black and blue and beautiful face.

The face of my dreams.

And nightmares.

"Actually, no," I say then. "I didn't pick you over him. I just never picked *him* over you. Because there was never really any choice. No choice for me but you. And I wish I'd known that, you know? I wish I was smarter. And I always thought that I was. I mean, I read books. I was, am, a bookworm. I'm a writer. I write in my journals every day. And people who write are very self-reflective. They're very self-aware. Very in touch with their inner selves. But as it turns out, I wasn't. And I guess that's because I always put too much pressure and emphasis on what is supposed to be. What I'm supposed to be doing. How I'm supposed to be making other people happy. How I'm supposed to be doing the right thing and make my boyfriend happy. And so in all of that, I never found out what *I* really want.

"And what I really want is to not be with him. What I really want is to not be his girlfriend. What I really *wanted* when he asked me out was to say no. Because I wanted to go out with you. What I really wanted, when I went to those soccer games to see him, was to see you. When I named my diary Bandit, it was because instead of a diary, I wanted to tell my secrets to you. When you looked at me so cruelly and condescendingly, I wanted to smack you in the face and tell you that I want you to look at me like I'm the only girl you see. And then every time I'd wear a pink dress, knowing that he wouldn't like it, I did it for you. That even though I kept my eyes away from the window of your room, I always kept my drapes open so I could know that you were there. That I could see you with just a turn of my head, a quick side glance. What I really wanted, Reign, when he kissed me for the first time, was to kiss you. And so I did. On the night of my sixteenth birthday. But you were wrong.

I didn't do it because it was a secret forbidden wish, kissing my boyfriend's best friend. I did it, I did all of it, because I loved you.

"I owe you an apology though. That I never figured it out. That I didn't realize that I loved you when I first met you. And so I made you suffer. But I did. I did love you. I loved you when you pushed me away and made me hate you. I loved you when I was with him and I love you now when I'm not. And I will love you even when you leave. Even when you reject me and storm out of here, thinking that I betrayed you when I told you that I'd be your good girl. That I'd go back to him at the end of all this. I won't. I'm sorry but I won't.

"And to answer your *whys*, why I wanted to fix things for you with your brother and with Lucas. Which you probably think has something to do with my good girl complex. It did. But only when I was trying to fix things with Lucas. I realized I was trying to fix things for him because I had the guilt of a good girl. But I'm not a good girl anymore. *Or* a bad girl even. I'm just a girl. Who wants to love a boy and who wants to take all of his pain away. And so she'll do anything to fix his problems, to mend broken things, to heal his bruises. Because to her, it's not fixing or saving. It's loving. Because that's how a Bubblegum loves her Bandit. Because that's how *I* love *you*."

I wish I had water right about now.

Or tissues.

Or both.

Or maybe a little bit of strength left to go on. Or at least just stand here.

Because it hurts.

The way that he's looking at me. The way he's *still* looking at me.

Like he doesn't know me.

Like he doesn't know anything.

Like everything is a revelation to him

And then, he hurts me more.

By saying, "It's over."

I knew that. I knew he'd say that.

But that doesn't mean it doesn't hurt.

That doesn't mean it doesn't make me furious.

It does.

It makes me so fucking furious that I don't have to find the strength to go on. It's already there, in my anger, in my pain, as I ask, "Why?"

His fists on his sides vibrate. His chest vibrates.

His whole body shakes as he growls, "Because you don't understand what we're doing here. Because I told you that the minute you make this into something more, something it's not, I'd leave."

I can't believe he just said that to me.

After everything that I told him, he has the audacity to make it about something as silly and petty as sex.

And not only that, he takes a step back from me.

Which I close in the next second.

In fact, I close all the distance and bridge all the gaps and stand toe to toe with him. "No, *you* don't understand what we're doing here."

His jaw clenches so hard that my own teeth ache. "Get the fuck away from me."

"No." I shake my head, fuming. "Not until I make you understand. Not until I get it through your thick Neanderthal skull that it *is* something more. That this is not just sex. You love me too."

"What the fuck?"

He looks so horrified right now.

So offended and alarmed.

Disgusted.

That it only fuels my fury even more. "Remember two weeks ago, that funeral we both went to? You lost your shit when you saw my ex-boyfriend take me to a locked room. And then you pinned me to the bathroom door and fucked me like you wouldn't stop. And before that, do you remember how you tried to blackmail me into giving you my virginity? How you read my diary because you wanted to feel close to me. Not to mention, do you remember last week, Reign? When I wouldn't stop talking about NYU and you got so upset."

He did.

All because he saw a purple and white brochure on my desk when he came over: an NYU brochure.

When he picked it up and started to leaf through it, I went on a tangent talking about how excited I was, how I was so looking forward to going and how I'd just gotten information about my dorm room and accommodations and my course list and whatnot.

Yes, I admit that I might have overdone it a little bit.

Just to get a reaction out of him.

Because he hasn't said it yet, but I know that me going to NYU is sort of like his self-imposed deadline. That is when he's planning to let me go and be with my ex-boyfriend.

And when I kept talking and talking about it, he got all agitated and upset. He fucked me before we went on our ride. He fucked me, right by the lake. Then he ate me out right after that. And then he brought me back and fucked me two more times.

Through all of that, he had his mouth fused to mine.

He had his mouth eating me and kissing me and stealing all my breaths.

He wouldn't let me go. He wouldn't give me a break.

"All that, that wasn't just sex. That was you being jealous. That was you being crazy, irrationally possessive. That was you not dealing with me leaving for college soon. Because when I leave for college, I leave you as well, don't I? That's when you think I go back to him. That's when you think I start my happily ever after. With the right guy. With the guy I'm *supposed* to choose. But you don't want me to. Because you want me for yourself. You want me to live my happily ever after with *you*. You call yourself sick because you want me too much, don't you? Because you're obsessed with me. You want to protect me from everything. You want to kiss my tears away. You want to take me on bike rides, help me climb down my window. You want to listen to my ramblings about my books; you want to watch movies you hate; you want to *fix things* for me, make me smile, send me to NYU on your dime and make my dreams come true. *Don't you?* But most of all, you want me to choose a guy you think is better than you. The guy you think would give me all the things that I want. It's because you love me. This is love. You're lovesick, and I wish…"

Just like that, all my anger drains away.

I become exhausted and heartsore.

Heartsick.

And I know that the only thing that will make me better is his arms around me. The only thing that will make *him* feel better are mine around *him*.

But I know he won't allow that.

So I wrap my arms around myself and whisper, a tear falling down my cheek, "And I wish that was all that you were."

He follows it with his reddish-brown eyes, his rapidly healing face going all tight and… anguished.

Because I know he can't see me cry.

And I also know that he doesn't know how to make it stop.

"But you're not, are you," I continue, another tear falling. "You're also a second son. A disappointment."

He flinches at that.

Drawing back. Taking a step back from me as if he's afraid of me now.

As if a crying girl, in her pink nightie and disheveled braid, dipped in pink love and heartbreak, is something to be afraid of.

"Don't go there."

"That's what you've been told all your life," I say, sniffling, ignoring him. "That's what your dad, that horrible man, has told you. That's what he's told the world. And so that's what they believe. They create all these rumors about you, all these lies. They misunderstand. And I have to admit that I misunderstood as well and again, I apologize for that. That I let you lead me astray, that I let you push me away rather than standing firm in my belief that there was more to you, the bandit that I met in the woods that first night. But that's not the worst part. The worst part is that you misunderstand yourself too. You believe all the rumors too, all the lies about yourself. You *believe* that you're a disappointment. That that's what you're capable of. You actually believe that you're all bad, all irredeemable, all sinner."

I sob and press a hand on my mouth to not be too loud.

To not be too heartbroken.

Because I can see that it's affecting him.

I can see that it hurts him to hurt me.

"But I want to tell you something, something that *you* told me. You told me that I can't be all good all the time. That I can't be all perfect. That I'm allowed to be whoever I want to be. I'm allowed to be myself. So I'm telling you that you're allowed to be yourself too. You're allowed to be who you want to be and *not* what the world believes you are. Not what your dad believed you are. And what you are is an abused boy who tried to survive the only way that he knew how. What you are is a loyal friend who saved a new kid from bullies. You're a boy who's learning to be a good brother, who's struggling with it but still learning and *growing*. But most of all, you're a boy who taught a girl how to be herself.

"You taught *me* how to be myself. How to be happy. How to love without guilt. You taught me that, Reign. You're the reason I know myself. You're the reason I know what I want. The kind of love I want. The kind of a relationship I want.

You've shown it to me, these past few weeks. *You*. So even if you don't believe anything that I've said today, I want you to believe that. I want you to believe me when I say that you're not a disappointment. You never were and you never will be. Not to me. *Never* to me. To me, you're worth loving. You're worth believing in. You're worth choosing and I choose you, Reign Davidson. I will always choose you. Even if you don't want me to."

CHAPTER FORTY-ONE

Who: The Bubblegum
Where: The second-floor bedroom in the carriage house on the Davidson estate
When: 1:53 AM; the night Echo tells Reign that she loves him

Dear Bandit,
You left.
And it hurts.
My body. My heart. My soul.
I hurt.
I've lied about things to you but I didn't lie when I said that I believe.
And I do.
~Echo

CHAPTER FORTY-TWO

I made him bleed one day.

On his shoulders and his upper back.

A little bit on the side of his neck too, and he told me that that wasn't the first time I'd done that.

That I did that a lot. Made him bleed.

"I do not," I gasped, straddling his body, sitting on his back and eyeing my handiwork.

His face was turned to the side, his cheek resting on his folded arms. "That's what happens when you fuck a hellcat."

I pulled at his hair even as I traced and caressed the scratch marks I left him. "Does it hurt?"

Staring into my eyes, he replied, "Yeah."

"What, really?" Horrified, I took in the scratch marks again. "I'm so sorry. I'm —"

Instead of words, a squeal came out.

Because abruptly, he spun around and changed positions. And I found myself straddling his stomach instead of his back. And it was a loud squeal too, but that was okay. We were in his gray motel room instead of my pink bedroom.

Grabbing my waist, he murmured, "Well, sorry doesn't cut it now, does it, Bubblegum?"

My hands landed on his bare shoulders. "So then what does, Bandit?"

A light flashed in his reddish-brown eyes, a mischievous light. "I have a few things in mind."

Oh no.

I knew that look. I *knew* that tone.

I shook my head. "No."

He chuckled. "Yes."

"Not in a million years."

"Million years, huh. Now we've got something to work with."

"Really? A million years is something to work with?"

"It's better than never."

God, he made me laugh.

And that's why I kept shaking my head. "No."

His lips twitched. "Come on, Bubblegum, don't be such a crybaby."

I swatted his chest. "I'm allowed to be a crybaby about this."

He pulled me down toward him. "Just the tip."

I bumped our noses together. "No."

He bumped them back, his hand creeping under his black t-shirt that I was wearing. "How about a finger? Two fingers."

My breath hitched when those fingers of his found my bare ass. "Nope."

"One finger," he said, tracing the crease of my ass now, making me squirm.

Making me rub my pussy on his ridged stomach. "No."

Then they stopped, those fingers, right where my puckered ring is. And tracing that with his digits, he went, "How about a thumb?"

At this point, I guess he knew that I was simply teasing him.

That one day I'd give it up.

My ass to him.

Of course I would've. I would've given him anything.

But playing with him was so much more fun right then.

I bit my lip. "No."

"I promise it'll feel good," he whispered against my lips. "I'll *make* it feel good, baby. It's the least you could do anyway, yeah? For making me bleed."

I think I said that he made me bleed too, when he took my virginity.

But I don't remember now. All I know is that I ended up both laughing and going horny out of my mind. Weird combination but he does that to me.

Or did.

He *did* that to me.

It's in past tense.

Isn't it?

He and I are in past tense. It's over now. He's gone.

He's been gone over twelve hours.

Or is it thirteen? I can't remember that either.

All I know is that I feel like I'm bleeding like his back and shoulders. I feel like my heart is bleeding both inside and outside of my body. And I'm coloring the world pink and red with it.

Who knew I'd turn out to be a scratcher during sex?

Who knew it would hurt so much when he left?

I mean, I had some idea. But even I didn't expect for it to feel this way.

One second it feels like I'm dying and bleeding out, and that my world has ended. And the next it feels like it did after our fight about his brother. I was angry after that fight, and sad. But I knew that it wasn't the end. I knew he'd come back. I knew he'd call or text or tap on my window as soon as night fell.

And he did.

We fought on a Monday and he came to me on Tuesday.

He came and I cried and then he soothed me the only way he knew how.

The only way I needed him to.

I need him now too.

I need him to come.

My mom thinks I've come down with a fever. She says I look tired. My eyes are all swollen up and I am running a light temperature. She says I look pale too. All the color has leached out of my skin. I wish I could tell her that the reason I'm no longer pink is because I'm bleeding.

And the boy I was made all pink for has left me.

I have no reason to be pink now.

I have no reason to get out of bed.

So I stay in it all day, under my pink covers, hugging my pink pillow and muffling my sobs with it. Because my parents are home and I don't want to alarm them more than I already have. I wouldn't even have let them know this much — I'm used to being a good girl and taking care of myself when I get sick; no money for babysitters and too many jobs for my parents — but I guess that ship has sailed. So when they go in and out, checking on me, bringing me soup and medicine, I dutifully accept it all. I be a good patient for them.

Even though what I have isn't explained by science.

What I have is a sickness. Of the heart.

And the drama queen that I am, it's fitting that I'd suffer physical symptoms of it.

It's fitting that I'm dying from it.

It's fitting that I'm chanting his name into my pillow, trying to summon him, trying to make him appear.

And suddenly he does.

Suddenly through my silent tears, I hear my window opening and sit up in the bed.

With wide eyes and a trembling heart, I watch him climb over. I watch his feet land on the hardwood floor and the moment they do, I'm out of the bed in a sudden burst of energy.

In a sudden burst of wakefulness.

I cross to him and stand before his tall and barely breathing body.

I say barely breathing and I mean it.

I also mean it when I say that he looks like me.

All sick with heartbreak.

His hair all disheveled and sticking up on the sides. His eyes red and dilated. The scruff on his jaw thicker than usual. His cheeks hollower too.

Yeah, he looks like me.

I bet if I touched him, I'd find that he's running a fever too.

"You came," I whisper.

His features tighten up for a second in response.

"What... What are you doing here?" I ask, my voice trembling.

My voice *hopeful*.

Could it be that he's here because he believes it?

He believes that he loves me and that we should be together?

"I'm here," he says, thickly, "to make you finally understand what we are not."

Oh.

He's not here for what I want him to be here for. He's here to tell me the opposite.

To *prove* to me the opposite.

Which is when I realize that I was wrong. He doesn't look like me.

He looks much, *much* worse.

Because not only is he *not* dealing with our break up, he's *not* dealing with the truth as well. The truth that he inevitably and irrevocably loves me.

So all my exhaustion washes away.

My own heartbreak set aside in favor of his crisis.

"My parents," I whisper as my heart begins to beat for the first time all day, picking up speed with every second that passes. "They are... They're downstairs."

It's not his usual time to come over.

Usually, he comes when my parents are deep in their slumber, dead to the world, oblivious to what their daughter is doing in her bedroom. And even though it's nighttime now — I don't know where the time went but I can see the moon through my window — they're well and awake, busy downstairs.

"I know," he says, his lips barely moving.

"Okay," I say.

Wondering what I'm doing.

I haven't forgotten what happened last time.

How two years ago on a night much like this, he'd come over and everything went to hell.

But the thing is that everything *had* to go to hell for things to fall into place. Everything had to fall apart and break into pieces so we could be remade.

So we could be here today, he and I.

So sick in love but also at war.

Me in my pink nightie much like yesterday, looking like love incarnate. And him, dressed in black, again much like yesterday, looking like summer and hate.

So maybe this time it'll work too.

So by the end of this, everything will fall into place as well.

I take a step toward him and it's as if something inside of him has broken loose.

Some bond, some chain, and he's free.

To breathe, his chest moving on a large wave.

And to pounce, his arms snapping around me in a death grip.

We're kissing each other then.

Which is how all things start with us, with a kiss. With our mouths devouring each other, our tongues licking and lapping, our teeth smacking, our fingers pulling at each other's bodies.

Soon, he's picking me up off the floor and throwing me on my bed.

Next he's kneeling on the mattress, a very masculine and dominating creature on my very feminine and submissive bed. Propped up on my elbows, my thighs limp and open, I watch him snag the back of his dark t-shirt and take it off, revealing his muscled torso.

That mysterious tattoo.

1510.234 3023.456

With a pang, I realize that I may never know what it means now. If he gets his way, if he wins today, I may never know what these numbers mean. But more than that I may never know the heat of his skin again, the feel of it. The texture, the smoothness, the solidity of his summer-like body.

So I break into action then.

I scramble up to my knees and press my mouth on his clavicles.

I run my fingers through his six pack, through that V, through his sleek obliques.

I kiss and lick him all over. I flick my tongue over his tight dark nipples, each and every number of his tattoo, trying to decipher it through its taste.

I kiss his abs next, his belly button, kissing and licking each rung of the tight ladder of his abs.

And I would've done more, so much more, but he grabs my untidy braid and pulls my mouth away from his body.

I look into his blazing eyes and whisper, "Tell me what your tattoo means."

"No."

I dig my nails on his chest. "Tell me you love me."

He tightens his grip on my hair to the point of pain. "No."

"I love you," I whisper.

He clenches his jaw. "Shut the fuck up."

"I love you," I say again because I won't.

And so he shuts me up with his mouth.

Punishing me with little bites and deep sucks, trying to prove to me that he doesn't love me.

And I kiss him back with all my soft tongue and plush mouth, trying to prove that I do.

But then I have to break away from him on a gasp.

Because he just did something crazy.

He just tore my nightie off.

He twisted the spaghetti straps of it so hard that the stitches ripped. And while I'm reeling with that, he pulls on the fragile neck and tears that too.

Ripping my nightie right down the middle.

Growling and straining.

"This was my..." I scratch his shoulders. "Favorite."

His response is to grab my tit and squeeze it all possessively. "I know."

I scratch him harder. "This was your favorite too."

It was.

Light pink with white daisies. That's why I wore it today.

To feel closer to him.

"Don't give a fuck," he rasps, tugging my nipple harder.

"I —"

He comes closer then. "I brought my belt."

My eyes go wide at that. My breaths falter.

"Your b-black leather belt?"

"Yeah."

"To tie me up?"

His response is a clench of his jaw and I know.

That yes, that's why he's brought it.

I swallow.

He's talked about it before, of course. Multiple times. Mostly playfully, sometimes with serious intent. But he never did. Because I guess he knew how much I liked touching him.

Scratching him.

Not to mention, how much he liked that as well.

He still knows that. He still loves that.

Just because we fought yesterday and ended things doesn't mean he forgot.

But does he really think that this would change my mind?

That this would defeat me.

Disappoint me?

"Okay," I whisper. "I trust you."

He hates that.

My easy acquiescence.

But tough luck. I don't care. I do trust him. I do believe in him and if he doesn't like that, he can suck it. So before he can say anything else, I go in for a kiss.

And then we start it all over again.

Kissing, biting, devouring, going crazy over each other.

Going sick and obsessed.

Like we've been for the past six years.

At last, he lays me down on the bed and goes up on his knees between my open thighs. He takes his belt off with slow, deliberate movements as if giving me time to back out. Giving me time to say no.

But all I do is watch him.

With bated breath.

With *anticipatory* breaths.

As much as I know I'm going to hate not being able to touch him, I also like the thrill of it.

He's always protecting me, isn't he?

He's always trying to keep me from harm even though he knows very well that I can take care of myself. Well, now I'm going to be really helpless.

I'm going to be really trapped, with my hands tied up and caged under his big muscular body.

I can't wait for him to take care of me then.

I *can't wait* to see how he protects me then. How he grows frantic with his need to keep me safe.

That alone is making me all wet.

It's making my pussy all drippy.

Plus the fact that he looks so sexy, taking that belt off. He looks so... commanding and dominating and such a deliciously frightening figure when he wraps that belt around his veiny forearm the way he wraps my braid.

My lips part. My bare tits jiggle with my breaths.

When he growls, "Arms up."

I don't know how I do it but I lift my arms, body arching up, my spine bowing. And when his eyes flash and his muscles shudder with my surrender, I don't know how I manage to not jump up and seek his mouth for a kiss.

He comes down at me, moving like a warm shadow like he always does, and loops the belt around my wrists, the leather feeling all kinds of hot and soft and supple. Erotic.

Just like his hard and smooth body over me.

Three loops, no, four.

Before he has a tight grip.

Tight enough that I won't get free, that I won't get the use of my hands back.

Good.

All helpless and flushed, me.

All dominating and protective, him.

When he's done, he looks into my eyes. "Keep 'em there."

I nod, speechless.

But my eyes are doing the talking.

My eyes are wide and unblinking and staring up at him with all the love.

Which he does hear like he always hears me.

"Jesus *Christ*," he growls, his brows furrowed and angry. "Stop fucking talking."

"I didn't say anything."

"Then stop looking at me like that."

"I can't. I love you."

He clenches his eyes shut as if my confession has actually pained him. Then, opening them, he goes, "Let's see how much you love me when I fuck you in the ass."

Now that he's settled between my open thighs, I lift them up and wrap them around his hot waist. "I'll love you more."

Framing my face with his hands, he growls, "You're fucking delusional, aren't you?"

"No, you are."

"And a drama queen."

"Yes. But you are too."

His grip on my face pulses. "You think you'll give me your forbidden little asshole that I've been dying to fuck for days now, and I'll magically declare my undying love for you."

"I don't know," I say, my fingers fisting up above me. "There has to be something magical about my forbidden little asshole if you've wanted to fuck it for days now. So I sure hope so."

He doesn't like my sass and it's obvious in his clenched words. "It's gonna hurt. I'm gonna *make* it hurt."

"You won't. You'll do everything to *not* make it hurt."

"You —"

Something occurs to me then. "Oh, my panties."

"What?"

"Stuff them in my mouth so I don't make a sound."

His eyes rove over my features for a second. "No."

"Reign —"

"Let them hear. Let them fucking come. Maybe they'll knock some sense into you when they see me raping your little asshole, you stupid little reckless girl."

"Not a rape and I'm a stupid little reckless girl *in love*," I lift my face up to his, "you big bad bully in denial."

Our teeth smack with our next kiss.

Our bodies smack too.

And then he proceeds to do what I always knew he would. What I've been waiting for him to do.

He takes care of me.

He protects me.

Prepares me. For his brutal invasion.

He kisses and licks and sucks every single part of my body. He leaves little bites on my tits. Little nips on my trembling tummy. He rubs his scruff on the inside of my thighs as he eats me out.

He fucks me with his tongue. With his fingers.

First my pussy and then my ass.

He tries to widen me as much as he can.

And the best thing is that he's so patient.

He's so gentle and tender that I don't know how to tell him that maybe this is not exactly making his point. Maybe him being so *excruciatingly* loving and wonderful with me isn't going to convince me that he doesn't.

But then, it's not as if I can make words right now.

It's not as if I can think right now either.

All I can do is squirm and twist and writhe under his hands, under his ministrations.

But I do remember to keep my arms up above me and keep quiet. I do remember to not make a single sound. I'm even quieter than on the nights he does stuff my mouth with my soaked panties. I'm even more careful. I'll be damned if anyone dares to harm him.

By the time he's done preparing me, I've come three times I think and I've soaked him, my thighs, my sheets that many times as well. And I'm so mindless and hungry for him, my asshole clenching, that I hardly feel any pain.

When he enters.

When he rocks in and out and gains entry one inch at a time.

Or maybe I do feel the pain. I do feel the stretch of invasion, of being conquered by his monster dick, but the pleasure, the victory of having him there, the fact that I did it and he helped me get there, wins over any discomfort that I might be feeling.

My love for him wins over everything else.

And I whisper, all sweaty and flushed, my head lolling side to side, my vision blurry, "I l-love you."

I can't say what happens then.

Because I don't know for sure.

Because I'm too delirious to know anything except the stretch of my asshole and throb of his dick inside of it as he moves in and out. But I feel him shudder. I feel him go all hot and heavy and... relaxed even, his sweaty limbs rubbing against mine, slipping with his strokes.

I hear him moan and grunt and then I feel his lips on mine.

Pressing tender kisses. Drooling kisses.

Sloppy kisses, slippery and wet.

So wet that when we break apart, we're still attached by the threads of our spit. Saliva from his tongue pools into my mouth and I think we're one. I've never been this close to anyone, exchanging breaths, exchanging fluids, exchanging love.

This is love.

So wild and sick and so pretty.

And I don't know how it's possible but I come once again, clenching around his rod in my ass, and I feel him coming too. Filling my channel with his cream.

And it's wonderful.

And we both love it so much that we don't stop coming for ages.

Even when we do stop coming, we don't stop kissing.

We'll never stop kissing.

We'll never stop...

But we do.

And we do it with a bang.

A crash and a scream and then my vision is reduced to flashes.

Reign being pushed away from me. My mother's horrified face. My mother's *crying* face. Reign being dragged out of my room by someone. Someone I can't see because my mother is now bent over me. My mother's doing something to my hands. When my hands go free I realize that she was untying the belt.

But I don't want her to untie the belt.

I *didn't* want her to.

I'm trying to show Reign that I love him. And that he loves me too. And now that he's taken my forbidden little asshole, he'll declare his undying love for me. Because it was magical, as I knew it would be, and so it's time for him to face the truth.

It's time for him to *believe*.

I want to tell my mom that.

But then she's sitting me up on the bed, all the while crying and screaming and saying things that I don't understand. When she drapes a blanket over me though, covering me in the kind of warmth that I don't want, my fog lifts.

My coma-like state breaks and I realize what's happening.

I realize that the door…

The door wasn't locked.

I always lock the door. *Always*.

After what happened two years ago, I always make sure to lock it. Doesn't matter if I'm reading inside or sleeping or being with Reign in the middle of the night. My room is *always* locked. And it wasn't today because my mom and my dad were so worried about me.

And so of course, the worst has happened.

Of course in my foolish recklessness, my nightmare has come true.

I push my mother away then.

I don't know where I get the strength from but I push her away so hard that her arms come loose from around me and I'm running out of my room.

"Echo, stop," my mom's screaming. "Get back here."

But I need to go.

I need to save him.

My dad's going to finish what he'd started two years ago.

So I rush down the stairs and tear down the hallway to get to the living room. Where I realize things are even worse. Because it's empty and the front door is wide open.

And oh my God, I see *people*.

I run out the door and my heart drops down to my stomach.

It drops down to the ground.

Because my dad is punching Reign and he's letting my dad do it. My dad is literally beating on him and Reign is doing absolutely nothing to stop him.

No one is doing anything to stop him.

All these people — I don't even know where they came from — are simply standing there, gasping and watching, without lifting a single finger. It's exactly like the night of the fight.

And just like that night, my feet move forward as I scream, "Dad, stop."

But I can only take a couple of steps before I'm stopped. Again, much like that night.

This time, by Mom.

She's caught up to me and is holding me in her arms. She's trying to shush me but I won't be silenced. "Dad, please. Stop it. Stop hitting him." I struggle against her hold, crying and sobbing. "Dad, please. Oh my God, stop. Please stop."

But he won't listen to me.

My dad simply won't listen and by now, Reign's on the ground and my dad's kicking him in the stomach. And there's so much blood.

There are bruises blooming and coming alive on his bare torso.

And so I turn to Reign. I direct my pleas to him.

"Reign, fight back," I scream, still struggling, still trying to push Mom away. "Fight back, please. Just please don't..." I turn to my mother now who's crying. "Mom, please. Stop Dad. *Please*. He's going to kill Reign. Please, Mom, stop him."

Something about what I said gets through to her and she loosens her hold on me.

Probably to go to Dad.

And I'm ready.

I'm ready to go as well, but then someone else grabs a hold of me.

And it's Lucas.

Lucas.

What is *Lucas* doing here?

At which point I realize that *he* was the one in my room.

He was the one who took Reign away.

I want to ask him what he's doing here. But I decide that I don't have time for that. I don't have time for questions. So instead I say, "Let me go."

Seeing my mother intervene, some people have come forward too. They're trying to make my dad stop. And I'm so relieved, if anyone could call it that, that at least Reign isn't getting beaten up on. Yet again, I try to go to him but Lucas won't let me go.

In fact, he drags me away.

He drags me inside the house and he's so much stronger than me or even my mom that I can barely resist it. I can barely get him to stop. Not to mention, I can't do much even if I wanted to because of the stupid blanket. Because if I struggle too much, I'll lose the tiny bit of dignity that I have left.

After what just happened.

What even happened though? Who came into my bedroom?

What is *Lucas* doing here?

But again, I don't have time for stupid questions.

So as soon as Lucas gets me in through the door, I go, "What are you doing? Why'd you pull me away? Why'd you..." I try to side step him. "I need to go back out there. I need to go to him."

He grabs my arms and makes me stay put. "You don't need to see that."

"But I —"

"Did he hurt you?"

"What?"

"Your dress. Your..." He frowns. "Your hands. They were tied up."

"Oh, Jesus Christ." I try to twist away from him again. "That's... That's none of your business."

"It is," he says, tightening his grip. "If he was hurting you. If he was ra —"

"No," I scream, horrified. "He wasn't. That wasn't..."

Oh my God, what's happening.

What do I...

How is it that Reign is out there, going through all the crap right now, and I'm standing here, half-clothed, answering my ex-boyfriend's ridiculous questions about rape?

"I wanted it, okay?" I tell him, my whole body both blushing and shaking. "I wanted it. Can you please let me go now? I need to go now. I need to —"

"He was at The Horny Bard."

"What?"

"Last night. He was at the bar, Echo," Lucas informs me. "He was out there trolling for chicks."

"No, he wasn't. He went there with his *brother*. He…" I look up to the ceiling. "Oh my God, why are we talking about this? Why are we —"

"I knew he'd do this."

"Do what?" I clench my teeth. "Do fucking *what*, Lucas? He didn't do anything."

"I knew it from the beginning. I knew he'd ruin you. I knew he'd be bad for you. I've been friends with him since we were kids. I've seen him go through girls just like that and when you showed up, he went all crazy over you. I could see that. I could fucking see how much he wanted you. But I guess he had some decency left in him that he let you go and didn't make a move on you. And thank fucking God because it would've been easy for him to. Because you were so completely under his spell. You were *completely* infatuated with him, Echo."

"What?"

"I could see that," he says. "You'd look for him at school. You'd search for him, trying to pretend that you didn't. You'd stare at him when you thought no one was looking. And I… I had to put a stop to that. I had to protect you, do you understand that now? I loved you from the very first sight, Echo. And I had to save you from him. I had to save you from yourself and I wish… God, I wish you'd just listen to me because look what he did."

I blink at him. "You knew?"

He frowns. "I did, yes. As I said it was easy to see that you were —"

"No, about him. That he liked me. You knew that?"

"Yes." He sighs sharply. "You don't have to look so surprised. Like he did. Fuck, seriously. What did you both think, that I'm a moron? That I wouldn't notice these things, your looks, your longing-filled sighs. Yeah, I knew."

And then I ask a very strange, off-topic question. I don't even know why it made it into my brain but it did and I say, "And the Halloween party?"

"What?"

"The one when you said he got you drunk and set girls on you. He," I take in a trembling breath, "didn't do that, did he? He didn't…"

Lucas's frown is thick, his features crumpled up. "What difference does it make now? That was years ago. That was —"

"Answer me," I snap. "Did he or did he not do that?"

Another sharp sigh from him. "No, he didn't. In his usual fashion, he was playing the babysitter that night, okay? I got drunk and I was very close to kissing this girl. And he stopped me. He reminded me that I had a girlfriend I needed to think about. Who wouldn't kiss me, by the way. But that's in the past, all right? And we've already talked about this. I don't care about all that. And you shouldn't either because I didn't. I didn't kiss anyone, and so can you come back to me? Can you finally see that I'm the right guy for you?"

"It was me," I say then.

"What?"

"I kissed Reign that night. I was the one who started it. And I did it because I'd wanted to kiss him for a very long time. Because I loved him. Since the beginning. And I love him now."

He freezes.

Goes still. At my confession.

That I only gave to hurt him.

Yes, I can admit that. I can fucking admit that I did it to hurt him.

Because he hurt *him*.

Didn't he?

He hurt my Reign. He's been *hurting* my Reign for years now.

He knew everything.

Everything.

He knew that his best friend — his brother — wanted me. He knew that I wanted his best friend too. Not to mention, he lied about Reign. On so many occasions. Because that Halloween thing wasn't the only time he'd lied. It wasn't the only time Lucas had told me something that Reign had done and my hatred for Reign increased.

And he did all that because he knew I liked Reign too, didn't he?

He saw how crazy we were for each other, right from the start, right from the beginning.

But he still came after me.

And while I don't care about myself in this scenario, I do care about him.

My Bandit.

So yeah, I did it to hurt him.

"You fucking bitch," he breathes out, his eyes all harsh and angry.

And then I don't care. I don't care if my blanket slips or I lose all my dignity, I go for him.

I go for his face. His hair, his chest. His fucking groin.

I go crazy on him. I go nuclear.

And I don't stop until I hear sirens.

Cops.

CHAPTER FORTY-THREE

The Bandit

"You okay?"

"Yeah," I say to my brother, looking out his car window as he drives and I watch the world go by.

He sighs, shifts on his seat. "They're not going to press charges."

"Doesn't matter."

"Because, well, we're not going to press charges."

"There's nothing to press charges for."

"He did break your nose."

I shrug, choosing to remain silent.

There's nothing to say except I wish he had broken more than my nose.

For a little while there, when Mr. Adler was kicking me in the ribs, I had high hopes that he'd break at least one of them. But no such luck.

I came out mostly unscathed.

A few bruises, one broken nose and a night in a holding cell.

That too only because I insisted.

I said I'd go back to the Adlers' and finish what he had started, and so they kept me inside until I was sufficiently calmed down. And well, because I told my brother to not throw his weight around and lawyer up.

If my dad was alive, I'd stay there forever; he'd make it so.

As it is, he's gone and my brother has this delusion that I'm a good guy and don't deserve to spend my life in jail. Not to mention, he has enough money to make these things happen and here we are.

Me riding back in his Bentley after spending a night in jail.

"You could've fought back."

"No."

"Don't you go to that boxing gym? So it's not as if you don't know how."

"Didn't want to."

He makes a non-committal sound. Then, "Well, maybe this will help with your dwindling street cred. Given that your old bruises were fading away and now you have new ones."

"Yeah, meetings should be interesting again."

I hear a chuckle. "So you love her."

I watch a tree with pink flowers go by. "Yes."

No use denying it.

No use calling it something it isn't.

It's love.

Although I've only recently been informed of this.

That the thing I feel for her is called love.

This irrational jealousy. This insane obsession. This crazy need to get close to her, to somehow get inside her body and live there. To somehow get her inside mine so she could live wrapped around my heart.

If I had my way, I'd call it sickness.

But I guess love works too.

Or maybe on someone like me love does look like sickness, I don't know.

All I know is that I do.

I do love her.

"And the problem is?" he prods.

"Me," I tell him, still looking out the window. "I'm the problem."

A couple of minutes of silence.

Then, "How's that?"

"I'm not you," I reply.

"What?"

I sigh, my ribs throbbing with a dull pain that I know has nothing to do with the beating I took — it was nothing; I've had worse — but from this love inside of me.

"I'm not good," I tell him. "I'm not responsible. I'm not a rule-follower like you."

"Okay. So?"

"So I'm the second son. I'm the disappointment."

Another couple of minutes go by before Homer asks, "And?"

I sigh again, this time sharply. "And I'm *afraid* that I'll always be that. I'm afraid that I'll disappoint her like I do everyone else. And she deserves better than me."

That's it, isn't it?

That has always been the case.

What she deserves and what I am.

I mean, look what happened. Look what I fucking did last night.

Not only did I violate her body, I fucking violated her privacy.

Instead of leaving her alone like a decent human being, *protecting her* like a decent human being, I exposed her to the world. All because I couldn't handle what she'd said to me.

I wanted to purge this angst inside of me.

That her words had caused.

And the only way I knew how was to go see her.

Prove to her that I'm not the guy she thinks I am.

And well, I did, didn't I?

So yeah, I'm the problem.

"I never wanted to run the company," Homer says.

"What?"

"I never wanted any part of this."

"Yeah and that's why you trained so hard for it all your life."

He chuckles again. "I never said that I *knew* I didn't want it."

I frown, still looking out the window.

"It wasn't until he passed away and I truly became the boss... Actually," he backtracks, "it wasn't until I left college and went to graduate school that I realized I didn't want to do this."

I finally turn to him. "What the fuck are you talking about?"

He glances at me for a second. "I realized that I didn't want to sit in an office all day and run meetings. I didn't want to read reports and make deals and everything else that goes with it. I thought I wanted it. I was *told* that I wanted it. And when people tell you something, every single day of your life, you start to believe it. Their beliefs become your beliefs. And then before you know it, you're trapped. You're caged and you don't know what to do. You don't know how to get free, *if* you can get free even if you tried. So you're stuck. Sometimes you're stuck forever. Sometimes you don't get the opportunity to become unstuck."

I stare at him, my big proper brother, in his three-piece suit, with no hair out of place.

Everything appropriate and perfect.

He glances at me again, his lips quirked up in a humorless smile. "He told me that I was the heir. That I was supposed to be a certain way, and I believed him. You believed him too, didn't you?"

I swallow thickly.

When she had said the same thing to me, I was angry. I was furious.

That she had the audacity of throwing everything I'd shared with her to my face. I showed her the parts that I myself don't acknowledge are there and she took them and shoved them at me.

The abuse. The rumors. The fucking lies that people believed about me.

But now, looking at my brother, I don't feel the same anger.

I feel... fear.

I feel that he — and in turn she — might be right.

"I know you did," he continues. "I don't blame you. He fooled us both. And that's because he's the disappointment."

"What?"

Another glance at me. Then, "It's not you who's the disappointment, Reign. It took me some time to see that. It's not you, it's them. It's the world. The world has disappointed you. Our father who was supposed to be a loving, patient authority figure, abused you. Our mother who should've looked out for you, protected you, let him do that. Even now, where the fuck is she? Vacationing in Italy rather than being worried about her son. Your brother, me, again who should've looked out for you, ignored you. And your best friend. Who stood up in front of the cops yesterday and said that you were trying to force yourself on someone. He lied about you to the cops. He tried to ruin your life. What do you call that, if not an epic fucking disappointment?"

Lucas did tell the cops that.

That when he opened the door to her bedroom, he found her tied up and crying. He found her clothes torn off and me on top, forcing her. Raping her.

That is a disappointment, isn't it?

I knew we weren't on good terms. I knew that.

I knew he hated me. I hated him too.

But I never expected him to do what he did. It actually surprised me for a second that he'd do that. But then like always, I accepted it.

I accepted it because I thought he was telling the truth.

I *was* abusing her.

Not in the rape-y way but in the way where I've been selfishly using her.

Where I've been selfishly, purposefully, keeping her with me to sate my own needs.

So I believed everything he said.

I *believed* it.

"She didn't," I say then.

"She didn't what?"

...*didn't believe the rumors. The lies.*

She actually never did. Not even back when we'd first met. It was my asshole behavior that pushed her away, that finally convinced her that she should hate me. Not the gossip about me.

She didn't believe it yesterday either. When again, I was trying to do the same. Trying to show her who I am underneath.

In fact, she stood up for me.

She stood in front of everyone, her parents, the people at the manor, the cops, Lucas, and said no. She kept saying that she loved me. That she wanted me, wanted it. That Lucas was lying. Everyone was lying.

Except me.

Swallowing again, I answer, "She didn't disappoint me. *Hasn't* disappointed me. Ever. In fact, she told me that I wasn't a disappointment at all. Not to her."

"Yeah," my brother agrees. "Which can only mean one thing."

"What?"

"That she loves you back."

My chest hurts again.

And again, it's not from the beating I took. It's from the thing that I feel for her.

Love.

She loves me.

I know she's said it a lot of times now. But I'm only now letting it sink in.

She loves me.

She fucking loves me. She's loved me since that first night.

She's loved me even when she hated me.

Even when I made her hate me.

"So my question again: What is the problem? What the fuck are you doing?"

Exactly.

What *the fuck* am I doing?

She loves me. Apparently I love her too.

I believe that I'm a disappointment. She doesn't. Even my brother doesn't.

She says I believe the wrong thing. I believe the wrong people.

And if I can believe the wrong people, if I can believe the world and my piece of shit father, then why can't I believe her? The only person who's never disappointed me. The only person to ever love me despite everything.

Why can't I believe what *she* believes about me?

Holy shit.

Holy fucking *shit*.

I look at my brother, the pain increasing in my chest. "Nothing."

"What?"

"There's no problem. I mean, I'm the problem but there's really no problem."

And if I believe her, if I keep believing her, then maybe one day...

One day I can believe it myself.

That I'm really more than what I was told I was.

I'm really more than a second son.

"Thank fucking God," Homer mutters.

"You cursed. Again."

"Seemed like the occasion for it."

My lips twitch.

"It's not going to be easy, just so you know," he says then. "Going after her, I mean."

"I know."

Not only did I not protect her last night, I also made sure that I'm on her parents' permanent shit list. The kind of shit list that I may never get off of.

But I'm going to try.

And I'll keep trying until I do.

Because like her, I'm not going to give up.

Not on her. Not on myself.

Not on this love.

"Because getting caught buck naked in their daughter's bedroom is not the way you want to start out with her parents," Homer adds for good measure.

I scrub a hand down my sore and bruised face. "I'm going to need a tie."

"You're going to need a lot more than a tie, but we'll start with that."

"Why do I get the feeling you're enjoying this?"

"Because I am." Then, "Besides, being good gets boring."

And then I break down and say it. "I know."

"You know what?"

"Why you wanted me to work with you for a year."

He stiffens. "So you can earn the money."

"No," I tell him. "So you can earn my trust and get to know me."

His fingers tighten over the wheel.

"And I don't blame you."

"No?"

I shake my head, chuckling humorlessly. "Because I never would've given you a chance otherwise." Then, "I don't trust easy."

His posture remains rigid. "I know."

"And it's not your fault."

"What isn't?"

"That you weren't there. I never told you. You didn't know. And when you did," I pause to take a breath, "you came for me."

He takes his time responding.

Probably absorbing my words.

The truth.

Because I don't blame him. Not anymore.

It's hard work, blaming someone who's trying to do the right thing.

Who's trying to be more than what you always knew them to be.

He makes another noncommittal sound, which means he didn't believe it. The truth. Which is fine I guess. I'll just keep telling him then.

Until he does.

Then, "If your soccer club offer still stands, I'd love to join you."

That makes him relax.

It also makes him smile a little bit. "Yeah?"

"Yup. Would love a chance to kick your ass."

He chuckles again. "Yeah, we'll see about that."

I chuckle too.

And then I think about how happy she'll be. When I tell her.

That I'm doing what she always wanted me to do.

That I'm bonding with my brother.

But more than that, I'm believing.

I believe.

In what she told me. In her.

And the fact that I'm in love with her. I've been in love with her for years now. And I'm finally, *fucking finally*, going to make my move.

I'm finally coming for her.

My sweet, pink-loving, sassy, drama queen Bubblegum.

CHAPTER FORTY-FOUR

He lied.

For me.

In all of this, that's the only thing that I can think about. That he lied to Lucas.

About the kiss.

Who started it. He told Lucas that it was him. And he did it to protect me. To keep me safe. To somehow make Lucas and I reach a reconciliation.

And I never would've known.

If Lucas hadn't blurted it out last night.

I never would've known that he protected me even then.

But then am I really surprised?

He's always protected me. He's always watched out for me, even when I thought he was the worst thing in my life.

He wasn't. He never was.

He was the best thing to ever happen to me. The most magical, transcendent thing.

My Bandit.

Which makes what I did last night even worse.

While he protected me since day one, I let my anger and pettiness get the best of me.

And that's why he's in jail, isn't he?

Or rather, that's why he had to spend the night in a holding cell.

Because in my vindictive fury, I told Lucas the truth. And that asshole took it out on his best friend. That *asshole* that I thought I loved. That I wanted to get back together with. Not to mention, he's the asshole that I still felt guilty for.

Despite knowing that coming clean with Lucas at the funeral was the right decision, I still felt that my utter blindness and lack of self-awareness had hurt him in the worst way. Like, all of this pain could've been avoided if I'd only known who and what I wanted.

While that's still true, fuck him.

Fuck him and his *fucking* pain.

Fuck him for taking it out on the guy who always, *always* supported him. Stood by him and loved him like his own brother.

He accused *that* guy of the worst crime that you could think of.

The absolute *worst*.

And I had a hand in that. *Me*.

If I hadn't let the truth about the kiss slip out, Lucas would never have done what he did.

Plus I left the door unlocked, didn't I?

"Hey."

I blink my eyes at the voice — Jupiter's — and focus. I guess I've been staring at the window of my bedroom for a while now and have started to worry my friends: Jupiter, Poe, Callie and Wyn.

They're all here today; they came over first thing in the morning when I called Jupiter to tell her everything that had happened last night. The fact that they all abandoned everything going on in their life — Poe and Wyn are moving to New York soon with their boyfriends, Callie has a newborn daughter, Jupiter abandoned her little sister, Snow, after already regretting the fact that she's been away from Snow for two years; Jupiter loves her sister to pieces — and came to my rescue is enough to make me break down and cry, and thank my lucky stars that I somehow met them.

"Hey," I say.

She smiles sadly. "Anything?"

My fingers tighten around the phone in my lap. "No."

"Well, maybe he's just," Callie shrugs, sitting in bed in front of me, propped up against the bedpost, "busy."

"Exactly." Poe nods, who's sitting right next to me like Jupiter. "Maybe he just got out and he hasn't had a chance to check his phone."

No, we all know that he got out first thing in the morning and it's evening now. But I understand her need to make me feel better.

I understand all their need to make me feel better.

Not that they can, but still.

"Or his phone died," Wyn offers from beside Callie. "That's a possibility. He spent the entire night in a holding cell. He couldn't exactly charge his phone."

They all murmur their assent and I give them a small smile. "Thanks, guys. Maybe you're all right. Maybe he hasn't..." I clear my throat. "And you know, you guys can leave. I'm going to be —"

"No," Jupiter says with determination. "We're not going anywhere."

"We're going to stay here with you," Poe adds. "For as long as you need, okay? We know how it feels. A thousand thoughts must be racing through your head right now. All of them bad. You don't want to be alone with them."

They're right.

I don't.

But I also feel bad for putting them out like this.

"When Reed," Callie begins with sadness flickering in her blue eyes, "wouldn't admit that he loved me, I'd be so miserable, you know? Like, here." She presses a hand to her chest. "I used to feel like a piece of my heart was bitten off or something. Everything would look so colorless and bleak. So yeah, I know. We all do. Which means we're staying for as long as you need us."

"Yeah," Jupiter agrees. "Not to mention, all the crap that you went through with the cops and the stupid, ignorant people."

Wyn nods. "Same thing happened to Conrad. Because of my parents. My dad actually had him arrested." She shakes her head. "I still can't believe it. I still can't believe that he was taken away like that. So we're staying."

Yeah, it happened while we were still at St. Mary's.

While I wasn't friends with Wyn or any of these girls except Jupiter back then, we did see a couple of guys arriving and taking Conrad, or rather Coach Thorne, away. Wyn's dad used his influence to have him arrested for being involved with her.

So she does know.

And a tear streams down my cheek.

Both for myself and her, because now that I know how it feels, seeing the man you love being dragged away like that, handcuffed and bleeding... I wouldn't wish this on anyone.

"Okay, thanks. I know that's not... enough, but..."

"Shut up." Jupiter gives me a side hug. "You don't have to thank us. We're best friends and that's what best friends do."

They all agree, and I tell them that I need to go to the bathroom to freshen up. But really, I'm going because I can't get rid of the images from last night.

They come and go, see.

The flashes.

The fact it actually happened, *every single thing* that happened, is still surreal to me. It still feels unreal. Bizarre. Nightmarish.

An outlandish joke.

First that it was Lucas — yet again — who found us like that.

Apparently, he'd come over to talk to me because I'd sent him those two stupid texts a couple of days ago. My parents told him that I was sick in bed, and since they've always trusted him and liked him, they let him go upstairs and knock at my bedroom door.

Which he did, but I hadn't heard.

And so he opened it to check on me.

When he found what he found, he alerted my parents, and my mom came running up. The fact that it was my mother and not my father who saw me like that, is probably the one consolation that I could take from this.

Then came the crying, the beating, the screaming while the whole world — or at least *my* whole world — watched, and Lucas dragging me inside.

And fucking telling me the truth.

Showing me his true colors.

I'm not sure who called 911 but whoever it was probably saved Lucas's life, much to my dismay. Because before that, I was hell bent on killing him with my bare hands. I was *hell bent* on exacting revenge on Reign's behalf.

On how for years, Lucas took advantage of him.

For *years*, he let Reign suffer. He let Reign be tortured and be agonized over the fact that he wanted me, his best friend's girl. All the while spreading rumors about him. *Lying* about him to me.

But then as I said, I made a grave mistake going after Lucas like that.

So when the cops came, I did everything that I could to correct it. I did everything that I could to convince them that I loved him. That everything that happened was consensual. Everything that happened between us last night was so *far* from that ugly, horrifying word that Lucas was accusing Reign of, that I didn't even know how anyone could've thought different.

How anyone could've thought that it was anything other than love.

I was loving him, and he was loving me even though he didn't know it.

That was *love*.

It has always been love, this thing between us.

They still took him though.

And now I can't get ahold of him. He's not returning my texts. He's not picking up my calls. An hour or so ago, my calls started to go to his voicemail.

Despite what my friends say, I think I know why.

I think he's done with me.

He was done with me the night I told him that I loved him. He came over to tell me that, *to prove to me* that it was over. And just because everything went to pieces yet again, doesn't mean that he's changed his mind.

So yeah, it's over.

And I think I'm dying.

I would've too. Standing here at the bathroom sink, staring at my pale and lifeless body in a pink dress, my trembling legs would've given in, and I would've dropped dead to the floor, if I hadn't heard a knock at the door.

"Echo?" Jupiter goes, urgently. "Whatever you're doing in there, which I know is not what a bathroom is used for since you know I've got those senses, you need to come out. Right now."

I grip the edge of the sink. "I'll be... I'll be out in a second. I —"

"No, not in a second. Right now." She even jiggles the knob. "Get out here. Right the fuck now."

"She's right," Poe says, knocking at the door. "*Get out here*."

Which is followed by the same sort of commands from Callie and Wyn. And confused and also alarmed because who knows what new hellish nightmare this is, I open the door.

"What's —"

Jupiter grabs my hand though, cutting me off, and begins to drag me. She takes me out of my room, down the hallway right to the landing and yet again, I want to ask what the hell does she think she's doing.

But suddenly, I don't care.

I don't care about anything, not a single thing in this whole world, except that.

Except him.

Standing at my door.

No, *filling* my entire doorway with his broad shoulders and that towering frame that since day one — even when he was only fifteen — has fascinated me.

And not only standing and filling my entire doorway, he's *standing and filling my entire doorway* with a rose in his hand.

A single white rose.

And God, he's wearing a tie.

A black tie on a dark maroon dress shirt.

And — *and* — he's clean-shaven.

When was the last time I've seen him without his stubble? I can't remember. *Plus* his hair's all short and spiky now as well, like it was the first day he crashed back into my life at The Horny Bard.

Over the past few weeks his hair had grown out, snaking down to the side of his face, looping around his collar. And while it still wasn't back to the length that it was when we still lived at the manor, it was getting there and oh my God, I loved sinking my hands into those dark strands.

I loved tugging at them, pulling at them.

In fact, that's what I was doing the whole time last night and...

What am I *doing*?

Why am I simply standing here, staring at him, when he's here?

He's *here*.

What is he doing here?

"I went out to get you something to eat," Jupiter whispers in my ear, as all my girls stand around me, watching. "And the doorbell rang while I was on my way up and he was there. Just like that, and so I ran to get you."

I'm about to do the same, run I mean.

When I hear this:

"What are you doing here?"

That's my mom.

And I realize that he's not alone. As in, he's standing at the door with a rose and a tie, and my parents are standing before him. And they're staring at him much like me. Much like all my girls around me.

His chest moves on a breath and I fist my hands.

Because it looked like he flinched.

Like his breaths are hurting him and it's because of all the beating, isn't it?

All the punches and the kicks and God knows what else my dad visited upon him by the time I got to them. And so again, I'm about to run downstairs to him but Jupiter grabs my hand, followed by Poe grabbing the other.

They both shake their heads, and I don't understand.

Why are they stopping me? Why...

"This is," he begins, and I hold my breath, "for you."

He offers my mother the rose and I notice her shoulders stiffening. I also notice that she doesn't make a move to take it.

And he continues, "I have to admit it was my brother's idea," with a small self-deprecating smile. "I'm not very good at these things. But he told me that I should bring something and the only thing that I could think of was a rose. A white rose. For peace."

My mother still doesn't make any move to take it and I've had it.

I try to go again.

But again, my friends stop me.

Jupiter mouths, *Not yet.*

Poe goes, *Wait. Let him do this.*

Let him do what, I want to ask.

He doesn't need to do anything. What he *needs* is me right now, going to him and apologizing for what I did. For my hand in what happened last night. But my dad chooses that moment to step forward, breaking my thoughts, and I grip my friends' hands tighter.

"What the hell are you doing here?" my dad asks, all threatening like.

But my mom's there to calm him down. She puts a hand on his arm and goes, "Scott, don't."

My dad's shoulders stiffen but my mother doesn't care. She turns to Reign and finally, *finally*, accepts the rose. "Thank you."

He gives her a short, somber nod before turning to my dad, who I know — even though his back is turned — is seething right now, and says, "I came to apologize."

"We don't need —"

My mom stops him again with a low, "*Scott.*"

I watch Reign's jaw getting tighter for a second before he breathes out again. "I understand that. I understand that this must be difficult for you. I'm probably the last person you want to see standing at your doorstep. Especially when this is the first time I'm doing this. *Standing* at your doorstep." He keeps his eyes on my dad, his shoulders straight, his feet apart. "And that's the first thing I'd like to apologize for. That this is the first time. That in the past, I violated the privacy of your home, by coming into it like a thief. By *sneaking* into it like a thief. You deserved better and I never gave that to you. I never thought how disrespectful all of this was to you."

"No, you didn't," my dad bites out and I notice my mom's hand on his arm growing tighter.

This is unbearable to me.

Me, not being able to go to him. Not being able to take *his* hand and stand beside him. While he faces my parents like this.

But I think I understand why my friends stopped me.

I think they're right; he needs to do this.

He *needs* to apologize to my parents.

It's clear on his face — on his beautiful and yet again bruised face — that he needs to tackle this head on, what happened last night. That he needs to say the things that he's saying, and no one knows it better than me.

That he feels things deeply. So much more deeply than anyone I've ever known.

Regret. Guilt. Loyalty.

"I didn't," he goes on, shifting on his feet. "And that's on me. That's something I'll have to live with. But the worst thing that I'll have to live with is the fact that I," he pauses to take another deep breath and God, I can see how much it hurts him, "failed to protect *her*. I *failed* last night," he says, his eyes clouded and his voice low and rough. "And I can bear anything in the world, anything at all, except that." His jaw clenches for a bit. "Ever since I met her, your daughter, I... Well, I've done a lot of fucked-up things. I've done a lot of things that I regret where she's concerned. And I always chalked it up to who or what I am. A disappointment. I've always been that. I've always taken great pride in that, but..." Another clench of his jaw. "This is the one thing that I'll never be able to forgive myself for. The *one thing* that I don't want any forgiveness for. That will haunt me forever, me not being able to keep her safe. Me not being able to keep her from harm's way."

At this, it becomes really difficult to simply stand here and let him do this.

Really difficult to not go to him and put a stop to this.

I don't care if he wants to do this. If he wants to apologize or make things right or whatever it is that he's doing right now.

I *don't* care.

I have to let him know that it was me who failed. It was me who'd left the door unlocked. It was me who provoked Lucas.

Me. Me. *Me.*

Not him.

"You didn't," my father says, his words sounding clenched. "You did fail to protect my daughter. You made *me* fail to protect her too. You're right. You're the last person we want to see on our doorstep. Because you not only came into my house and disrespected my family, you led my daughter astray. You turned her into something that we don't recognize anymore. A stranger and —"

"Scott, stop," my mom says sternly.

"But I —"

"No, not right now," Mom says to Dad, before addressing Reign. "We appreciate you coming here and giving us the courtesy to apologize. But as you and my husband have already said, you're the last person we want to see or have anything to do with. You're the last person that we want to think about. Because yes, you *have* turned our daughter into a stranger. A stranger who keeps secrets and tells lies and goes behind our backs. That is not the daughter we'd raised. We raised her to be good. To follow the rules. To be responsible and take care of the family. But..." She sighs. "You're not the only one."

My dad shifts on his feet again but thankfully remains silent as my mother continues, "I realized last night that we had a hand in this too. We had a long talk, Echo and us, last night. And I realized that while we did teach her to be good, to take care of the people she loves, we forgot to teach her to be good to herself, to take care of herself. *I* forgot that. A daughter learns from her mother, and I was always a good girl, growing up. I was always a rule follower and that's what I taught her. That's what I showed her. Maybe because my mother showed that to me as well, I don't know. But growing up, I taught Echo to be like myself. It was important because we always struggled with things, and then with my husband's accident, I had to make compromises and concessions and I relied on her a little too much perhaps, in order to keep things running. So yes, I forgot to teach her how to put herself first, and that's my regret. That's something that *I* will live with."

My vision is blurry but I can see that my mom's holding herself rigidly. My dad too. And I wish I hadn't told them all this. I wish I hadn't had that long talk with them last night.

When I confessed everything that was in my heart.

I came out of hiding and told them about my relationship with Lucas, how broken it was and how I didn't even know it. About the mistake that I made two years ago that led me to St. Mary's and how much I regret it, but I really would like to put it behind me.

And then I told them all the things that I struggle with, have *always* struggled with.

Being good. Being perfect. Being happy and not guilty all the time.

And they listened, silently, carefully.

Well, my mom did. My dad was interrupting with his own anger. But they both paid attention to what I was saying and as difficult as that conversation was, I did feel relief at the end of it. I did feel like it was an important conversation to have.

Plus I could finally tell them about St. Mary's, my friends, my time over there. Which is how all my friends were able to come over and spend the entire day with me.

But I also don't want my mother to blame herself for things in the past. I also don't want to see her in pain. I just want to move on. I want our family to look to the future.

"And Echo told us that you were the one who showed her that," she continues. "That she needs to take care of herself. That she needs to... put herself first and I... I'm thankful to you for that. And also, for NYU. For getting her a second chance and —"

"She deserved it," he says with determination. "She deserves whatever she wants."

My mom's shoulders inch up and down on a sigh. "She does. But again, that doesn't mean that this is easy for us, having you here. Having our daughter say that she loves you. That she wants to be with you. Especially when we know, when we've always known things about you. When we've heard things, seen things."

At this point, my mother has grasped my dad's hand and they're standing there as a team, and gosh, I want to do that too.

I want to make our own team. With Reign.

I don't want him to stand there, all strained and all alone, his hands fisted at his sides. I want to slide my hand into his and stand beside him. Now and forever.

But my friends still won't let me go and my mother begins to speak.

"Echo has told us about that as well. About the rumors and how they're false. Or exaggerated. How the truth is different. About you and Mr. Davidson. She never gave us any specifics but it's hard for us to believe, you understand? Because we owe a lot to your father. Most of us here do. But despite recent events, we're choosing to believe her. Which means that when she says that she's in love with you —"

"What are your intentions toward our daughter?"

That's my dad and I can't help but scream out, "Dad! No."

That wasn't how I wanted to make my presence known. Screaming from the top of the stairs and shocking everyone, including my friends standing beside me.

But I had to do it.

I had to stop my dad from asking the inappropriate questions.

Well, not really.

I mean, I get why he'd want to ask this, but I don't want him to.

Because I don't know what his answer is going to be. Because I'm afraid his answer is going to be something I won't want to hear. Because I'm... just scared out of my mind.

And I've had it.

I want to go to him. I *have to* go to him now.

While both my mother and my father turn around to look at me, I keep my focus on the guy I love to pieces. Whose eyes have come to rest on me, and they look so intense and shiny that it's not a gaze anymore, or a stare or a look.

It's a touch.

A pull. A gravity. A force.

His reddish-brown eyes are the life running in my veins and my bloodstream that give me the push to run. To tear down the stairs and all the while I'm running to him, I can see.

I can see things moving inside of him as well.

As if my own brown gaze, my thumping footsteps are affecting him the same way.

Are making his chest shudder, his feet shift, his mouth part.

And then I'm there.

Between him and my parents.

I take him in, his shaven jaw, his short hair, those eyes. The bruises. His split lip.

Then I step up to him. I step *beside* him.

I grasp his hand.

I clutch it — or rather his fist — like I wanted to all this time and turn around.

To face my parents. My dad and his seething features; my mom and her somehow both compassionate and cautious eyes, holding that lone rose.

That has the power to completely break me down.

It's slightly intimidating to be doing this, facing my parents like this, but I'll do anything to support and stand by the boy I fell in love with when I was only twelve.

I take a deep breath and go, "Mom, Dad, I love you both and I really appreciate your concern. I also get where it's coming from, and I can see that this is not easy for you by any means. But you don't have to interrogate him like this. He's standing at the *door*. You haven't even asked him to come inside and —"

"To fix it."

He speaks, cutting me off.

He also unfurls his fingers and threads them with mine. And I have to lock my knees together to keep standing. At the sheer joy, the sheer relief, the absolute delicious heat and roughness of his hand, sliding into mine.

My parents have switched their eyes over to him now.

And even though it hasn't gone unnoticed that I'm holding his hand, they choose not to comment on it.

"To fix all the things I've done in the past," he says, his voice grave, his features determined. "To fix what I did last night. To not only somehow make it right but also to make sure that it never happens again. And it won't." His grip tightens. "It will *never* happen again. I will never put your daughter in a situation where she can be hurt; where I can't protect her; where I fail to keep her safe. You don't have a lot of reason to believe me or believe whatever promises I make but someone once told me that a promise is an oath. It's a pledge. It's a word of honor. It's a covenant, a commitment and a vow. A promise is a bond and my intention is to protect that bond."

I'm scratching him.

I'm scratching the back of his hand, his knuckles. His fingers.

I don't intend to but it's involuntary.

It's out of my control. Much like how it's out of my control, those tears that well up in my eyes again as I look at him. As I see his determined face. That angular jawline dipped in strength. Those high cheekbones, all laced with willpower. His stubborn nose. His resolute frown.

And then, I break down and plead. "Mom, Dad. Please can I talk —"

"I'd like to ask your permission to speak —"

We both say it at the same time and we both stop at the same time too. But while he has the patience, the resolution to be strong, I don't. Because as soon as he stops, his fingers still clasped in mine, I start up again. "Please, Mom. Alone. Just for a little bit even. I —"

"Fine." My mom nods.

"Annie —"

"Let them," she tells my dad. Then, to Reign, "But as Echo said, only for a little bit. We still haven't forgotten what —"

"You don't bring her back to us within thirty minutes, I'm coming after you," my dad threatens, and with that, he lets go of my mother's hand and stalks out of the room.

My mother sighs and gives me a look. "No more than thirty minutes. And you will both stay out here."

That makes me a little mad. Like Reign isn't fit to be let inside the house, and I'm about to protest — for someone who didn't argue or confront her parents at all, I've become really free and accustomed to doing it since I opened up last night — but Reign beats me to it.

"I understand. I'll have her back in time."

My mom nods and then steps back to close the door.

As soon as she does, I pull at his hand and turn around.

And start walking.

CHAPTER FORTY-FIVE

I'm not sure where I'm going or even how it's possible that I'm dragging him behind me — the guy who can manhandle me very easily and has on numerous occasions — but I need to get far away from my house. I need to get far away from the people who look at him like he's a criminal.

Like he can strike any second now.

When I get to a place in the woods where I can only see flashes of my house and the stucco roof, I stop and spin around. I don't give him a chance to speak as I say, "I didn't tell them the whole thing."

"What?"

"About your dad," I explain, my fingers tightening around his. "As in, I didn't give them the specifics. I didn't give them all the details. Only that he wasn't a good man and —"

"It doesn't matter," he says, his eyes staring into mine, his fingers clasping mine just as tightly. "Fuck my father. I don't care now and I didn't, the other night as well. I just... It took me by surprise, and I got pissed off."

I understood that.

I would've gotten pissed off too. I *did* get pissed off when he'd told me that he'd read my diary and then he went ahead and used it against me. While my intention was never to use his deep secrets against him, I can see why he would've gotten a little taken aback.

"I just got really tired of everyone blaming you," I tell him. "Everyone thinking that you're the bad guy."

A bruise pulses on his face. "I'm not a saint either. I —"

"Does it hurt?" I cut him off because I have so many things that I need to tell him and ask him.

A myriad of things, and I don't know how much longer I can keep them inside of me.

It's as if he understands it too, my restlessness. My need to worry and fuss over him. And so, he patiently shakes his head and says, "It's fine."

I step closer to him, taking in the new bruises on top of the old ones. "It does, doesn't it? Your face is like... I know it hurts, Reign, okay? I saw you. I noticed. You can't breathe without flinching. It's your ribs, isn't it?" I glance down at his chest, my hand flying out of his hold and reaching his chest where I rest it very, *very* gently. "Are they broken? They are, aren't they? Your ribs are —"

He cradles my cheeks then, making me look up, his rough hands scraping against my soft skin, as he repeats, "It's fine."

"Reign —"

"Nothing's broken," he says, pressing my cheeks tightly. "Trust me. I had 'em checked out. I had to. Homer wouldn't leave me alone. So as I said, I'm fine. I've had worse. It's going to be okay. *I'm* going to be okay."

A breath escapes me, my eyes fluttering closed in relief.

He's going to be okay.

"Now, I need to —"

I open my eyes. "It was my fault."

"What?"

I grip his wrists and look him in the eyes. "I told him."

"Told who what?"

Reign already knows that it was Lucas who'd found us and why he'd come over in the first place; Lucas was plenty clear and *loud* about that last night with the cops. And while Reign knows that, he doesn't know what role I played in last night's debacle.

"About the kiss." Then, as if the truth wants to come rushing out, I keep going, "I told him that I was the one who started it. That I kissed you first. That I always wanted to kiss you because I always... and I did it to hurt him. I did it because I was angry. I was furious. Because he knew. All along he *knew* what you felt for me, and he let you suffer. He let..." I swallow thickly, my fingers tightening around his wrists. "I'm sorry, Reign. I'm... I *never* wanted to come between the two of you. That was the last thing I wanted. I never wanted to break up a friendship. I —"

"You didn't," he rasps, his nostrils flaring.

"I —"

"It was never a friendship." He swallows. "Not like I thought, at least."

He's right.

And that's the tragedy, isn't it?

That the guy Reign thought was his best friend, his brother, was nothing more than a snake. He was nothing more than a jealous and weak and pathetic human being who not only contributed to rumors about him but also tried to ruin his life last night.

God, and to think that I *wanted* to mend their friendship.

I wanted to make their differences go away. Enough that I actually texted Lucas behind his back.

"Why didn't you say anything?" I ask next. "Why didn't you tell me?"

Why did you take this burden on all alone?

Why do you always do that?

He works his jaw back and forth, narrowing his eyes as if in thought. Then, "Because I didn't know how to. I..."

I wait for him to gather his thoughts.

"I'm not," he shakes his head once, "good at sharing. I'm... And it hurt. But then I thought maybe I deserved it. For everything wrong that I've done in my life. So there was no point in telling anyone anything."

I bite the inside of my cheek.

I purse my lips.

I do everything that I can do stop myself from bawling. Sobbing and wailing.

For him.

For the pain I see on his tightened features. For all the pain that he's gone through. At the hands of the people who should've been the closest to him.

"So not your fault. Whatever he did, it's on him. Not you." Then, almost soundlessly, hesitantly, he adds, "And maybe not me either."

My voice, on the other hand, is completely loud and vehement. "Yes. *Not* you, Reign. It's not on you. You don't deserve that. You don't deserve to be betrayed like that."

Something changes on his face then.

His expression gets rearranged. His eyes both melt and become determined. Like they were back when he was talking to my parents about his intentions.

He rubs his thumbs over my cheeks. "I believe you."

I step back then.

I get out of his embrace. I put some distance between us.

Four steps worth of distance.

But then I decide I need two more. So I move back two paces further.

And all the while I'm moving back, I watch him.

I watch his fists tightening up at his sides. His eyes narrowing. His Adam's apple jerking with a swallow. His features becoming all kinds of brittle and pained.

While I hate to see him in pain like this, I also have to take a moment to myself.

I also have to prepare myself for whatever comes next.

I believe you, he said.

But I don't know what he means by that. Does he mean now, today, what I just said? Or does he mean all the other things that I've wanted him to believe?

So with my heart hanging from the ceiling, hanging in the balance between us, I whisper, "You came."

"You called," he says, without missing a beat, without making me wait even a single second.

A lump forms in my throat at the answer.

The one I've wanted him to give me ever since I became his.

Even so, I lift my chin and stay strong. "I didn't. I-I couldn't. Your phone... It was —"

"Dead," he says, his eyes direct and frank. "I think, at least. Haven't looked at it all day. Didn't even think to look at it all day. It took fucking hours at the fucking hospital and my brother wouldn't get off my back and then... Then I came here."

I look at his haircut. His clean-shaven jaw. His tie.

That rose.

Swallowing, I whisper, "To apologize to my parents."

"Yeah."

I fist my hands as well. "Is that... Is that all?"

"No."

"Then w-what else?"

At this, he makes me wait a little bit and I think it's because he has the same problem now. Like I did before. Where I had so many things to say, so many things that were clawing to come out. He has a lot of things too, to say, to get out.

It both scares me and thrills me.

Because I don't know what exactly those things are.

"Everything," he says finally.

"I don't..."

Know what that means.

"They're coordinates," he says then, his eyes penetrating.

"What?"

He opens his fists and brings a hand up.

He puts it on his chest. On the left side, his fingers open wide.

And I know.

What he means.

"The numbers," he confirms. "They're coordinates."

I'm... glad. That he told me about the tattoo on his chest.

But I'm also confused because I still have no idea what that means.

"Uh, coordinates. You mean," I wrinkle my nose, "like, of a place?"

He jerks out a nod. "Yeah."

"What place?"

"This place." Then, "Here."

"I don't... understand."

His eyes rove over my features, taking me in with a deliberate slowness. Then he sighs, lowering his hand, fisting his fingers again and goes, "You're always thanking me for things, aren't you? So I guess it's my turn now. To say thank you."

"For... what?"

"For never believing," he says, "the rumors, the gossip. You only believed what I showed you, never what you heard. You hated me because of how I *behaved* with you rather than what people talked about me and I... Yeah, thanks for that. And for last night too. For standing up for me. For defending me. No one has ever done that before. No one has ever stood by me and faced the world for me. *With* me. But most of all, no one has ever believed in me, Echo. *No one.* Not before you."

He pauses and my eyes well up with tears. "That's because people are stupid and ignorant."

And I hate them.

And I love you so much.

And please say that you love me too. Please.

His lips twitch slightly. "You know how you're always saying that I turned night into day, the first time we met?"

"Yes."

He shakes his head slightly. "I don't think it was me. I think it was you."

"M-me?"

"Yeah." He nods, staring into my eyes with such intensity that I'm all breathless. "You turned my night into day. The night that I'd been living in for fifteen years. It was you who made me see the sun that night. You made me see summer. Watermelons and lemonade and sunshine. All because you walked into my life with a pretty pink dress on." Then, shrugging, "Well, I thought it was pink at first. But as it turns out, there are about a hundred and fifty shades of pink: candy pink, cherry blossom, dusty pink, French pink, chestnut fucking rose. And the one that you were wearing that night was something called carnation pink. I looked it up later that night. I mean, who the fuck knew there were so many shades of pink. Who the fuck knew that pink, of all colors, would become my favorite. It would become the color with which I'd see the world. The color that I'd see in my dreams. It would become the color of every thought I had, every breath I took, every beat of my heart. But then, I shouldn't be surprised, should I? Because that's what you do. You change things. You change the world. You changed *my* world. With your books and words. With your diary. God, your fucking *diary.*"

He chuckles softly, lost in memories. "And I thought, *fuck me.* I thought, who the fuck is she? I thought, how is it that I've only now found her. The girl who's not only pink and pretty like a fucking flower but also who writes in a diary. Like me."

I blink. "What?"

His eyes are all liquid now, shiny and molten and deep pools of emotions. "I always hated it. Writing in a diary. Made me feel like a fucking pussy. But it was something that I picked up in a therapist's office and it was so hard to break, the habit. But when I met you, like so many other things in my life, it didn't feel so bad. It didn't feel like a shameful thing. It felt like... connection. With you. It felt like something tied me to you. Something secret but powerful. Something like magic.

"But anyway, I stopped it. I stopped writing when everything happened because I didn't want that connection anymore. I didn't want to be tied to you. I didn't deserve to be tied to you and that's the thing, isn't it? What I deserve. What I think I deserve. And what I *think* I deserve is not you.

"You were right," he says, shifting on his feet. "When you said that I believe what the world believes about me. I believe all the lies, all the rumors. I *believe* that I'm a disappointment. And if I disappoint everyone, then what's stopping me from disappointing you? What's stopping me from breaking *your* heart, crushing *your* dreams and making *you* miserable? And I could bear anything in this world, Echo, anything at all but *that*: Disappointing you. Disappointing the girl who changed my world. Who made the sun rise on my dark, *dark* life. Who made me see everything through rose-colored glasses. Who fucking taught me that there are a hundred and fifty shades of pink. I mean, that wouldn't have been fair, right? To her. To *you*. So I always thought my only option was to push you away. To *keep* you away. But that's not true. There is one other option. Something that I didn't think of. Not until now. Not until today."

He puts his hand on his chest again. "And that's instead of carrying you in my heart, carrying the place where we met the first time and the world turned pink, the world turned into something worth living in, I walk beside you. I take your hand and I walk this world *with* you. I care for you. I protect you. I keep you safe. I destroy every hurdle that comes your way. I kill everything that hurts you. The other option, Echo, is that I *believe*. You. That I believe you like you believe in me."

His nostrils flare with a long breath.

A breath so long that even his throat moves with it, as he gulps it down.

His stomach contracts and moves with it as well.

"My father, when I was growing up, he tried to change me, see. He tried to make me into something that was acceptable to him. But I didn't change. I *made sure* that I didn't change. So I don't know if I *can* change now, but I want to believe that I can. I want to believe that I can give you all the things that you deserve. That I can be whoever you want me to be. Or if not that, then I want to believe that I can fix it. Do you understand? That I can fix things for you. That I can fix what I break. I can fix all the tears that I'll make you cry. I can fix all the times I'll make you mad; all the times that we'll fight because I'm acting like a jerk. I want to believe that I can make things right for you.

"And so, I promise you that I will. I will believe. It will be hard, and I will probably fuck up a million times. But I promise you that I'll *keep* believing like you keep believing in me. I promise that I won't give up like you don't give up. I'll have faith like you have faith. I promise you that I will change your world, Echo, like you changed mine. That I'll turn every season into summer and every night into day. That I'll feed you fucking watermelon and lemonade for the rest of your life. That I'll keep you warm and in the sunshine. Or I'll fucking die trying. And you know that I'll keep my promise because it's you who taught me that a promise is a bond, isn't it? It's a commitment and it's an oath. A vow. And that's my vow to you: to believe. So I guess..."

Raw and intense emotions move on his features for a few seconds.

Then, "So I guess what I'm saying is that the reason I came here today is not only to apologize to your parents but also because I wanted to ask you something."

"Ask me what?"

He opens and closes his fist. "Something that I should've asked you the moment I saw you. Even though you were too young for me."

I'm opening and closing my fists too.

I'm also breathing very, very hard. While blinking, keeping tears at bay.

Because I want to see his face. I want to *remember* his face when he asks me.

"What, Reign?"

At this, he unfurls his fists and leaves his fingers like that, open and vulnerable. Much like he is right now. "Will you be my girlfriend, Echo?"

It's not my intention to make him wait.

To keep him on pins and needles for my answer.

But I don't think I can speak yet. I'm too overcome. I'm too emotional.

I'm too *everything*.

Six years.

I waited for this for *six years*. I waited for it when I didn't even know that I was waiting for it. And so I just... breathe.

I just soak it in. Like sunshine. Like summer. Like all the lovely things that he's promised me.

Things that I don't even need but I know he'll give me anyway.

Because that's who he is.

The boy I love.

The boy in black that I stumbled upon in these woods.

"Why?" I ask then and he knows.

Exactly what I'm asking.

And he gives it to me.

The words.

"Because I think I love you."

This, I need to absorb as well. And I do it with my lips parted and my eyes closed.

I do this with my fists open as well, letting every word, every sensation seep into me. So I never ever forget the moment he finally *admitted*.

He finally told me that he loves me.

I think I love you...

I snap my eyes open then. "You *think*?"

He studies my features. "Yeah."

I clench my teeth, my happiness, my too many emotions forgotten. "Seriously? *Even now*. You think?"

And oh my God, just look at him.

He's amused.

I can't believe he's *amused*. That his lips are twitching, and his stupid pretty eyes are twinkling.

And then he takes a step toward me. "Yeah. Because I don't think love's the right word for what I feel for you."

I narrow my eyes. "So then what's the right word?"

Another step. "Obsession. Because I'm obsessed with you."

I deflate slightly. "Oh."

Yet another step. "Crave. Because I crave you with every breath I take. I have craved you with every breath that I've taken since the first moment I saw you."

I swallow jerkily. "What else?"

Step number four. "Insanity. Because I'm insane for you."

Oh God.

"A-and?"

Step number five. "Life. Because you're the pulse that beats in my veins."

I hiccup. "I..."

He reaches me then, on step number six. "Sick. Because I'm sick for you. Because what I feel for you, Echo, doesn't have a name. It can't be described in words. Not yours and definitely not mine. Because what I feel for you isn't something that anyone has ever felt for anyone before. But if you like, we can call it love. And I can tell you that I love you every day. Until in all your logophile glory, you invent a new word or a whole new vocabulary that fits it all, every single thing that I feel for you."

And I realize that he just took six steps.

One for each year that we've known each other.

That we've *loved* each other.

And isn't that the most poetic thing ever?

Who cares about love when the guy I fell in love with is making poetry for me, right out of thin air? Who cares about love when the guy I'm obsessed with and insane for and live for and crave with every breath I take just told me that he's been carrying me in his heart?

He told me that, didn't he?

That he's been carrying these woods where we first met in his chest.

I mean, love seems so silly and small when you think about it all.

He's right.

I put a hand on his chest, where his tattoo is. "They're *really* coordinates of where we met?"

His chest moves up and down with a breath. "That was the only way I could keep you close. Or rather, the only way I allowed myself to keep you close. After everything."

"Because you..." I fist his shirt. "Stopped writing in your diary."

"Yeah."

Holy God, he has a diary.

A *diary*.

Just like me.

I mean...

What are the chances of that?

What are the *fucking chances*?

"What color is it?" I breathe out.

"Black."

"I want to read it."

"You can."

"And not just three lines."

"It's yours."

"You know why?"

"Why?"

"Because I think..." I step up to him. "I think this is how you fix it."

"I will," he says with determination.

"This is how you fix not telling me. All this time. Hiding this crazy connection between us. This crazy and huge and massive and gigantic connection."

"Yeah."

My heart twists. "And I want you to start writing in your diary again."

"Okay."

"Because I want that connection with you," I tell him, breathless. "I *want* all the connections with you. I want to be so connected to you that no one, not even you, could ever tear us apart. Because you did that. You tore us apart. So many times, Reign. For *so many years*."

Finally, he brings his hands up and frames my face. "I won't. I promise."

So I stand there like that, staring into his eyes, barely breathing, barely holding it together.

Barely being able to comprehend that this is real.

That he really loves me.

No, he doesn't actually.

He feels more for me than the word 'love' could ever explain or describe.

"You know, you don't need to do all those things for me," I tell him next. "Everything that you just said. I don't need them from you."

"I know." His lips tip up in a small lopsided smile. "But I'll give them to you anyway."

I bite my lip. "What color is it? My dress."

He keeps staring into my eyes. "Fuchsia."

I shake my head. "I can't believe you know that."

"Couldn't sleep that night. So that's what I did. Counted pinks."

I clench my eyes shut. "God, Reign."

He comes closer too.

Until we're grazing against each other.

"So will you," he asks, "be my girlfriend?"

I open my eyes and whisper, "Yes."

It's a simple word.

After all the beautiful and heartfelt words that he's said. After how he created poetry for me.

But I guess it's enough for him.

Because he shudders.

His forehead drops over mine. Then, "I meant what I said, Echo. I *meant* it. I'll believe, okay? I'll be a good boyfriend to you. I promise. I'll fix everything. I'll... And I know there's a lot that I need to fix. From last night. I didn't protect you. And God, I... I fucked you in the ass, baby. And then I didn't stick around to make sure you were okay. And even before that, I used you for sex. I —"

"We're even."

"What?"

I bring my hands up to his rigid jaw. "I lied to you. I kept secrets from you. And a girlfriend doesn't do that. I texted him behind your back and I'm so sorry. And then I attacked him. So we're even now. And you didn't use me for sex. That was love, remember?"

"Love."

"Yeah." Then, "And also, I took the pills."

"You did."

"Yes," I whisper, smiling slightly. "I knew you'd be beating yourself up about it. For not being able to take care of me after... So I took the pills. And I'm fine. There's no pain."

A relieved breath escapes him. "Good girl."

I shiver. "I love you."

Another breath.

As his eyes flutter closed for a second. Like mine did when I wanted to absorb it all.

"You're wearing a tie," I point out the obvious with my own twitching lips.

He chuckles, his warm breath wafting over my mouth. "I am."

"You hate ties."

"Yeah."

"You cut your hair."

"I did."

"And you *shaved*."

"Didn't wanna look like a criminal in front of your parents. Or at least, not again."

"That was very cool."

"What was?"

"That you gave my mom a flower."

"It's the least that I could've done. After what I was hoping that she'd do for me."

"What?"

"You." He presses my cheek. "Give me a chance to at least talk to you."

My heart squeezes. "I love you, Reign."

His jaw tightens up before he says, "I love you too. So fucking much, Echo."

And then, we both make the move.

We both reach for each other and kiss.

We kiss and kiss and keep kissing.

Until it's time for me to go.

He walks me back to my door and leaves me with my parents like he'd promised. He tells me that he'll call me later. Because he's my boyfriend now. And even though I don't want him to leave, I still let him go and shut the door with a smile.

Because I'm his girlfriend now.

Finally.

After six long years.

EPILOGUE

He looks like magic.
Of course he does.
Just look at him.

Zipping across the field with his dark hair, now much longer — as long as it used to be back then — flying in the air. Zooming from goalpost to goalpost with a speed that should be impossible. Much like the ball that he's dribbling and kicking. And made the first goal with at six minutes into the game.

We're at the thirty-second minute and the score still remains 1-0. And I know, I *know* that there's still a long way to go and anyone who knows anything about soccer *knows* that things change with seconds to spare in this game.

So I probably shouldn't be overconfident.

But I am.

Because it's him and as I said, he's magic.

Oh, and the Daredevil, who does impossible things, things that no one ever does.

"So are you sure? As in, really sure about your living situation."

I look away from the game to focus on the girl sitting beside me. A couple of years older than me, Maple Mayflower is gorgeous. With whiskey-colored eyes and wheat-blonde hair, she has to be one of the most beautiful girls I've ever seen.

I also have to say that at first, I didn't like her at all.

Even though she's one of the sweetest people I've ever met.

"Yes," I say, sighing, my heart clenching in my chest.

"It's going to be hard."

"I know."

"I do not envy you guys."

I look back out to the field. "Me neither."

"Especially when you think about how you guys just found each other."

Like about four months back.

Which honestly, feels like yesterday. It feels like I blinked, and the time simply vanished. And we went from kissing in those woods to me, sitting here and watching him be the star of the game, talking about our impending separation.

Maple bumps my shoulder then. "But you'll get through it."

I look at her again. "You think so?"

"Yes, of course," she says, throwing her arm across my shoulder and hugging me. "If anyone can do it, it's you two."

I swallow. "Yeah."

She's right.

If anyone can endure this separation, it's me and him.

It's *us*.

I mean, we've endured a lot. We've gone through a lot of things over the years and we still made it to the other side. So I know that we'll get through this as well: me staying in New York to go to NYU and him, getting picked to play with the LA Galaxy.

Well, the drafts aren't until next month but it's almost finalized. Actually, a lot of teams have showed their interest in him over the years — more so in the last few months, ever since he expressed the desire to enter the drafts — but the Galaxy have seriously courted him and made him the best offer.

And I know that he wants to go there.

He loves their team. He loves their offer. And from what I understand from their numerous meetings and phone calls and whatnot, he has the most room to grow over there.

Plus that team has Arrow Carlisle.

He's one of the best players who has a bright future in the European league, and he's one of my boyfriend's personal favorites. The more surreal thing though is that Arrow happens to be the boyfriend of one of my St. Mary's friends, Salem.

While I never got a chance to get to know her before this, we've come to know each other over the past months. With a couple of trips that he and I took to L.A. — and had *so* much fun by the way, traveling together as a couple — and a handful of times that they flew out to the East Coast, we've managed to come closer.

And I totally love her.

We talk about soccer a lot because Salem's an excellent soccer player in her own right and knows everything there is to know about the game. And I'm determined to learn as much as I can to support my boyfriend. Not because I'm compensating for something but because I want to hold his hand and stand by him in everything that he does. Like he does with me and my books and my writing. Oh, I started writing a novel too; in fact, he was the one who encouraged me to.

But anyway.

Salem also turned me on to the greatest artist ever, Lana Del Rey, and her haunting and romantic and melancholic music. Which has been a great inspiration for my work. So that alone makes us best friends forever.

But what I was trying to get at was that even though I hate that we'll be separated soon, I know — I have full faith — that we'll get through this.

And I love Maple for saying that.

I can't believe that I hated her at one point. Like, way in the beginning when I met her for the first time. But only because she seemed so close to him, the boy I love. And so I was jealous. But then I found out that they're more like siblings, so all my reservations were gone.

Not to mention, she's kinda engaged to his older brother.

Engaged and hopelessly in love.

Which even if I hadn't known already, I'd know when a second later Homer appears in the stands. All suited up and polished.

Because she freezes.

Like really. With her eyes wide and her lips slightly parted. She also ceases to breathe while she watches him wade through the unruly and shouting crowd to get to where we're sitting. Only taking a breath and looking away when he reaches us and takes a seat beside me.

Then, she does everything in her power to ignore him.

While blushing furiously and chewing on her lips.

But I know she's listening when he says to me, "Did I miss anything?"

"One goal."

"Shit." Then, "Him?"

"Who else?" I say in a braggy voice.

His lips twitch. "Hell yes."

Mine do too.

Because it's funny, curse words coming out of Homer Davidson's mouth. He has to be the most put-together guy I've ever seen. In an expensive three-piece suit with a perfectly knotted tie, a handkerchief in his pocket and not one hair out of place, Homer looks like the epitome of a successful and debonair businessman.

He looks intimidating to people who don't know him, but not to me.

Or at least, not anymore.

To me, he simply looks like a big brother.

A proud and a happy big brother who attends every single game that his younger brother plays in. Sometimes he's late, like today, but he always makes it. Who talks to his brother and discusses game strategies and what team his brother should go for. Who right now is watching the game like nothing is more important in the world except his brother on the field, playing both their favorite sport.

God, it makes me so happy.

It makes me overjoyed that they have a relationship now. A good one at that. The kind two brothers should have, where they support each other and include each other in the happenings of their lives. But more than that I'm overjoyed by the fact that the guy I love finally admitted to loving the sport that he was forced into.

It took a while and a lot of nagging from me, but he got there.

For the record, I always knew that he would.

I had faith. Plus he promised me four months ago that he'd try. That he'll believe, and I knew he never breaks his promises.

So this is perfect, this moment.

The only thing that would make it more perfect is if I wasn't sitting where I am. Between the two people who I think secretly want to sit together, Homer and Maple.

Only the problem is that if they had been sitting together, Homer would be rigid as a rock and Maple wouldn't breathe at all, which would probably lead to her fainting and maybe more.

It's very strange.

Their dynamic.

My boyfriend — I love saying that — thinks that if Homer doesn't feel the same for Maple, then he should break off the engagement and let her move on. But *I* think that he pines for her too. He just never makes a move and I wonder why.

I've often thought about interfering because I know how it feels when you love someone but you hold yourself back for whatever reason. But of course, he has forbidden me to do anything. He thinks it's none of our business, their relationship, and that they're both adults and they will sort this out on their own.

I personally don't think so.

I think people need help from time to time, a nudge in the right direction. So when the game's over — 3-0, in favor of his team — I'm quick to get out of the stands, leaving them both behind to contend with each other. Maple gives me a look, but I wink at her and mouth 'good luck.' Her furiously blushing cheeks and glare are the last things I see before I turn around and start making my way to the spot where I'm supposed to meet up with him.

Although I've said it to him a million times before, that he doesn't need to cut short his interviews or conversations after the game to come to me, he still does. He's probably the very first player to get out of the locker room and leave.

So I quickly make my way through the slow-moving crowd and reach the locker room entrance just as the steel doors are bursting open. I'm already grinning with joy, ready to congratulate him by jumping into his arms, when I see that it's not him.

It's his best friend.

Or rather, ex-best friend. Or better yet, the guy who should never have been his friend to begin with.

My smile falls off and he comes to a jarring halt at the sight of me.

Of course, this isn't the first time I'm seeing Lucas. He goes to this college. He plays for the team and since I attend every game, I do see him around. But this is the first time that I've stumbled upon him like this, when it's just him and me.

And I have to say that it makes me nauseous.

Also angry.

As angry as I was on that night.

Needless to say that my fury at him hasn't calmed even in four months. I still remember his cruelty, his sheer evilness when he accused Reign of such a heinous crime. Which makes me think — and I think about this often enough — that this must be way worse for Reign, running into Lucas all the time, playing with him, sharing a locker room with him.

Not that the guy I love has ever said anything about that, but still. It sucks that Reign has to see Lucas around all the time. And as much as I'm dreading our impending separation, I want it to come faster so Reign doesn't have to see him anymore. Because Lucas is probably staying in New York.

"Hey," he says, his gym bag slung over his shoulder, rubbing his hands together to ward off the chill.

While I'm burning and seething in my pink peacoat.

I take a step back from him in response, remaining silent.

When he understands that I'm not going to say anything, his mouth curls up in a small lopsided smile. "Well, it's good to see you too." Then, "You're waiting for him, I presume."

"Always," I say, which I do get sounds a little childish.

But I think I'm allowed a little pettiness here.

Especially on behalf of Reign.

Lucas chuckles. "So everything's going well, I take it."

"Everything's going great, yes."

He nods, his eyes on me. "Fantastic. Although from what I hear, he's leaving soon."

"So?"

"So," he shrugs, "you always loved NYU a little too much. That's gotta throw a wrench in everything great."

"You know, I think we'll figure it out," I tell him, my heart drumming with anger. "Because I'm coming to realize that when you love someone, you do all kinds of things for them. Things that you never thought you would. And happily too."

And then it occurs to me.

That I'm right.

You do *do* things for people you care about, things that you never once thought you'd do. And that's both the beauty and the curse of this thing called love. And while it has always been a curse because I'd never known where to draw the line, I think this time around it's more of a beautiful thing.

I hate that this is only now occurring to me. And especially after talking to Lucas. But I'll take the epiphany as it comes to me.

"And you know a lot about love," he murmurs, his features both harsh and loose with something akin to nostalgia.

"I think so," I say, nodding. "At least, now. He taught me."

He did, didn't he?

In the short time that we've been together, he's taught me a lot about love and relationships and loyalty. And the crazy thing is that he's the one who thought that he didn't know anything about it. That he still doesn't.

It's okay though; I'm on a mission to make him believe.

At this, the door bursts open again, and he finally appears in a fresh dark t-shirt and gray sweatpants and only a hoodie; God knows how he manages to stay warm in that but he does. His own gym bag is slung across his chest, his hair all wet and messy. His reddish-brown eyes light up when he sees me, but then he notices Lucas and those pretty eyes of his begin to shine with a different light.

As I knew they would.

He hates it when a guy so much as looks at me wrong. And so I'm pretty sure talking to my ex falls under that category. Actually it would be a category of its own.

When he takes a threatening step toward Lucas, his stubbled jaw all tight, his eyes narrowed, I make my move. I go up to him and, winding my arms around his neck, I lift my face and give him a kiss.

He's frozen at first, probably shocked at me attacking him like this. But then he gets with the program and winds his muscular and safe arms around me and kisses me back.

In fact, he kisses me better.

His arms squeezing around my body, plastering me to him, his tongue thrusting inside, taking and owning every inch of my parted mouth. And the kiss that I started mostly to distract him turns into something else.

Something more.

Which is always the case when it's us.

We break apart, probably years later — or at least it feels like it — when some of his teammates cheer and clap and whistle around us. Blushing, I hide my face in his warm chest and he tells them to go fuck themselves. From the corner of my eye though I do see that Lucas is gone.

Good.

When he's sent all his laughing friends away, he looks down at me. "You okay?"

"Yeah."

"Was he bothering you?" he asks, his eyes flicking back and forth between mine, slight anger still lingering in them.

"No."

His chest moves on a tight breath. "Because if he was, I'd —"

"He wasn't."

"And you're sure."

"Yes, I am." I kiss his jaw. "Besides, I didn't just kiss you to distract you from beating him up and thereby ending your streak of four months, one week and four days of no fighting and no bruises."

Which I'm hoping will turn to forever. The streak I mean.

Because I can't even express how happy I am that his beautiful face and his magnificent body are bruise-free. That he doesn't subject himself to the kind of pain he used to.

"So then what else?"

I bring my hand up to his face to cradle it. "To fulfill your fantasy."

"What fantasy?"

"The one you had," I lick my lips, "about making him watch."

He gets it then.

And his eyes go intense. "Yeah?"

"Yes," I whisper, smiling. "You told me once that if I was yours, you'd do everything to make everyone around you including him jealous, remember?"

"And you're mine now," he says all roughly and possessively, his arms flexing around me.

"I am. So, I figured I'd better catch up and give you everything that you've ever dreamed of." Speaking of, I blurt out, "And so I've made a decision."

He narrows his eyes in suspicion. "Decision."

I nod. "Yes."

"About what?"

Taking a deep breath, I reply, "About going with you. To LA." He stiffens but I keep going, "Look, I know what you'd say. You'd say that I shouldn't compromise on my dreams. That I always wanted to go to NYU and so I should. But the thing is that dreams don't have to be so rigid, you know? Dreams should be fluid and ever-changing. And yes, when I was with... him, I never thought that I could give up NYU and follow him to the ends of the earth. And that's because I never felt for him what I feel for you. I love you, Reign. You're the love of my life and now I know what that means. It means that I'd do anything for you. I'd follow you anywhere. My dreams include you now. My dream-like *life* includes you and I never ever thought I could be this happy. To love you and be loved by you is my happiness, Reign. And so, I'm going. I'm going wherever you are going. So you can save all your arguments because I've made up my mind."

Oh gosh.

It feels so good, *so freaking good*, to finally say that.

Over the past couple of months, every time this topic came up, he'd tell me to follow my dreams and do whatever I wanted to do. And since for the longest time my dream was to go to NYU, I thought that was what I should do.

But I know I'm right now.

I know what I just said resonates more with me than anything else.

Because yes, dreams change.

Because *you* change. Because once in a while, someone comes along and changes you. Once in a while, someone comes along, and he makes you see the world in a different way. In a hundred and fifty shades of pink and through summer-tinted glasses.

He teaches you what it means to love and be loved, and to build your life with someone. So I'm going. Not because he wants me to or because that's what a good girlfriend does but because *I* want to. A difference that he taught me himself.

"I'm not going to LA."

"What?"

He takes my face in for a few seconds. Then, "I've rejected their offer. Or rather let them know that I won't be accepting it."

"What?" I ask again but much more shrilly.

In his usual annoying way, he makes me wait for the answer. And I'm about to go all crazy on him when he sighs and steps back, murmuring, "Fuck it."

"What? Fuck what?" I ask as I watch him walk backward, taking his bag off and dropping it on the ground with a thud.

He comes to a stop after a couple of steps before he goes ahead and takes my breath away.

He completely hijacks it and leaves me frozen and breathless.

As he comes down on his knees.

Well, one knee.

"What…" I breathe out. "What are you doing?" Before he can say something though, I go, "Are you giving me another anklet?"

Because that's what he did.

The last time when he came down on his knee, in those woods where we'd first met.

"No."

I curl my toes and shift on my feet, as if to feel the one I'm wearing around my ankle. Then, uselessly, "Because you don't have to."

"Good. Because as I said, I'm not giving you one."

"I love the old one," I say, again uselessly.

"I know."

"How?"

His lips twitch. "Because you never take it off."

"I don't. Because I love it."

"You said that already."

"Right." My heart's pounding. "S-so then what are you doing?"

"Asking you something."

"Why are you d-doing it from down there?"

"Because it's the kind of thing you ask when you're down on your knee."

Oh God.

Okay.

Okay. *Okay.*

I figured.

The moment he went down on his knee, I figured that this was different. This was — *is* — so fucking different than before.

For one, his expression is way too intense for just a casual knee-drop. For another, we've always been so in tune with one another and what we're thinking and feeling. So yeah, I figured.

It involves a question like he said. And an answer.

Oh, and a piece of jewelry.

That goes on your finger.

And the moment he went down on his knee, I knew what my answer is going to be.

"Yes," I blurt out, completely ruining the moment.

Completely.

You idiot, Echo.

"Yes what?"

"I will marry you," I say because he was right.

Fuck it.

I mean, it's already out there, my yes. And I know guys like to be in control of these things and whatnot but the thing is that I'm uncontrollable. These things inside of me that I'm feeling are too wild to be controlled or contained by rules.

Too wild. Too untamed. Too euphoric and happy and pink.

And too fucking wonderful to be contained within my rib cage.

"I didn't ask yet," he says, his features flashing with amusement.

"But I'll marry you anyway."

"Yeah?"

"God yes."

"So then, you gotta chill and let me ask, Bubblegum."

I press both hands to my cheeks, trying to chill. "Okay, yeah. Right. Sorry."

He takes another few seconds to study me, my breathless form in a pink peacoat, my honey-blonde hair tied up in the kind of intricate braid that he likes.

And of course, my blushing cheeks.

Those, he takes in for the longest time and with the gravest of expressions.

Then, "I bought this ring," he fishes one out of his pocket, "four months ago. The day I decided to believe. The day I came to see you. And I've been carrying it around in my pocket since then. I sleep with it. I eat with it. I write about it in my diary every night. I even bring it to practice and put it in my locker because I can't... I can't bear the thought of ever being apart from it. I can't bear the thought of it disappearing when I'm not looking. I guess I have this crazy notion that this ring is somehow *you*. That I'll blink and you'll disappear. That these past months would turn out to be a dream. Well, they've been a dream. Better than any dream I've ever had but yeah. I..."

Then, staring down at the ring, he says, "All I know is that I want you to wear my ring. I've wanted you to wear it for a very long time now, probably way before I bought it. But every time I thought about giving it to you, I thought it wasn't enough. The words I'd planned to say. Or the moment I'd planned to do it in. Or just the fact that I haven't fully showed you yet, all the things that we can be together. All the ways I can love you or cherish you or be the kind of a boyfriend you deserve. But fuck it, yeah? Because I figure if you wear my ring, I could show it to you for the rest of our lives. So even though everything that I've just said is not enough, this moment isn't enough, and I've got a ways to go, I want you to have this ring."

He looks up then, his eyes liquid and his face vulnerable. "Because I'm insane for you. I'm obsessed with you. You're the life in my veins and you're the thing I crave more than air. I'm sick for you, Echo, and I want you to marry me. Will you?"

At this point, I'm just crying.

I'm bawling and I realize that I was wrong.

I didn't ruin the moment.

Because he just saved it.

With his beautiful words and beautiful face and beautiful soul.

And I'm proven right — that he saved the moment — when suddenly I'm in his arms. And I'm drenching his hoodie in my tears as he rocks me back and forth. And when I still don't calm down, he does the only thing that will get me to chill, that will lull me into submission.

He kisses me.

He puts his soft and warm mouth on me and drugs me with it. And again, it feels like we keep kissing for years and years as the world passes around us.

Coming up for air, I whisper, hiccupping, "You're right."

He frames my face with rough hands. "About what?"

I hiccup again. "I'm a drama queen."

He plants a hard but sweet kiss on my lips. "You're my drama queen."

"I totally ruined your hoodie."

"All my hoodies are yours to ruin."

I sink my fingers in his hair. "I can't believe you've been carrying around a ring for four months now."

"This was the only thing keeping me sane and you safe."

"Safe from what?"

His eyes flash. "From me kidnapping you and taking you away."

"Like a bandit."

"Yeah," he whispers, his fingers buried in my hair and flexing. "And forcing you to marry me."

"You don't have to force me."

His lips twitch. "No?"

I bring my hand away from his hair and put it on his chest. Looking down at it, I whisper, "Do it."

He glances down as well, and untangling his fingers from my hair, he goes ahead and does it.

Puts his ring on my finger.

I bring it closer, staring down at it with all the love in my heart. A solitaire diamond sitting in the midst of tiny ones on a silver ring.

"It's beautiful," I say.

"Yeah."

I look up and find him watching me and I know he isn't talking about the ring, as always.

And I realize, yet again, that I was right.

While I was hell bent on staying at NYU and feeling trapped when Lucas had asked me the same question, now all I feel like is throwing my hands open and laughing with joy. Now all I feel is this crazy urge to jump up and down and fly like a free bird.

I guess it's not the question, it's the person asking the question.

And my person is him.

My Bandit.

Which makes me even more determined to go to LA. with him.

"Reign, I —"

"If I couldn't bear the thought of being apart from the ring," he says, his features tight and sharp, "what makes you think I can stay apart from you when you're wearing my ring?"

"But Reign, your dream. Your —"

"Dreams change, yeah?" He clutches my hand wearing his ring and brings it back to his chest. "It wasn't even my dream before you came along. I wouldn't even *know* that I had this dream, if not for you. So I don't fucking care. I don't fucking care where I get to play as long as you're with me. If I'm as fucking good as they say I am, my future is bright anywhere. I'll *make* my future anywhere. Besides, it's my turn."

"Your turn for what?"

"To compromise."

"What?"

He shrugs. "We streamed *Die Hard* last weekend when you wanted to watch *Notting Hill*. So this week, it's my turn to give you what you want. Remember?"

I do.

We have this system where we take turns compromising. Because we realized as soon as we started dating that even though we have a lot of things in common, we have a lot of things that divide us as well. He likes action movies, while I like romantic ones. He loves Chinese food while I love Mexican. He likes to go on hikes and do athletic things while all I want to do is sit around my couch and read or write. He has no interest in books while I can't stop talking about them.

So we devised a system where we both take turns to do the things that the other likes.

And yeah, it was my turn last week to compromise, which means it's his turn now.

I fist his hoodie. "This is more than a movie and takeout, Reign."

His jaw clenches. "I know. Which means it's going to happen, so you need to get with it and soon."

My heart is squeezing in my chest. "I can't... I can't believe you'd do that for me."

His grip on my body flexes. "I'm doing it for me. I'm sick, remember?"

This guy.

I love him so much. So so much.

"I'm sick too," I whisper, placing a soft kiss on his mouth. "Which means when I graduate, it's my turn. To go where you go. To do what you do."

And then before he can say anything, I go for another kiss and this time when we come up for air, our foreheads are resting together and I'm up in his arms with my thighs around his waist.

Smiling, I whisper, "So I don't think you're my boyfriend anymore."

"Yeah, so what am I?"

My smile widens. "Fiancé."

"Not for long though."

"Why not?"

"Because I'm thinking Saturday."

"Saturday for what?"

He squeezes me with his arms. "For getting married."

That gives me a pause. "You mean this coming Saturday?"

"Yeah."

Fisting his t-shirt at his shoulder, I inch away from him. "That's only a week away."

He makes a face. "Feels like fucking years but we'll live."

I fist his shirt harder. "Are you insane?"

"For you, yeah."

"No," I tell him. "I'm not getting married to you in *a week*."

"Why the hell not?"

"Because I can barely tell everyone I know by Saturday, let alone put together a big, lavish wedding."

Not to mention, now that my parents have started to like Reign — my mom more than my dad — they would want in on all the planning and stuff. And oh my God, I cannot wait to call her tonight and tell her, and all my friends too.

He raises his eyebrows. "There's going to be a big, lavish wedding."

"Um, yes." I roll my eyes. "I want a big wedding. And I want music and flowers and cake. I want cake, Reign. And I want birds flying and people dancing. And I want to wear a pretty white dress and you to wear this gorgeous tuxedo. Plus the wedding invitations with ornate filigree. Yes, I want a big wedding and..."

I trail off when I notice that his lips are on the verge of smiling and that he was totally pulling my leg. I punch him in the shoulder. "You jerk."

He chuckles. "Well, I would've married you Saturday but if you want a big wedding, I'll give you a big wedding, Bubblegum."

I paste on a fake smile. "Thank you, Bandit."

"But you gotta give me the other thing."

"What other thing?"

"About who gets to tell the kids."

"What kids?"

"Our kids." Then, with a smirk, "About how once upon a time, Daddy climbed into Mommy's room through her window. And how while Mommy was writhing under Daddy and screaming in Daddy's ears about how good he makes her feel, they got caught and —"

"You asshole! I can't believe —"

He bursts out laughing and that's how he claims my mouth.

Still laughing and happy.

And okay, fine. I'm happy too.

Even though he just brought up the most embarrassing day of my life. The day that I thought I'd never be able to think about without breaking down and crying and being sad.

But then, he's magic, isn't he?

He can turn night into day. He does impossible things.

Including blocking out everything around me. Which is why I only now hear all the claps and hoots and cheering around us, making me realize that the whole world, or at least our world, witnessed his proposal.

So yeah, I'm happy and I'm laughing because I'm in his arms.

My Reign. My Bandit.

My soon-to-be husband.

>Who: The Bandit
>Where: Reign's college dorm room in New York
>When: 3:03AM; the day Echo says yes to Reign's proposal

She said yes.

She fucking said yes.

I wasn't sure if she would though. I wasn't sure if it was too soon. But I had hope.

These days, I'm hoping.

Thanks to her.

Although I do have to say that I wish I could've done it better. The proposal I mean.

I didn't lie when I told her that I'd been carrying this ring around for months now. That I'd been trying to find a perfect moment, orchestrate a perfect moment, something worthy of her and what I feel for her, but I hadn't been able to find one. But today I definitively said no to the LA Galaxy and then she was going on and on about how she'd move for me, and I had to do it.

As disappointing and lacking it was, she says it was perfect though.

That she couldn't have imagined a better moment than the one I'd randomly picked. She says she'll always love winter now — a season she isn't a fan of — because winter is when I gave her my ring.

But I believe her.

That's the other thing I'm doing these days: believing.

Not to mention, my girl is very easy please. Everything that I do is somehow perfect for her. I can't fathom it but yeah. That doesn't mean though that I get to slack off. That I shouldn't try to do more, give her more, be more for her.

My Bubblegum deserves the world and I'm going to give it to her. As I promised.

Which means starting tomorrow, I need to start planning the wedding.

Her perfect wedding.

I know wedding planning can be girly and embarrassing and whatever the fuck. But I'll do anything for her. I'll pick out the flowers, the wedding band, the cake, the wedding fucking china, if it makes her happy.

For now however, I need to go.

She's sleeping – naked; like I'd ever let her wear clothes in my bed especially when we have the room to ourselves – and if I don't cuddle with her during these winter months, she starts to get cold and restless. And she has an early study session in the morning, meaning she needs her sleep.

But yeah, tomorrow.

Tomorrow, I begin planning the perfect fucking wedding with the girl I fell in love with when I was fifteen. The girl who makes my world spin. Who lights it up with her smile, with her pink dresses, her stories and drama.

And her love.

My Bubblegum.

THE END
(For Reign and Echo)

ABOUT THE AUTHOR

Writer of bad romances. Aspiring Lana Del Rey of the Book World.

Saffron A. Kent is a USA Today Bestselling Author of Contemporary and New Adult romance.

She has an MFA in Creative Writing and she lives in New York City with her nerdy and supportive husband, along with a million and one books.

She also blogs. Her musings related to life, writing, books and everything in between can be found in her JOURNAL on her website (www.thesaffronkent.com)

www.thesaffronkent.com

CPSIA information can be obtained
at www.ICGtesting.com
Printed in the USA
BVHW041320210123
656723BV00004B/775